U3O8

by
George Macras

PublishAmerica
Baltimore

First printing

This book is entirely a work of fiction. The names, characters and incidents portrayed in it are the work of the author's imagination. Any resemblance to actual persons, living or dead, events or localities is entirely coincidental.

ISBN: 1-4241-0460-2
PUBLISHED BY PUBLISHAMERICA, LLLP
www.publishamerica.com
Baltimore

Printed in the United States of America

To

Dorothy Rosaleen Gibson

An unexpected telephone call from his irascible chairman in London signified one of two impending developments. "Chop" or "hop". Sir Francis Clayton, a *wrinkly* who combed his remaining strands of hair sideways was about to change forty-nine-year old David Bradshaw's world overnight.

Options? None. When the chairman spoke you listened. Very carefully. Staying on as head honcho at a copper mine in war-torn Rhodesia was out of the question for David Bradshaw. Someone influential on the board must have complained about the group's uranium mine in South Africa's remote Northern Cape that had turned into a financial black hole. Its product, U308 alias "Yellowcake" to the masses was reviled by international environmental groups and sanctions lobbyists desperate to close it down and to prosecute its customers. A replacement general manager who knew what he was doing was urgently required before disgruntled shareholders got in on the act.

After spending fifteen years in Rhodesia, a country of intoxicating beauty, leaving it was going to be a wrench. Few mining men worked their entire career on one mine so David accepted that eventually he had to go…this was it. Still it was a major upheaval, easier for him to wrap his head around, but for his wife Pam? Forsaking close friends along with her beautiful garden and Cape Dutch house that she'd nursed into perfection was a tough call to thrust upon her at such short notice.

"Our board feels," the crusty chairman oozed, "that you have the necessary wherewithal to pull our problem mine into profit. A change will do you good don't you agree young man? It doesn't pay for you to get too comfortable what?"

Put another way no other candidate within the London-based group had rushed to apply for the position. Desert locations were least favored among mining cognoscenti, especially one that was associated with a low-grade rogue mine whose dismal failure to produce anything like its potential had assumed laughing stock status among mine conglomerates around the globe.

Sir Francis had visited neither mine that David had worked at. The only time that the two men had met was at a seminar in London three years previously. David remembered the patronizing septuagenarian well—a bottle-of-malt-whisky-a-day man. In his opening address the old man had made no sense when mouthing meaningless idioms for blank-faced attendees to digest. He did though spur into action moving executives about like international chessmen when failing mines queued up outside his corporate sick office. Well into his seventies, he could have been forgiven for his reluctance to stray from his palatial eyrie in West London. Marshalling resources from those corridors of comfort was the easy part. It didn't do for underlings to deny the chairman his command.

David faced the hard part, reinventing a limping mine in the back of beyond. His reward if successful? A pat on the back and personal satisfaction of yet another errant mine he had brought to heel. What if he failed? Dismissal or "offer" of transfer to a non-job in a state of limbo bathed by a neon sign flashing *"Failure! Failure!"* loomed large as an unwelcome alternative. If that occurred he was headed for pariah climes guaranteeing that no other reputable mining enterprise would touch him. To say *nay*, David took for granted, meant that he was as good as dead within the blue-blood international Chater group of companies.

2

"Good Lord!" a dismayed David groaned when surveying widespread dilapidation that passed for a uranium mine. "What a mess! It's a bomb site—I have my work cut out here!"

Pam had uncomplainingly set about straightening matters at home taking it for granted that her husband's working hours promised to be protracted in perpetuity. Initially he surmised that antipathy toward English mine owners extended to employees using the mine's previous name, *The Thuringia*. After a week on the job he realized that it wasn't so, rather a term of mild affection, a remembrance of past German mining expertise that had discovered the desolate ore body eighty years previously and seen to its emergence under a number of under-capitalized suitors.

Animosity among employees bestrode the mine like a black colossus whose presence was best described as a desert scar fifty kilometers inland from *Thuringia Bay*, a small town on the infamous South Atlantic "Skeleton Coast." He'd realized before taking on the job that changes were ordained but had not banked on swift wholesale rearrangement to stem the rot.

Wisely he'd got written into his contract a "Free hand" provision that eliminated time-wasting wrangling with individuals at London head office who seldom fully comprehended on the spot pressures. David had long since discovered that head office denizens measured their importance in terms of how many operational situations in the field they could poke their noses into without being held to account. When things went haywire the top man on the ground got it in the neck. If he proved successful? Then of course silky characters at head office would jostle for kudos and more perks to underwrite their status as serious players in The City. Not this time—David had ensured that he was a step ahead.

On site David steeled himself for inevitable castigation once he began to tame his runaway cost monster. As an old Africa hand, cries of "Racism!" he expected as a hardy annual—and got. "Colonial Englishman!" too surfaced as did, "Nepotism!" but inane mutterings of "South African lackey!" stuck in his craw. He'd fought discrimination all his life so to be accused of it hurt him deeply.

A month after his arrival at the mine, it happened—a fatal accident in the open pit during a Sunday night shift. No one had informed David of the tragedy at the time. Only when arriving at his office on Monday morning did his secretary, Joey Schneider, tell him the bad news.

"Killed?" a shocked David reacted. "Are you sure Joey? Who? What happened? How did it happen?"

"I heard about it on the bus Mr Bradshaw. A haul truck driver did not radio his foreman to collect him to take him to an ablution block. The poor man must have been desperate because he squatted behind some rocks. There was a secondary blast, then a rock slide crushed him. He never had a chance."

Killed! A man killed pulsed in David's head, an event that mine general managers the world over dreaded. He'd paid little heed to tales about the infamous *Thuringia Mine* but bad news so soon? Why him? *Oh God...the state mines and minerals department would go mad;* such catastrophe reflected badly on him since the buck stopped at his desk. Facing a host of critical officials did not enamour him. *A man* *killed, unnecessarily…on his patch…*he could never live with that.

"Terrible! Do you know what time it happened?"

"Yes. Just after the third shift came on last night. Elevenish."

"Right!" he exploded. "I'm changing into my khakis. Ring Mr Moyne and tell him I'll be in his office in fifteen minutes."

It was an affront from the Mining Manager, Mike Moyne, an open challenge to David's authority not to have immediately informed him about the fatality. Moyne was a bully, an odious individual who invited confrontation and usually got his way through heartless intimidation, not that his results were wondrous; despite his frequent boasting and chest beating he seldom met his production plan. Labor turnover in his division was high due to his poor people-management skills.

When entering Moyne's office David found his quarry seated behind his desk surrounded by smirking, fawning cronies slouching with arms crossed, a posture blaring hostility at outsiders, and that included David.

Khaki-clad officials returned David's "Good morning" with barely audible mutters and baleful stares. Their pristinely polished steel-tipped safety shoes advertised that they had not entered their open pit that morning. *Strike one* David thought. They'd obviously been expecting him and were getting their stories lined up with their boss.

David placed his miniature tape recorder on Moyne's desk, switched it on, but remained standing in front of his seated quarry.

"We lost an employee last night in very unfortunate circumstances," he addressed Moyne. "What is his name?"

Moyne, who was seated, averted David's gaze choosing to fiddle with his pencil and said nothing.

"Anybody?" David said to Moyne's men. "Speak up someone. One of you must know something about your own employee."

Silence reigned followed by inevitable sounds of embarrassed throat clearing and feet shuffling. No one chose to look him in the eye and an eerie silence reigned. It seemed that the entire pit had stopped working.

"Who conducted the accident investigation?" David probed further. "Can anyone tell me what happened and why? What went wrong?"

Silence in any mining environment was a rare experience. Mines operated twenty-four hours a day. Constant noise signaled the daily life of a mine, a mix of voices, machinery and equipment going about winning and treating ore. An experienced mining man picked up the throb but silence bespoke malice and malcontent afoot. Mike Moyne ran a sloppy show and he was well aware that his inane posturing didn't fool David.

Still no one spoke up. The atmosphere dripped malice.

Moyne behaved as if David was not present and let a sneer adorn his fleshy features.

"Whom did he work for? One of you at least should know that much about him."

"Hell man!" Shorty Pienaar the pit superintendent burst out, "the stupid buggar worked for me. He deserved to get raspberry-jammed. Man these blokes don't know how to behave hey!"

Pienaar's florid face featured a scraggy ginger beard. His jutting stomach and shortness declared him a passable imitation of a music hall comedian—with a difference. He was a well known bar habitué who with his boss spent hours after work each night at the mine club drinking before going home to abuse his long-suffering wife and family.

"I see…" an infuriated David mused. "*Stupid buggar…raspberry-jammed.* That's how you feel about one of your own men. Very unfeeling reactions I must say, not to mention unfeeling in the extreme. And you have not held an accident enquiry yet?" His voice oozed venom. He intended that it would. In his long mining experience in different countries he had not encountered such flagrant disregard for life and that it had been rolled in layers of overt

11

racism was his prompt to eject its practitioners there and then.

David noticed Moyne's acolytes' arms crossed postures giving way to nervous hitching of sagging trouser bands. Sullen men stared at their boss who absently continued fidgeting with his pencil.

Someone farted. Nervous giggles broke out.

"*Aghh* no man, the stupid buggar's history man. What's the rush hey?" Pienaar snarled, making it sound more like a challenge. "There's plenty more where he came from."

David could not believe what he was hearing. "Did anyone contact the man's next of kin? Speak up!"

"What for?" Shorty declared irreverently. "That's bladdy personnel department's job. I'm no bladdy office boy." Shorty took heart from Moyne's smile and jutted his jaw. Then came his death wish. "I don't deal with bladdy blacks."

Shorty blanched when staring at David's unblinking vivid blue eyes. He saw extreme anger lazering back at him. He saw loathing and only then did it finally dawn on him that he'd opened his big mouth an inch too far.

David let a minute pass allowing ominous silence speak for itself and looked each man in the eye. *"Gentlemen,"* he announced tonelessly, "I've got news for you. This is 1984, a time when we are supposed to be building bridges of understanding and common decency. This includes knowing who works for you and with you. Color does not enter the equation and for as long as I'm here it never will be the case."

Moyne had leaned back in his chair, pretended to yawn and lit up a cigarette, blowing his smoke towards David in a gesture of ill-concealed contempt and resumed toying with his pencil.

"For your information," David continued, "the dead man's name is *Emanuel Hoabeb*. His family of two wives and eight children live in Upington. That did not take more than five minutes for me to find out. It's what any normal concerned person would do before preparing to visit the bereaved family."

"Visit?" Pienaar blared. "Visit bladdy blacks? What the hell for? It was *his* bladdy fault hey!"

Moyne raised his head and stared at Pienaar, a signal to zip his mouth.

Too late. Far too late.

"Obviously none of you value life like any normal person. You *gentlemen*, are racists. You are unmitigated buffoons whose very presence soils this mine. You are an affront. A disgrace to any decent company. You all are, as of now, discharged. *Fired*. Be off these premises within one hour."

"Hey! You can't do that!" Moyne spluttered into life and stood up exposing a good deal of bloated hairy belly that had burst a shirt button. His thick lips were quivering and lank hair had slid off his balding pate. He had to lean on his desk to keep his balance. "It's informal! I mean it's illegal!"

"Bladdy Englishman!" an unbalanced Pienaar muttered. "What the hell do you know hey? Buggar off!"

Hostility had given way to open panic. The stricken mining men realized that they were not fireproof. Moyne had been mercilessly taken down several pegs before their eyes and Pienaar reduced to a state of immense shock, shaking his head like a wild man. Looks of consternation were exchanged and everyone began gesticulating and hysterically firing questions at Moyne.

David turned to leave and retrieved his recorder. "One hour. A minute longer on site and you will be forcibly removed by security. In your case Pienaar you will go to court. This tape will convince any sane judge to put you behind bars. Within the hour I'll have your site-clearance and blasting license revoked. You're finished in the mining industry in this country."

He'd gone further than he'd intended but David was resolute that he'd made the right decision. He found himself shaking with rage, more so since such behavior had obviously been endorsed by past management. It was no wonder that the mine's industrial relations were in a bad way. Laying that ghost once and for all was going to take some doing.

He knew that the news would have spread like wildfire. So what? He wasn't sorry. The message would have fanned out, "Talk and act racist buster with this new GM, you're toast man!" Good. He jumped back into his car and headed for security to inform Victor Grey, the security superintendent of events.

When back in his office, he called Joey in. "Joey, please telephone a Mr Frank Fielding in Rhodesia. He's mine manager at the *Eagle Copper Mine* in *Banket*. I want to talk to him like yesterday. Then get in touch with all open pit assistant superintendents and tell them to come up here. We have to make a few management changes."

"Yes Mr Bradshaw. Right away."

David's eye fell on the yellow note Joey had left on his desk. *9.00 am. Sir Francis rang you.* He checked his watch. Allowing for the time differential with England the chairman had telephoned him at eight o'clock British summer time. *Must be urgent* he thought. *Early for the chairman. What now? Another move?*

Sir Francis picked up immediately.

"David Bradshaw returning your call Chairman."

"Oh yes Bradshaw. Good man. What's this business at the mine? You fired that fellow Moyne and his top team did you? He's just been blabbing to me. Threatening legal action and blustering that he will wipe the floor with Chater Mines out there. Not the best publicity I have to say so I hope you put a lid on it in good time."

"If we want a mine that means business chairman, Moyne and his racist thugs have to go."

"Annoying business this what? And I'm still in my pajamas! He said he's been there from the start. He says he won't be treated like this. *Did* you fire the fellow?"

"I did chairman. For very good reason. And his idiot hangers-on, got the push too. Do you want to know why?"

"I shouldn't really get involved in these domestic issues," Sir Francis sighed. "But you might as well tell me what happened."

Afterwards David picked up a more obsequious tone in Sir Francis's voice.

"Unbelievably uncouth this man, this Moyne character. The effrontery of the fellow! Dear me! Make sure he bally pays for his call to me. Yes—I agree no individual with such attitudes can work for us. Good heavens the press will make meal of it if we encourage such maverick doings."

David was relieved. "I'm pleased that you agree Sir Francis."

"While I have you on the line, there is something else I want to float across your bows."

"Yes Sir Francis?"

"An acquaintance of mine," the chairman coughed, "in fact a mine consultant, made it known he's available if we can use him somewhere in our group. He's kicking his heels seeing that the entire industry is in the doldrums. Merrick Marriot. Ever heard of the fellow?"

David felt tempted to answer truthfully, chapter and verse. Any mining executive worth his salt knew all about Merrick Marriot—a poisonous serpent of the mining world. Here was a man fired by a previous mine employer for illegally filling his pockets with gemstones and touting them to shady dealers in the Middle East. Such was his sinister character, a man who played self-serving politics, he was well known in developing countries for setting government and mine developers at each other's throats—his way of getting back at hated mine employers. Having him anywhere near a mine paralleled employing a hundred Pienaars' doing their cancerous worst.

"I do know of him chairman. I have a good idea of his fields of expertise. Should anything in his field crop up we can keep him in mind."

"Very well," Sir Francis replied crisply, irritated that chairman or no chairman he'd been expertly brushed off.

He'd had little choice. Bruno Gerber had been trapped by his copious contract conditions into staying put for five years. Jobs had been scarce to find particularly for a newly qualified greenhorn mechanical engineer. Severe economic downturn had seen to that.

At age twenty-four Bruno was still stuck with his university debts. At last, a job! He grabbed it with both hands grateful that the South African gold mine that he'd applied to for a sectional engineer's job mine had taken him on more for his rugby-playing abilities than his technical expertise.

He soon learned that it was all about repetition. No innovation. No expansion; the mine and its workings were ancient and to make matters worse, its ore grade was abysmally low. His job boiled down to managing gangs of highly demotivated artisans and foremen to whom it was news that their mission was to avoid outdated machinery from creaking to a halt. Wholesale desertion by American banks from the country had ensured crippling sanctions against South Africa eliminating old sources of supply, so what machinery was available simply had to work until kingdom-come.

A child of the Eastern Cape Bruno had come to terms with living away from his beloved sea and tried to find redeeming features about the flat, barren, uninteresting Highveld terrain he now existed in.

"Well Mariette," he informed his pretty wife over dinner at the end of his first week, "it's a start. We can eat and save some money. Next time my sweet, I won't make the same mistake. I'll have a good look at the papers before signing anything."

Bruno's patience had been stretched from day one. He'd arrived for work ten minutes early and found not a soul in the personnel building. Everyone arrived late including the general manager, the big boss to whom employees all but bowed and crossed themselves.

The personnel people had not been ready for Bruno and had it not been for his copy of his acceptance letter that he'd signed they appeared none the wiser as to who had orchestrated his employment.

On the job he received incredulous stares from his manager when asking about his budget.

"Budget? What budget? No man. We just fix things when they break down and the office blokes take care of money and spares. Forget budgets."

"Yes, but what about capital equipment replacement? There must be money for that. No machine works forever. Everything I've seen so far is crocked."

"All I know man is that the general manager decides where money goes," his sour boss replied. "Our bladdy job is to keep everything clanking away. Just enjoy it. Don't make bladdy waves or we'll all get bladdy fired hey! Just play your rugby and have a few drinks in the bar with the workers!"

Playing rugby on what passed for a field left him with permanent grazes. He was the only engineer pitching up for practise so he became a target for the men whose backsides he'd kicked on the job. One outing was all he needed.

Mariette found it difficult making friends among women in the mine township. Women segregated their friendships according to what seniority their husbands had on the mine. As for associating with people of different hues? *Horrors*. White society frowned on that. *Against the law*. It was her first experience of a mine township, one vastly different and unwelcome to what she was used to, living on a farm where no one gave a hoot about color or "position." It was the *person* who mattered. She wished her time away preferring to concentrate on golf and tennis, excelling in both sports so filling their tiny house that stood in the shadow of a giant tailings dump, with useless silverware and cut glass trophies.

"Bruno man, all everyone does here is drink and gossip hey. And they all talk politics and who's sleeping with whom. Everyone wants to know your business. Your general manager…"

Bruno pricked up his ears. "Yes Mariette what about him? What's he done now?"

"I don't like him. At club do's he flirts with all the women in front of his wife! He's got wandering hands the lecherous old bugger! He must kiss himself goodnight! Everyone knows he's carrying on with his personal assistant. What an awful man!"

Bruno stifled a chuckle. "Mariette, listen to yourself. You are the one who's gossiping."

"You're right," she retorted and held up her hands to her cheeks in mock horror. "I can't wait to leave this dump; let's face it. It is a dump Bruno. We even live next to a bladdy dump."

"Patience my sweet," he smiled. Mariette was putty in his hands because he never raised his voice to her and lived his life for her. "Patience. There must plenty of good things in store for us."

Christmas 1984. Three months before her husband's contract was due to expire, while sunning herself on their tiny patio Mariette spotted a job advertisement in her Sunday newspaper. They'd had a miserable time since anyone they had made friends with had fled to celebrate festivities on the steaming, humid Natal coast or to the warmth of their beloved Cape coastal area. Bruno had been stuck with duty manager responsibilities so he'd had no choice but to stay on call for the mine.

"Look at this Bruno man. Here's a great job for you in the Northern Cape. Near the sea," she said excitedly and passed him the newspaper indicating the section she'd ringed.

"Atlantic Ocean," he smiled when reading it. "That's great fishing territory. On the opposite side of where we were born!"

"I have a good feeling about this one Bruno. Anything to get out of this hole of a place."

After a few minutes he looked up and smiled. *"Thuringia Bay!* I'm excited! I'm going to apply for it. I've never heard of this *Chater Mines* outfit but it looks good. Come inside with me Mariette. Help me draft my application."

To begin with Frank Fielding could not get enough of the bush. Solitude and peace. Dry, dusty with its unique smell. He felt that he'd lived in it all his life. Then civil war had reared its ugly head sparked by insurrection of differing black movements all intent on snatching power and evicting "White settlers."

The Rhodesian bush war had become the bane of his life. At first his army call-ups were simply for shows of military strength but the war soon escalated into massive insurgency containment, carefully planned attacks and counter-intelligence operations. Mere mention of it frightened him. More and more demands were thrust upon him and his men to stop work, don camouflage uniforms, take up arms and go off chasing terrorists who had become past masters at laying waste to remote farms and settlements and slaughtering their inhabitants. The awful part was when some men did not return, burdening survivors with overwhelming guilt.

Insurgents competed with each other to wreak atrocities on hapless citizens white and black, gory sights that turned the guts of hardened police and soldiers. Satisfying mine shareholders who wanted their profit and satisfying Rhodesian army *brass* were mutually exclusive demands as far as Frank was concerned.

His natural ability to handle men and extract the best from them had soon earned him senior officer rank in the Territorial Army. In his opinion the war was a futile waste of lives because politicians had got it all wrong, a view that he had he have expressed officially would have landed him in hot water.

He loved and admired his wife Yvonne for not giving him a hard time since he was more often away from home than not. Miraculously he managed to run a tight mining operation in Rhodesia whose rebel declaration of unilateral independence had outraged the entire African continent along with a host of international detractors jumping on the bandwagon. An exacting mining engineer, Frank expected perfection from his men who worked the open cast mine—and got it. His men joked that Frank's motto was "Frank's my name, you play my game or else, buggar off!"

To begin with life had been as close to perfection as he imagined. His house and grounds were the size of an entire country estate back in Yorkshire. When at home in his new environment he had a swim every day in his own twenty-five-metre pool. Gardeners maintained three acres of verdant lawns and flowerbeds. Most meals were taken outdoors, usually shared with visitors who had popped in for "Sundowner" drinks and chat. That was the Rhodesian way of life. In the sun. Until war reared its ugly head. Afterwards it hung heavy on residents that they did not know whether they would survive from one day to the next. Returning to a darkened home after a night out raised lumps in everyone's throats for every resident knew someone who had been murdered by waiting terrorists.

There was a bright side for the country—a material one. Despite United Nations sanctions consumer goods were freely available having been sourced from South Africa. When it came to financing spares and equipment though, tightening international sanctions made life difficult for the mine's owners and management.

Local currency had become worthless outside of the territory, an unwelcome development for Frank both personally and business-wise. He spent a great deal of precious free time thumbing through professional journals looking for the one job that instinct told him would suit him.

Both he and Yvonne were agreed that it wasn't a case of "If" they departed, but "When" unless of course increasing ravages and horrors perpetrated by "terrs'" wasted him, her, or both of them, first.

His prayers were answered when David Bradshaw 'phoned him out of the blue.

Politics meant very little to a consultant. To Cecil Lonsdale what mattered was earning "real" money and hanging on to his job.

When approached by his senior partners in London to fly out to Southern Rhodesia with his wife Marlene, Cecil needed no second bidding to oblige them. A two-year contract to install training facilities and methods throughout the customer's many enterprises? What a pleasure! Fleeing interminable drizzle and cold of English winters had much to do with the couple's decision as did being paid in tax-free USA dollars by the company's London head office.

Two years shot by, then three, then five and after seven years in the territory Cecil admitted that he was irretrievably hooked on Africa. How could tiny, damp England remotely compare with his adopted country of rolling savannah, mountains, forests, rivers, dams, game, sun and space of gargantuan proportions?

He had no unsocial inhibitions about black people. He'd never understood why so many civil servants and European immigrants distanced themselves from the very people that they were supposed to be developing and helping. That's why the colony had been formed in the first place—to help and to protect; not to develop lifestyles of Croesus and put down roots of European culture that abjured all things black. Black people out of frustration were now making it plain that perpetual subservience to colonial masters was on its way out and Cecil understood why they felt that way.

Cecil enjoyed working with black people and admired their infinite patience and courtesy. Developing such a bond made it easy for him to learn local languages, his fluency surprising old hands who had lived in the territory for decades but whose exertions into lingua franca extended to a limited thesaurus of swear words and condescending views about people of colour.

Sights and sounds of his new surroundings were manna from heaven for Cecil. Living through heady days of unilateral independence in 1965 was an experience of a lifetime, an unwise political act in Cecil's view. He foresaw that after gung-ho political utterances had taken their course a debilitating war had to ensue, exacting a wasteful, heavy price in death, mutilation and destruction, aside from inevitable disastrous effects on the economy.

Marlene wasn't too happy when he too was called up to do his bit fighting "the enemy" year-in and year-out. *Enemy?* They were stampeding in from all fronts; from Angola, from Zambia, from South Africa, from South West Africa, from Zaire, from Malawi, from Botswana and from Portuguese East Africa, whose collective atrocities and cross-border raids had bludgeoned the entire Rhodesian population into entrenched fear and apprehension. Even the CIA and several of its European counterparts were sending in operatives whose inability to disguise their real masters had become a standing joke among regulars.

Frothing politicians at the United Nations and in Westminster proved a waste of space and time advertising that the British were bent on forsaking the territory at all costs. They'd milked it to the core and now they wanted to run off into the sunset and leave the colonists to their fate. If oil wells had existed in the territory it would have been different. The Brits and the Brits and Americans would have fallen over themselves to control matters. The new *Rhodesia* had to go and Whitehall made no bones about it. It was just going to get worse and Cecil fretted about his and Marlene's survival. Of prime concern was that when venturing out on military "ops" he had to leave his beautiful brunette wife alone in a small Rhodesian town where men slavered at the very sight of her.

Cecil did not take kindly to young people fighting old men's wars. Eighteen-year old lads were dying and leaving grieving parents behind who too in many instances also ended up gruesomely tortured and butchered by insurgents. He didn't relish the thought of becoming a war statistic. Damn it! He sympathised with people who wanted free elections. Why the hell did he have to fight them?

"Time to go," he informed his wife. She had no argument so he set about looking for another job. Applications to England were simply ignored or return posted, confiscated or stolen. Waiting for the South African SUNDAY TIMES to arrive became a weekly highlight and he loitered at the corner café on Sunday mornings until the truck roared up to unload newspapers. Scanning the appointments supplement heightened his expectations and when spotting something he thought he could handle he wasted no time applying.

Christmas 1984 he spotted it, an advertisement for a job that suited him. "About bloody time Marlene," he breathed, wreathed in smiles. "Look at this one. This is for me. *Manpower Manager* wanted in the Northern Cape, South Africa. Right up my street! Blow using the normal post. This one I'm going to 'phone in about."

His historic "Winds of change" predictions in 1961 by Harold Macmillan the bloodhound-eyed and droopingly mustachioed British Prime Minister when facing a dour South African cabinet in Cape Town had sparked racial turmoil throughout Central Africa with meteoric speed.

Harry McCrae, a born and bred Rhodesian, among many did not take kindly to being abandoned to the mercies of a projected black government. Democratic credos adopted by newcomers to the British Commonwealth had proved to be masterpieces of meaningless fulmination that after day one of "independence" had been overtaken by one-party states whose swollen ranks of corrupt self-seeking ministers and officials had ravaged their countries' coffers not to mention eliminating and killing their opposition side by side with making life near impossible for white residents.

Harry had reluctantly accepted that such changes were inevitable. Any sane person had to accept that and when pushed to the point where they had nothing to lose, black majorities had to react adversely so life had to become exceedingly cheap as a result. It was the way of Africa. On the practical side the thought of being trapped in a black state whose headlong trip into penury and reverse racism sobered him. He wanted to keep his European standards. That was his right but he knew that there had to be a price to pay.

Chairmen of the big copper mines sniffed the political ill-wind and took up the call, since profits were paramount. "African advancement" they uniformly advocated. *African* meaning black people, so the message was clear to people like Harry, *get yourself qualified or suffer the consequences.*

He did. Doubly—as a cost accountant and corporate secretary followed up by a year at a redbrick university in England reading for his MBA before returning to the Zambian *Copperbelt*. Six years after the country's independence in 1964 it was clear to Harry that he and his family had to leave for safer climes. White professionals were a threatened breed, legislated against, hassled by ever-increasing and intimidatory legislation and rapidly diminishing civil liberties. Worse was fast-failing security and belligerent politicians backed by lawless youth brigades who hunted in hyena-like packs that thought little of attacking and burning white residents alive and raping their women.

He was pleasantly surprised to learn that his finance, systems and computer knowledge had equipped him take on top positions in South Africa. Within a matter of a month from the time he had made his decision to emigrate he was snapped up by a big company in Natal and two months later he and his family crossed the famed *Zambezi River* for the last time when heading southwards by car.

Living barely a stone's throw from the beach was a big plus for Harry and his family. No longer were they afraid to traverse the countryside and explore the coast. Harry threw himself into his work, delighted that his efforts met with speedy promotion and welcome salary increases.

Only when working outside the mining arena did he appreciate how much he missed it. Such rumination sunk in after he had had a mild heart attack on his thirty-fifth birthday. "Don't kill yourself at work young man," his doctor told him. "Your family won't thank you." Harry yearned for the masculinity of mining, being associated with ore wrenched from the ground to wend its way through crushing, leaching, concentrating, refining and smelting to take on new life as a copper ingot or gold bar, a heady experience compared to manufacturing consumer goods and being embroiled in associated marketing gymnastics to increase product market share.

Three years down the line by when he'd earned senior manager status he was in the running for an operating company director slot an unexpected approach from a blue-blood South African mining conglomerate arrived. He had nothing to lose by meeting the officials concerned at the prestigious "Men-only"' Rand Club in down town Johannesburg. Captains of industry used this august waterhole and Harry was in awe of familiar faces, men whose actions affected the country's economy.

Very little came out about what it was the mining group wanted him for—until coffee and cigars were served. *"Top financial job...various directorships...you have the background...we heard good things about you..."*

"Yes, but where is it?" Harry queried. "And to do what?"

"Oh, my dear fellow didn't we say?" the urbane individual who had contacted him said. "In Botswana. I'm resident director there."

Harry blanched. *Botswana?* Among the poorest countries in the world. He'd seen enough of it when traveling through by train with his parents years before on their way to Cape Town for holidays. A wasteland. *Kalahari Desert* country was a far cry from the lushness of Natal and its pristine beaches.

"Our main show there is in diamonds. It's a fairly new investment. Latest equipment and modern methods. It needs careful handling. We want you to base in *Gaborone*, the country's capital. Close to government you see, in the south, close to the South African border. There's a lot more on the cards…copper, nickel, platinum. We want the right man in there to organize company finance and treasury functions."

Diamond mining….a process easier to win final products from but a lot more complicated when sending gems through tortuous paths of international contracts, markets and sales. Knowledge of international tax treaties was mandatory as was ensuring that the state got its fair share of cash flow.

"Just set it all up," the resident director drawled over his Cuban cigar. "And we'll be forever in your debt."

As for international promotional possibilities, it all sounded wonderful. Every one of the pinstripes present nodded sagely on that score.

"When I'm away Harry, of course you act for me as the next senior man there. When I go out on transfer in two or three years time, you're next in line" the resident director expounded. "It's quite a social whirl too you must appreciate. Your time will not be your own. You will inter-act with government and all the ambassadors. We must fly the old company flag mustn't we? International contacts are our life blood."

At three times the salary Harry was receiving in Durban and becoming a director of the mining group's Botswana operating companies he was going to service, it was an offer impossible to refuse. His *Copperbelt* experience had served him well to take on the role of financial director.

An ensuing four years of intense effort resulted in a smooth operating financial and administration function at one with government and his head office's expectations and one that took cognizance of training local citizens and setting their career paths.

Then the unexpected happened. The old school tie system kicked in.

A chum of one of the main board members was moved in over Harry so quickly and so shamefully executed that any member of the firm's hierarchy whom Harry attempted to counsel about this unwarranted ignominy, showed him cold shoulder.

From the moment their eyes locked the two men disliked one another on sight. Harry was no "Yes man", guaranteed to infuriate the pustule-faced interloper who expected unquestioned obeisance from personnel beneath him. The man was a clown and was left in no doubt that Harry knew as much. To rub it in, a local citizen was also appointed. "Lining him up for the top job," the new resident director snidely informed Harry. "After I've done my stint he's going to replace me. You're wasting your time here old boy."

Harry didn't like that message at all and insisted on seeing the group chairman in Johannesburg.

"He's busy!" his protective secretary condescendingly informed him. "You will have to make an appointment."

"Is he hell?" Harry barked and burst into the fat man's office to catch him joyfully picking his nose and rolling green goo between thumb and forefinger before flicking it on to his Persian rug.

"You can't...what do you think..." the startled official shouted. "Get..."

In as florid language as he could muster, Harry informed the snot-smeared chairman what he thought of his conniving, two-timing ways.

"You will rue the day you cursed me. I'll make it my business to interfere in your career. I'll break you," the affronted official declared, even unhappier when hearing Harry's "Get stuffed you fat prick!" as he walked out and slammed the door.

"How about Canada?" a dejected Harry told Doreen. "This place is on its way out. No point sticking around here is there?"

As if by divine intervention an unsolicited offer arrived from an old Botswana government contact now working on a nickel mine in Sudbury, Ontario. Harry grabbed it. Perhaps this time he thought that in the New World he'd work in an environment devoid of old-boy politics where only ability to get things done mattered.

It was not to be. His Canadian venture turned out disastrously for him. Immediately after landing at Toronto International Airport he'd learned that the mine he was to join had been sold and that its new owners were not interested in honoring the written commitment he'd received. Taking it to law? That meant years of expensive litigation, a slow and uncertain process. He didn't have anything like the money required.

He took the opportunity to have a good look at the country finally deciding that it was not for him or his family. All that snow….ice…tire chains…fur coats…layers of clothing…rows of identical suburban houses. Dog droppings in the snow…

What made up his mind once and for all was listening to Doctor Christiaan Barnard, the famed South African heart surgeon on a late-night talk show in Toronto. The great man's soft drawling Cape accent sent shivers of loneliness coursing through Harry. Once and for all he accepted that he was an African. His soul was African. His thoughts were African. He was part of Africa's soil. He just had to get back there, to South Africa whether it wanted him or not for it was the only place where he felt at home, to start again. South Africa wasn't so bad that he'd have had any trouble finding a good job, unlikely though in his preferred field — mining.

He didn't like to enunciate it but the thought that persisted in his head was that what had happened in Zambia would befall people like him in South Africa. Blacks there had to be looking for the country to be handed back and when the apartheid government fell how could life there ever be the same again? Would a third generation white be considered part of the landscape? Still, he had a crust to earn and children to put through school and university. If he had to, he assured himself, he'd have resigned himself to working in the fires of hell so long as his family did not suffer. Planning a long-term future had to be a luxury for any white African, that much dawned on him.

1984 developed into *Annus Horribilis* for Harry. His seventy-five year old father had fallen, knocked unconscious and frozen to death during a biting South African Highveld winter. A dull ache gnawed at Harry when picturing his father's emaciated body being carted away by ambulance men.

Harry blamed himself. He should never have succumbed his sister's insistence that "their old man" when visiting from Cape Town stay with her and her husband. They set out for work at seven in the morning and returned at seven in the evening to their corrugated iron roofed farmhouse that had seen better days sixty years previously.

No one else frequented a forlorn six acres that supposedly had attracted its current tenants because they had wanted to *"…be in the country to grow things you know."* Who could the old man, who spoke read and wrote seven languages, talk to during the day? An itinerant gardener high on dope who slept in a discarded concrete sewage pipe in a weed-strewn field?

No one called at the smallholding languishing thirty miles south of Johannesburg. What for? In flat uninteresting country it was the wrong side of the city for anyone upwardly mobile to take seriously and as for getting to it and away from it by road, a nightmare because one had to journey through ramshackle suburbs and ever-expanding squatter camps where filth mounted daily and roadsides were havens for human dross.

No wonder the old man had resorted to swallowing valium pills to doze and pass time away until someone came home for him to talk to. He'd been excruciatingly lonely. The only luxury he had was to take a hot bath. He had slipped in it and it had killed him. He'd died alone—unconscious until frozen to death, a waste of a gracious, wise old man who had given joy to all who had known him.

Several weeks later Harry's wife, Doreen keeled over in a shopping mall. No one came to her assistance but miraculously she kept muttering a number. She managed to stagger into a chemist shop and someone 'phoned the number. Her doctor.

"Brain hemorrhage," her doctor diagnosed within minutes of arriving at the chemists shop and summoned an ambulance. "We must get her to a hospital. It doesn't look too hopeful."

"It's your choice," Doctor Terpolsky solemnly informed Harry following his examination at the Princess Nursing Home in downtown Johannesburg. "I can't lighten the load for you. It's serious. If she has another bleed it will be the end for her. If we operate it's a complicated procedure because the bleed is deeply seated; if she survives she could come out severely mentally handicapped. There is only one man in the country who can tackle this operation. Mr Farnham. I must have your decision quickly. He's standing by."

Harry kept asking himself, "Is this really happening?" Not in his worst nightmares had he countenanced something so terrible happening to his beloved wife. If anyone had to suffer he thought it right that only he should have endured it. He'd been the sinner...not his wife...not his children. *Rather take me Lord* he prayed. *Take me.* He forced himself to sign the indemnity form authorizing the operation. He didn't want to concede one iota of probability that his wife could die or be struck down to resume "life" as a vegetable. "No!" he convinced himself, "'she doesn't deserve it. She's a good Christian. No! No!"

It had been touch and go during her twelve-hour micro-surgical ordeal. A month later she was sent home, exhausted, but miraculously in possession of all her faculties.

"She's better than new!" a pleased Mr Farnham had proclaimed.

During his bad weeks while Doreen hovered in intensive care Harry had found out who his friends were. Precious few. Robin, a boyhood friend and parish priest had given him spiritual sustenance. His neighbors could not have been kinder. The Byrons', friends for a lifetime had stood by him as had the Steads', but very little by way of "just being there" had sprung from Harry's relatives. Father Robin's plea to members of his congregation to pray for Doreen resulted in a flood of "Get Well" cards and kindly messages from total strangers. Some had even taken the trouble to visit her in hospital. Not one of Harry's relatives had bothered to do so.

Emotionally, Harry suffered severe knock. There was no way he could go to pieces with two young daughters to care for. Within six months streaks of grey had appeared in his leonine black mane and frown wrinkles aged his appearance by ten years.

Only when his wife was at death's threshold had Harry fully realized how dependent he was on her. Two teenage daughters desperately needed their mother and Harry with his twelve-hour working days was a poor substitute. He gave thanks that Doreen's mother had flown out from Dublin to nurse her allowing him to concentrate on how he was going to pay for costly medical treatment Doreen had received. He reconciled himself to cashing in his insurance policies, selling their house and probably their furniture. He'd have sold everything without blinking to save his wife.

"Not a cent," the financial director of his company informed him when Harry tremulously asked what the amount owing was. "You did us a big favor because the penny dropped how under-funded our medical scheme is. We've fixed that so you don't owe us anything. We just want your wife to get better."

That was the only time in the whole worrying, mind-blowing, agonizing period of Doreen's trauma that Harry couldn't stop his tears of relief. God had been on his side and so had his employers been.

Christmas day 1984 had turned into a joyous occasion. Over grace

Harry reminded everyone that it could so easily have been otherwise.

The Byrons' and the Steads' were present to celebrate Christmas lunch with them. Father Robin made a late appearance after Mass duties had wound up, feeling sufficiently at home to remove his collar and sup a cold beer. A mellow afternoon was spent chatting under a sun-bathed full-blossomed cherry tree in Harry's front garden.

"Christmas in Jo'burg," a relaxed Vin Byron oozed, "the weather's perfect and we had a great lunch. By the way Harry, did you see last Friday's financial pages?"

"No," Harry replied. "Why do you ask?"

"I spotted the perfect job for you. Back in the mining world. Working in industry doesn't suit you Harry. You're a mining man through and through."

"Really?" Harry perked up and took a hurried gulp of wine. "Where is this job? With what company?"

"Northern Cape. The mine's fifty kilometres into the desert from *Thuringia Bay*, the nearest town. *Chater Metals* is looking for a top financial man. Uranium yellowcake is its main product. It's right up your street judging from what I read. Divisional manager rank too."

Harry's initial excitement subsided. *"Geez*, Vin, that's rough country, desert and scrub. Blazing hot. My kids wouldn't thank me if I took them to the middle of nowhere. They'd be bored out of their minds."

"Well my gut feel is that it's shouting for you Harry. How many mines do you know about where you can live beside the sea? Your girls will love it I'm sure."

"Maybe so," Harry nodded. "I suppose it's academic because Doreen needs to be close to good medical attention. I've got a good job but I have to admit there's no magic in producing processed foods. Who would have thought I'd be running a foods factory?"

"Listen. You said Doreen's good as new now Harry. Let her doctor guide you if and when it becomes necessary."

"Strange isn't it?" Harry sighed. "Fate seldom allows you to have everything. I love Jo'burg. We have a beautiful home and wonderful friends. But job-wise I just can't get my foot in the door anywhere here in the mining business. Ever since I told you-know-who what I thought of him he's put the word out and I'm being shafted at every turn. Usually I make it to the last two candidates and then I get mountains rolled in my path, not boulders."

"Yes, he does seem to have it in for you all right," Vin mused. "Who knows, this could turn out to be a different proposition? I visited the place a few years back on a Rotary tour. It's not bad at all. Different. It's a combination of the real Africa you tell us about and Germany. You've got nothing to lose. The mine's owned by a United Kingdom consortium so you get paid in sterling."

"Follow your instincts," Father Robin commented. "If you don't try how will you ever know what kind of proposition it is?"

"Perhaps you're both right" Harry said, his hopes rising. "Thanks. Do you have the advertisement handy?"

His friends' words had fallen on fertile ground. *He had nothing to lose.* At forty-two he hadn't honed into a career path with a company whose sense of timing coincided with his. Yes, he'd gone up the ladder and had earned promotions. He remained unsettled. Whatever represented Utopia, he hadn't found it yet. It gnawed at him. He couldn't explain it…was this his chance?

Once he had read the advertisement he conceded that it did look promising. He was young enough and fit enough to deal with new challenges. The mine was small by *Copperbelt* standards. It wanted someone "to hit the ground with his or her feet running." He felt eminently capable of doing that.

He talked it over with Doreen once their two teen daughters had gone to bed. He'd learned that he tended to be the impulsive one in their marriage. Often he'd made decisions before without counseling her and had paid the price. Doreen had the gift of studied response. Some acquaintances considered her manner aloof. Not so, since she thought about her words carefully to avoid giving offence even if thoroughly deserved. More and more Harry relied on her good judgment and that such a beautiful woman chose to be with him continually astounded him.

"Apply for it Harry," she urged him. "Take one step at a time. They're bound to interview you because you have the experience they want. Size it up carefully. I'll support you whatever you decide."

"God, Doreen,'" Harry whispered, "I don't deserve you. You're such a nice person. I wish that I was blessed with even a tinge of your good nature. Thank you."

The next day he posted his application. Surprisingly a week later a recruitment official telephoned him at his workplace.

"Mr McCrae? Our general manager wants to interview you and your wife as soon as possible. It's just over an hour on SAA to Kimberley where the company 'plane collects you up and flies you to the mine site. Another hour in the air."

"You didn't waste much time!" an effusive but grateful Harry said. "Yes. Thank you. We can go at any time. For how long?"

"Normal form is to fly up early Friday and return midday Monday. On the Sunday you're left to your own devices to get the feel of *Thuringia Bay*. I'll make travel arrangements and arrange for everything to be delivered to your home."

A January Friday. Both Harry and Doreen had resolved to enjoy their impending trip and their minds were at rest since Doreen's mother was happy to look after their girls.

Perhaps it was because they were undertaking a unique adventure, an unexpected event with the promise of better things to come that the couple strove to enjoy every waking moment. A solicitous SAA crew had served up two gourmet business-class breakfasts. Not a wisp of cloud sullied the bluest of skies as their

Boeing 737 approached Kimberley, as arid a location as one could find. It didn't exactly lie in true desert but no one argued that it was uncomfortably hot for most of the year.

Compared to eternal hubbub at Jan Smuts International Airport in Johannesburg, Kimberley Airport was eerily quiet. It stood ten kilometers outside the town, on the nearest stretch of flat ground, surrounded by dry scrub dominated by thousands of desert sentinels, stark, spiny aloe bushes, in red bloom. Heat visibly bounced off the tarmac. An aircraft service crew bathed in sweat waited for the engines to die before steps were abutted to the 'plane and its doors thrust open.

During their brief walk to the terminal building the happy couple felt they had entered a sauna bath. The air was so clear and the sky so blue, they could see for miles. No smog ever came from somnolent Kimberley a town whose fortunes had apexed in the nineteen twenties when its diamonds had all but disappeared.

Their 737 was the only big jet in sight and one small 'plane stood on the apron opposite the Departures Hall. Air-conditioning within the building was a welcome release, not enjoyed for any length of time because formalities were quickly attended to and they were directed by airport staff to a gateway opposite where the *Chater Mines* shuttle 'plane waited.

Once over the Kalahari Desert Harry had no illusions that beneath him stretched some of the harshest terrain on the planet. He began to have misgivings. *I must be mad to consider coming to this back of beyond — it looks like outer Mongolia...no way I'm coming here...leave Jo'burg for this?*

A massive bank of mist appeared just as the small aircraft began its landing approach to the mine's airport. Crosswinds had the small 'plane bucking and Harry felt bile about to reflux out his mouth, combined with severe nausea. If he could have he'd have ejected himself from the 'plane to end it all he would gladly have done so. Doreen was unaffected and held his hand to reassure him.

When the aircraft finally parked in its hangar, propellers cut and door hefted open, Harry bent over and held on to his stomach. "Thank God" he muttered. "What a nightmare!"

At the foot of the steps stood a beaming young woman clutching a folder to her breast. "Hello, I'm Melanie. From Manpower Division," she proclaimed cheerily as the couple disembarked. "Mrs McCrae, this is your program. I shall be escorting you to *Thuringia Bay* to show you around."

"Thank you Melanie" an animated Doreen responded. "You are very well organized. I'm looking forward to it."

"Mr McCrae," Melanie continued, "our chief pilot will drive you to the mine site. Our General Manager Mr Bradshaw is waiting to see you. He has a full program lined up for you."

A white-faced Harry accepted his envelope preferring to wait until he was in a car before opening it. He kissed his wife's cheek and looked up to see Don South waiting, captain by rank who had effusively greeted him and Doreen at Kimberley's airport and shepherded them to his two-engine, unpressurised Piper Chieftain.

During the short drive Don turned out to be a font of information. He'd been associated with the mining venture from its start, some ten years, including the prospecting period when geologists were sweating to determine the size and grade of the ore body.

"We've seen them come here," he announced blandly, "and we've seen them go. No one's really managed to tame this mine so far. It always rears up and kicks us in the balls when we least expect it. General managers have been two a penny and as for divisional managers, herds of them flitted in and out over the years. They came here laughing and left as mental wrecks. You won't believe the shady characters who worked flankers here. But now that Dave Bradshaw's arrived, well, things do look a little better. I think he knows what he's doing."

"I must say," a still nauseous Harry replied a little sternly, "you hardly make the prospect of living here sound attractive."

"Don't mind me. I tell it like it is. David Bradshaw is quite new at the mine. He worked for a few years in Zambia, then in Rhodesia."

"You all seem to have had a rough ride."

Don grimaced. "That's no lie. There were a few times when we feared for our jobs. Money dried up. Customers complaining. And the government is none too pleased either. I was flying officials in and out here from Kimberley. The main problem seems to be keeping the production going. It's forever breaking down. Our mining guys say the metallurgists get it wrong and the 'Met' guys say the opposite."

Repeating his story brought beads of sweat to Don's forehead. He knew that he'd been lucky to have retained his job. It was only the remoteness of the mine that had ensured the 'plane had stayed. For emergencies. And ferrying people in and out of the mine since no commercial service had existed to fill that gap. At his age, pushing forty, finding a worthwhile flying job posed problems and commercial airlines were always laying people better than him off.

Harry took in his desert surroundings during the drive. There *were* plants of a sort, hugging the sands, stringy bushes and *narra* melons, food for the klipspringer and odd few springbok in the area.

"Once you get to know the desert, you'd be surprised at how much life it has in it," Don told him. "You do have to be careful. A stranger could get lost with disastrous results. There are plenty stories doing the rounds about people who disappeared without trace. The golden rule is that if your car breaks down you stick with it. Otherwise the sun fries you alive."

"I'm not exactly a stranger to deserts," Harry smiled. "The same applies in Botswana. There're some tracts up there that hardly a vehicle a month visits. Anyhow, there must be water in this desert if it sustains life."

"You're right. It's a combination of mist precipitation that rolls in from the coast and underground water. You have to get to know the river courses. The mine's water comes from underground river sources miles north and south of here and is pipelined in. The first thing our new general manager did was to put in recycling measures and anti-evaporation chemicals onto mine ponds. We were paying a fortune for water."

"I'm impressed. You're well informed. Your general manager sounds like an interesting man."

"He is. He's not a gusher."

"*Gusher?* That's a new one."

"Yes. You know people who spew words for the sake of it. We get lots of gushers pitching up here. Self-appointed experts, usually wasters who don't have a clue. And then guess what happens? They fly back to their bases and we're left here none the wiser still scratching our nuts. There's no one our GM wants to impress. He was transferred in here six or seven months ago to sort it all out. Before he came, the place was sinking like a stone."

"I'm glad to hear it. On the *Copperbelt*, mine general managers were akin to gods. Once at our mine the queen mother visited us and next to her sat the governor of the country in his Rolls. The GM got a bigger cheer than she or the governor did."

"Is that so!" Don laughed. "Relax brother...our GM's 'hands-on'. He walks his patch at all hours. You could never call him or his wife snobs. Nice people. He knows each employee's name, all two thousand of us. He actually tells the work force what is going on by issuing a weekly broadsheet. Before he arrived it was all rumor and gossip here. Backstabbing like you never saw. Management just went its merry way and kept everyone in the dark unless there was a reprimand to be handed out. Oh, oh, we're at security reception."

Don pulled up at the reception gate and bade Harry to exit. A huge blue and white signboard stood sentinel at the gates on which appeared, "180,000 HOURS WITHOUT A LOST TIME INCIDENT".

"You have to sign in," Don instructed. "It's a government safety requirement and you sign an indemnity form. And a security one. You probably read in the 'papers about the bomb blast in *Thuringia Bay* last year."

"I did sure enough. Some people were killed and a few badly hurt. Were the culprits ever caught?"

"No. Everyone says it was a terrorist thing. When something awful happens everyone assumes that blacks are responsible. They talk so much about getting rid of our government I suppose they set themselves up. A lot of residents took fright, called it quits and pushed off. You know this is a pretty lonely spot, literally the end of the line because the railway stops right on the Atlantic Ocean. That's about as far west as you get in Central Africa. So when something like that happens, well one wonders when your turn will come. Or to your family."

Harry had long learned that first impressions were usually accurate. Who was this David Bradshaw? He did not remember any person by that name when living on the *Copperbelt*. Apprehension disappeared when ushered into the General Manager's office. For starters the décor wasn't a testimony to self-importance and behind a very ordinary desk stood a beaming David Bradshaw, a picture of raw health. The man radiated goodwill and Harry felt cheered. It was his first positive reaction up to that point.

Fifty'ish. Liverpool traces in his speech. Well built. Dressed in khakis—the antithesis of *Copperbelt* general managers who paraded in starched collars and suits and expected everyone to pedestal them.

"Mr McCrae!" David exclaimed through a toothy smile and heartily shook Harry's hand, a firm grip Harry was prepared for.

"Thank you for coming at such short notice. We do appreciate it."

"Our pleasure sir," Harry responded. "Thank you for inviting us."

"*David* please. Keep the "Sir" for someone a lot older and wiser than me!"

"Thank you. My Christian name is Harry."

David nodded towards his corner sofas at right angles to each other. "Please sit down. Make yourself comfortable. I want to hear all about you."

No preliminaries. No *how was your flight?* Harry liked that. He felt kinship towards his host. The man was clearly very methodical judging from the piles of documents neatly stacked on his desk.

"Are you a Christian?" David opened with.

It wasn't a question that Harry expected but he was unfazed.

"Yes. I most certainly am. A Roman Catholic. Proudly so."

"Why?"

"It gives me sustenance. It's the mainstay of my life. I have its comfort, particularly in a crisis."

"Crisis? Have there been any?"

"Yes. There have." Harry explained what had happened to his father and about Doreen's recent travails.

"You have been through the mill Harry," a serious-faced David said. "You probably know by now that this mine is having severe problems of its own."

"Yes I believe so. We see mention every now and again in mining journals."

"I worked at *Bancroft Mine* in Zambia in the fifties and sixties. I know most of the referees you mentioned. I saw from your CV what systems work you had done and I know the truth of it. Do you remember a chap called Trevor Lee at the mine where you worked?"

Harry was surprised. "I do indeed. I was very much a junior at the time when the country was still called *Northern Rhodesia*. Trevor was a mechanical engineer. I remember playing inter-divisional cricket against him. Years later we crossed paths when I was in Botswana. By then he was a consulting engineer at group headquarters in Johannesburg. We were both on the same boards."

"Indeed...what did you think of him?"

Harry took his time answering a potential mine field. "He'd survived an air crash at a prospecting site much further north. Amazing man. No one becomes a consulting engineer in the world's largest mining company by mistake. He did very well for himself I have to say."

"Yes, but what did you think of him?"

"To be honest I thought he was in a bit over his head. He had a huge desk to watch over within a very demanding company. Frankly, knowing who his boss was, a man I did not respect, I don't know how Trevor managed it."

"Interesting," David again mused. "I spoke to him about you. He told me that you were a financial genius."

Harry gulped and felt his face flush and his mouth run dry. "It looks like I owe him an apology,' he said lamely. "And to you. Me and my big mouth. I am sorry."

"No you don't." David's relaxed manner was encouraging. He looked Harry in the eye, his riveting gaze taking in every gesture, every nervous tic. "I asked you a question and got a straight reply. No apologies are necessary. The previous six candidates I talked to about this job told me what they thought I wanted to hear. I must have a team that understands what transparency is. Duckers and divers have no place here. The risks are far too great."

"I understand."

"You were honest, so that's in your favor. In like vein let me explain what our problems are and then you can have shot at telling me what we do about it after completing your tour. This is mainly a uranium mine, yellowcake extraction and production, supplemented by rare earths. You must know the mine has suffered a long history of stop-start operations. We are an open pit outfit, extract ore and treat it on site. Metallurgical operations are varied and complex. That means we employ a big fleet of haul trucks, mining shovels and dozers along with a maze of metallurgical processes. It all cost big money and costs even bigger money maintaining it all."

"I see."

"Every square inch of this territory was scoured and fully documented by German geologists well before the First World War, an enterprising breed of men who found this ore body. Only in the fifties did a small operator open a one-horse mine. He named it after his home area in Germany. *'The Thuringia,'* it's more popular nickname. That speaks for itself. *Chater Metals Group* in London acquired it eight years ago. Suffice to say a lot of money was spent on more equipment and plant but cost over-runs are an enormous problem for us. Shareholders are desperately unhappy. Our job is to stop the bleeding, honor our final product contracts, get into the black and stay there despite all the lobbies who want to close us down."

"Is there a problem with cash flow?"

"Yes," David answered. "Good question. We have to fix that. I need to a first-class team to help me do it. I need experienced men who get on with the job and who can handle and motivate staff. For divisional managers, this will not be a training patch. They must kick in from day one and stick at it. I must have people who withstand pressure and make decisions fast."

"Oh, I didn't think that things were so bleak for you," a dismayed Harry said. "What sum is it all capitalized at?"

"Two hundred and ninety eight million dollars."

Harry whistled. "That's big money. Ten per cent return on that investment per annum is a big ask in any language."

"You learn fast young man. We're plagued with production and mining breakdowns. So unit cost goes up when we do manage to make final products but unfortunately our sale prices are pegged. Our products are desperately wanted by USA and Japanese clients. We've got their orders but we can't make what they want fast enough. Which forces us to go out to the spot market to buy products or we're in breach of contract. When we do make the stuff it has to be at a cost less that contracted prices."

"*'Spot market'*...I can imagine the cost. You must be paying big premiums." Harry began to have doubts. Listening to David's travails were not what he had expected but on second thoughts gave the man credit for being honest with him.

"We are. My concern is to get this mine operating round the clock all year round. If we don't, it's obvious what's on the cards.

Understand that up front there's a big mountain to climb and we haven't much time to do it in. I have to admit that there are a few directors who want shot of us because from day one this place represented nothing but problems. Most mines have problems but get over them Not this one. Five years after start-up it's still in deep marshes. If you prefer a more sedate working environment this is definitely not the place to look for it. You have to know that right away."

"Well that's perfectly plain," Harry answered. "No, the last thing I'm after is a robotic civil-service type position. Problems are there to be licked. It gives me immense job satisfaction."

"I'm very pleased to hear it," a relaxed David responded. "There is one important aspect about working in this country that I have to tell you about. It has to be factored in to your thinking should we offer you the job."

Harry chose to say nothing except nod.

"There is no racial discrimination on this mine. In certain government strata our ethos does not sit well. Be prepared to take big stick from conservative quarters in the community at large. We also get stick from underground political parties."

"What kind of 'stick?'"

"Independence movements among others. Some label us 'Western lapdogs!' So you see we don't please everyone. That's pressure. The big ask in my book if you join us is not to dilute your time sprouting politics. Just concentrating on the job is your main task. There can be no subsidiary interest that overrides commitment to your work."

"Can I ask what the promotional opportunities are within the group worldwide? I expect no one stays in the same job forever."

"I can only mirror our chairman's view. Sir Francis Clayton. He says that when you become a divisional manager within this group you've arrived. Anything more than that is a bonus."

Harry was taken aback and showed it, uttering a lame "I see."

David noisily swilled his cup of tea. "Right! Today, you will spend going over the mine. Ask any questions you want. I don't mind who you upset. Stirring up a hornets' nest often gets adrenalin going. Tomorrow, you and your wife will be out and about in *Thuringia Bay*. I want you to talk to some of the town's elders which includes our very entertaining mayor, a few businessmen, headmasters, medical people and so on."

"I look forward to it."

"You have to size up *Thuringia Bay* as a place to live with your family. As a manager I expect that your wife will live with you because she will be part of our team. Most people who come here learn to love living on the coast. A few people couldn't take its remoteness. It is after all part of the hostile Skeleton Coast we have all heard about.

"We found that long misty and damp days depressed a few unfortunate residents. They took up other pleasures like alcohol and drugs. It's just about the most remote stretch of coast outside of Antarctica, as pristine today as it was a million years ago. I must say that I enjoy it."

"Aside from the job my main concern will be education for my daughters and medical facilities for my wife."

"Good," David continued effervescently, "anything of note, write it down and we'll chat before we fly you both back to Kimberley. You will want to know where you stand before you leave. I promise you a face-to-face decision."

It was lot to digest for Harry. The desolation of what he'd seen so far had not infused him with wonder. Botswana's environment by comparison was a veritable Garden of Eden and had the advantage of being much closer to *civilization.*

"Thank you. You have gone to a lot of trouble for me. I hope I justify it."

"A note of caution. Save a little energy. You and your wife attend a dinner tonight with the managers and their wives."

"Oh! Thank you. I'm glad you warned me."

"Now, over to you. I see from your CV that you specialized in financial matters. *Financial Director* with our opposition in Botswana no less. Well done."

That remedial measures had begun on the mine was inescapable, but much remained to be done. Mindful that the mine was strapped for cash, Harry saw no point in labouring the obvious. Any fool could talk problems. How many could talk solutions? He'd acquired the habit of carrying a notebook and pen wherever he went. He had much to jot down. He'd noticed the new trend among younger officials who used the "F" word in almost every sentence. *Firing* people was no management technique to be proud of in his book without extreme cause.

He found that employees he met fell into three categories. The first welcomed positive leadership. The second group comprised a chorus voicing concern about "newcomers who did not know what they were doing." Lastly, the most insidious coterie groaned that their managers had not appreciated their massive abilities and given them a chance to strut their stuff.

"You know!" one sour demoted supervisor declared to Harry, "a manager called me 'A stupid f******g idiot!' when I met him for the first time! How could he do that based on a five minute interview?"

It took massive self-control not to answer *I can see why!* Harry did not discuss "Whys'?" What he wanted to know was what people genuinely thought about the mine and their jobs. In tandem with his walkabout he kept his eyes open and absorbed the state of the plant, open pit, equipment and materials.

At one pm he was delivered to the GM's office.

"Come and meet the rest of our management team," David smiled as he got up from his chair. "We take half an hour for lunch. It's a good opportunity to discuss how things are going."

Listening to the divisional managers' banter at the lunch table gave Harry a good idea of their mood. *Enthused*. No one was bent on scoring points. He was made welcome.

They chatted about mutual friends in the mining world. Both Frank Fielding, mining manager and Cecil Lonsdale, the manpower manager had worked previously in Rhodesia. Both men were in their late thirties but only Frank smoked like a trooper. They were comfortable with each other's company judging from Cecil's greeting to Frank, "How's my favorite troglodyte?"

"There's no point talking about saving cost if you can't quantify it," Frank commented when getting round to his first cigarette after eating. "Also, we keep running out of materials and then we have to pay an arm and a leg for them. Our mine stores are in a perpetual mess. That lot needs sorting out chop-chop because it adds to down time we can't afford. As for the accountants..."

Peter Gomez displayed a brooding presence. Although an engineer he was standing in from *Chater Metals* head office in London acting as metallurgical manager until David had found a permanent appointee on his wavelength. "We make the stuff," Peter quietly informed Harry, "and we have the most problems. Our plant machinery is a constant bugbear. We want acceptable ore grade from the pit and pit people shout, 'We sent it!' We need up-to-the minute production cost information but most times all we get is meaningless mulch."

Whoever was handling the financial portfolio Harry had to assume was not production-oriented; probably an auditor. He was right. Burt Burnett the internal auditor had opened up to him. The chief accountant had been an auditor who in Burt's books didn't show too much appreciation of finance.

Bruno Gerber the swarthy divisional engineering manager weighed in with details of his forthcoming Sunday fishing trip. "*Steenbras* are running this weekend," he jovially informed his peers.

"I'll bring you guys one each if you behave yourselves. Don't call me out whatever you do! Leave it to the duty manager hey!"

"I'm sure you buy the fish Bruno," Cecil said. "Go on, confess!"

Bruno ignored Cecil's derisory quip and addressed Harry. "So! Another Rhodesian? Man, you blokes are really multiplying up here."

Harry had to laugh but also remind himself that opinions were out of place. No newcomer could have gall enough to cast opinions on the back of a flying visit. To do so meant risking making ill-informed comment and upsetting someone. Word traveled fast in a small community. He assumed that David wanted him to size up his potential counterparts. He also saw that his potential counterparts were sizing him up. He kept his own counsel. He was to spend an hour with each manager later. That was when he anticipated getting into their heads.

An effusive Don South dropped him off at the Pelican Hotel at six-thirty. He had an hour to have a bath, dress and chat over events with Doreen. He'd got a good impression of the hotel, furnished more like an up-market country mansion and run as such by obsequious staff attending to their guests' every need.

Doreen was already dressed for dinner and had laid out his clothes and toiletries. "I liked what I saw Harry," she informed him while he set about shaving. "This is a nice place to live in. Melanie showed me the house that goes with your job. It's right on the seafront. Lovely position. How was your day?"

"Exhausting Doreen. My gosh, I learned a lot about what's going on here. This mine has always had big problems I can tell you that much. There's a good few years hard work ahead to get it on stream."

Her face fell and she stared at him for a moment. "Big enough to turn you off working there?"

He finished shaving and patted his face with a towel. "That's what I want to talk to you about. In my opinion it really boils down to how successful the GM will be. He is *Chater Mines'* last gasp so to speak. By the way some locals call the mine by its previous name, '*The Thuringia*' just to tip you off in case you wonder what they're talking about. Anyhow, if David doesn't get that mine making profits soon it's in big trouble."

"Do you think he'll fail?"

"He's an impressive man. He has a great track record in the mining business. I think that with a sound team around him he could pull it off. It's one of hell of a challenge."

"I'll meet them tonight won't I? Why don't we keep an open mind till the end of our visit? Then we'll talk it over."

"Yes. Good idea. David Bradshaw didn't pull punches. He told me that he'd give me a decision before we left. He pointed out the bad and the good things about the mine and the country. I must say I took to the man. He has a good way with people and he gets his hands dirty. I had lunch with him and the managers. There's no doubt that they respect him. One thing for sure, he's not a racist; anyone holding that line of thought earns a smart goodbye. He's had an ex-employee prosecuted because the guy's racial attitudes caused a major accident."

The couple enjoyed a quick walk, moseying down to the seafront. A rickety pier jutted out well to sea, its boulder-strewn sides lashed by angry waves that threw up spray into their faces. Smells of salt and seaweed invaded their nostrils. It was still light. On their way back to their hotel they took time out to photograph some of the late nineteenth century architecture bordering wide streets made of earth and rock salt, reminiscent of a *Black Sea* German resort.

Harry shook his head in amazement. "I'd never for a moment thought that we'd find a touch of Europe in the desert of all places. People really came here over a hundred years ago to put down roots. Even before diamonds were discovered further south. They made it into a carbon copy of a German village. It must have something special to have kept the generations here."

The town stood on a little palm-fringed bay carved out by the nearby Pelican River, named of course after the monstrously sized birds that flocked to the river mouth. The horizon had turned red with fading sunlight and a strong breeze rustled palm trees fronting the beach. The crash of the Atlantic Ocean all but drowned their conversation.

Harry smiled and breathed in deeply. "Ahhh, this sea air! It's fantastic! I never thought that I'd ever spend any time on the Atlantic coast, yet here we are. Fate seems to be dealing us a few decent cards for a change."

David's Granada glided up as they got back to the hotel steps. "Hello Harry. Get in."

When inside the vehicle introductions were hastily exchanged. David's wife Pam spoke with a pronounced Rhodesian accent.

Mid-forties Harry thought. An attractive brunette with piercing brown eyes and ready smile. She was attractive enough to eschew wearing jewellery.

"We have our own recreation club for employees just ten miles inland. Outsiders are welcome to join but not many do," David explained. "They're comfortable with their town associations. Our club puts on a dinner and a bit of a disco dance." He was in high spirits and clearly an afficionado of generous splashings of *Old Spice* after-shave.

"Be careful on this dirt road Dave," Pam warned and prodded his knee with her forefinger. "At this rate you'll be the first one to overturn going *to* the club."

"'I'm fine,'" he replied, "'I've got plenty of ballast.'"

"Rude man!" she joked. "'Don't mind him," she said to her guests over her shoulder. "It must be the sea air. I see so little of him since we arrived here."

A skeletal Roger Lacy the club manager was waiting at the club entrance. He'd demarcated a parking space for David and guided him into it.

"Welcome Mr Bradshaw. Mrs Bradshaw," he boomed.

David introduced him to Harry and Doreen.

"Your guests are waiting in the cocktail bar sir," Roger informed David.

David looked around the car park. "It looks like you'll have plenty business tonight Roger. That's good."

"Booked out!" Roger cheerfully replied. "Some joker let slip that we were serving free crayfish. In their dreams!"

Harry grinned and took Doreen's hand to trail their hosts inside.

The inevitable happened. After introductions the party split into two groups. The women. The men.

The manager's wives wanted to know all there was about Johannesburg from Doreen, some misty-eyed, awaiting an opportunity to warm up their credit cards once they hit the famed *Golden City*.

As for the men conversation centered on the one game that all men in the country worshipped, rugby, then on to Cecil's latest joke followed by matters more cerebral, *The Thuringia*.

David let it go for fifteen minutes. "'Hey you lot! No shop talk off duty!"

Roger reminded David that his table was ready. Harry recognized George Shearing's *Black Satin* piano pieces gracing the speakers. It was perfect silky dinner music as far as he was concerned. He found himself flanked by Pam and Marlene, Cecil's ravishing wife. Pam had little conversation but appeared to be in tune with what everyone was saying. It was as if she was in auto-mode, going through the motions. Marlene oozed grace. She did not have to do anything special to be noticed. Her presence had the same effect as if one was seeing a masterpiece for the first time, a painting that one could examine for eternity and always find something new, mysterious and alluring about it.

Opposite him sat Bruno's wife, Mariette, whose bubbly nature would have raised people from the dead. She reminded Harry of a swimmer doing the butterfly stroke, leaping out of the water with great energy ensuring that she had to be noticed.

Harry had a quick glance at Doreen saw that she was seated between David and Peter Gomez whose wife had stayed on in London. It was an open secret that she abhorred "The sticks." To underline her antipathy she had not endear herself to *Thuringia Bay* wives for saying, "The women there wear the same dress twice! Can you believe it?"

After completing the first Pam chivvied her party to change seats to allow the visitors an opportunity to converse with everyone. An hour later dance music began in earnest. Until then Roger had made sure that his uniquely long-haired and attired disk jockey had kept off his beloved *Commando* brandy, a quaint figure gyrating behind his rostrum to what he imagined was the beat of music Harry had never heard before.

At one in the morning, a weary David announced, "Come on guys, let's allow our duty manager to get in a few hours sleep."

Duty manager? That was Frank, well into his third box of thirty *Paul Revere* of the day and still nursing the fourth of his "ABF's", alias "Absolute bloody finals" comprising hefty tots of brandy.

"I'll go to work from here," he growled. "No need to break up the party."

"No you don't young man! Home you go, you need shuteye," David countered. "Yvonne, are you driving him?"

"Yep. Thanks David. We had a good time."

Lyrical goodbyes split the night air in the car park. A procession of tail lights picked their way through early morning mist barreling in from the sea.

At two in the morning Harry and Doreen fell into their beds at their swish hotel, utterly exhausted.

It seemed like only five minutes later that their bedside phone rang.

"Mr McCrae?" the receptionist trilled. "Miss Melanie Du Preez is here at reception asking for you."

Harry fumbled for his watch.

Nine-thirty. A bright sunny day.

As a potential resident to say anything adverse about the place he or she lived in was plainly stupid. Harry and Doreen were aware that it was up to them to cut through the verbiage that they expected to hear to draw their own conclusions.

"I was born here," Mayor Henrichs proudly announced, "as was my father and his father before him. Why should I leave? This is my home. My roots are here."

It came out with such vehemence that Harry and Doreen envied the man. Mayor Henrichs was in his mid forties, everyone's image of a typical German with blue eyes, blonde hair and oozing Aryan confidence. His neat attire bespoke hand-made apparel.

"Has the mine affected the town at all Mr Henrichs?" Harry probed.

"Yes! Of course it has! It has brought us wealth and opportunity. That is good for all of us. Good for our country too. Our young people will not have to emigrate when they leave school. Our families stay together."

"Did you find a job here when you finished your education?"

"*Jawohl!*" he grinned. "I was fortunate. My grandfather founded a trading business and a shipping company right here. He was an early dealer in guano that he shoveled off and shipped to Europe. You must see the guano platforms down the coast! What a *verdomde* stink! But the stink makes us good money. Then our trading stores expanded too. I started at the bottom. Because I was 'family,' he grinned, 'I was not paid a salary. I worked for free for ten years!'"

His exuberance was overwhelming. Here was a man totally content with the hand life had dealt him.

"This country," Mayor Henrichs went on, "soon it will change. Politicians talk and talk, most of it nonsense, but change is in the air. I welcome it if we get peace as first prize."

"No politics!" David had warned, so Harry obliged and listened to Mayor Henrichs outline his thoughts on impending independence.

If the headmaster of the secondary school was to be believed all his pupils were potential Rhodes Scholars and the great universities were on bended knee waiting for them to enter their hallowed halls of learning. Still, the man was confident and ran a tidy school. How potential matriculates coped without mathematics and science teachers worried Harry but he kept off the subject.

The doctors in the town's clinic struck a positive chord. The town's official hospital did not seeing that it was administered by aged nuns who were rapidly dying out and turning it into a sacerdotal sanctuary. Clinic doctors had big plans for expansion and did have the skills Harry and Doreen thought necessary. A select panel of medical men served mine employees on a contractual basis. Being assured that they had the ability to cope with neural matters allowed Harry a sigh of relief.

"We are waiting for the mine to make up its mind before we commit to a modern hospital," one doctor confessed. "We hear rumors that it might close. It won't be for the first time."

Harry toyed with the idea of exploring the comment but pretended he had not heard it.

The house intended for the "Financial man" enjoyed a prime position overlooking the sea. Amazingly it was surrounded by lush gardens managed by the mine's sole horticulturist and his crew.

Fresh water, Melanie informed them, was in plentiful supply within the town, "but boy does it cost!"

Harry couldn't get over it. Plenty of water in a desert town but nothing like it back in Johannesburg where despite frequent rains, rationing was imposed.

"Shops close at one," Melanie said. "They reopen at three until six, which gives our employees time to shop when they get off the buses."

Harry and Doreen needed no persuasion that *Thuringia Bay* comprised a very healthy community, financially speaking.

On the Sunday they accepted Cecil and Marlene's invitation to accompany them on an inland trip in their Land Rover to get the feel of a combination of desert, mountain ravine, rocky valleys and variety of game.

When barely past the town's outer limits they watched three regal Oryx antelope file past within ten feet of the vehicle. Their picnic lunch was a gastronomic revelation accompanied by an icebox crammed with drinks. For Harry and Doreen it might as well have been another planet that they were visiting, in terrain resembling a moonscape.

After lunch Cecil leaned back and muttered, "This is God's own country. I really love it here. All this space. Nature at its best. Most times I can hear my own heartbeat when I'm out in the wilds."

Marlene echoed his words, languidly adding, "There's so much to do! I'm attending a painting class at the moment. We go out into the desert to paint. From one day to the next colors change. I didn't think I had any ability, but it's coming. Nature inspires you. I'll have something good to show at our next exhibition."

Harry was dripping with sweat. The two women had kept out of the sun and began to talk to each other. Doreen, Harry noticed, had immediately struck a chord with Marlene. He was happy about that.

"Initially we were apprehensive about taking up David's offer," Cecil confided. "Not now! We've been here a year. It's the best move we ever made. Mark my words Harry our mine will go places! If you get a chance to join us, grab it."

Cecil dropped them off at six. "There's time enough for you to have a walk and take in the sun going down. It's a wonderful sight. Good luck Harry. I hope you do join us. We enjoyed meeting you Doreen."

After showering and a quick change of clothes they took up Cecil's suggestion. It turned out to be a hot, humid evening so they were in no hurry to vacate their bench at mid-pier while staring across a white-horsed sea and listening to the ceaseless whoosh of the waves. The end of the pier was a focal point for anglers continually casting into deep water. Every few minutes one struck it lucky and hoisted up a squirming fish, swung it on to wooden floorboards and clubbed it with a knife hilt before removing the hook. Once their catch was stowed away anglers baited up again in seconds to cast, gracefully sending sinker, hook and bait back into churning blue and grey waters. Harry noticed that anglers seldom spoke to one another preferring communion with their rods and the sea.

"It's a good time to talk," a thoughtful Cecil said. "What do you think Doreen? Could you live here? And our girls? How do you think they would react if we settled here?"

"I suppose that means you would accept a good offer?"

"I'm tempted right enough. The people I will work with? They make the right kind of noises. But if moving here upset any member of my family I wouldn't do it. If they are happy to remain in Johannesburg, so be it. I don't see why anyone should be inconvenienced because of my shortcomings."

"Don't be so hard on yourself Harry. You have to be happy in your job. With our girls getting ready for university perhaps it's an opportunity to save for their expenses. It's going to cost a lot of money. We can rent our house out and live in a company house here."

That she'd thought about renting out their house surprised Harry who duly said so.

"If you're happy to stop here, we will be happy," she assured him. "For what it's worth I think David is a sincere person. Our girls will settle in quickly seeing they'd have a lot more freedom. It's really your decision. Is it what you want? I know that if you do take this job on, you will be working long hours. You've always done that so I'm well used to it."

"Not forever. Three or four years tops, then it should ease up."

"In your place I'd have to think what lies ahead. At forty-two you have at best eighteen years left to work, perhaps less. Is there a risk that once you've achieved what's expected, your employer will slide in a favored son and do the dirty on you? You do the hard work and someone else benefits from it. It's happened before hasn't it? Think about your Botswana experience. That lot let you down terribly."

"You have a point Doreen. There are too many risks. I'll turn it down if it comes my way."

Doreen took his hand. "Listen to me. Don't make up your mind right now. Wait Harry. All I say is that you should be comfortable with your decision. Clarify issues with David beforehand. My feeling is that he will offer you the job. I watched the two of you chatting. He knows you've been round the block. He wants you badly so tell him what you want. What worries you. You can talk with him. He's approachable."

The arrangement was that Melanie was scheduled to collect Doreen at ten on Monday morning to head for the mine airport. Bruno was designated to pick up Harry at seven to drive him to the mine.

At seven on the dot Bruno cruised up in his BMW. "This mist!" he agonized, "is going to trap us behind the busses. Never mind man, we can have a good chat."

"How'd your fishing trip go Bruno? Did you catch that steenbras you were after?"

"I hit the mother lode," Bruno gleefully replied. "I caught a bagful of steenbras and kabeljou. The fishing here? It's the best. I had a hundred kilometers of beach to myself. I even filled up on crayfish for our cat!"

Bruno wore regulation khakis and the back seat of his car was strewn with safety gear. Hard hat...steel-tipped shoes...goggles...ear plugs...gloves. He noticed Harry taking it all in.

"If you do join us Harry, just accept that safety is big business. David is doing his best to raise awareness despite cash problems. I'm

59

limited by cash problems. Frank's always crying too. Peter Gomez is on a hiding to nothing keeping his plant going. Just be warned, we will be on your back looking for money."

"David's an experienced GM," Harry commented. "Safety has to be a priority now that legislation is tightening up. The mines on the Copperbelt never took safety seriously. My own father worked drenched in cobalt fumes and smokestack emissions for forty years. The poor old bloke got emphysema and no one gave a toss about him. His health was totally destroyed."

"I hope it doesn't happen here," Bruno replied. "We haven't achieved as much as we would like on environmental precautions."

"Any unions on the go here?"

"Not yet. They're coming, that's for sure. David doesn't want us managers to take our eye off the ball. That's production. He and Cecil will handle union issues as and when necessary. Cecil knows who's saying what on the subject. Lower grade employees are getting together and if they ask us he will help them set up a union. That will amaze them won't it?" Bruno grinned.

The time passed quickly. Heavy, swirling mist has prevented sightseeing on the way. After Bruno parked his car next to David's he shook Harry's hand.

"Mariette and I enjoyed meeting you and Doreen. Good luck with David. I'll deliver you to the lion's den."

David appeared preoccupied. "We suffered a 'Lost Time' injury at the weekend. Back we go to zero."

"Serious?"

"No. A cut on the leg that needed plenty of stitching. Through sheer carelessness. It could have been avoided. Anyhow let's talk about you. I enjoyed chatting with your wife. I think she'd fit in well here."

"Thank you. She asked me to say 'Thanks' on her behalf. She enjoyed her visit very much."

"And you?"

"I did of course. I had never appreciated how much this part of Africa has to offer. I must say that I go back home with nothing but good to say about it."

"Did you notice anything that you thought out of place? Rest assured that our conversation remains within these four walls."

Harry had a lot to say and reminded himself not to come across as a 'Wiseguy'. "David, it has to be subjective. An overview. I don't aim to wrongly despoil anyone's hard work or intentions. I could be way off beam and would hate to make an enemy."

"I understand but don't worry. I appreciate feedback. We take what we want and learn from it."

"Fair enough. I spent a few hours last night writing it up. One copy only, for you."

David stood and put the document on his desk. "Tell me about your main points."

"You most definitely have a cash flow problem. I saw a lot of idle equipment and machinery. There is no asset management system to speak of. I looked at your stores and materials. I don't think that having Kardex systems checking on a computerized systems is a good idea. That means too many people are employed checking instead of producing, aside from wasting money. Also, not a single person I spoke to really understands what 'added value' means."

"I'm not sure that I do either," a puzzled David confessed. "Enlighten me please."

"Gladly. If you ask an employee *'What value do you add to the company?'* they should be able to tell you and sound enthusiastic about it. If they can't, then one assumes that they are not necessary so why keep them? With my current employers I must tell you that philosophy applies from the board downwards. There are no 'Old boy' directors. No expense is incurred unless it has a proven and positive connection to production."

"I'd love to say the same about our board," David responded. "We have directors who sit on as many thirty boards. I wonder how they can do justice to all those responsibilities."

"It struck me that there are no yardsticks here when it comes to productivity," Harry continued. "Men and women who produce get no more recognition than those employees that the systems hide. My impression is that there are surplus employees. I'd recommend that as people leave that they not be replaced unless you get a cast iron cost-effective case for their replacement from the divisional manager concerned."

"Well!" David scowled. "I have to agree."

"There's more if you want to hear it."

"I do. Carry on please."

"If I was a production person I'd be demanding daily cost and production statistics against plan. They get none. Is it possible that you're treating ore that is not payable? If so, that's wasted money. How does one control yield against plan? No one could tell me. Your computer system set-up? The wrong people are running it. Production people should have their own IT resources."

"What! But data processing has always been under one roof!"

"Yes. I think that has to change. Data and information are different needs. There's a case for production people to run their own systems using engineers and planners. They need effective tools, in this case appropriate computers with masses of megabyte calculation capacity and speed to process technical information. You cannot do ore reserve planning on the same computers used for commercial systems. They're just to slow and incapacitated. Technical systems should interface with commercial systems to draw expenditure and commitment data, but I'd definitely prescribe that production people do their own thing with their own highly specialized hardware and software. Not nearly enough people are as computer-literate as they should be. I don't see a computer terminal in here for example. That means you don't have up to the minute information. That costs big money."

David's concern was obvious. "This is a new approach for a finance man. Lateral thinking is it?"

"No. I prefer to say, 'keeping up with the times'. Ahead of your opposition. With everything becoming so competitive you need fast, accurate information which saves making wrong, costly decisions. To me, it's common sense to have systems producing data that allow decision-makers to size up cost before it's committed or spent. Explaining what happened well after the event can be construed as a criticism of the board because in the last analysis it carries the can. In your place I would hate to report to a board that hasn't moved with the times. I know that anything to do with uranium is something of a secret, but you need appropriate back-up."

"It has to be for obvious reasons. We keep to the provisions of the Atomic Energy Act."

"That's even more reason to keep a tight control over data. I heard mention of possible saboteurs. I'd suggest that such damage is just as effective if information gets into wrong hands. You would also require disaster recovery computer equipment at a location to back up your processing. There's nothing like that on site. No one here has ever heard of it. I think your entire information philosophy has to be re-examined with a lot more care."

"I'm beginning to palpitate," a solemn David replied after taking a deep breath, "but what you say makes sense. What about commercial systems?"

"I saw results of systems, not the systems in any depth. Frankly producing monthly accounts ten weeks after the month ended is no use, particularly as provisions I saw on the balance sheet hide expenses that the accountants don't want made public. Or they didn't balance the books and stuck the questionable figures into provisions. My experience with tax people is that they don't like financial provisions. They would want to see what's in there for obvious reasons."

David remained stony-faced. Harry bit his lip.

"Go on," David said, "I must hear it."

"Your chief accountant didn't take kindly to questions. There is no debtor or creditor history to speak of. I did pick up when talking to people in town that the mine is a bad payer. That's not a good reputation to have. If in future the mine wanted something in a hurry you might risk delays dealing with unhappy suppliers. It hurts production. I don't detect trends towards accountants supplying timely management accounts data, but what is plain is unwillingness to work closely with production people. I don't think it has ever entered their minds to do so. They're far too hidebound and seem to ignore that production is the name of the top game."

"Did you form any opinion of production people lower down?" David probed.

"Yes. I think there will be big changes and I think that in most cases people will play ball. There are some pretty clued up men at section head level. A bit in the dumps, but I think they shout potential."

"Do you think some of them might not play ball?'

"One or two might not. In your place I'd pay them off if they blow an opportunity to change their ways. It's bound to be the case. The stakes are too high. That's my view. Get it over with. I get the impression that there are far too many people giving orders and too few carrying them out. I suspect a flattening of manpower structure merits your attention. Six levels from employee to GM has to raise eyebrows by any standards. If it was my own company there's no way I'd tolerate so many employee levels."

"Well, that was certainly to the point," David commented and sighed heavily. "The other six candidates who applied for this job by this stage were talking golf, rugby, money and overseas trips. You've given me an unexpected perspective, if anything underlining that we have a lot more work ahead of us than I anticipated."

"For your sake," Harry replied, "I hope that it pans out as you want it to. You gave me an idea about how big the problem is. It's big. You need lots of responsive backup and finance to carry it out and free thinking people brimming with ideas let loose in the process. Selling surplus equipment, material supplies and getting rid of what I saw in the scrap yard...I estimate will rake in at least fifteen million rands. Contract out non-core services and reduce investment in dead equipment and assets. A man on that as a special assignment would pay his costs ten thousand times over. Or woman!"

"Mmmm...Non-core activities you say? You mean housing and so on?"

"Definitely. Sell them. Clubs. Playing fields. If people want facilities they'll form their own clubs. Cecil has enough to do organizing training and career planning. Bogging him down with housing and administration, aside from huge cost incurred is wasteful of his talents. Get rid of it! If this were your business would you spend so much dead money? Clinics? Schools? My view is that everything that is non-core goes."

"Managers' houses?"

"Yes, those too. Go to an overall package deal. Any firm of chartered accountants will run that for you for a darn sight less than the cost of employing dozens of people in an in-house salaries section. Managers can build or buy their own residences. That's the way it's done in Canada and in the USA. Shareholders there wouldn't see it any other way. Keep computers for the important stuff like costs against plan, strategic planning, capital budgets and commitments. In short, for anything that interacts with production."

"I must think more about it," David said. "I'm sure I won't get any opposition from my board if we went that route."

"That's the golden rule. *'Does it affect production?'* If it does—it stays. You have a fortune tied up in infrastructure. That's a government responsibility, not yours. It will pay you hand it all to government for free and let it pick up the cost of future maintenance."

"Anything else while we're about it?"

"Yes. The mine does not get into tax until it starts making profits but you have to assure yourself it doesn't pay anything that it does not have to. There has to be some specialist tax knowledge here. There's none. There is a risk that you might incur a deferred tax bill that you did not expect and plan for. If you have cash problems that will make matters worse for you. Your chief accountant told me in no uncertain terms that this mine can never make money so why bother? Tax planning starts well before you have to pay it."

"Go on. This is interesting."

At noon David put his hand up to halt Harry in mid-speech.

"I have your notes Harry. I'm grateful for them. We've delayed the 'plane for an hour. Before you go let me say I'm very glad you came to site. You are a forthright person."

"We enjoyed it. I hope we will reciprocate at some time in the future."

"I'd welcome that," David replied.

"The job's yours if you want it."

"Oh!" Harry exclaimed, surprised. "Thank you very much. But we haven't talked conditions and…"

"I assure you." David cut in, "that it will be far more than you ever expected. What is your current annual gross?"

Harry named the figure.

"Treble it. That excludes free house, company car, travel allowance, free 'phone, free electricity, travel allowances, education allowances and free water. It's a divisional ranking job and you get a big salary. When can you start?"

"Two months time. In April."

"Welcome to my team. I'll draft your letter of appointment and send it tomorrow. Hand-delivered to your door."

"You know Doreen," an incredulous Harry whispered to Doreen when settled into the Piper Chieftan. "I didn't say whether I'd take the job. David took it for granted that I had."

"I told you Harry. You have what he wants. He needs you badly. What's more…"

"Yes Doreen?"

"Congratulations. I think you need this job badly. It will extend you to your limits. Go for it."

Slicing through a clear twilight sky on its return flight from Kimberley, at 15000 feet sky the lights of the mine were visible well before the Piper straddled it.

Anyone camped in the desert within twenty miles of the open pit had to hear unmistakable clanking sounds emanating from hydraulic Harnischfeger shovels and throaty growls of WABCO haul trucks about their business. Each shovel was fronted by a crane boom measuring forty meters. Attached to the boom a huge claw-like bucket swiveled to scoop up blasted ore the size of a house before hoisting and dumping it into the pan of a waiting, begrimed haul truck.

Drivers of these one hundred and fifty ton behemoths waited a safe distance away until radioed an "All clear" to re-enter their cabs. Slowly the haul trucks were piloted up twenty concentric benches from the pit bottom, each bench thirty meters high, to discharge their ore at the surface primary crushers.

One starlit February night proved the mother of all exceptions for the pilots. A giant fire flash billowed up from the mine plant area. Rapidly heat ascending heat buffeted the 'plane within seconds. Don immediately radioed mine security to report what they'd experienced.

The duty sergeant frantically answered, "Fire! Solvent tanks exploded. Mr Gomez is on it."

Two fire engines were immolated in seconds. All that hapless firemen could do was to flee in one Toyota Stout vehicle to breast a hillock and witness a fire-path being carved out by their deadly visitor from hell. Peter Gomez's immediate concern centered on evacuating employees from the affected area and taking a headcount.

Peter ordered the open pit crew to send up two 12000 liter water bowsers. Another huge explosion flared into the air. Petrol and diesel tanks at the garage exploded, rocketing debris into the stratosphere that tumbled to earth in a cascade of crimson sparks.

Despite their heavy-duty nozzles spewing at full bore, the bowsers proved impotent at arresting the inferno. Peter ordered pit engineers to hastily bulldoze an earth berm a kilometer ahead of the fire to prevent runaway molten debris careering into the open pit. The hastily contrived berm held fast forcing the deadly mixture of flame and molten debris to splay down a dry watercourse well away from the open pit.

David had broken speed records driving out to the mine. "What happened?" he asked a smoke-blackened fire chief waiting for him at the gate.

"It started at the solvent tanks sir. It's too early to say more," fire blackened Herbert Muhle answered. The back of his asbestos-lined jacket was hot to the touch. "Thank God this did not happen on day shift. That would have been a catastrophe. We'll know more in the morning."

"Any fatalities?" a pained David queried while taking a deep breath and screwing up his eyes at the prospect of hearing debilitating news.

"No. Mr Gomez made sure of that. He had a plan for evacuation. We accounted for everyone and bussed them home. No serious injuries to speak of."

"Okay," a relieved David whispered, "that's a blessing. We have to wait it out. Just keep me informed. But," he continued and put his hand on Herbert's shoulder, "you get some rest Herbert. I need you. Thanks."

One by one grim-faced managers arrived to assemble in the security superintendent's office.

"Bad one," Victor Grey grimaced. "The met plant's finished."

"Can someone see to coffee and tell Don South to stand by? I want a flight over whole mine."

David caught Vic's eye and nodded towards the car park outside. "A word Vic please."

"This way," the truculent official replied and led his boss out from where they could feel the heat of the blaze aftermath.

David had his hands in his pockets. "You know what's going through my mind don't you?"

"I have a good idea. Sabotage? I wouldn't jump to conclusions. Perimeter security is tight. We had no reports of breach and no alarms registered. We let the dogs go and they came up with nothing."

"When can you say for sure?"

"I have informants. By noon tomorrow I'll report back to you. My gut feel is that something went wrong with operations."

"I need to know Vic and the sooner the better," David said. "I can't allow the rumor mill to begin cranking. Where's your scrambler? I'd better put the chairman in the picture."

"My office. The blue handset."

"Can you make sure sightseers are contained? And local press?"

"Already in hand. I alerted police up country. They'll be on the lookout for odd bods or funny traffic. Trains and airports too will get some attention. We have it covered."

"Thanks. Can one of your chaps drive me to our airport? Don must be waiting for me."

The Piper was waiting on the apron with one engine idling. A worried-looking Don South stood at the foot of its steps.

"Thanks for hanging about Don. Let's get her up."

"No problem," Don replied and followed David aboard. He pulled the door shut and shuffled to the cockpit.

A grim-faced Larry Foyere was already in his seat doing pre-flight checks. "G'evening Mr Bradshaw," he uttered hoarsely and got a nod from David. Pleasant as Larry was he stank permanently of tobacco so anyone near him had a hard time not to gag. Larry's mitigating virtue was his reputation as a first-class pilot, always cool and in control.

Don eased the Piper on to the runway and headed downwind to the end of the tarmac strip. He did a tight turn to face into the wind, went though his compression and pitch tests before releasing brakes. At five hundred meters the 'plane jerked upwards sweeping to starboard Don rightly guessing that David wanted to inspect the open pit first.

The pit was fine. No damage. David's problem was that activities had come to a standstill, yet another massive setback to production. If there was no metallurgical plant to send ore to there was no point in blasting it. Stockpiles already stood at capacity. Stagnant equipment cost big money in increased unit costs. Informing fed up customers too came into the equation. Having to wait much longer for final products was hardly likely to improve relations.

The fire had turned the metallurgical plant into a smelted orange and crimson mass of lava and black smoke. David mentally sent Peter Gomez a thousand thanks for his quick thinking, saving the open pit and extricating terrified, milling employees from the runaway monster. A normally dry water course splitting the plant from the pit, nature's blessing if ever there was one, glowed menacingly back at him.

Periodic explosions cannoned spectacular flames into the sky.

"Bloody hell!" David cursed, "what a sight!" He pictured his board's reaction. Despite insurance cover, a goodly few more directors would not have batted an eyelid at closing the mine. They certainly had a strong case now.

71

Already the road from *Thuringia Bay* was swamped with vehicle headlights…sightseers—all stopped at the mine turn-off by security personnel.

David pictured everyone's reactions. Directors? Big problem—some of them were guaranteed to go ape. Employee morale had to skid to a new low. Inevitably police had to stamp over the site to determine whether "terrs" were in the picture; Newspapers? A field day for them. He needed all this like a hole in his head.

Harry sat bolt upright when news about the mine burst on early morning television.

Doreen took her cue and also sat up, riveted to the screen.

"'*Problem Mine*' the announcer called it," a concerned Harry said at the end of the bulletin. "He certainly revved the incident up, unnecessarily so for my liking. I'm beginning to believe that's a hoodoo mine all right. David Bradshaw has bad news coming at him from all angles. The poor bastard can never win."

"Perhaps you should 'phone him," a visibly upset Doreen replied. "I feel for the man."

"You're right. Things could have changed for us if it goes belly-up. I need to know where we stand." Harry disappeared to his study and emerged half an hour later. "There might not be a mine much longer Doreen. It doesn't look too good."

"Oh?" an anxious Doreen probed. "What did he say?"

"He's flying to London shortly to see his board. He did tell me at the mine that one or two directors wanted to close it down so this fire is manna from heaven for them. An enquiry has to be held to find out how such a disaster could have happened. It's in the lap of the gods."

"That hardly sounds hopeful. David deserves better."

"If it does close down Doreen a lot of people will lose jobs, including him. Politically it won't look good either. That region of the country needs that mine to remain open. If it closes the negative effect on all those communities will be devastating."

Doreen sat back and sighed. "Of all the rotten luck. How did you leave matters with him Harry?"

"He'll 'phone me when he gets back from London. I don't envy him explaining such a disaster to a board that has different agendas."

"What will you do?" a worried Doreen enquired. "Can you rescind your resignation if you have to?"

Harry got up and poured two cups of coffee. He handed Doreen hers. "I'll cross that bridge later. David Bradshaw is a persuasive fellow. I think he'll win his board over. When he does, just watch that mine's smoke! *Oops!* Let me rephrase that. Under David Bradshaw that mine will make it."

June in London was normally a pleasant experience. This time round David was filled with dread. Sleep had evaded him during his flight and he was glad to vacate the 'plane when docking at London's Heathrow International Airport.

Chater Metals PLC head office complied with the usual image of an international mining headquarters; excellent location in *Onslow Gardens*, Kensington; a grey edifice of no known pedigree, that was deeper than it was wide. Inside its five storeys lurked echelons of corporate "suits" whose wealth was made on the backs of minions who ran mines "in the sticks" so condescendingly referred to by Peter Gomez's London-bound wife, Carrie. The atmosphere in the building resembled that of a cathedral, gloomy, somnolent and forbidding, whose inhabitants seemed to be under permanent orders not to smile under any circumstances.

Within the somber boardroom reposed several familiar faces. Stern expressions left David under no illusion that attendees resented being summoned to this extraordinary general meeting. He'd requested it to apprise the board of developments and to receive a decision on whether to continue mine operations.

A quick check established that a quorum was present and at ten a.m. the chairman walked in puffing at his trademark cigar, all of eight inches long.

"You made it Bradshaw! Not too tired I hope," Sir Francis Clayton rasped while dropping ash on the carpet. "Kindly proceed will you? Tell us what you did to that blot of a mine of yours."

It was plain to David what was running through the chairman's mind.

"May I have a seat please chairman?" David responded. "It would help." He was aware that the chairman was needling him to let him know who was boss.

"Insolent fellow," David heard the chairman say to his vice-chairman. "The bounder did not greet me."

The company secretary rose to his feet none too quickly to remedy matters, pushing a chair in next to Sir Francis for David.

David put his papers on the table, sat and faced his audience. Sixteen apparently hostile directors glared back at him.

"Good morning gentlemen. *The Thuringia*…"

"Chater!" Sir Francis angrily intervened. "Chater! Native non-de-plumes are foreign to us!"

"Forgive me chairman," Harry ruefully smiled. "The Chater Mine is a sizeable investment. Some two thousand jobs are at stake and closure would be devastating to the North West Cape. The mine is the backbone of the economy in that region."

"Bradshaw," Sir Francis testily broke in again and emitted a plume of blue smoke, "our role is to invest on behalf of shareholders for an acceptable return on capital invested. We're not a charity operation. Mining is a risky business don't you know. We don't require cotton wool from you. *Profit* is not an event that so far we accord to your mine. We have waited long enough for it."

At it again. The chairman's infuriating patronising manner. David kept his composure.

"I understand Sir Francis." David paused to retrieve some papers.

"The cause of the fire gentlemen—our insurers wasted no time bringing in assessors, all experts in their own fields. Forensic specialists too arrived on site as did police. They were all agreed on their findings."

"Which was what?" the touchy chairman whinnied while examining growing ash on his cigar.

"The fire was **not** due to sabotage despite what some of the press printed. No sabotage."

"Out with it man!" Sir Francis barked. "What exactly happened?"

"The cause was ascribed to undetected solvent leakage in the metallurgical plant area over the years. Investigation determined that solvent tanks were installed by original contractors who omitted a second stainless steel skin as specified in the tender."

"'Undetected' you say," the vice-chairman warily commented, wisely not emulating his principal's caustic approach. "How did that occur?"

"Outlet pipes were not welded according to specification. That meant that seals over time rusted from the inside out. Even in the desert, salt content in the air is manifestly high. Solvent leaked into surrounding areas, shorted underground electricity cables and blew the plant sky-high."

David sensed tension in the air. Sir Francis appeared decidedly uncomfortable and expressions on a few other faces exhibited fear.

"Extensive attention was given to the acid stocks by investigators. At any one time a hundred thousand tons of sulfuric is tanked on site. Again, original plans showed that stainless steel lined moats surrounding tank areas were to be installed at construction stage. They were not. Concrete moats were built but without stainless steel lining protection. I did detect this shortly after I took up my appointment and applied to the board for capital to remedy matters. It was refused. Unfortunately, the solvent leak played havoc with electrics and a short got to one acid tank. There was a spill but it was contained. That solvent explosion caused most of the damage. If it had happened on a day shift we could have had huge personnel casualties and an environmental debacle."

The chairman sat rigid, his cigar suspended in mid-air. All the directors appeared frozen to the spot.

"If all that acid had blown it would have launched international concern, aside from hundreds of lives lost and not only those of mine employees. Insurers compare such potential disaster as worse than a two hundred thousand ton oil tanker going down in a marine reserve."

"This is all the more reason to call a halt to that dashed mine," one director loudly intervened satisfied that he was following the party line. "It's been cursed from the start. We were duped into buying it. Let's get shot of it! Close the bloody thing before we take another financial bath!"

David suspected what he had to say was about to be glossed over.

"Officially gentlemen, the damage resulted from cutting corners at design stage. Additional expert observations were that plant design and layout left much to be desired. Production flow, safety and environmental aspects were all patently done on the cheap. *Their words* not mine."

"Yes, yes, don't labor the point," Sir Francis testily intervened. "Some of us might not take kindly to such unjustified surmises."

"Their conclusions Sir Francis, were that the plant was erected on the cheap but premium prices were paid to contractors. Our insurers will have something to say on that score. It will be the largest ever claim in African mining history."

"Go on! It doesn't look like 'on the cheap' when you see what's on the balance sheet," Hilton Walsh ventured, a combative Australian mine developer who had bought into Chater Metals in a big way. If Hilton bought in anywhere, a rush to buy shares ensued on the Stock Exchange, such was the fifty-year olds' reputation.

Sensing an ally, David continued. "You may recall that

construction of *The Thuringia*, sorry, the *Chater Mine*, was supervised by experts appointed by this board. The project team did not call for open tenders. The award was made in-house so those officials concerned will be called to give evidence at an enquiry along with original contractor personnel involved."

Was it his imagination or did he sense extreme discomfort among certain board members who were frantically scribbling notes to each other?

"When I arrived at the mine ten months ago," David continued, "I checked its insurance cover and picked up that *Force Majeure* cover was not included. Nor was consequential loss cover included. Chater's headquarters here in London placed the original policy. I took the liberty of canceling it after obtaining cover elsewhere including attending to previous omissions at half the original premium cost."

David turned to catch the eye of the particular director who had placed the original policy. "The Name".

Tie loosening, sideways glances and whispers being exchanged and worried frowns escaped their bearers.

"Any questions so far?" David invited. "Gentlemen?"

"Yes, there bloody are!" Hilton Walsh bellowed. "There are. Plenty. And damn serious ones too. Who were the original insurers?"

David told him, his answer studiously recorded.

The Lloyds "Name" was taking noticeably short breaths.

"And what are the names of this company's *experts*?"

David pretended innocence. "Before my time sir I have to say. There is one other potential bit of bad news I must inform you about."

"Haven't you given us enough to worry about? What is it this time?"

"I'm only a messenger Sir Francis. Not the culprit. It concerns radiation. In the short period that I have been on the mine I discovered five employees with cancers, three of whom died. Cancer of the brain. Bones. Pancreas. One baby was born with spinal bifida.

For a small community these incidents are more than medical statistics suggest should be the case."

"Ah well you see those are examples of inherent risks in mining," Sir Francis scoffed. "It's a demanding business. If people don't like the heat in the kitchen then they should get out."

"I'm afraid the insurers don't quite see it in such superficial light. If they prove that cancer was contracted before our new insurance cover was taken out, claims will be rejected. The mine will have to make provision for any such claims."

"What!" the chairman exploded. "Over my dead body!"

"Chairman, there's a lot of talk about radiation but we have no money for testing and protection measures. Radon readings are high throughout the site and my enquiries established that several buildings rest on foundations of radioactive ore. That's a big risk to employees working in those buildings. If we continue operations, suspect buildings will have to be demolished and re-sited. We are expected therefore to upgrade our radiation screening procedures."

No comment arose. The directors were in shock. It was plain no one present wanted to associate with such unwelcome information. Or were they mulling over what adverse reports the press was capable of and the effects on Chater's share price?

"As for plant and equipment," David said, "insurance will finance damage and consequential loss if a rebuild is on the cards. Should closure be your elected route, then consequential loss payments will be negotiated downwards taking account of equipment and plant disposal proceeds. There are substantial loans and debentures to be repaid. Paying off our work force will need a sizeable tranche of cash flow as will certain environmental containment costs. Either way, there is much planning ahead and procedures to be installed, taking account too of authorities who want to know what we are going to do. If we do rebuild there is no time to lose."

"Can you do it?" Hilton Walsh queried. "Rebuild that renegade mine? And get it into profit?"

"Yes sir. This time we won't cut corners. My buyers tell me that we can source almost everything we need from South African suppliers. At far less than original cost too."

"How long will it take to get up and going at rated capacity?"

"Twelve months. There is one condition to this."

"Oh yes!" Sir Francis groaned, "I might have known. What might that be?"

"Our main product is uranium. U3o8. We have to commission a proper evaluation of the ore body. Ore reserve with a twenty year minimum life of mine must first be proven otherwise it will prove uneconomic to continue operations."

"But surely that was done before the mine was bought?" Hilton Walsh erupted, aghast. "What on earth was it mining? Waste ore?"

"There is a document on the subject sir," David replied. He was glad that Walsh was getting stuck in; no one else present gave the impression that they were capable of making constructive observations. "Subsequent core samples retrieved and ore extraction to date show that our London planners got it wrong. I did ask for it to be re-examined after my arrival but got no response. Yes. You're right. *The Thur...*, Chater Mine treated substantial quantities of waste rock."

"Unbelievable!" Hilton Walsh uttered and shook his head in disgust. "Abso-bloody-lutely unbelievable! When are you flying back to South Africa? And don't call me "Sir". The name is Walsh."

"Tomorrow night Mr Walsh. When I return the Government wants a statement of intent from me. The press is looking for a story too."

"Will that be all Bradshaw?" an imperious Sir Francis asked. "All this chit chat. I must say this is very bad news altogether."

"Yes Sir Francis. You had to know the extent of it."

"Before you go Mr Bradshaw," Walsh broke in. "Where are you staying?"

"At the Grosvenor House Hotel."

"Make sure that you're contactable if you go out. May I ask that you be back here at three pm tomorrow?"

David Bradshaw had hardly closed the boardroom door when Hilton Walsh stood up and spoke.

"You do realize Chairman that Bradshaw fingered this entire board as a bunch of clowns. We're in a right mess."

Including cigar-puffing Sir Francis, all present were slumped in their chairs.

"That's a matter of opinion sir," Sir Francis croaked. "I'd say he's overdoing it. These fellows often go 'bush' when they hang too long around in the sticks I'm told. I'm sure that we just witnessed a prime example of it."

"No. I don't think so," Hilton Walsh replied tartly making sure that his chairman was aware of his refusal to brush matters away. "He's a solid mining man. He's got excellent form in this business. You know that chairman, because you offered him the job to fix the place. There's no point saying you got it wrong is there?"

Sir Francis took none too kindly being chastised as to his own shortcomings. "Well Mr Walsh, what do you suggest that we do? If you ask me Bradshaw provided us with a cast-iron case for closing that mine, particularly as we lose nothing. Not a few members present say that it's been blight fodder from day one; that is apparent is it not? Bradshaw had his chance. We'll ring-fence its accumulated loss globally and write it off. It won't cause even a blimp on our consolidated balance sheet."

Hilton Walsh's ice-cold blue eyes bore in to Sir Francis. This was one old man in Hilton's eyes who'd pushed his boat out too far, way past what his degenerated brain was capable of. No person present in the room doubted that Hilton was not going to toe the chairman's line of least resistance. That Hilton was stinking mad was plain to see, a sight of raw malice, disgust and seething anger about to erupt. The old man was first to drop his eyes under guise of lighting up another pungent cigar with shaky hands.

"Allow me to tell you what I intend doing chairman," a steely Hilton Walsh exclaimed and rose to lean on the table. "I am going to do some digging during the next few hours. Right here in this building. I'm going to upset a lot of people in this nest of West End complacency. If Bradshaw is remotely right in what he says, I suggest that board members who had under the counter dealings have their resignations on this table tomorrow morning along with those of the officials responsible for causing this catastrophe. As we have read in the press, shareholders are out for blood these days when directors mess up. We are not going to pay for incompetence. Bradshaw's not the man who put Chater Metals into skunk limelight. He did his job by giving us the facts to decide what remedial course we follow. We have to do our job now. And to make sure that it never happens again anywhere in this group."

"Now listen here my dear chap..."

Hilton irritably cut a scowling Sir Francis off. "If they do not comply, I'll call a press conference to announce my reasons for selling my Chater Metals shareholdings even if I do take a big loss. My name is that important to me. I may drive a hard bargain but I operate above board. An appropriate term in the circumstances."

"Don't you think you are a tad over-reacting?" an edgy vice chairman said. "Let's not be hasty my dear fellow. We shouldn't make a rod for our own backs now should we?"

"You don't get it do you?" Harry replied in a raised voice. "What a load of mush you sprout! This board has been tumbled. **Us!** Evidence is available right now that could earn us high-profile court cases brought against us from several quarters. Damage control is on the table."

"Oh come on!" Sir Francis guffawed. "'*Damage control*' indeed!"

"When The City sniffs it out, and it will, guess what happens to our share price? What bloody idiots authorized a mining investment of such magnitude without being assured of sustainable ore reserves? If a hundred thousand tons of acid had gone washing around the countryside do you think for a moment that this board would have been absolved? As for this insurance business—it stinks to high heaven! *Employees contracting cancer and dying!* That alone will hog bad headlines for years. If we walk away and pretend it never happened this group will be dogged by environmental zealots and lawsuits. Have you any idea what that costs? Compensation? We're talking potentially hundreds of millions of dollars!"

Aside from Hilton members present presented a sorry sight. No one wished to look him in the eye. The company secretary looked like he was about to expire and Sir Francis's sagging jowls seemed to have grown six inches.

"Nothing that I heard today suggests that this office behaved according to accepted norms," Hilton barked. "No, no, *gentlemen,* I'm not associating myself with this fiasco. It smells. In fact it damn well stinks and you know it! I had nothing to do with it. I want heads to roll. I want it all out in the open before someone else does it for us. At midday tomorrow I'll be back here and I suggest that you all do likewise. That's damage control!"

"For what reason Mr Walsh?' Sir Francis huffily enquired. "May I remind you that I am the elected chairman of this company. I decide on when meetings are held."

"'*What for'*" you ask?" Hilton replied grimly. "I thought it was obvious even to you. You and your cosy pals are out. We need a new interim board to stop the rot."

Sir Francis's jowls quivered with rage as he watched Hilton Walsh storm out the room. He poured himself a generous glass of blue label *Johnnie Walker* and gulped it down in seconds. Sullen cohorts stayed put waiting for a lead from their liver-spotted master who was contemplating throwing back a second tumbler of whisky.

Back in his hotel room David went over the sequence of events. He'd played it fairly. It was asinine to think that the entire board would ignore the more unsavory facts that he'd put on the table. Something had to happen. He sensed that Hilton Walsh was keen to tackle the mess, but Sir Francis? He'd always been an enigma to David. Perhaps the old man was past his "Sell By" date. Whatever was bugging him, he surely had not made David feel welcome.

He'd talked it out with Pamela before leaving for London. "Pam, if our mine closes down we obviously have to go. My conscience will be clear because I would have given it my best shot. Then I think we start again in Australia. If it stays open and nothing is done about scams that were pulled here, I have to resign. If I don't, quite rightly people will assume that I was part of the plot. I can't work with that hanging over my head."

Spending a night out on the town did not appeal to him. If anything he saw it more like cheating honest-to-goodness employees back at the mine depending on him to return with good news. He fell asleep in front of the television set.

Only twelve board members were present. Sir Francis was not among them, nor the financial director; nor "The Name".

A smiling Hilton Walsh greeted David as he entered and bade him sit down. "Mr Bradshaw," Hilton opened, "you have had a torrid time of it. What remains of this board wishes to commend your efforts."

Remains! Oh, oh! Sir Francis got the chop! David thought. *Was he next in line?*

"There were some among us who took stock of rebuilding a mine in a country beset with political pressures, sanctions and difficulties finding and servicing venture capital. This board is well aware that it could walk away with minimal financial penalty thanks to your assiduous efforts in plugging the insurance gap."

All this sweet-talking…Why don't they just tell me. The mine has had it…I'm out. They're letting me down gently…

"Certain board members felt that they did not have the stamina nor inclination to go for the rebuild route. Including Sir Francis. I shall be acting as chairman until our next group annual general meeting."

David mumbled a surprised, "The mine stays?"

"Yes. But before our press conference is called we must ask you again. Can you bring it to full production and into profit within twelve months?"

"Subject to proven, viable ore reserves," David replied, "we have an able team to do it."

"How long do you think it will take to get proven ore reserve assessments behind you?"

"I asked our mines commissioner back home the same question. He's a geologist more familiar with the terrain than me. 'Three months' he said for a mine our size. He recommended a Professor Koenig right here in England to do the job. If I delay my return for a few days perhaps I can get to see the professor to discuss matters with him. He lives in Oxford."

Hilton stared at him for a few seconds. "Prof Koenig is no mug. We've come this far. Go ahead. Stage one—three months at the outside—viable ore-reserve based on no less than a fifteen percent discounted cash flow return on investment based on twenty years ore reserves. I will give you the commodity sale prices for the payback formula. If the figures work out then go ahead. Rebuild. If not—no sweat, we close it down. Clear?"

"Very" David smiled. "Thank you."

8

Professor Erich Koenig in the flesh did not remotely match David's mental picture of him. In his sixties, the professor spoke unaccented English despite his East German origins. A full head of black hair that was greying at the temples gave him presence. Questing green eyes and lithe physique of a tall man suggested that he was closer to forty years of age.

"Thank you for seeing me at such short notice Professor Koenig," David said after shaking hands, "I have heard so much about you."

Awash with charts, papers and computer printouts the office certainly looked busy. An entire corner was devoted to a bank of *Perkin Elmer* and *Cray* mainframe computers, compact mainframes with huge number-crunching capacity that had backed the USA moon-shot and Mars exploration missions.

He was easy to talk to, a kindly man devoid of images of his own self-importance. David gave him a rapid summation of events.

"No wonder," the professor smiled wryly afterwards, "that you are worried. I have seen it all—developers carried away with the first flush of mineral samples taken from a supposedly prime yield ore body. Then what happens? Salted mines...no worthwhile ore-bodies to speak of, suspect proposals that hoodwinked boards of directors who did not ask questions. I could talk for hours on the subject. For an international mining house to act in so cavalier a manner mystifies me. It was clearly been badly advised and of course you tell me that the shareholders are wising up. A bit late it seems."

David winced. The thrumming coming from the computers got to him too for surely they were doing what his predecessors at *The Thuringia* should have done—their homework.

"Professor, I believe that you mentored Gerard Dresser at Heidelberg University. He is an experienced mining man whose geological knowledge I respect."

"Ah yes, Gerard…I do remember him. Let me see, yes, he came to me in the late sixties. He struck me as an earnest young fellow. He always asked probing questions. How is he keeping?"

"Very well. He is Mines Inspector in our province. A committed individual who is making a great contribution to the industry."

"That sounds like Gerard," the professor smiled.

"We inherited a badly contrived ore reserve plan professor and Gerard is aware of it. He recommended you as the sole expert on ore-reserve verification and planning who could pronounce with certainty whether our mine is viable. Would you consider establishing what our grades and ore quantities are? Our main mineral is U3o8. The existing reserve plan makes no sense at all. We have yet to match actual results to theoretical readings. Processing as much waste ore as we do is not good news."

The professor steepled his hands for a good minute passed before replying. "We are talking about nuclear materials. You appreciate that globally it is a very sensitive topic. I have lost count of the number of monitoring bodies involved when the word 'nuclear' crops up."

"I do. I don't get involved in politics professor. My task is to produce final product tonnages required by our London sales office within an agreed time frame. Matters worsened when that fire broke out and wiped out our metallurgical plant. When taking into account all the head banging, the question our board faces is does it sanction rebuild or stop the mine it in its tracks? It's no secret that some Chater Metal executives are sick of it. If it was left to them they'd close it down in an instant."

"I am not surprised. Mining hosts capricious individuals. How they survive beats me. Yes. By all means close it if facts suggest as much. There is no shame in doing that."

"My sentiments entirely professor. Getting the facts. If we do start up again, it has to be from a sound base. I have fifteen months to accomplish a successful rebirth, presupposing that we have proven ore reserves to begin with."

"So. You want me to assess it. A detailed viability…The bad news is that I am heavily committed. All my people on six continents will tell you the same story."

"It would have surprised me sir if that was not the situation. I beg you to do this viability study for us. My new chairman Hilton Walsh has given me his financial return on investment criteria that you will need to factor in to your calculations. If there is a hint of viability then our ore body must be excavated responsibly. There is no suggestion of high grade mining to satisfy greedy shareholders or that we dance to the tune of errant directors."

"I am pleased to hear it." The professor sympathized with David appreciating the strain that he was under. "As it happens I was planning a long overdue vacation starting next Monday—six days time. I could fly out then if that is acceptable to you."

David heaved a sigh of relief. "That's wonderful news professor. What do you want us to get ready for you?"

"I require a recent aerial survey of your mining lease area. Add core samples down to three hundred meters taken at intervals of hundred meter blocks covering your entire lease areas. Is that possible?"

"Yes. Most of that work is complete. We have the core samples."

"We also need ultra sound equipment and cameras aboard an

aircraft large enough to carry them. You should have a sampling laboratory dedicated to the exercise with at least three analytical chemists and a dozen geological samplers working round the clock."

While scribbling it down David was thinking where he could lay his hands on the missing items of equipment.

"On hand must be all geological records no matter how old, all relating to the lease area and details of who compiled them. I require a list of all your mining, geological and metallurgical people in supervisory positions and their background experience and qualifications. It would help too if you had a scientific computer on site with at least a million gigabytes of processing capacity."

"Like yours?"

"Not quite. Mine has ten times that power. But it allows me to feed back data here for extrapolation on my computers. I must ask for assurance that I will not be countermanded by anyone when asking for something to be done seeing that we will be working within such a critical time frame."

"You have it Professor. The minute I leave your office I shall relay your needs to site. We must arrange for your accommodation. Any idea how long you will stay with us?"

"It is impossible for me to say accurately. At a guess, no less than two to four weeks, backed up by subsequent periodic audits. I have read about ore bodies in your part of Africa. They are unique mineral composites but I do not know them through personal experience. Give me your contact address and telephone number. I suggest too that you treat my visit as low key."

"Yes, except that I have to put my managers in the picture before you arrive."

Less than twenty-four hours after visiting the professor, David was seated at his desk. He'd got no sleep during the long flight to Johannesburg, one that took three hours longer because South

African Airways had to fly out to sea, way off the West African bulge to avoid invading air space over hostile nations that politically abhorred South Africa and its mandate over South West Africa, though curiously enough, they comprehensively traded with both polecat countries.

Aside from the tediousness of the flight the enormity of what actions he'd committed to began to sink in. It would have been easier to have couched his report so that everyone in London rejected the rebuild out of hand. His reputation would have remained intact. He could still have looked himself in the face. Australia beckoned. That's where new high-tech operations were opening, crying out for people with his experience. *No. I have to fix this one first* he told himself. *It affects a lot of people. Then we'll see…*

First order of business on his first day back at work was to wait till eight o'clock chimed and then telephoning Harry McCrae. Ten minutes later Joey Schneider his secretary entered carrying a tea tray.

"Thanks Joey. Please ask the managers to meet me in our conference room at nine. No excuses."

Joey nodded. "Mr Dresser will be here at eleven. It's his normal quarterly appointment with you. I prepared everything that he wants. They're on your desk. Will there be anything else?"

'Yes. One thing. Should a Mr Hilton Walsh from London office want to speak to me, put him through. He's our new chairman. It doesn't matter what I'm doing or whom I'm speaking to at the time. Put him through."

"I understand."

David welcomed his team who were waiting at the conference table, talking in muted tones. He saw one uniform expression on all their faces. *Worry.*

"Before I fill you in on events to date gentlemen you have to promise me to keep a lid on what I'm about to tell you."

Frank lit up another cigarette and got straight to the point. "That fax you sent us? All organized. Are we still in business?"

89

"Yes. And no. We're in business, and this particularly applies to you Frank, if we can put a proven but payable twenty-year plus ore-reserve plan on the table. I stress *payable*. You know that the present version isn't worth a row of second-hand beans."

"Jeez!" Frank exploded. "But that takes time…"

"Who wants to throw money away? You've read your journals. Mines are opening up in Canada and Australia with ore yields twenty times ours. The chairman's given me his investment criteria. Only if we match it, then we're in business."

"Excuse me," Bruno Gerber interjected, "it sounds like you have a plan in mind."

"I do. I managed to see Professor Koenig."

"Prof *Koenig!*" Peter Gomez whistled. "An ace. How did you get him? The man's a legend."

"So everyone tells me. He's arriving on site next Tuesday to spend a few weeks with us. Learn from him gentlemen. Give him your every support while he does whatever he has to do. If he doesn't throw us a lifeline, kiss this mine goodbye once and for all. Obviously it is not the kind of news that I want you spreading about the place."

"But if he does," Frank said, "what then? I hope our London office doesn't get in on the act."

Recalling his hostile treatment by Sir Francis, David grimaced. "No. They most certainly won't. We have a new board headed by Hilton Walsh the Australian magnate, until the next annual general meeting. He's one tough cookie, but he gave us his support. He's not keen on head office staff getting involved in site operations."

"The old geezer, Sir Francis?" Frank queried. "What happened to him?"

"Gone. Stepped down. He and a few of his pals are history. I suppose you could say there's been a palace revolution. When I laid out all the aspects of the fire, including details of short cuts taken by the original contractors and how useless the ore reserve data was, Sir Francis got both barrels from Hilton Walsh. It was a consummate demolition job. Sir Francis and his mates couldn't stand the thought of potentially re-vitalizing the mine, so out they went. Besides which, they might have to answer to shareholders for a few strange decisions concerning the initial construction phase."

"I see," Frank smiled. "So *Walsh* is our top man now? That's a step in the right direction. He's a mining engineer. Not some finance guru in a suit sprouting textbook trivia. About time too."

"If we verify reserves within three months we've got another twelve months to get up and running. Profitably. I said that we can do it if we have the reserves. Are you with me?"

Relieved expressions that David saw on his managers' faces was endorsement enough for him.

Gerard Dresser arrived punctually and was shown through to David's office.

"Gerard, good to see you," David beamed and shook his visitor's hand. "You saved me Gerard. You saved me."

Gerard appeared perplexed. "Oh! That is good. How did I do that?"

"By suggesting to me that I should contact Professor Koenig. I did go and see him. A lot depends on what he has to tell us."

"Good. Impressive character isn't he?" Gerard said, genuinely pleased. His unusual accent was typical of Cape-born people with German backgrounds.

"He'll be on site next week. He wants to meet you."

"Well, well, well...my old mentor is coming out here. Man, that is a bonus." Gerard shook his head. "You were lucky. I know people who have tried to land him for years as their consultant. Why exactly is he coming here?"

"To reassess our ore reserves. I want to retain him permanently if we pass muster."

"You mean there is a risk that this place might go under? Hey man, the politicians will go mad if that happens. They need some cash from you first."

David was well aware of political implications stemming from a mine that had delivered nothing like the cash flow it had promised earlier.

"Don't remind me Gerard what politicians think or what they want. To me they're scavengers, vacuous superficial incompetents who can't hold down a normal job so they prey on the public and innocent investors. I'm a miner. My prime concerns are satisfying the expectations of this mine's shareholders. I have to be sure we can cut the mustard. I don't want to waste investors' good money."

"Who would argue with you but we cannot wish them away. My job is to help you because the longer your mine stays open, the better for all of us, not just your shareholders. Besides which, if you wind up operations, I lose my job. Imagine what the press will say if it sniffs something about you pulling out? This province will die. Man, the thought is just too terrible to consider."

"Please Gerard, Professor Koenig asked that we treat his visit as low key. It fuels up expectations in a variety of quarters if we mention his visit and the last thing we want is to tip off our opposition that he's here."

"Of course," Gerard replied. "I would have loved to have boasted about him visiting our part of the world. It will be a great honor for us."

"Perhaps later. The next few weeks will be a crucial time for us."

"Okay man. I must tell my boss something when I go home. Our politicians are frothing at the mouth. Unemployed miners shouting in the streets is not a pleasant thought for them."

David brought Gerard up to speed. Ore reserves. Cutting corners. Scams. Acid risks. Cancer deaths…everything…including board machinations. "I leave it you Gerard. You pick out what you want to say as long as it is the truth."

"God!" his thunderstruck visitor joked. "You made them wet their pants! The South African news association printed something this morning about Chater's new board. Fancy that! You caused it man! Well done hey!"

David emptied his teacup. "Your mining and lease returns Gerard," he said and passed the envelope over. "Plus our cheque covering our quarterly lease rentals."

Gerard's expression magically changed. "I have something to tell you. You did not hear this from me Mr Bradshaw. Are we agreed?"

Formal use of *Mister* was warning enough. Both parties were officially at arms length.

"If it's about politics I don't want to know. This mine is all that I'm interested in."

"In that case." Gerard hesitated, "forget it. I'm running late for my open pit inspection. I hope that I see a big improvement on the safety side."

As data flooded in Frank's geologists finessed computer programs at the Professor's request.

The professor wasted no time being flown to the mine's airstrip,

where David had met him and driven him down to Frank's offices. The big hole had taken on an eerie resonance. Minimal sounds were emitted from Caterpillar bulldozers tidying up waste dumps but the huge shovels lay dormant, their booms stretched flat on the ground, inert, like graceful mechanical giraffes hanging their heads in submission. Mine workshops too stood quiet with only a concerned caretaker crew tending to three lines of parked-up giant haul trucks.

"What if?" the professor proclaimed frequently once among the geologists, "you must never tire of asking 'What if?' As we unlock this ore body. We will peel it back like we do an apple to isolate its rotten parts."

At the managers' lunches the professor left everyone under no illusions about the scale of their problems.

"I doubt that pit roads were lineally derived and built accordingly. This means large sectors of payable ore could be trapped forever. The crushers could be sited in the wrong places. At a glance I can see that your entire conveyor set-up is far too elongated. You are needlessly wasting time, power, money and materials."

That's what the insurance assessors said, thought David. *Will we ever get some good news?* He wrestled with the task of keeping himself motivated. One off-key expression or comment by him in public risked launching fires of discontent among his employees. If ever his leadership skills were being tested it was now. He just had to see it through. *I must. I must* he promised himself.

"I obviously arrived at a bad time," a wary Harry McCrae commented when ushered into David's office. His new boss looked careworn but brightened when seeing him.

"The mine's in choppy waters by all accounts," Harry said. "Everyone looks so down in the dumps."

David was pleased that his new finance man had arrived. Some of his pressures were about to be relieved. He'd learned enough about Harry McCrae to know that he was not one to tread well-worn paths of standard performance.

"As I told you before Harry, I hope not. Quite the contrary — you arrived at a good time with Professor Koenig here. We'll know soon enough where we are headed. Your wife and daughters? When will they join us?"

Harry warmed to David's jocular manner. No signs of resignation or defeat were apparent. "In a month's time. At the start of the school term here in *Thuringia Bay*. My girls had no intention of staying in Johannesburg as boarders. I'm happy about that but it cost me two Honda 50 cc motorbikes to bribe them on to my side."

David laughed. "Your colleagues won't thank you. Their kids will come running looking for motorbikes. In a small town word gets around quickly."

Harry rubbed his hands together animatedly. "I'm raring to go. I want to get stuck in. I have a good idea what I want to do. I did my homework on all those papers you sent me; they were a God send."

"The sooner the better. I called a meeting for ten this morning with your department heads. Introductions, a quick pep talk and then over to you. Set them a cracking pace because I can tell you our technical guys are almost dead on their feet from catering to the prof's needs."

Professor Koenig put the cat among the pigeons at the Friday managers review with his latest request.

"Diagonal drilling?" an amazed David reacted. "But why Professor Koenig? Surely vertical derived core data is sufficient for you?"

"I do not think so. I have never seen an ore body like this one. It is not soft travertine we face here. This is *cordeirite gneiss*, the hardest ore known to man. It is inconstant. Lava flows do not show a standard pattern of repose. I have to rely on diagonally drilled data to give me a foolproof total picture. Diagonally drilled cores will pick up chance malformations that vertical results might have missed. It reduces risk of excavation in the wrong places."

"Diagonal drilling?" Frank mused. "You think we might be mining crap in other words?"

"Diagonal drilling will answer that question once and for all. We need accurate base ore grade data. Only then you can we talk life of mine with certainty, depending what financial results you want. My computer model will make short work of the analysis but I must have those drilling results first."

"My problem Professor," a worried Frank said, "is to find the right kind of drilling equipment. Diamond drillers in this country just don't have that kind of specialized kit on hand. Neither is it available anywhere in Africa. What do you want me to do?"

The Professor opened his personal organizer and extracted a business card. "Take this. This is an iron ore mine in Finland that will help you with specialist drilling equipment. Contact its managing director. Doctor Maskell—that's his name on the card. Tell him I asked you to telephone him. He will lend you the equipment. You will need to charter a big cargo 'plane to get it back here."

Frank looked at David. Bewildered. "Hell! This will cost an arm and a leg. We're not exactly bursting with cash. Harry will have his work cut out finding out how to pay for it."

"Do it Frank," a tired David ordered. "'We came this far. Let's get it right. Harry will find the money somewhere. Won't you Harry?"

Harry swallowed hard. "I have to don't I?"

"How long will it take professor, once we have the equipment on site?" David enquired. "To get an idea what this ore body looks like."

"A day or two for positioning; a week for one square mile of diagonal drilling—two days computer analyzing core results. Let us say we pencil in a date two weeks from now to talk factual ore reserves. Total job—three to four weeks."

To David, "four weeks" sounded better four months.

Harry McCrae found it hard to smile. "I might have known. It will look bad on my CV if I only last another four weeks. Oh well, let me go and *rev* my guys while I can."

Victor's weekly meeting with David perpetuated tradition from earlier days when the top security man reported directly to the GM weekly to discuss developments. Victor's new boss Harry had no objection and sat in on the meetings. Victor's written report usually proved no more than a list of thefts from mine site, some culprits caught and most unknown. No mind-boggling revelations.

"Let's talk about what you didn't write down Vic," David said. "My grapevine tells me that we are being targeted overseas. It seems a lot of people don't like us. Do you get any feedback on loonies who we need to know about?"

"Yes, yes, I hear it all the time," a truculent Victor replied, "along with rumors of bombing raids, attacks on the mine, kidnappings, rail sabotage, putting poison in the drinking water and blowing up our trains as they shunt out of here. If we took too much notice of nut cases none of us would get our work done. Bar room gossip starts these things off. Before long the tooth fairy too will crop up in the chat and Adolf Hitler will also make his reappearance."

"Assuming that what I heard was right, what do you do about it?"

"This," Victor said and withdrew a hand-written sheet from his folder to hand to David.

After a quick eyeball of the document, David passed it to Harry.

"I see. You're a step ahead. Pinch a bit of yellowcake? Is that all?"

"Yes. These objectors are not militia or religious *born-agains'*. They want to embarrass a multi-national company but not bomb it into oblivion. We all know their ploys off by heart. 'Capitalist pigs exploiting the natives.' It's a well-worn anti-colonialist cry along with 'Kill the boer!' What better way to do that than toss radioactive material at our chairman or other senior official if and when an opportunity arises? Better still, another scenario, like a film showing what a bad lot we are."

"Oh yes! Film? What kind of film?"

"One that shows where our final product comes from and where it is sent to. Who gets paid backhanders and how much. That stirs up the greens no end. Uranium oxide going to rogue states like China, Korea, Iran and Iraq—they lose a lot of sleep over that thought. Then there is always talk of the phantom product, *Red Mercury*, that supposedly makes uranium oxide look like small bananas when it comes to priming nuclear bombs. We know that it's tripe. But the readers out there? They lap it up by the bucketful. The entire free world is looking for commies under their beds."

Harry's eyes were agog.

Victor was deadly serious. Lugubrious feedback was old hat to him it appeared.

"What do we do about it?" David enquired. "Presupposing that someone over here is not so well disposed towards us?"

Victor sighed heavily. "For anything serious to happen, someone on this mine has to be in on the act. I'd suggest that our London Public Relations keep their ears open among television companies overseas. That's where a film is likely to be commissioned, a documentary for example that will alert us if any strange folk pitch up here to visit us or linger around *Thuringia Bay* asking leading questions."

"I don't want to get into the espionage business," David said. "We have enough on our plate to cope with."

"I know, but there's no harm in being aware what the risks are. We need to check everyone on site, particularly employees with access to yellowcake in production and shipping. All procedures to be vouchsafed and test run again. I've started doing some checking. Now is as good a time as any to tell you what I turned up so far. You're not going to like it."

A meeting scheduled for half an hour metamorphosed into a full-blown enquiry that took up the rest of the morning.

Victor had listed eight employees with bogus qualifications, eleven others who had adopted aliases, nineteen who had undeclared criminal convictions, two registered psychopaths who had deserted previous milieus elsewhere in the country and four individuals whose medical history showed them as confirmed schizophrenics.

"That lot," Victor declared, "slipped through when idiot cowboys were running this mine. A spymaster's dream. He'd easily find a turncoat among them. One of these aliases has been running a lucrative temporary staff supply business from Cape Town. We brought plenty of *temps* to site. Guess who got the fees? One of Cecil's crew."

"They have to go!" a horrified David exclaimed. "I know them all. Their wives—their children. What a disaster!"

A disappointed Harry noted that of two names that fell into his division. Bogus accountants. "I'll deal with my two. I must admit that I had my suspicions judging from the work they turned out. No qualified accountant would have made such a mess. All of a sudden those salvage yards sales I was asking about...it all falls into place...the buggers! They must have creamed off a fortune for themselves."

"Inform the other managers Vic," a suffused David ordered. "I want these blots of humanity off the site by midnight. I take it that you will arrange with local police to keep an eye on anyone who makes threats?"

"Yes. Don't worry. The culprits will go quietly if they know what's good for them. They'll fade into the background and crop up somewhere else where they will probably cheat as well. It's genetic. These characters have no respect for themselves so why worry about anyone else's scruples?"

10

Despite the late hour his house was ablaze with lights. He sensed something was amiss. He'd hoped that Pam had not waited up for him. They seldom had anything in common to talk about. He accepted that it was mainly his doing. Night after night he'd burned midnight oil. Only the thought of not meeting his challenge spurred him on. Pam had definitely been victim to an agenda not remotely of her making.

They'd been together for thirty years. It was her who had proposed to him. At twenty-two she'd been older than him by three years. She had worked all hours as a nurse to pay his university fees. He had wanted nothing more than to become a mining engineer. She'd made it plain that there was one condition to her offer. She wanted him to marry her. He'd accepted her proposal on the understanding that after he qualified he would pay her back. His obsession had become his career. He had made it a point to run the extra mile, in the process learning not to be impulsive. Such dedication and hard work ensured that he had clawed himself up the ladder to one level below a main board appointment.

Pam might have been petite but in her tiny frame reposed a will of iron. Unlike her peers she'd kept her lithe figure and had not allowed her skin to be crisped by harsh African sun. She dressed sensibly and by day looked much younger than her years. When asleep her features gave way to tension, lines appearing and though her eyelids although closed, flickered, wakefulness barely a second's response to the slightest unnatural noise. Africa's increasing beat of violent changes had ensured that very few people managed a normal night's sleep.

Pam's conquering of David with his inherent strong personality she'd accepted as her prize but she was under no illusions that when age had atrophied her, for women aged quicker than men, almost all his affections were destined to be manifested in his work. He was not one for affairs, the scourge of many a powerful individual. Weak women loved strong men. Sure she knew that many women had flung themselves at David. He had simply ignored them. Work was his mistress. Challenge. Work. Licking problems. Running an honest show for the benefit of someone else.

The couple's initial showers of hugs and kisses had gradually descended over the years into mute acceptance of each other's presence and while he accepted this status quo he had rightly expected that eventually Pam would cool towards him. Put bluntly, his wife had enough wealth now that her late father had left her a tidy sum, not to be agreeably and permanently subject to pressures that his career wreaked on her.

She was waiting on the sofa, absently thumbing through a magazine as he entered the front door.

"Your dinner's in the fridge. *Again.*"

"Thanks very much Pam but I'm not hungry."

"David…We must talk."

A serious chat with a surly wife was furthest from David's mind. Heavy mist had curled in from the sea, having delayed his homeward drive by half an hour. Worrying about what Professor Koenig was going to say nine hours later drained him of his last vestige of energy. Were they in business or were they not?

"I'm sorry Pam for keeping you up so late. Is something the matter? Just let me fix a drink for myself. You?"

"No. Not for me," she replied coldly.

He got up and mixed himself a whisky and soda. "I looked forward to this all day. What a relief." He sounded tired and his movements showed as much. He's acquired a grey, pinched look and his shoulders were hunched.

Although it was late, she was immaculately attired, giving the impression that her evening was about to start. She waited for him to settle in his recliner. "I've been thinking."

"Oh yes. About what?"

She tossed her magazine on to the coffee table and turned to face him. "You…Me."

"Me? Why? Now what have I done?"

She waited for him to look at her so that she could stare at him. "You have a mistress. I can't stand it any longer. I'm so mad I'm going."

"What?" he shouted and shot to his feet spilling his drink in the process. "What are you talking about?"

"That damn mine of yours David. That's what I'm talking about. It's possessed you. It rules you. You have no life outside of it. Face it. We don't have a marriage any more. It's dead and you know it. I seldom see you. Our children are gone and I ask myself what's left for me? You know what the answer is? *Nothing*. I've had enough of mines and all the tripe that goes with it. You are stranger as I must be to you. I am not going to see my life out floating in a cloud of indecision and growing further apart from my husband. It's driven me insane."

"But Pam," he pleaded and put his glass down. "Have a heart. You know that I've got a lot to contend with."

"You always say that. So have I David. So do I have a lot to contend with! There must be more to life than this. I'm sick of it. You married to that heap of steel. It sees more of you than I do. I'm not going to hang around here waiting to see how much time you can spare me. Enough!"

"Stuff and nonsense! Come on Pam. You're over-dramatizing. Why are you dressed up? Are you going somewhere?"

"You noticed! Halleluiah! I most certainly am going somewhere. My car's packed. I'm leaving right now. I had to have this out with you first."

I'm not hearing this he told himself. Please God I'm not hearing this. Make it stop.

"Please Pam you said we have to talk. Let's talk. Tomorrow, well I..."

She got up and angrily brushed past him. "Stop David. It's far too late to do anything. As you say, you have plenty to worry about. I need to get out of here. I'm driving down to Kimberley. I'll take it easy and catch the morning flight to Cape Town. Don't try and stop me. I have made up my mind. I'll leave my car keys with the airport manager."

David ran his fingers through his hair and shook his head with disbelief. "Just like that. You're walking out on me. You're off after all our time together." He didn't know whether to be relieved or angry. He was confused. *Women...*

"Yes. Just like that. I'll rent an apartment. I need time to think and actually mix with people who know me and have time for me. You know, a normal life, like doing normal things together. Not this eternal round of attending company functions flying your company's flag and talking to corporate robots. I don't know who I am any more. I've been stripped of any feelings of worth. I've become a plaything dictated to by your mistress, that bloody mine!"

"Pam, please, I'm very tired. Can't we talk about this later?"

"Talk to who you want. I'm leaving. Right now."

Dumbstruck he watched her flounce out their front door, heard her car door slam and listened to her accelerate into the misty night.

"The old man's not looking so good," Cecil whispered to Frank and Harry. "What's wrong with him?"

Both men glanced at David, noticing how beaten he looked. His cheeks had sunk in and his pallor had taken on a grey hue

"I don't know. It's his business," Frank replied and lit his next cigarette from the butt of its predecessor. "Whatever it is it's got nothing to do with work."

Professor Koenig joined them in the training lecture room.

"Everything set up Mr Lonsdale?"

"Yes professor."

"All our managers are present Prof," David announced, "shall we start? Over to you."

Long experience had taught Harry much about body language. Little about the professor's posture suggested that bad news in the offing. The man had looked and sounded decidedly upbeat.

Frank was dying to cut through the preliminaries and ask the professor "Do we have a mine or do we not?"

Cecil sensed that the prof's cheery manner signified good news and gave Bruno a wink.

Bruno took it or granted that the mine was there for all time and Peter Gomez gave no hints about what was going through his mind.

Just David, slumped in his chair, appeared to be the odd man out staring blankly at the professor.

"My job was to look at this ore body and compile an accurate three dimensional picture of its mineral contents. Thank you all for working with me. Let me show you a computerized disposition of your ore body. Dim the lights please somebody."

Cecil obliged and the carousel projector clicked into action.

"This shows that your mining lease area has plenty of low-grade uranium ore evenly distributed at various levels. Host rock for this is *cordeirite gneiss*, the hardest rock known to man. Your extractive and processing equipment will need hardened steel to deal with this geological monster. Waste ore is evenly distributed throughout the lease area so simplifying its removal and disposal. It means that mobile waste in-pit crushing can be implemented allowing you another income from sale of aggregate. I'm ignoring modest quantities of rare earths and minerals like silver, titanium and selenium that metallurgical operations can recover from secondary treatments and flue residue refining that will make a hefty contribution to your cash flow.

"One area," he pointed at his picture, "hosts a highly concentrated lode of high quality gypsum. You may pull that out and sell it at a premium to a discerning German market. Besides yellowcake sales, you should earn enough from by-products to finance your mining equipment and machinery operations for a good few years. A further bonus," he said stopping to peer at his picture and point to a blue section, "is that you have a sizeable underground water supply waiting to be tapped. It is fresh water of potable quality so you will have to inform your government water affairs department about it. You save a lot of money if you tap it and recycle it."

"Any idea how much water?" Frank enquired.

"Equivalent to eighty years consumption at your peak production needs, disregarding natural underground replenishment that must occur periodically. If you had mined into that by accident, you would have incurred a calamity."

"I'll be a witch's wig!" Frank bellowed. "Fresh water! There's not a mention on that London-produced ore reserve map."

The professor waited for the hubbub to die down. "Your previous ore reserve plan data is confirmed therefore as a trifle lacking in accuracy."

"Why am I not surprised?" Peter glowered.

"I'm very pleased about the water Professor, but have present extraction operations affected access to payable ore?" David queried.

"Partly. Bench faces have to be re-sited. This must affect your road system, added to which your primary crushers are wrongly sited. They straddle the only high-grade ore reserves close to surface. Diagonal drilling yielded those facts gentlemen so that alone made the exercise worthwhile. The remainder of high-grade ore rests at eight hundred feet below surface in the southeast area of your mining lease. Based on peak capacity for final U3o8 product, lower grade ore gives you a life of mine of no less than forty years. There is an option to access some high-grade ore to supplement low-grade yields, but this must be done with due care and consideration."

"No high grading if we can avoid it Professor," David interjected.

The professor smiled. "A responsible attitude Mr Bradshaw. This three dimensional picture shows you tonnages of ore distributed within your lease area. I did compile costings, playing different tunes with ore grade and return on investment percentages. I believe that you can meet board investment criteria subject to certain aspects that I shall refer to later. Had you have continued on your current path you would have cut off sizeable areas of the pit for later excavation and faced making permanent losses. You acted just in time. Also, you would not have had the data to plan for excavation and processing a range of secondary minerals."

"I cannot tell you how relieved I am," David said. "Our new chairman will be equally pleased. We owe you a great deal."

The professor held his hand up. "No Mr Bradshaw, you do not. You acted in time. I sound one warning. Your sales prices to existing yellowcake customers are contractually pegged. Not to have negotiated an inflation-linked sales price was most inadvisable, a situation that your sales people must avoid in future. You will have to find ways and means of working smarter to offset annual inflation. Out here it is running in double figures and appears unlikely to be curbed in the immediate future. If you look at how exchange rates of all African countries fared since their marches into independence, this comment is underlined even more. The answer is to run everything for control purposes in USA dollars. That is the system in Brazil.

"It will not be easy to achieve. You have to increase employee wages annually or you will lose good people. Good skills. You cannot expect employees to contribute more and accept that their money will buy them less and less. It requires astute money management, personnel training, and sound leadership to keep this mine afloat. It is not simply a question of whether you have payable ore. It is a question of running a tight, smart, responsive operation. A suggestion for reducing costs is that you should look at electrically driven haul trucks because electricity is cheaper than consuming fossil fuels. Installing radioactive scanners that assess ore grade of each truckload before it gets to primary crushers saves you processing waste ore."

"If you were chairman Professor would you continue operations at this mine?"

"I am not chairman Mr Bradshaw. I would not presume to answer your question. A chairman has to deal with many other issues including politics."

"So we're in business," Frank said while rubbing his hands together. "Let's roll!"

"Yes Mr Fielding," the professor grinned. "I believe you are."

Bruno had been a key man during the rebuild. Without him critically pathing repairs and equipment replacement the mine was hardly likely to have risen from its ashes in time. He lived in aircraft ferrying to and fro South Africa chivvying contractors and suppliers to meet and beat deadline dates.

Road haulage fleets thundering along national highways to and fro the Northern Cape became common sights. Harry got his men behind the rebuild with streamlined cost control and reporting procedures, an essential requirement aimed at potential highlighting stray cost before it was committed. Many of his men had to adapt to shift work, a new development for administrators but it drew them closer to production people. Harry's particular headache was overseeing the necessary funds to back it all up without steering into red ink on the company's income statement.

David paid particular attention to improving environmental protection measures the money for which Harry had been charged with finding.

"That's bad news!" a pained Harry exclaimed, three *mill?* What does that do for production?"

"If we offset cancer starting in one employee Harry, it will be worth every cent. We have to be ahead of the game. It's only a question of time before questions come flying at us on the subject, aside from squashing drivel that left-wing lobbies are spewing."

"Just checking. We'll find the money lurking somewhere."

Frank, to his annoyance, had insurance assessors constantly peering over his shoulder. Assessors would not understand the necessity for some road rearrangement in the open pit. "We're not paying for that!" one official exploded.

"Suit yourself. If I'd left it where it was you end up paying out more on operating costs. This way," Frank explained, "you score. Check the figures. Ask the *prof* if you think I'm lying to you. So, in the meantime why don't you get lost!"

"Well, if you put it that way..."

"I know what I'm doing," a steely Frank informed over-anxious assessors. "Do you want to take over? Be my guest boyo."

Cecil had worked his network bone-dry tracking down competent employees to replace human dross that had been pushed out. Running multi-skilling training around the clock ensured that his wife saw little of him too. He'd also had an eye on the future and managed to profile with the help of South African university staff, a nucleus of high fliers two years away from gaining their degrees. By forming early bonds with chosen students and helping them out financially Cecil was assured of high hit-rates when it came to finally employing them.

Everyone on site enjoyed the sight of pieces being put back together and tested to their limits. One general foreman informed Bruno, "There's a big part of me and my men in this rebuild. There's no way we want people years down the line to point fingers at us. This is the best." Divisional managers were constant in their efforts to cajole, spur, motivate, congratulate and sometimes to scream at someone who had gone off course. Occasionally they had to back off and cool off, and met at the club after work to enjoy a few drinks with their men.

Harry ruminated about the enormity of what he had taken on. He had license to introduce whatever changes he wanted, subject to justification materializing. A complex change from outmoded computer equipment and systems to new technology had turned his hair almost totally grey offset by his satisfaction that he'd prevented an inevitable information earthquake when the mine could have least afforded a system collapse. More and more he had to struggle top find free time to do "normal" things like go out for a meal with his family, or spending time on the beach with them "letting it all hang out."

Bruno and Mariette felt the same way as did Cecil and Marlene. Bruno's impromptu invitations to come round for a drink at odd hours and Mariette's dinner parties were a culinary tribute blessed by her bubbly personality. Cecil's sharp wit, Harry's "put-me-downs" and ladies decrying their menfolk for their outrageous behavior also ensured that for a few joyous hours the mine took a back seat in all their lives.

When the managers and their wives appeared at the club for dinner the disc jockey's face fell a mile. Firstly, he was on caution from Roger Lacy to keep off hash and booze and secondly it meant that he'd have to hang around until four or five on a Saturday morning while "big bosses" made fools of themselves letting their hair down.

Harry loved to chat. He told his share of entertaining stories and in turn was regaled by what the ladies had to say about living with a manager. His first time at the club with the Gerbers, Mariette got him up to dance with her; she made it easy coaxing long forgotten steps back into action.

"Ah Mariette, you make me feel young again…"

"Oh you! Don't try and sound like a grandfather! There's life in there somewhere isn't there?" she said, eyes twinkling, accompanied by her infectious laugh.

At the Christmas "do", Harry's first, an event at the club that

David's personal assistant had organized, he was amazed that it was a black tie event. On the edge of the desert...black tie?

"Don't complain so much!" Doreen chided her grumbling husband as he struggled with his bow tie. "After all it's the one time that we ladies have to really dress up. We look forward to it. Don't go there with a long face and spoil it for everyone."

The superintendents and their spouses too attended most of who enjoyed interaction with their top team. Everyone left no later than midnight, some anxious to party back home with friends rather than hang around at the club self-conscious that they were keeping their host, the GM, well past his witching hour.

Inevitably most of the managers and their wives repaired to one of their homes to continue celebrations. No one was shy to have a drink Bruno did his inevitable break-dance routine—a rare sight observing a two hundred and fifty pound giant gyrating on the floor drunk out of his mind. Vigorous dancing soon gave way to slow music, an opportunity to for hardy stayers to recharge batteries in readiness for greeting a rising blood-red sun.

Spontaneous events had their highlights.

Just as Harry and Doreen were about to depart to visit a friend who ran a parrot farm in the Maru river bed further north, they had an unexpected visitor. Johnny Rowlands, a recent Sandhurst graduate busy hitch-hiking from England to Cape Town rang the front doorbell.

"Hello," the tousle-haired young twenty-two year-old beamed. "One of your friends in Jo'burg suggested that I should look you up."

Small world. He'd met up with the Byrons', good friends in Johannesburg. They'd suggested to him to detour to *Thuringia Bay* for the time of his life.

Harry and Doreen bundled him into their car—no Land Rover

needed this time, and trailed Bruno *en famil* , ninety miles North-East into the hinterland beside the *Maru* River.

"*Parrot farm?*" Johnny enquired. "How does one farm parrots? What for?"

"This country is full of surprises," Harry said with a straight face. "To eat them!"

"No!" Johnny shrieked. "That's disgusting!"

"Don't mind him," Doreen placated her visitor. "Our friend Chris started it as a hobby. It's grown so big he exports them all over the world. And he makes a lot of money while he's about it."

They stopped on the way at some garnet beds for Johnny to gathered ruby-like stones. He couldn't believe his luck. An hour later they halted again for "Elevenses" and out came cooked cold crumbed steenbras fillets, hot coffee and cheese sandwiches.

"What an incongruous sight we must be," Harry exclaimed. "Here we are in one of the remotest parts of this continent absorbing the quiet of desert and eating like royalty."

A breathless Johnny rooted in his rucksack for his camera to capture scrubland and gypsum-bound sands, lichens and dried bushes that a gentle wind blew along the surface.

"Hey man," a reverent Bruno broke silence and nudged Johnny, "overseas people pay big money to come here and do this. To get away from it all. If you step off the road onto the sands, your tracks will stay for all time."

"What's this *Maru River* like?" Johnny enquired.

Bruno explained that it was a remote, dry river that rose in the highlands but that its water ran underground when traversing the desert.

"It has deep water wells," Bruno informed him. "We tap them for water to pipe to our mine."

"What for?"

"It mines and treats uranium among other rare minerals. The guy in the street calls it *yellowcake.*"

"'Uranium?'" Johnny gulped. *"'Yellowcake?'* You mean for bombs and that kind of thing?"

The two managers glanced at one another and smiled. Both of them had the same thought. *Tell Johnny that buck around the mine glowed in the dark? And were twice normal size?*

Reason prevailed. "No," Bruno said. "To generate clean nuclear energy. Power stations. Coal is just too dirty and causes pollution."

Johnny shook his head and let out a deep sigh after taking a big bite of his sandwich. "You chaps live like lords!"

At their destination Johnny distinguished himself by taking Bruno's .22 rifle to expertly shoot two cooing birds flying overhead.

"Hey!" an angry Chris van Wyk, their host, shouted. "You just *bladdy* shot my *bladdy* prize fantails. What are you bladdy doing?" Chris whistled loudly and from nowhere *Amy*, his pet baboon loped in.

Johnny's eyes were the size of saucers. "Wh'what do you do with it," he faltered and kept his distance from the mangy animal.

"Her," Chris corrected and patted *Amy*. "Up!" he commanded and *Amy* jumped into his arms to begin inspecting Chris's scalp.

"It's an ape-thing," Chris informed Johnny. "She's looking for nits. That's how they clean each other. Here you try it."

Before a startled Johnny could make himself scarce, Chris snapped, *"Him!"*

Amy jumped off and flew onto Johnny's chest, holding on with one hand, while fingers of the other sank into the longhaired young Englishman's scalp.

"Get 'orf!" a hysterical Johnny screamed. "Get 'orf!"

"That will teach him to shoot my birds," Chris grinned to his guests, all prostate with laughter.

Johnny couldn't look at *Amy* whose array of lethal fangs hovered inches from his face.

"Come!" Chris commanded and *Amy* jumped off to bound toward Chris and clasp his outstretched hand.

"Look around the farm," Chris invited. "I'm going to give *Amy* her tractor lesson."

"'Tractor lesson?'" Johnny gulped. "A baboon driving a tractor? Go on! You're talking rubbish!"

"Of course," Chris answered with a straight face. "She's a fast learner. You want to come with us? *Amy's* union won't mind."

"N'no thanks," a hesitant Johnny replied, "I'll stick around here. I'll go and look at your parrots."

"Just don't you bladdy shoot any of my birds!"

They'd all just gone through a repeat of Chris's time honored ritual—his *Amy* routine.

A campfire outside the house on their first night and a braai were new experiences for Johnny. For a slim man, he put away a lot of food, particularly home-made farm sausage, Chris's specialty. Under a canopy of midnight blue and myriads of stars that all felt they could touch if they wanted to, a few drinks in their bellies, Johnny confessed was about as close to Heaven he thought that he'd ever experience.

"The best part comes now," Chris smirked. "When we go to bed."

"Don't tell me Amy sleeps inside?" a tremulous Johnny answered.

"No man. You funny chaps in England might sleep with baboons. We don't. We draw the line at such bladdy behavior."

"Ha ha. You're pulling my leg again aren't you Mr Van Wyk?"

Chris scratched at his beard. "No man. But we all sleep in one room. You have to get changed in the dark. And don't you bladdy snore hey, otherwise I'll let Amy in to shut you up!"

It must have taken a lot of courage on Johnny's part to exact his revenge on Chris who had been ragging his visitor all day and most of the evening. Sensing when Chris was about to remove his underpants in the dark to don his pajamas, Johnny momentarily shone a torch beam at him. All present bore witness to two ginger beards. The ladies shrieked and Bruno's hysterical laughter boomed out while Johnny sniggered.

"Who bladdy did that?" Chris shouted and dropped his pajama

pants by accident. He fell to the floor to retrieve them and on came the torch again for few seconds to expose a set of snow white buttocks. "It's not funny hey!" Chris's disembodied voice echoed.

"Oh my God!" his wife laughed, "It's the first time I ever saw his bum!"

Mariette's giggle was unmistakable and Johnny emitted strange sounds of repressed laughter.

"It's that bladdy Englishman!" Chris rasped. "Isn't it? I'll kill him! The bladdy bastard!"

"Who me?" a paralytic Johnny cried who at the same time moved near the door in case he had to run for it.

"Go to sleep Chris!" his wife commanded. "Or should I call you *Whitey*?" she giggled.

"Very bladdy funny!"

Next morning turned out a glorious sunny blue-skied Sunday. Everyone awoke to appetizing aromas of baking bread and strong coffee.

The men did what all people did on a Sunday in the middle of nowhere, lounging on the veranda while exchanging tall stories. They watched reluctant mist rise off a dry riverbed and sank a few tots of *Jagermeister* liqueur that Chris produced along with his .375 *Manlicher* rifle that he propped up in a corner.

"There's a pride of lions living in the river bed," Chris announced. "If the wind is right you hear them grunting and roaring at night. Sometimes early in the morning we spot the old ones limping back from the beach."

"Oh yes," a disbelieving Johnny broke in. "Ha ha! On the beach indeed! Coming back from sunbathing were they? Do they pop in here for a drink and snacks?"

"I'm serious man," Chris said. "They go down to the sea to scavenge, like jackals do. Their teeth are gone so if they get a chomp at a dead seal or whale washed up, they fill up. If they don't eat," Chris croaked ominously and stroked his rifle lovingly, "and they walk back up the riverbed, spot us, then have a guess what they might be thinking?"

"No," Johnny cried, "Not us surely?"

Harry produced a bottle of *Chivas Regal* and Bruno weighed in with a bottle of exquisite *KWV* Cape brandy.

"Nice to have a sip isn't it on a Sunday?" Bruno grinned. "No 'phones. No mine pressure. Man, this is the life!"

A sleepy-eyed Johnny agreed. "If I hadn't have experienced all this I'd never have believed it! Have you got a vacancy for me?"

Just then a plate of steaming bread appeared with a pot of salted yellow butter. The ladies made it plain that they were weren't too impressed with their men boozing so early on a Sunday morning

At midday Chris checked his watch. "Brunch," he announced and his beady eye fell on Johnny.

"Do you eat liver?" he asked. His huge ginger beard provided Chris with a big advantage for it hid his facial expressions. "I mean you chaps eat a lot of strange things don't you, like bladdy snails and brains?"

"I do eat liver," a suspicious Johnny answered. "But it must be fresh and slightly pink on the inside. Also…"

"No kidding!" Chris broke in, "this bloke is spoilt! Do you want it served by a bladdy butler too?"

"No. But it has to be floured and fried with onions. Topped by Worcestershire sauce. My old granny's recipe."

"Chris is at it again,"' Harry whispered to Bruno. "What now?"

"Do you want me to play the piano too?" Chris wheezed at his guest. "You like it with bladdy knobs on as well!"

The two managers knew better than to join that conversation.

Chris disappeared. Minutes an unmistakable aroma seeped through the farmhouse. A smiling Chris rejoined his guests holding a massive platter of fried liver and onions, hot bread and a bottle of *Lea and Perrins Worcestershire* sauce.

"Wow! *Miracle man*," Johnny whooped.

Johnny began fingering Chris's rifle after he'd had his fill.

"Give me that!" Chris said and snatched it from him. "I'm not serving up bladdy roast pigeon again for the bladdy British army."

"Ish hell in Africa," a decidedly drowsy Johnny muttered while on his fourth *dop* of brandy. *"Nishe shtuff shish..."*

"Where did you get it?" Harry asked Chris and nodded at his emptied plate of liver and onions. "That was quick work."

"Oh," Chris laughed, "I told my foreman to grab a sheep and kill it. It doesn't make any noise when you kill it you know. Just slice its throat, open its guts, and pull out its liver. Can't get fresher than that can we? I did the onions..."

"What!" Harry boggled, horrified, a hypocrite when it came to eating meat. "You slaughtered a sheep on our account?"

"Yes. What's wrong with that?"

"Any more?" Bruno enquired hopefully through grease-smeared lips. "That was great man!"

"Ish shell 'n Arfri..."' Johnny muttered before his head lolled to one side.

Next morning Harry put an unsteady Johnny on the Piper bound for Kimberley. That gave him a good start for his hitchhiking further south.

"It was like a dream," he said while taking a last look around him. "I can't thank you all enough. I have never had such hospitality in my life. I don't think I ever will again." Just as reached the top of the plane steps, he turned and shouted, "Give my best to Chris and his lady! And to Amy!"

12

"The chairman 'phoned you from New York," Joey informed a hot and bothered David on his return from his tailings dam inspection. "He asked that you to return his call as soon as possible."

Pressures did not upset Joey. Her placid exterior was sometimes mistaken by the unwary who assumed that she was a "pushover." No individual got past her desk without her consent.

It had just gone five o'clock, an hour later than he intended, but coping with demands for more tailings dam pumps had unexpectedly waylaid him. He'd been presented with no choice, yet another example of Peter Gomez's predecessor having slyly hidden his problem, understandably because his slip-shod tailings management had caused it. David was forced to condone more unbudgeted and very expensive Swedish pumps to prevent contaminated water seeping into the underground water system. At thirty thousand rands a time he had every reason to be angry and did not relish telling Harry to scrape up the money somewhere to pay for it.

"Fine thanks Joey. Give me five minutes to clean up."

After three attempts he got through.

"How are things going out there?" the chairman queried.

Harry gave Hilton Walsh a quick overview.

"Good. As I recall we have five months to go to our D-Day. July 1986. I spoke to a UN contact last night. The UN and South Africa are close to an independence solution for South West Africa. For obvious reasons I want to court these people in good time."

"I see chairman. May I ask why?"

"They're heavily involved in this South West African independence issue. My thinking is that they could add your mine to their itinerary when sending their working party to South West Africa and Angola. They're in deep with the Cubans in Angola. Kissinger's boys are pretty thick on the ground there. Three guesses why—it's all about oil. Our American friends change sides easily when it comes to ensuring access to strategic commodities. We should keep on the good side of all parties concerned. Angola figures high for oil and mineral prospecting. I'm looking well ahead. If there's any energy action in the offing there I want Chater to get a piece of that pie."

David paled at the thought of bogging down in one of the chairman's esoteric missions. Had he forgotten that he had a runaway mine to get up and going. Bloody *hell, where was the time needed going to come from?* "When will that be chairman? This working party visit you mentioned?'

"July…August this year."

"Politics chairman? I was hoping to keep clear of it."

"You can't this time. It's an opportunity too for your mine to put itself on the global map for the right reasons this time."

"How? We are really pushed for time chairman. We're doing here in a year what it took five years before to erect."

"I expected you to say as much Mr Bradshaw. No, I'm looking ahead. That's what I'm here for."

"But how will that help us?"

"In your case I have to take a long view for our shareholders. I think it's an opportunity for you to demonstrate what you achieved. It will pave the way when it comes to interim UN dispensations and US congress acceptance until South Africa attains majority rule. You could use positive publicity. I think the timing is perfect. It eases us into Angola, as I said before."

David remained far from convinced. He'd had plenty of experience of mealy-mouthing politicians. In his opinion politics was the repository of leeches fixed on the public purse. "We will do our best. I suggest that you wait for at least a month after commissioning to allow us to fine-tune."

"Ah thank you! I knew you'd see it my way."

Victor Grey stopped David when he cruised up to the gate at seven in the morning. "I have something to show you," he said grimly. "It's not pleasant."

"What's happened?" David exhaled as he hastily exited his vehicle.

"Read this, today's UK press," Victor replied and handed David a faxed news report.

Desert Rumblings

Reliable sources report that troubled Chater Mine in South Africa's remote Northern Cape will recommence producing of uranium oxide in July. This follows a major repair exercise caused by unexplained sabotage last year. Exploitation of indigenous labor has arisen and questions are being asked about radiation killing off mine employees. No comment has been received from the London based owners of the mine, the Chater group of companies.

Reported by Andrew Keinander.

"What utter rubbish!" David uttered disdainfully. "Where do they get such tripe from? Aren't they supposed to check their sources before they rush into print?"

"God knows, but appearing weeks before start-up date is no coincidence. I'll make enquiries. It could be anybody—opposition smears, environmental nutters, politicians...You know the scene," Victor mused.

"One thing for sure, the chairman will have read this," David said. "I'd better 'phone him to get his reaction. He might know something about this Keinander buffoon. We'll have to work on him."

Hilton Walsh's reaction? Prime Australian invective—bad news for the group's share price. More importantly, it chipped away at the board's credibility—and he was its chairman. At huge cost to his time and resources he'd been lining up Japanese clients for *The Thuringia's* products. Potential clients who embraced corporate probity had an excuse to either run for cover or force sale prices down based on Keinander's spurious article. The British Foreign Office had not contacted him yet but he knew that some starched collar would be "My Dear Boying" him at his club, usually prefacing another round of political mayhem in the House of Commons.

Hilton's mind raced over negation and damage control tactics. A UN delegation visiting the mine forthwith? That would restore credibility. He had enough clout to get South African foreign affairs people hopping about. Painfully aware that David Bradshaw was in his final lap and in no mood for distractions he blanched and then stretched for his telephone.

"UN! At a rededication ceremony...1st July! Chairman...you can't be serious! I dismissed the article as lunatic press ravings." David had expected reaction but none that immediately involved him.

"Keinander is no lunatic. He's a Fleet Street heavyweight and someone must have slipped him a few bob to publish it. We have to knock him off his perch. At this stage, we're not concerned with post-mortems. Remedial measures—yes. Help me out here David. You won't believe the damage we face on the stock exchange and losing customers unless we act fast to shaft these reporters."

"I suppose Chairman that in your place I'd do something similar," David relented. "My managers won't be volunteering handstands when I tell them what you want. Preparing for a visit of that magnitude is some ask on top of what we're contending with."

"You have a good team. Let me tell how many visitors I expect to go out there."

An hour later David summoned Joey. "Something totally unexpected is in the offing Joey. I need your help."

"If I can. What do you want me do?"

"Our chairman is coming out here with a United Nations group to visit us. It's very short notice, but we want a rededication ceremony. I want you to handle it aiming for July first. I can't spare the time and you appreciate that our managers are spoken for. You're the only person I can trust to do this without stepping on toes."

"Wow! Four weeks time. How many visitors do you expect?" Joey calmly asked her boss.

"Only the chairman from London office. No hangers-on. He's divorced. Six UN members and a dozen shadows; security and UN press. A dozen senior government people, plus twenty or so press. It will be a fly in, fly out function. We will have to arrange air transport Cape Town so Don South is heavily involved. The entire party needs to tour mine operations, with particular emphasis on environmental aspects."

"What about our managers?"

"Of course! How stupid of me! Involve all managers and their wives. And I'd say all employees on site must attend the actual rededication ceremony."

"Outside guests? The Mayor?"

"Thirty. Use your discretion Joey."

"I'll do my best. I take it there is money budgeted for this?"

"No, but after I've spoken to the managers, have a word with Harry McCrae. He'll see you right."

13

Joey roped in local artist Chantal Mallis whose imaginative input was sorely needed. She undertook to paint several water colors of "the mine at work" for a limited edition of prints to be assembled into leather-bound VIP presentation folders. Designing appropriate invitations to the rededication ceremony and special certificates of congratulation for each mine employee also fell into her remit. Victor Grey weighed in with accelerated clearances from national police authorities required for all guests and Don South got cracking touting for suitable aircraft at knock-down hire rates.

Joey prepared a press release for David to who predictably initialed it without reading it. "You know the game Joey," he said. "Thanks."

One meal had to be arranged to cater for all tastes…vegetarian, Muslim, Jewish, Hindu…necessitating trucking in a giant marquee from Johannesburg, along with the caterers and equipment because no one locally wanted to tackle such an important event at short notice.

Joey commandeered a lecture-hall in the training centre and equipped it with telephones, computers, fax machines, desks, pads and paper, along with a plentiful supply of soft drinks for press members. Liquor was not allowed on site by law. Bussing employees about the mine was no problem except that she had to isolate a venue large enough on site to accommodate employees during the dedication ceremony.

"I know! What about the open pit?" Don suggested to her. "All the mining people have to do is tidy up the top bench near the primary crushers. We can put up temporary covered stands for staff and visitors. That's what it's all about isn't it? Mining? Television crews will lap it up. Right in front of the big hole. With a bit of luck one or two of the buggars might fall into it!"

Finessing an event program was hard. She had to arrange for a bus and test-drive each guest route. Allowing for settling down time, speeches and leeway for the unexpected resulted in each event being truncated to fit into the eight hours available. Arrival times at Cape Town and departure times from the mine airport were sacrosanct since they had been politically negotiated. Then there was the question of tour guides and preparing nominated employees to supervise VIP passengers. Uniforms in new corporate colors, fawn and orange, were contracted to a delighted local cottage industry and as for a light-hearted moment, Joey had just the thing in mind.

Professor Koenig walked into her office two days before the big visit.

"Professor! How nice to see you!"

He shook her hand heartily. "Miss Schneider! So you are the brains behind all this activity. I have never seen the mine looking so neat and clean."

"Ah no Professor. Just doing my job and getting a lot of help. I've had to call in favors and I've forgotten what my boss looks like."

"Understandably," he smiled. "Working in this pressure cooker takes it toll. But then he lives for tackling and licking production hurdles. There are few men like him."

Joey listened closely. Evidently her visitor was not conscious of the wide esteem he himself was held in.

"Please pass my respects to Mr Bradshaw. I could not pass up being here for the opening. It almost equates to waiting for the birth of one's first grandchild!"

Just as well, Don South mused, that they'd laid on an extra aircraft. A DC3 in camouflage trim on offer at an excellent hire rate was too good to refuse, the very 'plane used to fly army generals about the country. It had appropriate luxury seating for sixteen people, so that meant the chairman and the UN group was taken care of. Two unpressurised twelve-seaters were available for the press contingent which freed up the mine's Piper for emergencies.

A holding pen had been set up in Cape Town's airport terminal for the press to interview UN delegates and chairman of Chater Metals PLC Limited. Government protocol officials orchestrated arrival proceedings, thankful that because the visit was classified as private, no official welcome bogged down with its extreme time-consuming protocol was mandatory.

Joey and Don were present to oversee proceedings while David consorted with waiting officials. He couldn't remember when last he'd worn a formal suit. It felt awful and he felt out of place. After cups of coffee were dispensed, a drum sounded, so loudly, everyone stopped in mid-conversation. A tiny, crouching bushman appeared clad in a skimpy leather apron over leather underpants. He was bare-chested and barefooted. His tiny wrinkled face all but enveloped raisin-like eyes. He carried a small bow, placed an arrow on it and drew back the hide string. He circled, trance-like, emitting a series of clicks and sucking sounds.

"He's demonstrating how he stalks an animal in the desert," Joey explained to a wide-eyed reporter beside her.

"Yeah," the man drawled, "just as long he doesn't fire that arrow head this way!"

"He's a bushman," Don intervened, pretending amazement. "They don't waste ammunition."

A tribal chief appeared adorned by a variety of leather attire highlighted with mud and cowrie shell fragments intertwined with his kernelled hair. He too was barefoot and his chest, legs and arms were splashed with red ochred mud. His handsome face evidenced tribal slash scars and his thin arms sported a variety of brass and copper armbands. Close by a tall graceful lady stood attired in a floor-length flounced floral dress that embraced long leg-of-mutton arms complete with matching head scarf, mirroring the influence and style of German women who had lived in the Northern Cape a century ago. An elderly gentleman exhibited his unusual mode of dress, an impressive spectacle with bandoliers that bestrode his torso as he proudly clutched an ancient *Mauser* rifle. Beneath the broad rim of his hat, one side of which was pinned up, he stared back at his open-mouthed examiners, his straggly drooping moustaches completing the effect.

"I hope these reporters pick up on the significance of a multi-cultural country," Joey whispered to Don. "It's not all about mining or black and white people. Our mine has to become a part of it."

"Look around you Joey," Don laughed. "They're all taking *pics* like crazy. No one is bothering with political heavies."

Don was right. Stiff-lipped, hair-slicked South African diplomats, most with trademark pencil-thin moustaches with a gap in the middle herded together, all of them wearing permanent frowns.

Don and Joey picked the right moment to move in and distribute the program of events awaiting everyone at the mine. Up to that point, she was still none the wiser who comprised the UN party.

"For security reasons," the Chairman had informed David, "no one knows their names. Being highly-placed UN officials should be sufficient."

When the chartered Lufthansa DC 8 from Frankfurt touched down the airport was abuzz. Uniformed security officers were the first to exit followed by UN officials, and lastly Harry Walsh. One UN member appeared in fetching garb, flowing robes and skullcap that signified him as a Nigerian. A tiny very slim lady wore a white silk sari. The remaining four men wore suits. Not one face looked familiar perhaps just as well Joey surmised otherwise press interviews risked delay if pressmen chose to explore other topics.

The entire party grimaced when feeling the biting chill of a cape winter's day. Before the party entered the terminal an unexpected voice blared out through a megaphone.

Without warning cries of "Independence! Independence! We want independence! Capitalist exploiters!" rang out. "Murderers!"

Cacophony in public enclosure was not helped by frantic officials running amok like headless chickens. A tin was hurled onto the tarmac, spilling yellow powder. A security official rushed to pick it up but when spotting a skull and crossbones pained on its side along with "POISON" he drew back. "Custard powder!" he declared minutes later, when taking a closer look. "Can you believe it? Some oaf chucked out custard powder!"

Unfortunately for stricken Joey, the press caught the incident on camera. Squads of security men failed to find the culprit.

"Aren't you at risk?" one excited reporter queried a UN delegate in the terminal. "That could have been acid thrown at you."

"It makes a change to rotten eggs and tomatoes," the urbane visitor blithely replied. "It goes with the job my man."

"What sir, do you hope to achieve with this visit?"

"Facts. First-hand facts. That's why we came here. To see it all for ourselves."

"What about independence?"

A smile spread across the official's face. "It's the new game in town...eventually."

A collective and audible gasp broke out. At long last someone of stature had committed openly to the independence issue. The last time that had happened was over thirty years previously when the droopy-eyed Harold Macmillan, the British prime minister had dropped his bombshell in Cape Town's parliament building for the benefit of outraged white Nationalist party members. Macmillan's poetic "Winds of Change" speech had clearly signaled British extrication from its African responsibilities. "Independence" to white South Africa flew in the face of government apartheid policy. South Africa had been launched as a polecat nation by Macmillan and now a UN man was openly hinting at its impending deliverance.

Joey heaved a sigh of relief. That welcome remark had deflected attention from bogus radioactive powder but she was not naïve enough to believe that the press would ignore the sensational incident. Hilton's smile bespoke his glee at the priceless public relations the UN official's comment had ushered in for his Chater group of companies.

15

"D-day" had assumed ogre status at the mine. On the one hand employees had feared its arrival but on the other, they wished that it was well behind them to allow them to get on with their jobs since time was tight.

On arrival at the mine's airport visitors were ushered to changing rooms to don safety gear. The Nigerian delegate using mellifluous English drew back and refused point blank to don steel-toed safety shoes, cumbersome footwear seemingly too indelicate for his sartorial tastes.

"It is for your own safety sir," David politely informed him when querying the delay. "You will be visiting operational areas where heavy equipment is used. We are bound by law to protect you from potential accidents."

The man demurred after several photographs were taken of him and fell back into line.

The UN party accompanied by the chairman and David was the first group to embus, accompanied by a few reporters and government officials. At ten-minute intervals the remainder of the party followed in three groups.

At each stop along the route a divisional manger waited to usher them through the area concerned. Explanations were crisp and questions arose aplenty. David had no gripes; Joey had planned it well and his managers had risen to the occasion. The plant and equipment in his view rivaled a spotless hospital ward.

"It looks good, "the chairman muttered to David. "Bloody well done."

Doctor Hannah took great care when explaining radiation hazards at the roasting plant where visitors saw uranium oxide for the first time, *yellowcake* being loaded into black drums the sides of which were emblazoned with the universal yellow nuclear "Danger" sign.

"Yes but it's still very dangerous stuff isn't it?" an unconvinced reporter broke in. "Nuclear power?"

"It is. Only when it's abused or mishandled. But human error is also a risk."

"Yes!" the reporter smirked. "I thought so!"

"Incidents in the Soviet bloc and the recent Three Mile Island nuclear power runaway in New York sensitized the world to increased safety procedures at nuclear repositories. Many people do not accept that nuclear power is here to stay. The unavoidable fact is that this planet does not have enough fossil fuel to service its energy needs. If it did, pollution would be curse so virulent it would poison the ozone layer and choke us all in the process."

"I'll need convincing about that," the reporter reacted. "We had a world before nuclear power arrived on the scene didn't we?"

Doctor Hannah decided not to debate the issue. Time was on short leash, a restraint that mildly irritated him. Deflection tactics were required. "During early operations several employees unfortunately contracted cancer but we did not understand the cause at the time. Since then we have counseled top international environmental experts and have acted on their advice."

"What for example," the Nigerian delegate queried, "did you do?"

"We installed massively increased protective measures, clothes and equipment several levels higher than prescribed international standards. Frequent testing of employees has not indicated further radiation-caused cancer cases."

Doctor Hannah was prepared for the question, "And what about the people who died? Will you bring them back to life?"

David recognized his questioner—a strident woman from a Johannesburg weekly finance magazine whose written diatribes usually provoked heated correspondence from all quarters.

"Madam, no sane employer knowingly kills employees. Ignorance of the process did. What would have been inexcusable is not to have done something about it. We did. As fast as was humanly possible."

"Did you pay compensation to their dependants?"

"Yes. Plus pensions for their spouses and families."

A stringer for a German newspaper surfaced. "*Mein Herr*, who are your customers? Will you sell your entire production of nuclear material and how much do you charge for it?"

"Out of my field," Doctor Hannah answered. "I do know that our competition would be over the moon to receive such information. We process low-grade ore. When we spend money we try to do so smartly. In other words we aim at controlling costs effectively."

"We have a UN dispensation to supply customers with whom we contracted before sanctions were introduced. They had planned on receiving it for their power stations."

Three hours later the various entourages were driven to the open pit site in which temporary multi-layered wooden stands had been erected. Employees had picked up on the festival atmosphere and helped themselves to food laid out on trestle tables shielded by a huge red marquee before taking up their seats. At the foot of the stand a table awaited UN officials, chairman and the management team and their wives. Only David's wife, Pam, was conspicuous by her absence.

Visitors had plenty to observe and all had plenty to say when peering into the gaping open pit where the hulking electrically powered shovels stood mutant, waiting for a signal to begin operations. Seven gigantic haul trucks had been parked fifty meters away from the stands, their ore pans raised, on the backs of which each bore a huge letter spelling out an eye-catching "WELCOME" in ten foot high letters.

Half an hour later David rose from his chair and to stand behind a microphone.

"Honorable United Nations members, guests, members of government, mayor chairman managers, superintendents and mine teams I wish to pay several tributes. Firstly, to our board of directors for supporting the re-awakening of this mine that we have all worked so hard to get back on to its feet; to our managers who unstintingly gave of themselves against all odds and to our employees who persevered through to finality.

"Our mine is playing its part in educating and training employees and bursary holders for the future, to take up jobs right up to board level and to contribute to the fiscus. We hold no secrets. If we make a mistake we will be the first to admit it, remedy it and learn from it. We aim to do what is best for our employees and for our shareholders along with assisting government as best we can. We would like our children to one day say, 'We were part of that great mine. We were part of history."

David waited for mild clapping to subside. "It is now my honor to invite our chairman, Mr Hilton Walsh, to address you. Chairman if you please."

Hilton got up and awaited applause to subside. "Anyone who has met this mine's people will understand the real meaning of teamwork. I defy anyone to point out a project of this scale that was completed within fifteen months and below budget. For that our insurers are eternally grateful."

A laugh from the audience relaxed Hilton. "We would deem it an honor if the honorable leader of the UN delegation pressed the start button with me to rededicate this great enterprise and wish it a long and fruitful life."

The Nigerian delegate sprang up without any prompting and put his hands on the chairman's to press the button.

Carefully sited ammonium nitrate charges began to rip out a kilometer of ore from the opposite side of the pit. Successive explosions and momentary flames of uniform height pierced the air unleashing a threatening rumble of nature's forces being disturbed. Within minutes dust clouds settled, signaling the shovels to awake. Haul trucks emitted menacing growls and began to trail each other to loading sites. Onlookers raptly watched primary crushed ore tumble on to a conveyor belt that reared up at a forty-five degree angle for fifty meters before tipping in freefall on to a conical mound beneath two widely spaced steel support columns comprising the "A-frame". Comforting sounds of prosperity had returned to the desert. The mine and *Thuringia Bay* were as one again.

A troupe of ululating barefoot chanting dancers burst out before the stands while frenetically stamping their feet to the beat of four massive cowhide drums behind which stood laughing drummers clad in loose white togas.

An hour later enthralled visitors reluctantly boarded their buses to depart for the airport where they were to remove their safety apparel.

Only when the last aircraft had wheeled out of sight did David turn to Joey. "You came up trumps Joey. It went like clockwork. I'm a lucky man to have you on my team. Thank you."

Harry McCrae was bit more circumspect. "A hundred grand that little jolly cost!" he muttered to Bruno when seeing off the last of the aircraft. "I wonder what it did for production?"

16

"David's been mightily distracted of late," Harry commented to Doreen after their daughters had excused themselves and gone to bed. "He's not his normal self. I can see that he's taking big strain on board."

"Who would blame him?' Doreen said. "Pam left him. She's been gone far too long so it looks like they've called it quits." Doreen heard two women in town discussing David and Pam's supposed travails but she had put it down to small town gossip. She wasn't about to repeat it other than to her husband.

"He's a difficult man to get close to," Harry said. "That's one of his problems. Being top dog? It's lonely. Who could he confide in without risking accusations of favoritism? If any of we managers get too friendly with him someone drops snide comments. You don't just drop in for a drink like we used to do in Rhodesia. Wives always have plenty to say about who they think is snorting up to the head man."

"Not to mention the men," Doreen shot back.

"Maybe," Harry said, "we do know from bitter experience it is all but unwritten law. Pity that. Mine communities are the same wherever they are."

"I hope he's not ill. He needs a good rest. All you managers do. It seems to me that you're all competing with each other now the mine is up and running smoothly."

"Competing? Now that's an interesting comment Doreen. Why do you say that?"

"This is only for your ears Harry. When I meet with certain wives they slip into conversation snippets about promotions their husbands are in line for. One or two have opinions about whom should get what job up the ladder and when. I must say I don't like it when wives begin to jockey for limelight. I'm sure if David knew what was being said he'd throw a wobbly."

"Is that so?" Harry smiled wryly. "Well I never...I thought that he'd pick up on something like that and put a stop to it. He's an amazing guy."

Doreen had hit a nerve. True enough, he was tiring quicker than he cared to admit, but to say anything to Doreen immediately caused her to worry. "All the managers would toss themselves to the sharks if David ordered them to do so. But you're right Doreen. I for one am going to throttle back. There is no need for overkill. I'll stop and smell the roses for a change."

"It worked out well for you didn't it?" Doreen was genuinely pleased for her husband. "You should write to Father Robin and tell him all about it. He's another one who works his socks off but he doesn't get paid for it. Invite him to come here for a break. He'll love it. And the Steads. And the Byrons."

On the South African west coast summer daylight faded at nine in the evening and watching the Atlantic crashing on to the beach never waned for Harry. Try as he might not to think about work, his mind remained locked on the mine, sizing up the obstacle of the moment and how to beat it.

"Thanks to Professor Koenig. That was good thinking on David's part. Getting him involved when he did. The chairman came up trumps giving us all a big bonus. Imagine that? Perhaps we can take that trip to California we always dreamed about."

"I must say," Doreen enthused as she cleared their dinner plates, "I can't remember when last time I saw you so content."

"With all this on my doorstep," Harry said and waved toward the sea, slowly disappearing behind a curtain of mist, "how could I not be? Sometimes I pinch myself to see if I'm dreaming. I'd give it up if you felt any differently Doreen. When and if it becomes a drag that's the time to opt out of here."

"Don't worry about me. We don't live in a city. Crime was a big problem in Johannesburg and getting worse. I'm very glad to be out of it."

At eight on the dot on the Monday after the rededication ceremony David pressed his intercom button.

"Joey apologize to the managers on my behalf and tell them I want them all in here at 8.30. It will only take ten minutes or so. Please ask Peter Gomez to come at 8.20."

"Yes Mr Bradshaw," she replied, sensing that something unusual in the offing. "Right away."

Harry's office was the closest so he waited till the operational managers cars drew up and met his colleagues in the lobby. Worried expressions underlined that no one liked being summoned to a meeting without knowing what was on the agenda.

"Where's Peter?" a frowning Cecil asked Joey.

"He's with the GM. Go in please."

Frank put his cigarette out before they trooped in to David's office and sat down.

David rose from behind his desk and joined them on a corner sofa.

"I'm Sorry to mess up your schedules. You must be speculating about why you're here."

"Have we had bad feedback?" Frank piped up. "Did we screw up somewhere?"

"No. Nothing like that. I have to tell you that Peter will be returning to our London headquarters. Our chairman wants him to take on to a new group project in Australia. We have to decide how best to plug the gap when he leaves us in three weeks time. It had to come eventually. You fitted in here like a glove Peter. It's about time you were back with your family. Thank you for doing your job so well."

Peter flushed but said nothing, exhibiting a cursory nod.

"I also asked you up here," David continued, "to explain about matters concerning my wife and I. We live in a small town and people begin to make assumptions if things aren't too transparent. I want to level with you. My daughter 'phoned me from England as did my son from California wanting to know about my 'Affair'."

None of his managers wanted to look him in the eye. Too embarrassed. *David? Affair?* Preposterous.

"I must ask you not to make the same mistake I made. We have to keep this mine up and operating at peak levels. But it must not be at the expense of your families. You chaps who are putting in long hours. I cannot ask you to do that day in and day out. You have to spend more time with your families. In fact, I insist that you do so."

"What's happened?" a hesitant Cecil enquired.

"Some time ago Pam made it plain that she's not putting up with me seeing so little of her. She accused me of having a mistress."

"What!"

"Yes. This mine. This 'heap of steel' as she called it. She's in Cape Town. I don't know any more than that. I haven't heard from her. What I do know is that it would weigh heavily on me if your wives think that you work here at the cost of your private lives. The same applies lower down. No impossible hours. No impossible demands."

"What are you going to do?" a serious-faced Frank responded. "You can do without that sort of pressure. How can we help you?"

"I've decided to fly to Cape Town to talk to Pam. That is if I can find her. If she'll see me. I hope that we can work something out."

"When?" Bruno said. "I have a lot of stuff I need your approval for."

"Tonight. I'll take the afternoon 'plane to Kimberley and then on to Cape Town on a scheduled flight. I want you, Frank, to act for me while I'm away. You must make whatever decisions are necessary. I have put the chairman in the picture and he is agreeable. I hope to return within a week or two. Is that acceptable to you all? Frank?"

Frank inhaled deeply from his eternal cigarette. "Yes. I'll do my best. I'll have plenty of support."

Not for a moment did anyone query David's choice of Frank to act for him.

"I'll put a notice out that you're on leave for a few weeks and that Frank is acting for you," Cecil said. "Everyone agrees that you need to let up."

David stood up and shook each manager's hand. "Good luck," he said cheerily and ushered them to the door. His eyes told another story and none of his team missed the sadness mirrored in them.

Two days passed before the managers were at the club having a drink together after work.

"I wonder whether Joey Schneider wears white socks in bed?" Des Irwin speculated while leering at Joey who was chatting with her friends. "She's a real cracker that one!"

"Hey man, what's with the white socks business?" an annoyed Bruno enquired while downing his pint of lager. "A fetish of yours? What do you wear in bed…safety shoes and hard hat?"

"Most German women wear white socks."

"In bed too? Expert are you, on ladies' clothes?"

"Get your head out of your pants Irwin," Frank growled. "If you want to say things like that then say it in front of the person you're bad-mouthing. Shall I call Joey over so you can entertain her with your question? You are a cheeky bastard."

Irwin flushed and slunk back to his cohorts at the end of the bar. "No Frank. Sorry man. Just joking."

Roger Lacy was helping out behind the counter, glad that his paltry weekday turnover was being lifted by Frank's unexpected largesse.

"I wish I had an expense account," Irwin sulked. "It's easy to celebrate when the company pays for it all isn't it?"

Roger shot the scrawny man a withering look. "You already put your big foot in it tonight Des. Don't do it again within five minutes of getting your backside kicked. Frank's paying. Out of his own pocket for your information. Pipe down!"

"David's badly stretched," Cecil muttered. "I think he needs longer than a few days to recoup his health. Have you heard anything from him yet Frank?"

"No. He's a hard nut. He wouldn't want us to take our eye off the ball. Let's start with "No shop talk"—his credo. We'll let our hair down. You guys should 'phone your wives. Tell them it's going to be a late one."

"Now you're talking Frank," Bruno said and energetically rubbed his hands together. "Roger! Over here! Yard of ale! Frank, you always boast you're the biggest drinker in town. I challenge you!"

"You're still in short pants Bruno on that score," Frank replied unleashing a sly grin. "How much do you want to bet mate?"

"Twenty rands."

Bruno lost his money.

So did Peter.

Cecil turned chicken and hid behind his whisky glass.

Harry cried off. "Have a heart! I'm duty manager this weekend," he claimed. "I can't go drunk to site. Old Vic Grey will put me in clink and Gerard Dresser would not be amused!"

Don South delivered them all to their furious wives after midnight and Roger arranged for their cars to be delivered to their houses.

The Fielding's home telephone rang at exactly six in the morning. Frank wasn't duty manager so he ignored it. It kept ringing. Fifteen minutes later an irked Yvonne got up and answered it.

"Yes!"

She listened intently and then her face fell. "Frank! It's for you. Some police official wants to talk to you."

Mention of "Police" shot Frank to his feet. His first thought was that something had happened at the mine. "Frank Fielding speaking. How may I help you?" Frank's features indicated that it was a very serious matter. He'd gone ashen and had flopped down onto the camel stool beside the 'phone table.

After a few minutes, Frank hung his head. "Are you sure Commandant? It definitely wasn't someone else?"

Another minute passed and Frank gently replaced the receiver. He gazed mournfully at Yvonne.

"David and Pam were involved in a car crash early this morning. Killed outright. A drunken slob smashed into them. That was the Seapoint Police in Cape Town. They found David's wallet. There was a photograph of both of them in it and his identity card."

"Oh no!" Yvonne shrilled and burst into tears.

"Sit down Yvonne. I have to 'phone Cecil and ask him how to contact their son and daughter. I'll have to break the news to them. What a bloody awful thing to happen."

It wasn't a nightmare. A tragedy has befallen an entire community. By the time Frank had contacted David and Pam's children, they already knew what had happened and were making arrangements to fly to Cape Town.

Hilton Walsh gasped when hearing it from Frank. "That man was going places. Awful business."

"I'll keep you posted Chairman."

"Please let me know what the funeral arrangements will be. I want to be there and afterwards I want to visit your mine. You and I have to talk face to face."

"The Chairman's attending the funerals," Frank told Yvonne when he got home. "Then he's flying up to the mine."

She looked at him…surprised. "The chairman? Coming here? What for?"

"He only spent a few hours on site during the UN visit. Perhaps he wants to really give it a good going over so that he knows it first-hand. He says he wants to talk to me face to face. It's a shame that it took a tragedy to bring him here. David would have liked him to have seen *The Thuringia* at its worst before we turned it round."

"I hope that we poor old wives can talk to him."

"I'll arrange something once he's here Yvonne. I'm sure he'd appreciate an informal get-together with the management team and their ladies."

Ten days after David had left for Cape Town, he and Pam were interred at the Goodwood cemetery. Patrick and Sarah, their two children, stood at the graveside, bewildered. Frank dutifully invited them to *Thuringia Bay* to clear out their parents' house. Neither of them were interested in doing so. Frank delegated the task to Cecil who had seen to funeral arrangements.

"Use your discretion Cecil. If you think they should have anything, box it and we can speak to them later when they're not feeling so distraught. The least we should offer is to pay for their travel to *Thuringia Bay* if they want to fly out later."

The chairman's flight had landed barely hours before the funeral ceremony. He exchanged words with Frank outside the Goodwood Chapel prior to the start of the emotionally taxing service.

"He impressed me," Hilton said. "He was the right man for the mine in its time of need. There weren't too many like him in the group. Now we have to think again."

"David? He was determined to get a good team around him to help him achieve it."

Hilton screwed up his eyes and stared at Frank for a good few seconds. "Perhaps…" he faltered, "perhaps…things will work out after all. You understand why I have to get the feel of the place? Why don't you and your wife hop a lift with me to the mine tonight? We can talk aboard the 'plane."

During his two days on site Hilton donned his khaki's and safety helmet and shoes to rove every nook and cranny of the site.

"He's no stuffed shirt, that's for sure," a worried Bruno informed Frank. "He wanted to check what the inside of an empty acid tank looked like. He even called for the specifications to check on its sealing standards."

"He grilled me about employee training," Cecil commented. "He'd agreed with David that we weren't doing nearly enough. 'No money' I told him. 'Find it!' he said as if the stuff grows on trees. We all know how many trees there are in a desert!"

Frank invited the managers and their wives to a barbecue at his house to welcome their august visitor.

Harry fetched Hilton a bottle of cold lager. That Hilton knew so much about him and each manager surprised Harry. He liked the man. There was nothing pretentious about him but no one doubted that Hilton Walsh was a hard taskmaster. Frank had put it well. "Get it right or it's *Bye Bye'sville* baby!" Harry asked Hilton outright.

"You bet! I like the clink of dollars! Being the bean-counter here, you must be pretty happy too."

Hilton conversed with each of the ladies, in some cases discovering mutual friends and acquaintances.

"Mr Walsh gives me a comfortable feeling Frank," Yvonne confided to her husband. "He genuinely enjoys talking to people. When I think of that loudmouth London sales guy who came here a year or so ago I have to say the chairman is nothing like him. At least he doesn't slaver over women in his company."

"Hilton's a miner," Frank reminded her, "a tough cookie who fought his way to the top. He knows the mining business inside out and he learned how to manage men. He is results-oriented and takes no prisoners. Don't build up false impressions about him Yvonne. He won't shirk a tough decision. He will do what's best for shareholders. If it pays, he likes it. If it doesn't, he sells it. Or closes it. Hilton Walsh is no sentimentalist."

"These Australians," a belligerent Cecil chimed in, "they're hard bastards. Just like Canadians. They slide their own people into their mines. I suppose they have to," he scoffed.

"Why?" Frank enquired.

"Well, they speak a special brand of English I for one don't understand. I hope I'm not out of a job before too long."

"Me too mate," Frank muttered. "The gaffer wants to say a few words after we've had a munch. Hold your breath."

Once their plates were empty Hilton tapped his glass with a spoon and stood up. "I have to sing for my supper," he smiled.

Frank lightened up. A smiling Hilton would have to be cruel to fire anyone.

"David Bradshaw made a big impression on us. He had courage to get to the root of problems on this mine and to face the board. That took guts. When you're sitting in an office miles away it's difficult to get to grips with what goes on at a mine site. It's no excuse. There were massive problems and David Bradshaw hid nothing from us. After meeting him I had no doubt that he would succeed."

Frank watched his men closely. His team. He saw no hint of doubt.

"David's death was a big blow to us. Before doing anything I decided to come here for a good look around and to talk to your employees. That's the only way I know how to get a feel for an operation. I must have upset a good few people isn't that true Mr Lonsdale?"

An embarrassed Cecil uttered a weak "No, not really Chairman!"

"I discovered spirit in a workforce raring to go, very much David Bradshaw's legacy. Not for an instant did I detect despair. I know of mines with half your problems that haven't a hope of making it because the wrong men run it. If a mine has no soul, it's dead. Only excellent management gears it up so that its employees love every moment that they spend at work."

While Hilton stopped for a sip of beer, Bruno nudged Cecil and whispered, "Hey man, it looks like we breathe again!"

A relaxed Hilton resumed his address. "I enjoyed meeting you and being with you tonight. David was right. He did assemble a top class team and that includes the managers' wives. My conclusion is that this mine still has a big future."

"Oh no, here it comes," a visibly alarmed Cecil whispered to Bruno, "some Sweet-talking Aussie bastard is going to jet in here. Then in trot his pals and we're shafted good and proper."

"Appointing the general manager of a mine with this scale of capital investment has to be a board decision. I believe that Frank Fielding in an acting capacity as general manager must have at least six months in the job before a permanent appointment is considered. A new boy at this stage will hold matters back and probably lose the plot. We can't afford the time. I'll be back here in six months with one or two of our directors to review the situation. Good luck to you all and thank you all for your hospitality."

17

"What a pleasure for us to identify with a known face. Instead of some faceless overseas board member who sprouts bollocks most of the time. No wonder Hilton's become the chairman. The man's a corporate dynamo."

"I have to say Frank, old Hilton Walsh doesn't have much of an opinion of accountants," a disturbed Harry complained at their Friday managers' meeting. 'Bean-counters' he calls us. Motivating stuff I must say!"

"Don't fret Harry. It's his Aussie sense of humor. The more they insult you the more they like you. Get used to it. Anyhow without him at the wheel, we would have gone to the wall."

"Yes," Bruno said, "the bloke talks bladdy funny but he's fair."

"Okay," Frank interjected, "he's very happy that he doesn't have to buy yellowcake on the open market now that we can meet our order book. But if we fall behind just remember we're big into the brown stuff. I don't ever want to be on the receiving end of a call from Hilton who might want to roast my privates. Our *Met* guys have to concentrate hard on getting that new plant fine-tuned, with your help Bruno. We need to create slack for plant back-up."

"Man, am I pleased to hear that," Bruno commented. "I need more time to put in detailed maintenance."

"We've a job to do," Frank continued. "Let's decide how we operate at management level in the long term. When David got back I was going to suggest that I handle both mining and metallurgical divisions. That would have removed one manager's post. Now that I'm acting for him we can't follow through on that idea. The question is, do we replace Peter Gomez at divisional manager level? Do I make someone act for me as mining manager? I have to be careful whom we appoint. We don't want to risk anyone like that idiot who was here before Peter came, the creep who lied his way in and lied his way out."

"Who did you have in mind to act for you as mining manager?" Harry asked. "That's an important decision."

"Des Irwin. He's way out in front. No other man could have licked that pit into shape and satisfy the prof. His men did the impossible."

"I don't know," Cecil muttered, "I grant you Frank that his men respond well to him. It just that…"

"What?" Frank said. "You don't like him?"

"Let's face it he's rough for a manager's position Frank. Remember when you asked him to host that Canadian visitor and his wife at the club? Des got drunk and got funny with the poor guy's wife on the dance floor."

"I heard as much. I gave him a good lashing about his behavior. I think he'll reform. He's not that stupid."

"It hasn't done him much good Frank. Des tries it on with any woman he meets and not a few husbands have punched him. He's a rough diamond if ever I saw one. He's not very discreet once he hits the beer."

"Okay. I'll put it on the line for him. Put yourself in his position," Frank rasped. "He's young. He's single. I saw for myself how women react to him. Giving him the eye. But you're right, he has to behave properly. I'll sort him out. His blasting ability is world-class. I want him to pass that skill on."

149

"Be it on your head Frank, you're taking a big risk." a doubtful Cecil retorted. "I hope that you're proved right."

"We'll see. Despite what we think of Des I think that the main issue is metallurgy. It's in limbo so we need someone on our wavelength to get in there and prime it up. Any suggestions gentlemen?"

"In your view Frank what is the main criterion for the job? Is it technical expertise? Or is it man-management skills?" a careful Cecil enquired.

"Both man!" Bruno interrupted. "You can't put a desk jockey in there. That will be a bad example. We want a bloke in khakis with fire in his guts. I'm saying that the appointment requires a special animal. Not a 'routine' person."

"A man with sound man-management abilities will do it," Cecil said. "Peter proved as much. Operating superintendents who survived David's putsch can be trusted to supply technical skills and if I might say so, have exposed a will to take on more responsibility. Give them a say on equipment and plant replacement and you'll not be sorry. They're all young and anxious to impress."

"Did you rehearse that speech last night?" Bruno playfully elbowed his colleague in mock wonder. "Sounds good man. I agree with Cecil."

"Who then?" Cecil probed.

"I don't think that any of our *Met* superintendents are experienced enough to oversee the whole divisional operation," Frank replied. "It looks like we need to bring in an outsider. I contacted the boys in London. No one obvious jumped up there. They're frightened of this mine so they disassociate from it. I wasn't surprised."

"Believe it or not I know someone who'd fit in here like a glove," Harry said, enjoying the surprise registered on his colleagues' faces. "I worked with a guy on the Zambian Copperbelt years ago called Walter Clark. He was a great cricketer too. When his mine was stumped over treating a mutant ore all their top brains couldn't sort it out. Experts flew in from Johannesburg and London. No dice, but they charged a big fat fee for bog-all results. Walter, six levels down the pecking order, puzzled it out without being asked to do so. He made the *Met* manager look like an idiot and as for the GM, believe it or not, he wanted to fire Walter! Can you imagine? Someone displays not a little initiative, saves your bacon and you want to fire him!"

"What happened to him?" Bruno enquired.

"An anonymous letter tipped off the chairman in Johannesburg. An outside consultant flew in to that mine and appraised matters. He confirmed that Walter had thought out the solution. He saved that mine make no mistake. Afterwards when it came to pats on the back no one upstairs had the grace to say "Thanks" or "Up your pipe" or so much as buy Walter a beer. Naturally he told them to stuff their job where it hurt most."

"Ouch!" Cecil quipped. "Is he still on the Copperbelt? I thought that place had all but collapsed since the country's independence."

"No. He pushed off long ago. He moved South but he's never been all that happy at his new employers. He's vegetating on a platinum mine in Rustenburg, bored stupid. 'Too structured' he told me just before I joined you guys. He has to ask permission to belch and sign a form in triplicate. You know the kind of organization, where everyone is posturing trying to outdo one another. If you pardon the expression he calls it 'ignoranus management'. Why not invite him and his wife Judy to visit us? She's a nice lady and would fit in well in our team. If I know Walter, he thrives on the right kind of pressure. If you give him his head Frank, he'll surprise you. He's an innovator. Unless he lost his brain we'll all be impressed with him. If not, then fire me!"

"Hey, if a bean-counter can remember a technical guy like that he must be good," Bruno cut in, "let's grab him."

"Hold it! Age?" Frank cut in. "We must be careful."

"Early forties," Harry said. "No kids. If you want I'll ask him to fax you his CV."

"Any other nominations while we're at it?" Frank invited. "Last chance."

"I'll get the details from Harry for you Frank," Cecil volunteered. "This Walter sounds too good to be true. Leave it with me."

"Okay, we're making headway," Frank said. "Get him on site Cecil as soon as possible, only after you've checked out his qualifications. Just be sure we're inviting the right man to come here. And his wife."

"Next item on the agenda. David had a point about everyone working incessant overtime. We put out a message to all employees to *work smarter*. We need to do the same thing with *safety*. Please don't encourage overtime. Besides the cost, the last thing I want is to upset the families. Let's get some inter-divisional sport going. Cricket. Bowls. Tennis. Fishing. You name it. We can help with start-up grants but the people who want recreation facilities have to learn to take over later."

"Everyone is so hyped up about their work Frank," Harry said. "I told my guys to use their common sense about working long hours. They don't like dropping things to rush for their buses at knock-off time. They have targets to meet and don't want to let the side down. I do have a couple of passengers. Overtime might suit them to get their act in order. I'm watching them but I won't let overtime be abused."

"It applies to you guys too," Frank snorted. "Yes, you managers. For a start I want you all to join Yvonne and I on Sunday to head up the coast for a spot of swimming and fishing. We'll handle eats. Bring your own booze. We've got enough Land Rovers between us. Who is duty manager this weekend?"

"Me," Harry answered. "Just my luck...no problem. I'm glad of the time. I'm preparing a case for more computer equipment and software. I'll be looking for money to pay for it."

"As the Chairman so often says," Frank rasped, "F..."

"Find it!" the managers chorused.

18

Impervious to scathing criticism from certain town residents who were upset that the mine was taking things too far, Frank and his team trumpeted their color-blind approach. Scholarships were awarded to candidates of all races to study further in South Africa and in the United Kingdom.

Vestiges of discriminatory legislation had remained on the statutes and as David had decreed, no mind was to be paid to it. He had relished the prospect of being challenged in court but none had arisen. *Thuringia Bay's* dissidents cursed him, his team and the mine, preferring to swim in their recalcitrant, racially obsessed cesspool.

At Harry's request Victor Grey investigated who among the town's business community had benefited from cosy deals struck with previously "bent" mine officials all of whom had been already dispensed with.

After carefully surveying Victor's report the managers' views were as one.

"Blacklist crooks for all time," Frank ordered. "We don't buy so much as a washer from them. If we have proof that any of our men who are still with us took bribes, they're toast!"

Harry informed his buyers of Frank's instructions adding, "Companies that run a clean show get the message that we award to the most dependable and cost-effective tender. We don't make funny deals. The only negotiating we do is to drive prices down. But," he said, eyeing his chief buyer and chief accountant, "I want you guys to pay our creditors on time. We don't put suppliers in a position of having to cry for their money. Pay by invoice due date and get a settlement discount. We'll need them to reappraise us as a solid firm to do business with. When things get tight and we have a breakdown we want suppliers queuing up to help us out."

"But it's normal to use other people's money for as long as we can," Mike Hardy the chubby chief accountant objected. "That means we use other people's money for our benefit. Pay on time? Sod them. I won't do it. You're off your trolley! We'll pay on statement only if it suits us."

"I see," Harry replied, glad that Hardy had finally cooked his goose but irate that the man had foamed with such hostility and before embarrassed witnesses. "In that case consider yourself fired. I'll get Vic Grey to personally escort you off the premises. Get out. Now."

"He got the benefit of the doubt to begin with Frank," Harry explained to Frank later in the day. "I have plenty of witnesses. Hardy was acting out his assumed role of 'big man' with an ear to the GM. It doesn't wash with me."

The news shot around the mine in seconds. Mike Hardy had finally shot his bolt, not that anyone appeared surprised.

"A bit harsh don't you think?" Frank commented testily after summoning Harry to his office. "The man's got a young family to look after."

"Harsh? He's not been a player. Getting him to do anything was a trial. The guy's so adversely reactive it's laughable. No ideas, no verve—stuck in the traces. He's spent a lifetime in his own legend. I don't think I've been harsh at all. I tried everything to swing him round to our mission but he assumed he was someone special in his eyes and in yours."

"Me? That's news to me."

"Frank for what we want to achieve he won't make the grade. It's a miracle I've managed to work around him to get his men to do what I want. He is a natural objector to all change. A liability. He wasn't a team man and bad mouthed whoever took his fancy. Too bad. We're well rid of him. He had plenty of time and opportunity to mend his ways."

"We need discipline," Frank growled, "I admit that. His previous managers were scared of him. He's come to me saying that he never meant it and wants his job back. He thought he had you tied up in knots."

"No," Harry replied. "It's far too late. I don't want him. He was part of the problem here. How the hell he survived for so long beats me He's history. Burt Burnett can stand in for him. He's better qualified and more reliable. He's one big asset. Hardy's definitely yesterday's baggage."

"Okay. Have it your way," Frank sighed. "We said that things had to change. You did not run away from your problem like your predecessors did."

Cecil's feedback on the mine's policy contained mixed blessings.

"The town boils down into two camps. The majority welcome benefits that our mine brings them. A very small minority are cancerous in the extreme. Whispering campaigns, rumors and libelous comments are in no one's interests. They meet in Hitler-like bars and plot. You cannot believe some of the stories doing the rounds about us managers and our wives. Some of our lower grade employees are being deliberately picked on while going about their normal business. Our public relations in town have definitely not gone down well with right wing die-hards."

"We have to win them over," a concerned Frank said. "Community spirit is vital. It's enough to be getting over racial discrimination but educated whites have no business stirring up matters for the sake of it. They need conversion. It will mean us, the managers, rearranging our priorities and making time available to rub shoulders with more *Thuringia Bay* residents of all colors. We'll educate the bastards!"

"Our main problem," Harry said, "are town crooks. They're going out of business because we won't put anything their way. Their tongues are naturally working overtime."

"What do you suggest that we do? We agreed that they be blacklisted. We can't back off otherwise we upset honest suppliers toeing the line."

"It's simple Frank. Prosecute them. If it gets down to defamatory statements and libelous comment, prosecute. That will shut them up. Whoever is the subject of a loose tongue must be amenable to taking a case to court. It could be you or a manager. The only setback is that it will waste valuable time aside from publicity it brings."

"I'll talk to the others," Frank said wearily. "Check with me before you knock off."

At 5.30 Harry 'phoned Frank. "Any decision yet?"

"Yes. We prosecute. No exceptions. Let the spoilers close down. We don't deal with shady characters. But the same applies inside the mine; any negative machination earns instant dismissal and the full force of the law."

19

"So Harry, what have you got for me today?"

Harry enjoyed his regular midday meeting with Frank. The custom had begun with David three years previously and there was always much to talk about. He could see that Frank enjoyed it too. Usually, ten minutes was spent on performance tracking indices; thereafter, they threw ideas at one another and agreed an action plan.

"I'm glad that you offered Walter the metallurgical manager's job Frank. I'm looking forward to working with him. I have a good inkling about what he wants from me. He'll keep me busy. I'm going to put a few more management accountants into mining and metallurgy to work with the production engineers. Things are hotting up."

"He checked out okay. He had good ideas. Walter Clark's got experience that young metallurgists dream about. What a pity he was kept to his three months notice. I'll keep him in the picture anyway. He will have to get moving here from day one."

Harry checked his watch. "Frank, I've got news. 'Sweet and Sour.' What do you want to hear first?"

Frank stretched for his box of cigarettes, withdrew one and lit up.

"I might have known. Let's get the 'sour' over and done with."

"Fair enough. You know that I had a good look at our materials in stock. Burt Burnett was a great help. When I asked him about acid stocks he told me that the metallurgical manager always looked after that side of things. One thing led to another…"

"No!" a shocked Frank broke in while spitting out a strand of tobacco, "don't tell me there's a shortfall."

"No. Nothing like that. It concerns transport of the stuff from Cape Town to mine site. I found it strange that it was contracted to one company for ten years. Five years is normally the longest period any company commits to, for obvious reasons. Peter Gomez, and no one would blame him, accepted the contract as gospel when he took up the job. I dug deeper."

"What did you find?"

"On paper, all the directors and shareholders are in South Africa."

"What do you mean, *on paper*?"

"We made enquiries Frank. Two of them do not exist. They were using aliases."

"Are you serious? Do you know their real names?"

"Yes. I got quite a shock. You will too."

"Who are they?" Frank's asked in a low voice. "Who are these conniving sods?" After inhaling deeply he again asked ominously, "Who?"

"When the mine was being enlarged after Chater bought it, an office was set up in Cape Town. Tenders were called for from that office and contracts were given out like confetti. Very nice—for the two phantoms, I must say. They were ex-mine employees who formed a company and awarded themselves the acid transport contract. Carlson and West don't appear on the company letterhead in their own names. What's more, they're living in Spain. Why Spain you might ask? It has no extradition legislation. The *Costas* harbor wanted criminals. As for the remaining six directors, they reside in South Africa and don't tell me that they didn't know what was going on. Oh a bonus for you—Mike Hardy signed as a witness to that contract Frank."

"The creep!"

"In other words Frank, there was a nice little carve-up going on at this mine's expense."

"Another scam," Frank hissed. "When will it ever stop?"

"I thought hard about it before coming to you. The mine has been ripped off to the tune of about fifteen million rands. If we go after the company in court, it gets into the newspapers. We look bad. In fact, we look pretty stupid. I needn't spell it out for you."

"What does Vic say? Have you told him about it?" Frank blurted through a puff of smoke.

"No. Not yet. So far just you, Burt and I know. I haven't discussed it with our auditors either."

"Goddam it! They were supposed to be professional men! I'll screw them to..."

"Hold on Frank. Hold on. Think about it. What do we gain if we rush in for the jugular? The main criminals are beyond our reach. We could spend a fortune trying to get at them and gain nothing."

"We can't let them get away with it."

"They won't. I read the small print on the contract. Having bogus directors is enough to cancel it out of hand. Right now."

"That's not enough. The mine gets nothing back."

"It can Frank. The *sweet* news is that the mine can get a little something out of it. *Acid Movers Limited* is a separate legal entity in its own right and a corruption and deception action can be brought against it. Its directors are jointly and severally liable for crooked administration. I say that we go for the company and buy it at a token price."

Frank looked puzzled. "I don't think so. We haven't got that kind of cash to spare."

"We do Frank," Harry laughed. "We do. We buy it for one rand."

"One rand!"

"Yes. And it pays all legal costs. Once its remaining directors are faced down by top counsel they'll sweat bricks at the thought of their names appearing in the national newspapers and finance journals. If the details leaked out, they're dead socially, in business and I suspect that tax authorities would have a field day with them. Their wives, kids and families become pariahs. Why? Because they committed the cardinal sin of getting caught Frank. Think about the prospect of prison in a country on the threshold of a black government? That's got to be the stuff of nightmares."

Frank's face had gone puce. "Are you sure about this? No comebacks? I don't want us to end up looking like prize dunces."

"Absolutely. Trust me. If you want, run it by your choice of lawyers. We have options. Sell the business or run it ourselves. But I suggest selling it because it's non-core activity. I had a look at its last accounts; it has nineteen million rands in moveable assets and five million in fixed assets. It has a price earnings ratio of five to one."

"What does that mean? It's Greek to me."

"It means that annual earnings per share exceed the share price by five times. Imagine that? A five hundred per cent return on its share price! Such a ratio means that the minimum going price for the outfit is around the eighty million rand mark. If this mine was a person, he or she would be laughing all the way to the bank. We can go out for tender on acid transport again but this time we screw cost down for our benefit. The mining world right now is awash with sulfuric acid and some producers are giving the stuff away."

While on his third cigarette Frank leaned back and took a deep breath. "Harry, talking to you is bad for my blood pressure. Am I covered by our company's board resolutions to make such a decision?"

"We're only talking *one rand* Frank. Of course you are. What board in its right mind would castigate you for moving against these thieves? Another plus, this will make your hair curl, is that we sell off *Acid Movers*. Imagine! The proceeds are free of tax because it's a capital gain. When we couple that with our excess stores and equipment sales and flogging scrap, you've got a cash mountain, besides what cash the insurance people still have to cough up. It will look great on our balance sheet."

"It sounds too good to be true," a suspicious Frank commented. "Are you absolutely positive?'

"I am. To put your mind at rest I suggest that you float it past our auditors. Listen, some of it can go towards financing training and your safety programs. We can repay debenture loans early. I need a few bob for computer and systems upgrades. Your mining guys are crying out for more capacity to cope with expanded ore reserve planning."

"If this is a dream, I hope I have more of them," Frank grinned. "Damn good work Harry. That's the kind of news that makes me happy. Go for it! But I must have written external auditor approval first. Hilton Walsh is going to love this when I tell him about it!"

"This mist is for the birds," a sour-faced Walter complained. "It's so damn depressing and it's not exactly warm is it? Can't you get that heater going? I'm freezing my nuts off!"

Harry was listening to the seven o'clock news on his car radio with half an ear while fixated on the tail lights of the car in front.

"You get used to it Wally. In twenty minutes we'll reach halfway and sunlight will hit us like a laser. How's your good lady settling in?"

"Judy? Not bad. She's missing our beloved Highveld sun though. But she's not locked into crazy routines like she was in Rustenburg. In the few days we've been in *Thuringia Bay* all we've had is this thick mist. To be fair, it's a welcome change from sapping heat. We both like the place. It has a relaxed vibe about it."

Harry switched off his radio. "I'm glad that I'm not the new kid on the block any more. You are mate. We hope Frank will be confirmed soon as GM. He'll be depending on you to keep customers happy. Metallurgy stopped blaming mining division for sending up inferior ore to treat. Prof Koenig's work stopped all that nonsense."

"Frank was thorough when he interviewed me I must say. I like his no-nonsense management style. GM's at the outfit I just left think no one except them has original thought. A corporate gook, you know the type, a typical head office wimp with black suit and driving a big Beemer, told me how happy he was to steal other people's ideas. To quote him it was, 'a sound management technique!' Hell am I glad to be out of it!"

"Me too. You can do great things here. Frank is a lot like our late David Bradshaw. As long as we're on plan he leaves us alone to get on with it. You and I are hard to please Wally. You know that? We're both too judgmental."

"Really? Why do you say that?"

"Face it. Routine is not for us. We thrive on being measured. We love to sort out difficult situations. We're builders and we're both experienced enough to get results."

"Yeah. I suppose you're right Harry. It gets up some people's noses though."

"Tough!" Harry snorted. "When this mine is running like a Swiss watch, that's our watershed point. We'll be bored out of our skulls. What then? We'll be too old to take on new challenges."

"When do you think that will be?"

"Frank asked me that question too. Four, perhaps five years. I suppose we're preparing the next work-force generation. The way I see it is that our standards will become bedrock. That's a good footprint to leave. Africa's changing fast. A lot can happen in five years. Its politics are heading for total reversal. Heaven knows how we will come out of that fog."

Sunlight suddenly pierced the mist. Sharp contrasts of brilliant desert yellow and orange hues were nothing short of dazzling.

"Aaah, we've reached our half way point! I can put foot now," Harry exclaimed cheerfully. "I never tire of the desert. I thought that the novelty would wear off after a year or two."

"I can see that it didn't," Walter said. "I expect Judy and I will feel the same way about it too given a chance."

"It's unique; plants, animals...snakes...The scenery is fantastic, but be careful. You must know where to go and learn the tricks of the trade. Get yourself a Land Rover Wally. I was here for a month and bought myself a beauty. The things last forever."

"I will. But I want to go fishing with Bruno," Walter cackled. "He catches fish I've never heard of."

"Yep. Bruno's our in-house expert sure enough. He's a laugh a minute. He knows the beaches and the desert like the inside of his hand."

Walter came back on a different tangent. "The pilot on the company 'plane mentioned that Hilton Walsh is due out here shortly."

"Yes," a surprised Harry said. "Our esteemed chairman likes his visits out here. You met him did you?"

"Guilty as charged. He's one piece of work. I think he eats steel for breakfast lunch and dinner. I presented a paper in Melbourne three years ago on ore dressing. He and his daughter joined me afterwards at my dinner table. He grilled me good and proper about my paper. More out of politeness I asked his daughter what she did for a living. She's one of these environmental do-gooders."

"Now that you mention it," Harry said. "I've read about her somewhere. Did anything happen?"

"It did. My first thought was why such an attractive woman bothered circling the globe protesting about strange issues. What for? Her old man's loaded. I put my foot in it with a silly comment concerning freaks taking up cudgels on behalf of strange minorities I'd never heard of. Well, she went bananas."

Harry chuckled. "I'm not surprised."

"I was dressed down by her. Man, what a mouth she has! Words came out like I never heard before. All very embarrassing in a five star hotel dining room I must say. Hilton stared at me as if I was the original bad smell and then they both took off. When walking out she was still flinging abuse at me over her shoulder. I'd better keep out of his way when he arrives. Talk about painful memories!"

"No chance," Harry laughed. "All managers see Hilton. In fact he insists on it. He doesn't ram his position down your throat. I doubt whether he'd remember your incident. If he does, he's not likely to give you a hard time. I'd say that if within a year at this mine you're not producing the goods then he might go for you. We all know he's driven by results, an ace control freak. Your first mistake on that score is your last as far as he's concerned."

"Let's change the subject," Walter said. "How are we fixed for finance?"

"Why?"

"I have a good project in mind. It has almost instant payback on an automated process system that I have in mind."

"Well now Wally, it's funny that you should bring that up," Harry grinned. "Have I got news for you!"

"Arrange it on day one so that we kick off in mining then follow the entire process sequentially. We want to hear from section heads what they've done. What they expect. Not managers or department heads. *Section heads*. They're close to the work face. We don't want tedious presentations, overhead projectors and man hours wasted preparing fine words for us. Just an informed feel of what's going on. Next morning, let's hear what your managers have to say, then it's your turn Mr Fielding. We will deliberate in the afternoon back at our hotel. The following morning we will meet with you and your managers to provide you with feedback."

Frank handed out copies of Hilton's fax to the divisional managers. "Pretty clear isn't he? Security-wise I don't intend informing anyone on site about this visit. The chairman's party must see the mine as it normally is, so don't paint and wash down everything in sight. Also, when asked a question impress upon everyone to tell it like it is. No *bull*. Okay? No marble polishing and foaming at the mouth. Any questions?"

"What do you think they really want?" Bruno asked Frank. "What is his underlying agenda? These Aussies are hard people. We need to know what not to say in case we get stick from them."

"You know," Frank replied, "I'm not making myself ill about it. Nor should you. Results speak for themselves. How could the chairman moan about this mine? We're up and running and making big money. Our order backlog is history. Cash flow is fantastic. What more could he want? If the chairman and his mates think otherwise then they have a problem. Not us. We've done damn well and proud of it we must be. Good question though Bruno. What *not* to say you ask. I'll tell you what you and your guys must not leave out. *That you're proud of this mine. You built it.* You can't say it often enough."

"Hey Frank," Cecil said, "it's rich of you not to tell us what long hours you've been putting in. I don't know too many general managers working forty-eight hour stints without sleep."

Frank pretended not to hear. "All I can say is that, well, I'm only sorry David isn't here to tell you what I just did. He's the guy who really gave us the opportunity to show what we could do."

There was no question of Frank hosting the chairman and his two directors for dinner even if they did spare the time. Such invitation risked being interpreted as a patent attempt at soft soaping, or *arse creeping* as Bruno had so succinctly put it. Instead, Frank invited his managers and their wives around to his home for a barbecue. It was a good excuse to break into fifty-year old port that he'd been hoarding for just such an occasion.

"Good stuff this Frank," an enthused Bruno said after tasting it. "Man, it's hell in Africa!"

The three visitors were ready for them when Frank and his team trooped into the conference room. Anthony Scobar, Chater Metals financial director had also done his share of roving the mine and asking searching questions. Bruno had spent the most time with this "head office suit" whom he proclaimed to his colleagues as "nobody's fool". Judging from Scobar's smile, he was happy. Edward Fuller, a much older non-executive director gave nothing away except a terse "Hello" and a mute Hilton Walsh absently twirled his gold *Cross* pen from hand to hand.

Frank noticed that not one member of the august trio had any papers in front of them. His heart began to thump. *Oh no. A bad sign. A quick brush-off and hey presto, next chapter!*

Joey had arranged coffee and tea. Wordlessly Hilton rose to close the door at eight-fifteen and returned to the top of the board table choosing to remain standing. He leaned on the table and looked sternly at each person in the room.

Damn! Harry thought. Hilton's going to launch nasties! What did we miss?

"This won't take long. I'm going to give it you straight," Hilton said gravely. "We had a thorough tour and dug deep. We wanted to make sure that the 'rebuild' as we understand it, is a fact of life."

Now what! Frank inwardly agonized. Is he going to screw us? The devil! We fix the mine and he wants to chop us?

"We're impressed. Normally after a visit like this I'd have a list a yard long that needs attention. It is not the case here."

Frank wondered if he'd heard right. Cecil was staring open-mouthed at Hilton turning over in his mind what he'd just heard. *Hilton was pleased!* Had he heard right?

Bruno's disbelieving face told it all and Harry's beaming face signified relief. *He still had a job.*

"We were pleased to see such tight financial controls. One or two other group entities could learn from you. I'm going to send a few people with corns on their asses out here to take lessons on the subject. Having so much cash in the bank is a welcome surprise."

Frank winked at Harry.

"Mr McCrae has done wonders on that score. Well done. And no more qualified audit reports. A big relief gentlemen. A big relief when you're facing down unhappy shareholders I can tell you."

The chairman glanced at Walter Clark who was hovering well away from the top brass. "We must finish our conversation on ore dressing Mr Clark. As I recall we were rudely interrupted when last we spoke."

Walter flushed. "Whenever you say so sir."

"You have been busy. Putting up a case for a centralized process control system so soon! Two million rands worth. Where will that cash come from? Not from our insurers I take it?"

"Er, not exactly Chairman," Harry coughed. "Not quite!"

"Ah yes! More fancy footwork is it!" Edward Fuller piped in.

"Oh!" Hilton feigned absent-mindedness and stroked his chin like an errant professor. "Mr Fielding?"

"Yes Chairman?" a suspicious Frank answered, choking on his smoke as he inhaled.

"Let me be the first to congratulate you on your confirmation as General Manager. We feel it is a well-earned promotion."

"Hey! That will cost Frankie a few drinks!" a delighted Bruno whispered to Harry.

20

Sandstorms howling from inland at eighty kilometers an hour had played havoc with transport, mine operations and employee tempers.

"It's the season," old-timers sagely nodded. "The first three months of the year we can't see for sand, then it disappears. There's nothing we can do about it."

The infamous East Wind was nature's reminder that she held sway. Equipment and machinery maintenance bills soared as fine dust wreaked havoc on their workings. Temperatures in town had rocketed to stupefying humid levels added to gale-force sand sheets that converted normally tidy *Thuringia Bay* into a begrimed red specter. Housewives fought a losing battle with dust piling in to their premises. Only electrical equipment repair shops rubbed their hands in glee when literally an ill-wind made them huge profits.

Magically the infamous East Wind abated in late afternoon like clockwork. A vista of sunset oranges, reds and yellows coated the horizon and the sea resumed its deep blue hue and iridescence.

One Saturday morning a gleeful Cecil rang Harry. "Up and at 'em Harry! We don't have an East Wind bugging us! What say you two, we and the Gerbers' head up the coast? It's a fantastic day."

"Walter will be upset," Harry grimaced. "He's stuck as duty manager and he'd kill to go fishing with Bruno. Great idea. Doreen's keen on a break too."

Two hours later the men had their rods in the water. The ladies hovered under sunshades happily coating themselves with tanning lotions before spreading themselves out to bake. Not a breath of wind stirred and the wave pattern in Bruno's valued opinion indicated "Plenty of fish!"

Predictably Bruno was first to strike and reeled in a fine Saint Joseph's shark weighing eighteen kilograms. "This goes back," Bruno told his jealous colleagues. "We can't eat him."

Harry more by luck than skill hauled in a *barbel* and wrestled to get it off his hook without impaling his hand on the slithery creature's poisonous spinal barb.

"Man, don't throw it back!" Bruno shouted. "We'll give it to our neighbor. The Germans smoke these things like herrings...tastes good!"

Cecil proved hopeless with a rod. All he contrived were frequent nests with his reel and eventually he gave up, preferring to swim, content that the *Benguela Current* was at its warmest.

To prepare for lunch the men set up a barbecue using driftwood washed up on to the beach. Bruno opened a few beer cans and handed them around while prodding at his stuffed *galjoen* on the embers. "Man this is a fantastic country. Here we are catching sharks and meters away people are swimming! Where else do you see that hey?"

"I agree. I'm old enough to appreciate it. This is bliss!' Harry chorused and took a long gulp of ice-cold lager. "All together now..."

"It's hell in Africa" the three men boomed out and swigged from their beer cans.

Mariette shoved a plate of salad into Bruno's hand. "Lazy devil! Put some fish on that and eat!"

"I trained her well didn't I?" Bruno whispered.

"Hey Doreen! Take some lessons!" Harry shouted at Doreen.

"In your dreams pal. It's my turn to be spoilt for a change."

Cecil opened a bottle of wine and handed everyone a glass. "Tasting time gents. Then I'm catching a few zzzz's."

To everyone's relief early afternoon ushered in a slight wind. Scorching sands barred bare feet from walking on anywhere not under shade or under water.

For some members who had downed several glasses of wine they lay beneath their sunshades. The sea rippled in the background rising to a crescendo every few seconds as waves strove towards the high water mark and whooshed back in a strong undertow, preparing for another attempt to sweep up over the beach.

Harry and Marlene chatted amiably. Bruno had put on a large sun hat and thong rubber sandals allowing him to stand in surf to cast and hold his fishing rod.

"If ever you want to see a happy man just look at Bruno contemplating his navel," Harry exclaimed. "He simply loves the sea."

"What's new Harry? It's in his blood," a relaxed Marlene drawled. "For him the sea is holy water."

Harry stared out to sea, a distant expression on his face. He liked Marlene because she was easy to chat to. She had no side and no wish to impress other than to be her normal self. Yes, she had outward beauty and outstanding ability to chat sensibly about most subjects to any person whether king or minion. He'd noticed that seldom did husband and wife really *talk* to each other. They displayed basic courtesies when in company, but Harry surmised, their relationship was their business. "I envy anyone with that sort of inner peace."

"Really!" Marlene exclaimed. "Don't you have it?"

He tipped his cap back. She'd lowered her sunglasses and sat expectantly hugging her knees.

"No Marlene. I admit not. I yearn for it. I feel as if there must be more to life but don't know what it is. Aside from my birthplace I've never lived anywhere where I felt totally at home. I can't go back to where I was born even if I wanted to."

"Oh! Why not?"

"The country's changed names. It's not the same place any more. It bears no resemblance to what I remember as a place of excellence. It's gone forever. What effort that went into building it up into the world's greatest copper region was for nothing. Most times I find myself talking to people whom I should understand and don't. We talk at cross-purposes. They see me as different and I see them as who I think they are."

Foam crested the waves creeping towards them. "Oh! Then I must be the lucky one! We're not talking at cross purposes now are we?" Marlene laughed.

She sounded happy enough but her big brown eyes told another story. Harry was convinced that she had her demons to deal with as well.

"No," he laughed. "I'm the lucky one. Just chatting with you, well, I find it very comforting. I feel I've known you for a lot longer than I really have. Perhaps a kindred spirit?"

"That's good of you to say," she said and patted his hand. "Thank you. What about living here? Are you just passing through? Yet another mining family on the move eventually?"

"I haven't given myself enough time to consider it. Maybe. After a disastrous spell in Canada some time back I decided to return to Africa. It's me. I'm a child of this continent but deep down I know that it doesn't want me. We have lived in three African countries and saw how quickly things can turn on you. White people are being marginalized. African democracy boils down to reverse racism. It's anti-white and we all realize it, the rest of the world knows it and turns a blind eye, but to say so is to invite vilification."

"I couldn't have put it better. Cecil of course disagrees. He thinks that eventually everyone in the 'dark continent' as he calls it will see sense and we'll all happily go riding off into a red sunset to enjoy our pot of gold. Some optimist my husband is I have to say."

"It's hard Marlene. History tells us that Africa has never enjoyed stability for any reasonable length of time. I'm old enough to accept that what we're doing right now, being on this fantastic beach, basking in our success at the mine, well, we'll remember it as a highlight in our lives. This spell we're having in South Africa? It will end and we'll never experience it again. I'm not arguing the rights and wrongs of it. That's the waste of it. We're gradually being pushed out, lined up to be thrown out like limp rags because black society judges us as white marauders. They want their own color at the top orchestrating events to their advantage whatever the cost."

"I really don't let it upset me," Marlene replied. "Why worry about what other people think? I want to enjoy my life."

"I can't help worrying about the long term. We can contribute so much but forces waiting to take power revel in mediocrity. Ineptitude and a grab for the fiscus is par for the course. What good did independence bring to this continent? More than half of it is permanently at war. Millions lie dead and the toll is shooting upwards. *Child soldiers*—God what a mess."

"But why let it get to you?" Marlene said while applying another coat of sun cream on her legs. "What can we do about it? Nothing."

"I can't help it. Africa is a permanent begging bowl and I don't doubt that international aid lands up in the wrong pockets. Tribalism is a scourge. Crooks here mess up their own countries then slope off to foreign climes. Look how many of them have pads in Europe and money in Swiss banks…. Yet, I want to stay here because I feel part of it. I ask that I be judged as a person. That's all."

"I'm not sure I understand you Harry. Are you saying that all whites are considered racists by blacks?"

"I'm breaking a golden rule Marlene," Harry checked himself and stood up. "No politics. It gets us into strange waters. I apologize for bringing it up. You're too nice for me to bore you with my mental meanderings."

"You do think it will radically change don't you?"

"Yes. Definitely in one respect. A long time ago a close friend on the Copperbelt told me that *'The mining world is a succession of hellos' and goodbyes'*. You make friends and bingo within a few years everyone moves off and then you start all over again." How true. It didn't happen for him though, the silver lining that we all want. He and his family were murdered by bandits. It must be wonderful to live in one place among friends from birth to death. People whom you trust. We made so many friends wherever we went. We miss them."

Marlene drew her knees up under her chin. "You had a few disappointments along the way. You're not afraid to talk about your emotions. That's good."

"Disappointments Marlene? We all have had them. And you?"

"Me!" she laughed loudly and jumped up to energetically brush sand off her legs. "I live each day as if it's my last. I squeeze all the joy I can out of life. Try it sometime."

"I do have my family and my job. I can't wait to get to work every day. There's so much to do. I ask myself though that when the day comes that I don't feel the same way about it, what then?"

"You're pushing yourself too hard Harry. Take a step back and reset your parameters for your own good."

"It's not a bad idea," he said ruefully. "I haven't had a day's leave since I arrived here."

"Now you're talking. Meanwhile old stick, it's time for a swim. I'm going to fill a bottle with seawater and chuck it over Cecil. That husband of mine will sleep his life away. That is what's left after that blessed mine has taken its fill!"

At four in the afternoon the wind had stepped up and the sand began to whip up and sting. Other vehicles along the beach too were packing up and nosing towards the main road.

"Time to go," Cecil announced. "Come on everybody before we leave I must take a photograph. Up against my *Landie*. Harry, stand at the back. Doreen! Here, stand in front. Bruno! Put your rod away!"

"Help me up," Marlene said and grabbed Harry's hand. "All good things don't have to come to an end," she whispered to him. "Remember that Harry."

21

Well after the 1986 deadline had expired, the mine monopolized Frank's waking moments; in his view his managers would not have expected less of him seeing that they were piling in changes, forcing costs down and increasing profits. Professor Koenig had become a frequent visitor whose invaluable contribution had become a company cornerstone. Frank had faced down widespread problems that would have broken many lesser men, but the prospect of flying to London to attend a Chater Metals PLC annual general meeting in August 1987 terrified him.

Invited to attend by the chairman was an accolade for the mine his managers told him. Despite his team insisting that he and Yvonne enjoy themselves in London Frank felt that he was playing truant. Hilton Walsh had put it more succinctly over the telephone. "You men out there met your targets. It's carrot and stick for you Frank. Come to the London and bring your good wife with you. One or two shareholders might want to talk about your mine. You need to be present to answer questions."

During their weekly meeting Vic Grey had let loose his penny's worth too. "Hundreds of shareholders attend the AGM so head office hires a hall in a five star hotel. They all come to say their piece, including the *weirdos'* whose number grows annually. They don't pitch up just for the tea and biscuits you know."

"'Weirdos'? What 'weirdos'?" Frank testily enquired.

"Odd investors who buy one share which qualifies them to attend so that they can shout their heads off. Environmental loonies will scream about minorities being disadvantaged and how we kill the earth. The press laps it up because it sells newspapers. Idiots in funky dress get their pictures taken and a good time is had by all. I don't think!"

"You're enjoying this aren't you Vic? Making me sweat. Get lost!"

Frank and Yvonne jetted in to Heathrow the morning before the dreaded meeting. It was a baking hot day with the bluest of skies, the effect of which dwindled when Frank bought a TIMES newspaper. It was plastered with graphic accounts of a huge oil spill in the Hebrides from an errant tanker. Damage to sea life was inestimable. Photographs of sorry looking, sodden seals and gulls stared back at him. Environmental lobbies were freaking out and lawyers acting for the vessel's owners were quoted making ridiculously defensive statements.

"Just my luck," Frank growled. "That's fuel for tomorrow's meeting."

"At last!" Yvonne declared after approving their hotel suite, "I'm going to do some retail therapy. It's a great morning for it Frank. Are you coming with me?"

Frank winced. "Me? Go shopping? No thanks. I'm not on holiday. I'm 'phoning Chater's public relations people. I want to know where the trapdoors are going to be tomorrow. Don't melt your credit card Yvonne. Remember I have to carry the stuff that you buy."

From Bruno's point of view Frank going to London brought him an unexpected bonus. He was acting for Frank as general manager and on his first day of acting, appeared on site wearing a suit. As far as he was concerned, acting for the big boss implied that he was Frank's ultimate successor. He was glad about that, as was Mariette who lost little time telephoning her pals to casually drop her bit of news into their conversation. The managers accepted that decision whole-heartedly and took Bruno for a celebratory "Yard of Ale". Mariette wasn't so pleased when Don South delivered her beer-soaked husband at midnight.

At the hotel entrance two burly men confronted Frank.

"Shareholder?" one man uttered tonelessly while barring the way.

"No. I work for Chater. In South Africa."

"Frank!" a familiar voice rang out. "It's good to see you." Hilton Walsh had loomed up. "You made it. Come in. Come in."

Unsmiling heavies stepped apart to let Frank enter the cavernous ballroom in the Park Lane Hotel.

Vic hadn't laid it on. Frank shook hands with his chairman.

"Directors and executive officers sit themselves at a long table on the stage," Hilton informed him. "We want you up there. Your seat has your name on it."

"Top table!" fearful Frank gulped, "but I thought…"

"Your mine might be half the globe away Frank but many people know about it and want to know more about it."

Frank fought down bile, glad that he'd made the effort to be briefed by *PR* people as to what lay ahead. Hilton's hint at impending grilling made the prospect sound less and less enjoyable.

"Sign in and get yourself a cup of coffee. We begin at ten sharp. This will be a lively one I think. Almost every seat is taken with fifteen minutes to go."

"To be honest Chairman tramping my patch back home is more my style."

"There's always a first time for this old son," Hilton smirked. "This is where it all happens. In the shareholders' bull ring. The herd is here to see blood spilled, so to speak. Besides gems of verbal virtuosity, a few tomatoes might come flying at us, so be warned. The funny thing is that it happens despite the group generating good profits. In my book, it's a circus."

Precisely on time Hilton banged his gavel called the meeting to order. Attendees continued filing in, some noisily, to the annoyance of those attendees already seated. Po-faced and beefy security guards, whose services Hilton informed Frank, were mandatory, ringed the entire assembly.

Frank had a good look at the faces focussed on the chairman. They seemed harmless enough and he sat back wondering whether Vic Grey had tried to spook him out of sheer devilment. Proceedings remained predictably dull while ordinary business on the agenda was sped through. Financial results, markedly better than forecasted, attracted questions, some asked and answered in the same breath, some so painfully ventured, few people present understood them judging from their vacant expressions.

Frank spotted a troupe of rowdy latecomers who positioned themselves at different spots in the aisles. His heart fell. *Oh no! Vic was right* he thought when taking in their ridiculous hairstyles and outlandish garb. *You must be crazy to appear in public dressed like that. Oddballs every one of them.*

"Any other business," signalled adrenalin to flow. Loud accusations instead of questions assailed the board, mouthed by an array of animated individuals, including women who sprouted choice invective and shook their fists.

As more unwelcome and plainly unjustified accusations rang out security men forcibly removed baying objectors and escorted them outside. The atmosphere turned baleful and wholesale malfunction threatened to envelop proceedings.

"Order! Order!" Hilton shouted while banging his gavel. "Order! Order please!"

Noise gradually abated. Hilton's eye fell on a grey-haired gentleman who was leaning on a walking stick.

"Sir. You have a question?"

"Thank you," came a faltering reply. "My name is Andrew Sumner. A year ago my son Brian, a healthy robust young engineer aged twenty-three, died of brain cancer at one of your uranium mines in Canada. My question is does mining uranium incur a greater risk of contracting cancer and if so what you are doing about it?"

The old man sat down unaware of many sympathetic nods rippling through the audience.

A longhair shouted, "I told you so! The bastards are killing us all!" and was promptly removed for his outspoken exertions.

"Order!" Hilton commanded. "Your question sir is so serious that it deserves an appropriately researched reply. I undertake to provide you with an appropriate written response concerning your son. I am very sorry for your loss."

Frank felt sweat pouring off him; had that question had been aimed at him he would have died a thousand deaths.

The old man nodded. An aide walked toward him to get the details.

"Yes Madam?" Hilton said a little stiffly when an attractive young woman stood rigidly, hand up, glaring at him.

Frank noticed that she was neatly groomed. Something about the glint in her eye forewarned him. *This one means business…*

"Ann Foster. Shareholder," she primly announced.

"Your question please madam."

"Why are your companies killing people in Indonesia, South America and Africa? Paying starvation wages, allowing children to drop like flies and burying them without saying a word? Your profits are blood money!"

Before Hilton could answer a loud chorus broke out around the room, so perfectly timed it must have been planned. "Hear! Hear! You tell 'em darlin'. Killers! Capitalist rapists! Shame on 'em. Imperialist dogs! Western lackeys!"

Rotten fruit cascaded onto the stage. Hilton brushed a squishy pear off his shoulder. A foul-smelling egg splattered on an official next to Frank.

"You should be ashamed of yourselves!" Anne Foster lambasted and stood defiantly while waiting for her answer, arms akimbo.

There was no opportunity for a reply. The meeting descended into further disorder as stern-faced security men moved in. Scuffles and fights broke out. Elderly attendees cried out in desperation, shielding themselves with their arms while creaking their way towards the exits. Pressmen slavered with glee holding up tape recorders and taking photographs of a melee right up their alley.

Frank was mortified at the scene. *Revolution…fruit and vegetables soaring at them…fists thumping…batons bashing…God Almighty what was going on…*This was London, the so-called civilized capital of the free world and people behaved like that? He'd never take Victor Grey so lightly again!

"So endeth the lesson," Hilton boomed and banged his gavel but no one was listening. "I declare this meeting closed."

A cleaning crew appeared to swiftly sweep up before clearing the hall and stacking chairs. All doors were shut except one where a guard assisted board members and company officials to exit the venue.

Frank was doubly shocked when Hilton caught his eye and shuffled towards him.

"So," Hilton murmured, "you saw it for yourself eh Frank? Four hours of revolution. Not a pretty sight was it? Up goes my dry cleaning bill."

"I was warned about what to expect Chairman, but I didn't believe it. It's the kind of outcry you expect in a third world country. What an utter disgrace."

"Ah well, let's say that bounds of normal behavior now take on new dimension. Mad hatters need to blow off steam. On the plus side it's better than attending a West End show. Mining company head offices are inured to being attacked for the world's ailments. And it gets worse. There's international pressure for multi-nationals to be brought to account when coups and revolutions break out. Business today? It's no picnic I have to say. You got off easy Frank and it's as well you were here to get it under your belt. Some people call it democracy in action. Holding up the London end of the business is no cakewalk."

"I believe you chairman," Frank said. "I'd heard the stories but did not take them seriously."

"You know, even our mail is infected with diatribe and one or two tabloids put shadows on us hoping for a quip they can headline to their advantage, or wait to photograph us at our worst."

"I had no idea," Frank repeated.

"Your eyes must have opened. Did you learn any lessons?"

"Yes. I think so."

"What about in particular?"

"I'm thankful that David Bradshaw had put his finger on the radiation issue. We installed a medical unit and screening procedures at great cost. I think we should tell the world what we're doing and not wait for the kind of attack you got. Anything to do with uranium is emotive stuff so there's no point being reactive."

"You're talking about Ann Foster? That's her stock in trade, embarrassing multi-national corporations. She does shove in the knife, no quarter given, even to her long-suffering father."

"Who might he be?"

"Me. I suppose I'm to blame for her outrageous behavior. I drummed into her never to back off from issues that she believes in. Feisty wasn't she?"

"When is our favorite troglodyte arriving Joey? I'd like to see him please. Pretty urgently."

"The 'plane landed twenty minutes ago Mr Lonsdale. He should be here at any moment."

Just then Frank breezed in. Despite his long Jumbo flight to Cape Town where the Piper had waited to collect him, he showed no signs of fatigue.

"Hello Joey. Cecil! Just the man I need to see. Come in. I have news for you."

"I hope that it's good news Frank. I could do with a bit more of it."

"Something out of the blue cropped up," Frank said when both men were seated. "I want to put it to bed."

He was smiling so Cecil relaxed. "What do you have in mind?"

"I want to tell you about a Miss Ann Foster."

Cecil listened carefully not expecting the punch line when Frank got to the part about her being the chairman's daughter, now divorcee.

"How embarrassing for him. Obviously her lift doesn't go all the way to the top," Cecil sniffed. "Why isn't she in a padded cell?"

"The way I heard it I gathered Hilton is very proud of her. He doesn't agree with what she's doing but admires her for sticking to her guns. I don't think he indulges her when it comes to the high life. She's on her own."

"He'd do her a big favor by committing her, judging from what you just told me."

"Far from it Cecil," Frank replied, pausing to light up a cigarette. "Pardon me. This is my first since leaving Heathrow," he smiled. "Bliss! Hilton knows that there is an element of truth in what she says about multinational companies."

"Come on Frank," Cecil scoffed. "Is it the old routine about abusing pygmies or is it the hoary annual about cartels ripping off the world? Or pouring acid into the Amazon? No let me guess! Someone is pinching the rain forests!"

"Unforgiving fellow aren't you? Nothing like that. But think about manufacturing contracts being placed in the East these days. Ask yourself 'Why?' Because labor over there is so cheap. Whatever way you look at it, that's exploitation. She's got a point. Kids working for a bowl of rice a day is acceptable practice there, and up to few years ago, no one in the western world gave a hoot about it. More people do care now because they're better informed. I hope you agree with me."

"I suppose so," Cecil said. "It's just that we hear more bad things about multinationals than good. When last did you read about a good news story, like what we're doing here with our training and human development? Oh no, the press don't publish that. That's not news. No corpses—no rape, explosions, riots and mayhem to hog headlines."

Frank grimaced. "Don't go over the top Cecil. Think about it. We're not lily-white."

"I don't see room for censure. We have all bases covered," Cecil interjected. Frank's observations had taken him by surprise. *Was Frank getting at him? What had he done wrong?*

Frank lit another cigarette. "'*Bases*'? '*Covered*'? Yes, if we look at ourselves in the context of where we live. Internationally? Not by a long chalk. We don't exactly pay our employees a similar wage to what they would earn in Canada do we? We're small change if we compare our pay structure to American mines."

"Yes Frank, but there is the law of supply and demand, and..."

Frank lifted a hand to cut him off. "Cecil, what I learned is that we must consider the global picture. If we don't do so that's how we get shafted by malcontents. No one wants to listen to our excuses about a low-grade ore deposit. Wage jumps from worker to manager here percentage-wise are monumental compared to America and Europe. I'd don't think even you could argue that one in open debate."

"I could, believe me, because productivity comes into the formula. Anyhow, what is it that you want me to do Frank?" a rapidly rising to combative mode Cecil enquired.

"Please ask your *PR* people to find out as much as possible about a Ann Foster. I need to know what she says and what context she is reported in."

"This is all very sudden. What for? What do you want it for?"

"I need to know everything about people like her. Persons who reject nuclear power. Environmentalists, freaks, whoever is so disposed and live in a fantasy world. We must get to know who is saying what about us."

"Why? It's a lot of effort just to get to grips with *brain-deads*."

"I want to write to one or two of them."

"Good heavens! Why on earth do you want to do that?'

"To invite them to visit this mine. At any time that they want to come, to go anywhere they want, and ask whatever questions they want to. I want them to make up their minds based on facts. I want to try and turn uninformed critics into allies. In case you were going to ask me, no, we won't pay their expenses to come here. If they pay their own way they will be free to tell it like it is. Whatever criticism we get we will either agree and remedy it, or disprove it. We must meet detractors face to face. If they don't come here after being invited to do so and they rant on about this mine, then they give us ammunition to shut them up."

"A note of warning for you," a dismayed Cecil said. "The more money we make the more visitors we'll get. Isn't there a risk that we'll be distracted from our main purpose? Surely production comes first?"

"Cecil, after what I saw in London not a few shareholders would close us down in a second, profits or no profits. If we don't encourage doubters to see for themselves mystique grows and so does opposition to what we do. They will ask, *'Do they run a clandestine operation? Why? They must have something to hide'*. Ann Foster accusing us of keeping local people down offends me. What's wrong with inviting anyone who is interested to witness first-hand what we've done in training local people and putting them in jobs? If they're honest, not a few should apologize afterwards for shooting off their big mouths."

"I have to say Harry and Vic Grey won't like it. Harry hates wasting cash and Vic will tell you that it heightens chances of saboteurs and opposition spies running amok. The more about us they see, the more they plot and scheme."

"I thought about that. Xenophobia is rife in this country, spy mania, telephone tapping and activities of official security battalions. There's a risk in becoming so reclusive because as I said, our detractors will assume we have something to hide. If we don't tell them about our operations without being forced to, it's easy for idiots to make up foul stories. We, the managers, our employees need contact with the outside world too. The last thing we must do is pedestal ourselves otherwise we will be badly taken down in years to come. If visitors leave here impressed with us then our employees will feel good. It's worth the effort in my opinion."

"You have a point," Cecil said begrudgingly. Frank had gone past the bounds of lateral thinking. It was more a case of three-dimensional futuristic planning. "I've been too wrapped up with this mine to consider what the outside world wants to see and hear. Okay, I have a good idea where you are coming from. I'll put something down on paper, a guideline on how we do this without spending too much money. You won't believe how many of our London brothers want to swan out here now that we're the bees' knees and trip around the country while they're about it, naturally at our expense if they get their way."

Frank sat back and lit another cigarette. "So you agree with me. The chairman does too I might add. How about bringing it up at our Friday managers' meeting?"

With deadpan expression, Cecil scribbled in his diary. "Let the games begin!" he murmured. "While I'm here Frank, there a few more mundane issues I need to bring up with you."

23

"I have been working here for one year," Andreas Mohtlane informed his unwelcome visitor whose dishevelled appearance and bodily smell spoke volumes, "long enough to understand that these people mean well. There are no white racists left on this mine."

All he'd wanted was a quiet drink before dinner in the single quarters buffeteria but the stranger seemed bent on talking to him. Judging from his accent and appearance Andreas classified the visitor as originating from the Rehoboth area in South West Africa, their northern neighbor, one engaged in a bitter war of independence between guerillas and South African overlords.

The stranger sneered but kept his voice low speaking a sing-song brand of Afrikaans unique to Rehoboth inhabitants, his accent tied in with his appearance, that of shifty eyes, crinkly hair, height-challenged, with dark brown skin.

"This mine funds the South African government. The government buys arms and ammunition for the regime's troops who shoot our people. Do you support them comrade?"

Andreas was uneasy. "No I do not. How can anyone on this mine say how taxes will be spent? The mine recruits our people and trains them. Some of our people have been appointed to top positions."

"Bah! Tokens! They accept money so that their black faces can be paraded to uphold a capitalist company! Sell-outs!"

"You are wrong. I see them doing real jobs. Soon there will be more trained *comrades* working on this mine. We see the benefits of good wages and in the towns and villages. The mine is educating me to become an engineer. I stand a chance of an overseas bursary. I have no complaints. My superiors treat me very well."

"I see. Then you are a sell-out too. A token! People like you are traitors. When the new government comes you will have some explaining to do—and your families."

Andreas was sorely tempted to query his strident drinking comrade but common sense prevailed. *Walk away.* He had no call to pick a fight. He stood up. "I have a long day ahead of me tomorrow. I must do two hours study before I go to bed. Good night brother."

His visitor scowled, finished his beer and took off into the night.

Two days later he met Victor Grey at a remote desert rendezvous well outside of *Thuringia Bay.*

"He's good!" he reported to Victor in perfect English. "I gave him a thorough going over. Checked his body language; he said all the right things—consistently. He's not hiding anything. I got his beer glass. His fingerprints don't check out with anything on national records. He talked about applying for one of the mine's new bursaries to study overseas. I did not detect any hint that he was a political sleeper. God knows, I riled him but couldn't reel him in. To be honest I liked the man. As far as I can tell Mr Grey, he's clean. A committed employee."

"Okay Major de Villiers, thank you. I've set him up at a few times talking to different people and they all said the same about him. 'He's clean'. You've been very helpful."

Since Gerard Dresser had tipped him off Victor had kept his eye on Andreas. If the young man had been planted by *agence provocateur* for no good purposes, he'd not given the slightest indication of other agendas. Until now.

"New bursary scheme?" Victor muttered and reached for his pipe. "What bursary scheme?"

Until he had a lead Victor had not wanted to waste Harry McCrae's time nor Frank's. That time had plainly arrived.

"New bursary scheme you say?" Frank frowned. "It was outlined in my fax to the chairman two weeks ago. I'm waiting for his reaction since I need his pull to get places at overseas colleges. Cecil prepared it for me. I'd better call him in here to find out what is going on."

Victor held up his hand. "I suggest that we play it down for the time being. Only the three of are aware of it."

"Four," Frank corrected. "Joey typed the final version."

"Five!" Harry corrected. "I'm here."

"To your knowledge has Joey ever leaked anything?" Victor asked Frank.

"Never. She's proved to be a confidential secretary in every respect."

"Well then, we have another player who we don't know about. Someone who feeds Andreas information. I wonder who that may be?"

"What do you suggest we do?" Harry asked Victor Grey. "This is serious."

"With your permission I want to install a time-lapse camera in your management block tonight. My staff and operating people are used to seeing me waltzing about at all hours so no one will fall out of his tree if they spot me."

"You think someone in this building is leaking information?"

"It's a distinct possibility."

"I suppose it had to happen some time. I don't automatically go with this automatic terrorist scenario," Harry interjected and turned

189

to Frank. "It's too convenient to blame everything on. Vic's right Frank. We might be surprised with what he turns up."

A week of time-lapse tapes evidenced human traffic everyone expected to see entering and leaving the management building. Frank's office was a programmed like a dentist's chair. *No wonder* that he took so much work home. The night cleaner, always the same individual, a grey-haired old colored man shuffled into the building at nine in the evening. He emptied waste baskets into black refuse bags, wiped down desks, equipment and telephones with sanitized towels, vacuumed carpets, washed up kitchen debris and departed, carting refuse bags outside to await collection by a nightly refuse truck that automatically mashed its contents once dumped into it.

"It doesn't show any leaks from your building," Victor informed Harry and Frank. "There is another angle that comes to mind."

"Yes!" a concerned Frank piped back. "Tell me."

"Frank, please don't take offence," Victor said. "You take a lot of work home. Did that include correspondence on your new bursary scheme?"

"Yes. I don't get time during the day to devote to matters outside production. I stack 'things to do' stuff until the weekend when I have time at home to do it justice."

"Do you lock your study?"

Frank swallowed hard. "No. You'd better put in a camera," he continued weakly. "Hell, I'd hate to think that our domestics are double-crossing us."

"I'll call round tonight," Vic said. "What time will be convenient for you?"

"Any time after dinner. We'll disappear to my study and talk."

Three days later Vic entered Frank's office holding a portable combined VCR and television set.

"You'd better look at this tape. Then tell me what you want me to do."

Frank picked up a tremulous note in Victor's voice and stood up. He went over to his sofa, sat down, lit a cigarette, inhaled deeply and leaned back. "Something tells me that I'm not going to like this. Okay. Switch it on."

It wasn't Frank's housemaid.

It wasn't the gardener.

What he saw was Yvonne sifting through his pile of papers and whispering into a hand-held dictating machine.

Frank sat frozen, his eyes glued to the screen well after the tape had run out. *His wife! Why? What the hell was going on?*

"You want to know what to do Vic," Frank said at last. "I'm driving home right now. I have to have this out with Yvonne. I'd ask you to keep it under wraps until tomorrow morning. By then I'll have a clear idea of what action to take."

"I'm sorry Frank," Victor commiserated, appearing to genuinely mean it.

At eight-thirty next morning Frank 'phoned Vic and Harry to come to his office.

"I thought she'd got that university demonstration streak out of her system years ago," Frank said grimly. "She was anti-South African government then and got heavily involved in reaction politics. Her sister was put under house arrest and one or two of her friends disappeared. Now I discover that she was feeding stuff to this Mohtlane individual. He was contacting an anti-multinational protest group overseas who must have persuaded him to work for them. I don't know Vic, perhaps he was intimidated. It happens. Perhaps Yvonne felt sorry for him. He impressed her when she spoke to him at our staff functions. She believed that what he had to say was gospel, so what did she do? She dropped him an odd tape with data on it. Only now, can she see how silly she's been."

"I'd never have thought it Frank. You must know what kind of information Yvonne might have passed on. Anything shattering?"

"I did deal with some very confidential data involving the scams we uncovered. Then there was sales data I put together for London office. That could have been valuable to our competition. That's the truth of it. Since one of her friends died from cancer she believed that this mine was the cause of it. She bottled her anger. It was her way of getting back at the company. There's little else that I deal with that is damaging should it get out. I mean we encourage people to come here to see for themselves don't we?"

"That's probably what happened," Victor replied. "We had a visitor on site sporting a hidden agenda. No doubt that's when Andreas was recruited. He's a young chap, so wave a few hundred rands under his nose and I'm sure he'd jump at it. Money for an extended family that has no work is a big temptation for any person."

"We all make mistakes Vic."

"Well then, that's it. I'll pick up this Andreas and have him explain himself. I want to find out exactly who he's been communicating with. And why."

"I am to blame Vic. I have to go. I've had a good few years here. As for Andreas he's probably miles away by now, but if he isn't, I wouldn't want to be rid of him. If you find him, tell him that he's been disloyal and it's his last time. If he wants to become an engineer then all he does is concentrate on his work. I'm sure he'll pull up his socks. You did your job and now I have to do mine. I talked to the chairman earlier and explained matters to him so the deed is done."

Victor was taken aback. *Frank leaving?* That wasn't remotely what he was after. "I think you're over-reacting Frank. No one would hold it against you."

A glum Harry agreed with Vic. "Frank...stay. You know no one can do the job as well as you. If you go we all suffer."

"I hold it against myself Harry," Frank said softly. "The managers will be waiting outside. For the good of the company I ask you both that this be kept between us three. If it leaks out, employee morale will take a hammering. We worked too hard these past four years to destroy what we built up."

"But Frank, you going just like that! It will have the same effect!" Harry said.

"I hope not. I'll tell the managers that I have to give three months notice, but I'm going to ask Bruno to act for me as of now. He knows this mine better than all of us. I'll say that I'm going to do my own thing and having decided so, I wouldn't have been able to keep my mind on mine matters. That would not have been fair on the team."

"Where will you go?" a glum Victor enquired. "What will you do?"

"I always fancied a spot of consultancy. The *prof* might help me out with his contacts. He's looking for someone to handle his South East Asia desk."

The news hit the managers like a bombshell.

Bruno refused to act for Frank. "You're not going man. This mine needs you. We need you here."

Cecil was dumbfounded. His best friend was putting distance between them and he'd had not a clue!

Walter was devastated. "It's the first time I worked for somebody who understood my language. I knew that it was too good to last."

All eyes focused on Harry. "It's happened again! Mining is just a succession of hellos' and goodbyes. Frank, there's still so much for us to do here. I'd hate to see you go."

"It's a done deed," Frank replied. "I've been running mining division with Des Irwin as acting manager. How do you feel about confirming him in that position? Bruno, I know you like him. Are you agreeable?"

"Yes," Bruno boomed. "He's young but you taught him well. He's grown."

"I'm going now. Thanks chaps. You were the best, but please, no farewell parties. By the end of the week we'll have our belongings moved out. You're all welcome to come and have a drink with us while we're in town." His was a wan attempt at a smile. "I have to put Joey in the picture. Bruno. Joey's a gem, look after her."

"Yes man. I will," Bruno grimly replied. "I will."

24

His bedside telephone rang. From reflex Harry woke immediately and sat up. He checked his watch. Six o'clock in the morning.

"Harry man! It's perfect weather to catch fish," a sparky Bruno blared.

Since being confirmed in the GM's job Bruno had been irrepressible. Mariette had gotten used to her gregarious husband, but there was just so much fishing that she could take. "Boy's time", she called it and rolled over when he shot out of bed at five-thirty on a Saturday morning.

Harry peered out his window. "In this thick mist Bruno? So early? Even the fish can't see where they're going!"

"It's the best time man," Bruno assured him. "I have a good spot in mind eight miles north. We can have our rods cast within half an hour. Come on man. I've got plenty of red bait; *galjoen* go crazy for it."

"Okay Bruno," Harry yawned. "You win. Doreen will take a dim view of me. She had other plans for this Saturday." Out the corner of his eye he caught his wife's arm signaling "Go!"

"Ten minutes, then I'll pick you up. We'll collect Johan Schmeldt on the way."

Harry was barely awake when boarding Bruno's Land Rover. Bruno looked as if he'd been awake for hours. "Grab a tot," he grinned. "Back seat."

Harry turned round expecting to see a flask of coffee. Instead all he saw was a basket packed with green *Jagermeister* miniatures, liquor that had three times the punch of whisky.

"Evil stuff Bruno," he grinned. "I'll wait. It's a bit early for me."

Minutes later they pulled up outside Johan's house. Mist lay particularly thick and Bruno's ageing Land Rover's headlights were of little use. Johan was waiting at his gate. Three emaciated dogs skulked past, a cat running for its life and a shadowy figure emerging from the domestic quarters of a house across the road amused everyone. Friedas, Johan's wife, still clad in her pink quilted dressing gown and pom-pom slippers, stood on their front step wagging her finger at her shame-faced husband.

"Your first Saturday off in months from that damn mine Johan and you go off bladdy fishing! Buggar you man!"

Johan infuriated her even more when he spotted the Jagermeisters, helped himself to a nip, opened it, toasted her and gulped it down.

"Man!" he declared and wiped his lips with the back of his hand, "a Jagermeister shot! That's the best way to begin a Saturday morning."

A convinced Harry joined him and Bruno stepped out too to have a sip of the potent liquor. Johan's next door neighbour emerged to see what the fuss was about. Piet Uys took one look at the Land Rover and shouted, "Wait for me!"

By the time an excited Piet stumbled out with his kit ten minutes later his three cohorts were into their third Jagermeisters.

"You'll be sorry!" Friedas shouted at Johan. "And you Bruno? What kind of example is this from the general manager hey? Drinking on the bladdy street! Harry McCrae! Doreen will bladdy kill you after I tell her!"

"Friedas my flower," Johan crooned through puckered lips, "I'll bring you a nice…"

"Don't bladdy *'my flower'* me! I'm going to my ma's!"

"I don't know," Johan informed his laughing trio of onlookers in a low voice, "what a pity my ma-in-law didn't join us. I'd use her as bait. The old crow!"

Mist had not let up so Bruno's "half an hour" turned out to be a tortuous hour straining through thick sand before he swung his steering wheel hard right.

"Don't worry man, last lap."

"Bruno," a fearful Harry chirped, "do you know where you're going? If we get stuck I don't want to drown!"

"Hey! Trust me man. We're close," Bruno shouted as he wrestled the wheel.

The roar of the sea drowned out conversation and suddenly Bruno put on anchors. "We're here. Bait up!"

All Harry could see was a sheet of white foam and seaweed piercing the mist by rushing up the beach fifty feet away to rustle back into the gloom leaving a trail of slimy seaweed and tumbling shells. It was grey and it looked cold. It was cold, incentive enough to fortify themselves with more Jagermeisters.

Bruno clambered out and got busy. Within minutes of baiting up and casting he yelled, "First one!" When he reeled in he discovered that he'd caught two sizeable *kabeljou* fish.

Heartened, Harry cast in. Within seconds he had a strike. A big *kabeljou*.

Piet and Johan each celebrated another Jagermeister before trudging along the beach, further south, disappearing into the swirling mist. They hadn't gone far because every few seconds Bruno and Harry heard, "Got one! Come baby come! Look at that one! He's a monster!"

At ten o'clock sunlight broke through, mottling the sea with yellow spots. Amazingly, as the scene cleared the quartet discovered a line of vehicles lining the coast north and south as far as their eyes could see. Word had seeped out. Fishing *bonanza* day. Dozens of fishermen were cashing in, no less fortunate than Bruno's party whose arms were weary from casting, catching, gutting and cleaning fish, including a good few *galjoen,* the biggest culinary prize of all because of its tasty marbled white flesh.

A few desert cowboys had appeared to rev their four-wheel drive vehicles through the surf now approaching high tide, enraging fishermen who suffered broken lines. Bruno's Land Rover was well known so no antics took place near his spot. Fishermen's garb varied, the more serious among them wearing heavy waders to standing chest-high in crashing surf. Others chose to launch ski-boats to fish in deep water without fear of snagging their lines.

"Too easy," Bruno said disparagingly. "All those creeps do is chuck out hand lines, lie back and drink neat brandy! By the time they get back ashore they'll be as pissed as newts!"

Squadrons of pelicans had landed and more were circling for space to land and gobble their share of fish entrails that excited fisherman were dumping.

"Time to leave," Bruno sniffed at three o'clock, he who hated sharing a beach with anyone except friends. "Let's see if our ladies are still talking to us."

Later that night at Bruno's house the "fishermen" gathered for a *braai*. Their ladies, had forgiven their errant men seeing that they'd filled their deep freezes with assortments of fresh, cleaned fish. Bruno insisted on preparing *galjoen* on coals having wrapped them in foil with onions tomatoes and herbs. The men stuck with their Jagermeisters, content to chat about anything except work.

"Man!" Piet Uys beamed, "I'm speaking English so well now I don't understand it myself!"

Coming from Piet his statement was hugely funny. Before the influx of English-speakers, his languages had been Afrikaans, German and local lingua franca comprised of a mixture of tribal tongues. Anneke, his wife gave no quarter, meaning that if anyone talked to her they had to use Afrikaans. Harry tried his best with his frequent mispronunciations, exploding Piet into hysterical laughter.

"One thing about living here man," Bruno exclaimed, "is that we get plenty of laughs hey!"

"Yeah." Harry agreed. "It makes a change from rebuild days. Then we cried for most of the time wondering what the hell we were doing. I still wonder how we managed it. These past four years flashed by. I've worked for three general managers here in that time. Isn't that an interesting statistic?"

"It sounds bad doesn't it?" Bruno muttered. "It must be a hoodoo mine. I'd better watch my step!"

"Forget it Bruno. Your star is rising. I just hope you and Mariette don't up and leave us," Harry said.

"Bruno!" Mariette shrilled, "no bladdy talking business hey! Leave that mine back in the flippin' desert! Go and make coffee!"

"Who me my sweet?" Bruno cried in mock astonishment. "I'm not talking shop. Shame on you!"

Obediently, he got up and headed for the kitchen. "She gives me a hard time!" he muttered.

"You!" Mariette gestured at a surprised Harry, "stick a tape on. Everyone must dance before you all get too drunk! Go on! Move yourself!"

"Guess who's coming to visit us?" Bruno opened with at the Friday afternoon managers' meeting.

"If it's Goldie Hawn I volunteer entertaining her," a chirpy Cecil said. "I'd love to show her our desert. It will be the first time that I get lost."

"*Anne Foster*. Does her name ring a bell?"

"Hilton's daughter!' a visibly aghast Walter said. "Oh no! The Queen of bloody Sheba! She's a bitch. I'm taking leave. When is she coming?"

"If I fax acceptance today she'll arrive in two weeks time, or close to it. What's your problem? She sounded very nice on the 'phone."

"Yes. Why does she stir everyone's blood?" Harry said. "She may be the chairman's daughter, but from what I hear he's the last one to treat her with kid gloves."

"Let me educate you, "Cecil said. "She's a rabble-rouser; a public relations virago who specializes in screwing multinational companies. Does the chairman know about her impending visit Bruno?"

"No, but I'll have to tell him about it," Bruno replied. "She's welcome but she pays her own way. She must know that we can't make exceptions for her."

"We have nothing to kow-tow to her about," Cecil barked. "Frank saw her in action at the AGM he attended. He tipped us off about her activities. She gets around, enrages blue-blood companies in return for plenty of press. She's not shy. The Chater Group gets blasted regularly by her hot lips. She says we maltreat our employees and kill their kids, She has no shame that one. In short she's bloody dangerous!"

"Is she single?" an urbane Des Irwin enquired. "I'll show her around the mine. Let me find out what she really thinks of us. More importantly what it is that gets up her nose."

"You Des? Are you mad? The chairman's daughter with *you!* We'll all end up being fired!"

"Very funny Cecil. Why not? You guys are too straight-laced and you'll be overly polite and fawning. It's natural. You will tell her what she wants to hear. She'll eat you alive and then spit you out. Why not let me have a go at getting into her head?"

"As long as it's not into her pants!" Cecil muttered. "Old Hilton wouldn't thank you for that."

"I agree with Des," Harry chimed in. "She won't be expecting someone to shepherd her around who isn't on his knees paying her homage. If she does the Queen of Sheba routine Des will bring her down to earth. He can save us all from that. I don't know about you chaps but I've got better things to do."

"I'm still taking leave whatever you do!" Walter declared. "She's bad news. I speak from first-hand experience."

He hadn't planned it that way. Des kept her waiting for fifteen minutes before she was ushered into his office by the public relations officer. His weekend production figures had needed disentangling as did eternal problems concerning ore grade sent to the plant, always his first ports of call on a Monday.

"Miss Foster, welcome. I'm sorry for the delay." He wasn't about to justify why he'd done so even if it meant getting off to a bad start with her.

"That's business!" she answered brightly. "I believe you're going to show me around Mr Irwin? Thank you."

"Yes. I assumed you weren't after an official program. You must have certain questions that you wish to ask. You might want to visit technical areas to get into the nitty-gritty. I'm in your hands for the rest of the day. Where would you like to begin? Ask," he smiled, "and ye shall receive."

"Where's Walter Clark?" she asked Bruno at the lunch table after having a good look around. "He's an old friend of mine." She was happy to nibble at an apple.

"On leave. He's fishing up our north coast."

"Give him my regards," she smiled. "We met some years back in Melbourne. He's a convincing metallurgist."

"How's it going?" Cecil enquired. "Is Des looking after you?"

"Yes," she said and turned to look at Des. "Very well."

"Answering all your questions is he?"

"Well, to give him his due he's trying hard."

"Right," Des exclaimed when noticing Ann had finished her coffee, "we're going to talk to the trainers and Doctor Hannah. Excuse us please. They're not expecting us so now's the best time to catch them."

"Why you Des?" Ann Foster queried Des that night during dinner at the Pelican Hotel. She'd dressed up, turning every head when entering the formal dining room. Female diners longingly took in her immaculate attire. Their mens' eyes roved her figure. Des had difficulty containing his mirth. Tongues were sure to wag in the community later that evening. She cradled her wineglass in both hands and sipped from it.

"Were you supposed to soften me up? Was that the plan? You didn't have to invite me to dinner. Your boss had told me that I was on my own."

"Nothing like that Ann. Don't flatter yourself."

Within an hour of meeting her they'd resorted to Christian names and he'd read the signs well; there was a spark between them.

"'Flatter' myself? You're a rude man."

"Suit yourself. I really don't take your bait. The only reason I asked you out for dinner is because I like you. Simple as that. I have No other agenda."

"You're supposed to explain yourself," she said and tossed her mop of auburn hair while assessing him with her wide green eyes. She didn't wait for him to top up her glass with Constantia red, and did so herself. And his.

"You look very nice."

"My God!" she exclaimed and sat back to stare at him. "Here I am talking to a grizzled miner and he's ignoring my questions! Come on Des! I love the flirting, but level with me please. What's your game?"

"Why?" he answered and sat back nonchalantly. "You came. You saw. Come again if you want. Any time. Bring your pals. There's no angle. We think we got it right here. You have to make up your own mind on that issue. If and when you do, we'd like to hear about it first. There's always room for improvement in any organization."

"You're an infuriating man," she said, but with little conviction. "Any men I meet are usually 'in your face' from the moment they open their big mouths. They can't stand the fact that women do have some grey matter. Men usually only have one thing in mind and its not gauging female intelligence."

"Your words not mine?" Des breathed. He was taken with the way her ivory temples throbbed but thought the better of telling her as much. Her sinuous hands too were works of art, especially when cradling a glass of wine. "I can understand that view."

"Oh? What do you mean, 'understand'?"

He took a deep breath and looked long and hard at her without blinking.

"Have you lost your tongue?"

"You really want to know?" he whispered. "You won't do a Walter and start screaming the place down?"

"Yes," she admitted. "I made a bad impression on him. Tell me. It promises to be a novel experience for me."

"Okay, mock me all you want. For openers, you upset important people."

"Me?" she retorted and rolled her eyes. "Whatever gave you that idea?"

"Yes, you. You seek confrontation and get a lot of international press in the process. The word is that big men in business pee their pants at the mere mention of your name never mind the sight of you."

"Is that so?" she replied coquettishly. "Wow! If that was '*for openers*', what's next then maestro?"

Again he looked at her, taking in her unblinking stare and compressed mouth which looked as if it been set like granite. He took in her exquisite silver peacock broach, her only concession to jewelery, but tastefully set against her black silk blouse.

"You're a very attractive woman Ann. With brains to die for. That unsettles many men. They fall in to two groups. Group one comprises old codgers who are well past their "sell by" date, one-hair lotharios who still fancy women young enough to be their granddaughters. Put yourself in their position. They verge on brain-dead and an attractive young woman peppers them, *publicly*, with embarrassing accusations. Few match you in open debate; they're eviscerated; being made a fool of in front of an audience that invariably turns hostile. They end up changing their laundry and seeing their therapists after crossing you."

"How prosaic. And pathetic. What about group two? I can't wait to hear this."

"Yes, let me see now, group two—here we have the younger desk jockey, corporate creepers who take for granted that every woman is theirs for the taking. In your case they want to make a pass at you but back off for fear of a royal verbal lashing; what do they do? They stand back to admire you from afar, or, chicken out by making excuses for their cowardice. *Your* fault. *You* pushed them away. *You* said that...*you* did this...We both know that it's not your fault. *The chairman's daughter*. That's held against you. Net result?"

"I can't believe I'm hearing this," she gasped through pursed lips. "Go on Doctor Des. Let it all hang out."

"If you insist. You rebel against corporate robots and their companies because it's a fair bet that such men have strange agendas that suit them first and stakeholders last. Believe it or not, I don't blame you for standing up and shouting the odds. Someone's got to do it. You do it very well but it costs you dearly emotionally. You're losing out on close relationships."

Her eyes shone. Was he mistaken? Did he see makings of tears? Her silence got to him.

"I'm sorry if I upset you. You did ask me. I answered you truthfully."

"You did," she said and patted his hand. "I wish that I could say otherwise."

Next morning Bruno rang Des. "I didn't get any feedback. How did it go with Ann Foster?"

"Ann? Fine. She dug deep wherever we went. She seemed happy enough. She's talking to the mayor and a few of his pals today."

"Is there any risk of something stupid appearing in the newspapers?"

"I don't think so Bruno. There's nothing on the mine or about it that she criticized, leastways in my hearing. Believe it or not I think she's a very nice person. Nothing like I expected. I'm sure Walter would agree this time round."

"That's good," Bruno aid. "She's on the Piper to Kimberley this afternoon and then on to Cape Town to catch the London jumbo."

"I know. I'm driving her to the airstrip."

At his Friday managers meeting after Ann Foster's visit, Bruno raised his coffee cup to Des. *"Ann Foster...I received a fax from her this morning."*

Cecil pricked up his ears. "Oh yes. What did she complain about this time? Not employing enough blind one-armed Afghan mountain guides who play ice hockey? We must have got it wrong somewhere for her to justify her jolly here."

"You are too hard on her," Bruno laughed. "Just remember we did not pay for her, so it was no picnic. She's not complaining. She was impressed with our environmental work and said that radiation screening is top class. She complimented you Des, on being so thorough and willing to please. Well done man."

"Thanks Bruno. She's no dragon, believe me."

Cecil had a quiet smirk to himself while taking in Des's ultra-cool feedback, restraining himself from commenting. *"Willing to please?" I do believe you mate!*

Harry did not have to wait long for testing times. The weekend after his impromptu fishing orgy he was rostered as duty manager for the week, putting him on call after hours and having to be on site Saturday and Sunday.

The "up" side was that it gave him a chance to catch up on his professional reading. Just after midday on Sunday the fire station hooter began to wail.

Harry froze. A serious accident. Seconds later his 'phone rang.

"Acid plant! Man dead!" a voice shouted hysterically.

Harry jumped up, raced to his car and gunned it to the acid plant in three minutes flat.

Too late, he saw a stretcher on which lay a body covered by a blanket. Grim-faced paramedics lifted the stretcher to carry it to a waiting ambulance.

"This looks bad. What happened?" he asked the shift foreman.

"He's a contractor artisan," the stricken man gasped. "He was repairing a weld on acid tank number seven. He was up a ladder and loosened a plate above eye level. The acid gushed all over him. It ate him alive!"

"What is his name?"

"Alan Jones."

Only then was Harry aware of an acrid smell and spotted a piece of burnt flesh lying on a drain grill. "Is the tank sealed off?"

"Yes sir."

"No danger from it or any others?"

"Yes. I mean *no* sir," the shocked foreman answered. His eyes were glazed and his body began to shake.

Harry sat him down on a railing and summoned a security sergeant. "This man needs to go to hospital. He's in shock. I'm going back to my office. I must put the GM in the picture. Bring everyone who was in the vicinity to my office in half an hour and don't forget to tell the shift engineer I need him there as well. We have to make out an accident report and then I'm to contact the mines inspector to fill him in. Got it?"

"Terrible!" Bruno cursed after Harry had 'phoned him. "Alan Jones of all people. He was a damn good artisan. I can't believe it! An experienced man."

"I take it there'll be a post-mortem Bruno?"

"There will be. I'll tell the police to go out and take statements and cover all angles. What time will you finish your accident investigation and report?"

"Walter's coming out," Harry replied. "He'll handle the accident investigation. I'll handle the report. I'd say by seven tonight we'll reach that point. Cecil wants details too before contacting Jones's next of kin."

"Okay. I'll 'phone his boss in Windhoek. Also..."

"Yes Bruno?"

"Change the board to *zero hours without an accident*. That's three years bladdy hard labor out the window. Up go our insurance premiums. David must be turning in his grave."

An unfortunate discovery was that Alan Jones had been drinking. He'd smuggled a bottle of Commando brandy past the security gate and had guzzled at it throughout the day, not expecting to be called on for any serious repair work.

Victor Grey roasted his entire staff. "You should have spotted it!" he shouted at a row of sullen officials. "A man's dead because you lazy dimwits didn't do your flipping job! Proud are you? I'll have you all doing first-aid and fire drill training till it comes out your ears. You all need to pull your bloody fingers out!"

The police examiner concurred. "Unfortunate accident" and signed his own inspection certificate a copy of which he handed to Harry.

"An awful way to die," the surly official informed Harry. "You blokes are slipping. What's all the publicity about your fancy *safe* mine?"

Harry lost his appetite along with his convivial personality. All he looked forward to was the comfort of chatting to Doreen. Her stabilizing influence, he freely admitted, had become his core, his standard of behavior, thinking and reaction.

"Harry, you were not to blame," she commiserated. "How could you look over the shoulders of a thousand people?"

"I know. I know. But Doreen it's a wake-up call. A man's dead whichever way we dress it up. *Dead*. We got it wrong. Things went so smoothly that we eased up on site. We're not as hungry for excellence as we were. That policeman got it right '...*you blokes are slipping*' he told me. We have to rejuvenate the fire in our bellies that David and Frank strove for. It's the only way."

"It's hard for Bruno following in David and Frank's footsteps. He's riding a wave of success. All you men did that. You got the mine up and running. What more is there for you to fix? Time to ease off Harry. Now you want what?—a tidal wave of excellence? It has to stop sometime. Unfortunate as that accident was, by tomorrow another dozen people will have had fatal accidents on the roads. It happens at the best of times."

"I feel it Doreen. God knows I feel it. A man was killed when I was duty manager. How can I ever forget it?"

"You can't. Learn to live with it."

Try as he might to banish gory images of burnt human flesh from his mind, Harry could not. Depression reared up to the extent that Doreen began to worry about her husband. He had shed twelve kilograms and had taken on a grey pallor. She was thankful that her children were not present to witness their father withering before their eyes. When telephoning them each night at Cape Town university, they picked up concern in her voice. "What's wrong Mom?" they asked, forcing her to resort white lies.

Harry took to driving to the mine at late hours, often working twenty-four hours without a break. He refuted claims that he was "over-compensating" and redoubled his efforts. His expectation that all three hundred people under him had to do likewise caused problems, problems that their wives queued up to complain about to Doreen.

Then came a body blow. One of Harry's section heads was killed in a motor accident—a man for whom he'd had high hopes for, a man with a loving wife and four young sons. It hadn't happened at the mine so mercifully Bruno did not have the soul-searing duty of informing Gerard Dresser of yet another fatality involving a mine employee.

Harry's dark moods worsened, turning him into a social zombie. Morose moods overtook his normally vibrant conversation until his very presence gave way to perpetual silence. Doreen's attempts to get him to talk proved fruitless. In desperation she 'phoned Bruno to confide to him her increasing worries about her dejected husband.

"I know Doreen," a sympathetic Bruno uttered, "we are all concerned about him. I told him to take some leave. I know what long hours he's been putting in. He won't go. I tell you what—he's earned a business trip a thousand times over. I'll find a seminar in America to send him to and you can go with him. I want him to slow down for his own good. He needs to get away for a while to rest up."

Days later Harry collapsed at work.

"It's not a stroke," a grim-faced Doctor Hannah informed Doreen after his examination. "He had a transient ischemic attack. A *TIA*. That's a precursor to a stroke. If he wants to avoid stroking out he's had his warning. Next time..."

"Thank Heaven!"

"But his blood pressure is sky high and that's not a good sign. He has to take beta-blockers to control what we call *'essential hypertension'*. He'll be on them for the rest of his life. He has to follow a strict diet. The fact is Harry's near killed himself working at three times the pace of a normal person. He'll need at least two months off work to rest up and then we'll check him again. This time he has no choice in the matter."

26

"All of a sudden Des is taking a few weeks leave," Cecil let slip to his wife while downing his early morning tea and toast. "Just like that. Two day's notice."

At six on a mist-less morning the sun had broken through and a light wind was deciding whether to wax or wane. Marlene was still in her dressing gown, sipping from her mug of coffee as they sat absorbing the sight of an ultra-blue sea showing tips of white horses breaking.

"Why don't you follow his example?" Marlene retorted. "Nothing wrong with that is there? While we're on the subject I need to go to Johannesburg."

"When?"

"It depends on what flights are available. I'll stay with Monica. You don't mind do you Cecil? You can go to bed with your 'In' tray like you always do."

Mere mention of her younger 'with it'" sister Monica immediately soured Cecil. He detested her over the top liberalism and the feeling was mutual. Marlene staying with Monica made sure that Cecil kept his distance.

"Her? I might have known. Let me see," he mocked putting on his schoolmaster's voice and stroked his chin, "who does cow-face work for now? Oh, I know! That fried chicken franchise...what's its name? You know—the one that sells only left wings and arse holes."

She ignored him. At his disparaging best Cecil excelled. Prising him away from the mine? About as possible as swimming to the moon. Small compensation was to drag him off for a few days to places like a hot springs resort that only local residents knew about, or the big red dunes further south that bordered a verdant game reserve; anything potentially longer than a few days away from work led to Cecil's stock reply "...too much on my plate..." In short, she was fed up to the brim with his preoccupation of corporate addiction.

"Or are you going to wait till you crack up like Harry? It's a miracle we still have him."

He ignored her. "Any sort of leave never entered Des's head before," he mused. "He hates his own guys sloping off for a few days. Now he's doing it and is pleased as punch I might tell you. He's up to something. I know it. Sly dog that man is."

Marlene decided to stir the juices of marital assertion. "He's probably looking for another job. Going for an interview is he? It isn't exactly Monte Carlo here, stuck being stuck in the desert. For a single man, it must be a terrible place to live seeing that there are so few eligible females and a thousand panting men are chasing after them. Des must have made a few bob. I don't blame him if he wants to enjoy himself for a change. He's probably decided not to work himself to death like you and Harry. Good for Des."

"Another job?" a derisory Cecil answered. "No fear of that...not a chance. Not our Des. No one pays the kind of package he gets here. He won't say where he's going. Don hasn't got a booking on the Piper to take him to Kimberley."

"Big deal. How long is he going away for?"

"Six weeks. From tomorrow."

Six weeks! Marlene stowed that gem of information to later cajole or shame her husband into doing something similar.

"Why flog it to death? He earned it. He's human you know. Anyhow it's got nothing to do you with Cecil. You're prying...that's a small town disease. Stop it."

He laughed and put his cup down. "You're right *Marl*...it's his business after all. He's taking us for a drink after work at the club so I'll be a little late home my joyous one."

"A little late?" Strange words for someone reeling in at midnight wined out of his mind, usually propped up by a sheepish-looking Don South.

"Why am I not surprised?" she spat back at him and left him to gobble his toast down. Minutes later she heard garage doors fly up and his *Beemer* engine roar into life, then she went back she went to her bed.

Des had never driven to Cape Town before. Nine hundred kilometers of national highway to most drivers constituted a dreadful bore, all the more reason to "put foot" to leave drab surroundings behind them. Not Des. He bowled along in sunlight at his leisure taking in arid countryside. He relished being off the leash...no production demands, no pressures to beat plan—master of his own time for a glorious six weeks.

Had he flown to Kimberley someone was bound to have grilled him about where he was heading. Within minutes it would have slipped into the town's gossip mill. *Cape Town! I wonder why?* He pictured one or two denizens scratching their heads, particularly Cecil whom he took perverse pleasure in baiting. Bruno hadn't exactly fished for details but had insisted on a contact telephone number. Des had already approached his brother in Durban to cover for him on that front.

Desert gave way to scrubland that in turn after eight hours yielded to golden wheat farming terrain of the Western Cape Atlantic seaboard. The main language was Afrikaans spoken with the quaint Cape drawl that storytellers mimicked. Any comparison with stark desert surroundings he was used to working in was like night and day. The Cape Peninsula scenically had no peer and visiting it after a four-year absence excited him.

At the pristine white Dutch-gabled guesthouse he glided into a parking space under an aged plane tree that had already begun to shed autumn leaves. He found no one in attendance at reception but he spotted a large white envelope lying on the counter addressed to him. He stretched for it, opened it and found a welcome letter from the manageress and his room key.

A bowl of fruit, cheese platter, biscuits and bottle of Chardonnay and two wine glasses awaited him in his suite. French doors to the veranda were open to reveal a vista of silky blue sea and the whitest beach he'd ever seen. A salty breeze compounded his "glad to be alive" senses. His euphoria was interrupted by a soft chime and he went to open the door.

"Hi Des! I saw your car outside. I'm glad you arrived safely."

Attired in jeans and cotton blouse she looked stupendous. She smiled broadly and removed her sunglasses.

"You were right Des. What a wonderful place! I never knew that *Melklbos Strand* existed until you mentioned it to me."

He reached out to embrace her. She needed no second bidding and flew into his arms.

"I've missed you!" he whispered hoarsely and held her close. "You're all I think about Marlene..."

Bruno's replacement as engineering manager hadn't worked out, nor had his successor's successor. On engineering matters Bruno was a hard man to impress.

Bruno had taken it for granted that incumbents had to maintain or improve on standards that he'd set. In return, he was eternally disappointed on that score and said so. Spending more time overseeing his former division than he wanted to irked him. But, he reasoned, as his other managers and their deputies were so strong, normally, it wouldn't have given him grey hair while he waited for Cecil to track down someone suitable to fill the gap.

Harry's resistance to virtually being boarded for two months on the one hand irritated him, but on the other, Bruno was thankful, for Harry was a huge crutch to lean on. Utilizing his abilities to appraise problems through unique eyes was a godsend. Ill as he was, Harry resisted attending any seminar just to get him away from the mine and *Thuringia Bay*.

"When I'm up to it Bruno I'll take my wife on a holiday overseas. I don't want to waste company money. I think conventions are swans at company expense. I won't let my own blokes attend them so I'll look bad if I don't practise what I preach."

As for Des wanting leave? Bruno could hardly begrudge him a good rest. Des had spent five years molly-coddling the mine; the man was plainly exhausted.

"He has to rest up Bruno," Doctor Hannah advised. "He's young, but looking at being heart attack material unless he puts in at least six weeks of *Gyppo PT* immediately."

Bruno felt like a spot of leave too when Des returned. He had over six months due to him so recharging his batteries seemed eminently sensible. He looked forward to informing Cecil that he was going to ask him stand in for him as general manager. He deserved it.

At dinner with the Gerber's Mariette came out with it point blank. "Why does Marlene spend so much time away from here?" she asked Cecil.

"She needs to see her younger sister every now and again to put that crazy woman on the straight and narrow."

Mariette persisted. "When does she get back this time?"

"Two or three weeks time. Otherwise there's no point spending all that money on airfares is there? Besides," he grinned, "I like a bit of time to myself so I'm not complaining."

Their time together swept by in a flash. Both of them loved their early morning jog on the pristine strand, as did several hundred other health-conscious athletes of all shapes and sizes. She was far fitter than him, a product of playing squash every day of her life and took pleasure in sprinting the last hundred meters back to their guest house to wait for him to pant in, chest heaving.

Across the bay, Table Mountain stood sentinel over a most magnificent sight, occasionally bedecked by its famous tablecloth of protective clouds. After a long lazy shower the couple sought out a different venue to enjoy breakfast together.

Four days shot by, four heaven-soaked days as far as Des was concerned and in Marlene's case, 'four days of sheer bliss'.

During coffee time at their last breakfast together Des broke silence. "It's gone in a flash," he breathed. "Marlene, what are we going to do?" he whispered while refilling her cup.

Marlene had prepared herself for his question. His sense of timing was perfect; they were seated beneath an oak tree in the courtyard of an aged hotel that had seen better days.

"About what Des?"

"You know very well Marlene. You. Me. Our lives together."

"Enjoy life," she answered unhesitatingly. "Enjoy every shred of love, affection and experience that comes our way and wring the neck out of it! Tomorrow we could be dead."

"My thoughts exactly. Marry me," he said and stretched to cup her hand with his. "Marry me. I love you. The question is Marlene, do you love me? I think you do. I'll tell Cecil that you're mine. That's it."

She took her time answering him.

"Well?"

"I asked myself that question. You gave me faith in myself again Des."

"Come on Marlene. No riddles please. Answer me.'"

"I love to be in your company," she sighed. "I don't love you. I don't really know what 'love' is. It's no recipe for marriage. I'm sorry Des."

His face fell but he held on to her hand. "I worship you Marlene. What more can I say?"

"I know," she whispered, "I know."

That evening she was gone. He'd taken her to the airport and watched her walk out across the apron to board an airbus bound for Johannesburg.

He whistled while driving on to his next stop in Hermanus. Who would not have? Sixty miles of the most spectacular coastline and wineries in the world sated his eyes.

At his hotel a pretty young receptionist effusively greeted him. "Your partner arrived this morning Mr Irwin. She said to tell you that she's roasting herself poolside until lunchtime."

"Wonderful! Des laughed. "Which way to the pool?"

She stood out like a red rose in full bloom amid a bunch of straggly weeds. Heads turned to take in the wondrous sight of a fair-haired young woman with a body like Venus, the only difference being that Venus had never sported a skimpy polka-dot tanga with such panache. When she saw him she rose languidly and turned to face him.

"You made it!" he gushed and embraced her. "That's great!"

"This morning Des. How did your seminar go?"

"Oh that!" he coughed. "What a bore. Just the thought of seeing you kept me sane."

"I'm flattered," she murmured and kissed him again. "I'm starved. Shall we go and change for lunch?"

"Good idea," he smiled and put her arm in his. "A very late lunch. Did anyone ever tell you what a fantastic vision you are Ann Foster?"

At the first Friday managers' meeting after Des returned Bruno lost no time informing his managers that he and Mariette were taking a Greek Island holiday.

"It's my turn to goof off for a few weeks hey," Bruno gloated. "I might even get in a bit of fishing!"

"How long are you going for?" a plainly pained Walter enquired. "This leave business is becoming an epidemic—everybody dashing off and deserting me."

"Three weeks. I want Cecil to act for me while I'm away."

"Me?" an animated Cecil all but shouted. "Did I hear right?"

"Yes. Is it a problem for you?"

"No...I didn't...well...it's a surprise. Wait till...Thanks very much. I must 'phone..."

"Marlene? She'll be pleased. But you'll need her to stay in town Cecil. Both of you will have a heavy social calendar to see to."

"I'm sure she'll love it Bruno. My wife is such a gregarious person."

"Congratulations Cecil," Des said and shook Cecil's hand. "We'll break you in don't you worry."

"Yes," Walter spoke up, "that's fine with me. Cecil knows this mine backwards."

Cecil walked on air back to his office. He couldn't wait to tell Marlene his news and hastily dialed home.

Engaged.

Minutes later he tried again.

Engaged.

Des had beaten Cecil to 'phoning Marlene the news. "You're flying in eagle circles Marlene," Des said. "You won't want to be bothered by the likes of me."

"Oh stuff and nonsense Des. We can still see each other. I'll invite you to dinner with the other managers and wives, just like Bruno and Mariette do. We'll still have a bit of fun won't we?"

"That sounds nice Marlene, but let's be careful. I don't want to risk getting on the wrong side of your big *bwana*," Des joked.

27

"To avoid tongues wagging," Hilton informed curious board members, "I considered it best for us to meet unofficially outside of the country. The press is too well informed about our domestic movements."

What he intended saying was going to unsettle a few of the grey-hairs who had coasted along, happy with Chater Group's profits to which they had contributed the square root of zero. For those attendees their accountabilities were going to rocket so they were bound to back off preferring an easier route of touting for knighthoods or lounging at their clubs writing obituaries for fellow peers in anticipation of their celestial departures. Correctly, he'd surmised that no one would complain at being ordered to spend a few days in Paris. Lodged at the prestigious St. James Club in the shadow of the *Arc de Triomf* hardly constituted a penance—more so since the chairman was funding the entire cost of their "holiday" out of his own pocket.

"Why the secrets Chairman?" a suspicious Anthony Scobar enquired when Hilton asked him to close the conference room doors. As financial director he got straight to the point, just like his boss.

"Gentlemen," Hilton barked. "Planning is not our strongpoint. It is cosmetic within the Chater group. Reactive stuff…I want *seismic* not cosmetic. This is mid 1988 gentlemen. 'Global economy' is staring us in the face. Our minds should not continue to operate like tariff barriers. Survival in our corporate world will require a great deal more forethought than we are practicing. along with an ability to shape financial rearrangements, yes even currency speculations for our benefit before someone else does it for us and we become its victims. This board has to compile a five to twenty year strategy that is not based on simply extrapolating past results. More pressure is resulting in more legislation to make directors more accountable to the investing public. We have to position ourselves in our chosen marketplaces well ahead of time. We're in iron ore…we're fine with that item. Our Japanese clientele are locked in for thirty years. Gold? It cycles but we're winning there. Silver? Too static for my liking. I won't list everything. We're generally fine with all our products except one."

"Which one?" a voice enquired.

"Uranium oxide. It's becoming far too topical and is not meeting the energy supply proportions that Chater's earlier strategies promised."

"Who's the culprit?" another voice rang out.

"This group has majority shareholdings in six uranium mines. We know that our Australian interest goes to the wall next year because unions won't see sense, so that operation closes down whether they like it or not. We have time to asset strip and get our money back. Our Canadian trio sport high grades and they're doing well so they're prime candidates to offload at premium prices. Our fifth mine languishes in Russia. It's making money but the Ruskies won't pay us in dollars. Barter business is not our game. That goes."

"That leaves our mine in South Africa," Scobar butted in. "We can't complain about that one surely? Low grade or not it's making damn good returns chairman."

Hilton stared hard at his finance man. "That is why we're here gentlemen. To toss our collective interests and skills into a hat, mix them with gut-feel assumptions to allow us to have another good look at ourselves well ahead of actual events. If we can market an illusion of a mine making eternally good profits, all the more reason to flog it at a premium. What we don't want is to rubber stamp strategic plans that line management submits to us, the latter usually resulting from a weekend foray at some exotic location at company expense. We're the damn directors of this company! It's our job to do the strategic planning. Operators do what we tell them. Otherwise gentlemen, shareholders don't need a board do they?"

"Would you give us a lead Chairman," an embarrassed Scobar prompted. "The kind of events you foresee that might have bearing?"

"Yes. This is what I'm tossing in. We have to relocate our head office offshore—to Luxembourg. That move streamlines tax issues."

"Good lord!" Edward Fuller the non-executive vice-chairman exclaimed, "our prime minister will do her nut! It's like moving the crown jewels to Moscow. I'll bet it will be the first time she swears in the House when she hears the news!"

"Secondly," Hilton continued, "I see huge changes coming among the Ruskies. Politics and nuclear power don't mix while super-nations are at loggerheads. Legislation, sanctions, more safety provisions and so on are going to explode exponentially. That costs gentlemen. It costs big. Then we have squads of madmen running about shouting more and more about nuclear Armageddon? Not a nice thought is it? We don't want to spend most of our time in congressional-type face-downs do we now?"

No one around the table took exception to Hilton's words.

"South Africa? Only a fool would say that there are not big changes looming there—uranium is a highly susceptible and sensitive product in a third world country. Armies of red tape specialists take over. Aside from the usual corruption, misappropria-tion of nuclear material makes bad headlines."

"Political change is overdue in South Africa right enough chairman," Edward Fuller said. "We all accept that. Is there another reason you want to be shot of it?"

"Yes. The threat of nationalization. It happened to the Zambian copper mines during the sixties despite prior claims to the contrary by politicians. You agree that's in a mess and likely to stay so? 'Variable Royalty' has since made its appearance thanks to US advisors running amok in developing countries, intended to collectively strip cash flow from the mines. The trend is to peg the mines to agreed rates of return. That penalizes productivity. It constitutes socialist claptrap at its worst."

"I'm beginning to see daylight right enough," a doubtful Fuller answered.

"Enough scare stories," Hilton interrupted. "The question is what products can we chase and make a go of with minimum fuss? Yielding no less than an annual twenty per cent after tax for at least twenty years?"

"Oil?" Scobar ventured. "I can't think of anything with that kind of margin."

"True, true...there are few fields in Alaska and Asia up for grabs. We can do a deal by exchanging proven mineral lease areas in different parts of the world for oil fields, should we want to get into that game. After uranium mines, oil outfits are next in polecat stakes. A big *but* is that there is one huge industry about to form under our noses, one that promises Croesus-like profits. Any suggestions as to what that might be? Think twenty-first century gentlemen. Think big. Think about your wildest dreams."

Faces stared at each other. Puzzled.

"Come gentlemen come, we're the friggin' directors," an irritated Hilton cajoled his moribund audience. "Kick-start your grey matter! We're supposed to be leading this group into the future. Let's have it no matter how ridiculous it might sound."

Silence.

"Well," Hilton sighed while assuming his characteristic pose leaning on the table with outstretched palms, "let me tell you. Plain and simple. *Communications.*"

"I must be thick," one head-shaking director confessed. "What exactly do you mean Chairman? *'Communications'.*"

"Think hard gentlemen about how computers revolutionized the workplace. Computers will shoebox in size and be a million times more powerful than the most powerful mainframes in existence. Why do you think I've spent so much time in the East? I'll tell you. Ten per cent time for sales. Ninety per cent time listening to new ideas and keeping my eyes open. The guts of computers are electronic. In California and Taiwan the race is on, to develop a microchip as the heart of a computer, so displacing electronics. An item no bigger than your thumbnail gentlemen, massively powerful, fast machines processing more data and more importantly, powering improved stellar 'phone systems. To do that one has to have new-phase software and satellites. We can get into those businesses. Instead of mining for metals we can mine the universal **mind** and transport information instantly. That's *communication!* Not to mention remaking newspaper and entertainment industries. If we get in first, we'll make money for shareholders that a thousand gold mines could not dream of and with a lot less hassle."

"Am I right chairman? You're saying we should plan on *moving away* from being a prime mining house?" Scobar enquired. "Dropping our core business?"

An exasperated "Whew!" escaped Hilton Walsh's lips. "At last! Got it in one Tony. That's precisely what I'm saying. We quietly diminish mine shareholdings without anyone in the market pointing fingers. We sell off mines at a profit while other companies lust after them, accumulate a cash mountain and buy into the future. We transform Chater Metals into *XYZ Enterprises* with global partnerships where politics don't dilute our efforts and profits. Chater Group PLC can become a restructured shelf company, in turn owned by XYZ Luxembourg; that way we lessen our tax bill. Reshaping. There's time to plan for it before our opposition begin asking the same questions of themselves and consider diversifying."

"I don't know…tens of thousands of employees who work for this group are not going to take kindly to such developments," Edward Fuller announced. "Buy-outs imply people casualties. As well as political after-burn. I haven't even mentioned what unions will say."

"It's a tough world out there right enough Edward," Hilton replied. "Let me say this, if we depart from here tomorrow night without an outline future strategy, I'll go it alone. Opportunity is staring us in the face. Seminal moments this size rarely happen. Let's not be standing behind the barn door. If Chater Metal PLC doesn't pro-act, it is headed for the scrap heap. Look what happened to the aero industry in England and its motor manufacturers. Kaput! I'm not going to be part of an outfit that drives carthorses when supersonic aircraft are creasing skies and men are flying to the moon."

"Now I know why we're in France to hear this," a colleague commented to Edward. "I'm in shock! I wouldn't dare having a heart attack here after what I just heard from *Captain Marvellous!*"

Anthony Scobar stood up, removed his coat and draped it over the back of his chair. "It seems we have job to do," he informed his fellow directors. "I want to be part of this future. We can shape it."

A reluctant Joey had let him into Bruno's office when he told her it concerned an important matter.

"A pal I worked with years ago in Botswana 'phoned me last night," a preoccupied Harry informed Bruno. "He's a vice-president with a Canadian outfit."

"What about?" Bruno replied and turned away from his computer. "Good news? Is he offering you a job man?"

A scowl embedded on Harry's face gave Bruno his answer. "No

Bruno. If what he says is true it's not good news. I hope I don't relapse if it is true. Six months back in the job and struck down with fright."

"Sounds grim. What did he tell you?"

"He says that The City in London is rife with rumours about Chater Metals doing plastic surgery on itself. For starters Bruno, it's getting rid of its mines. Including uranium mines."

"No man! Including us?"

"I'm afraid so. That's real news as you can imagine. One of the companies involved is his, so he dropped me a wink."

"You're not bladdy joking are you?"

"No Bruno. I don't joke about matters so serious. What do you know about it? My contact is rock solid."

"It's news to me too man," an upset Bruno replied. "I know nothing. But I'll sure as hell find out what's going on."

"You're the only one I've told about this Bruno. If it's true you can imagine our employees' reactions. They should hear about it from us first. I don't have a good feeling about it."

"Neither do I man. Leave it with me." Bruno said and waited for Harry to leave the office. Minutes later Bruno stretched for his scrambler telephone and dialed a London number.

"Scobar here," an urbane voice silked out.

"The news is out Mr Scobar."

"Good show. Keep me informed will you Gerber?"

Harry popped his head in to Bruno's office the following day. Wednesday. "Anything in from head office Bruno?"

"No. I tried again and got the same message. The chairman's always out swanning somewhere."

"Bruno, to give Frank his due, he was under no illusions about Hilton Walsh. The man does what's best for shareholders. If he sold us off it must be for good reason. For Chater to dump us after we rebuilt this mine and got it into profits, doesn't make sense to us, but it might to him. The risk is we'll lose top people and then history repeats itself. We're pawns Bruno—that's the truth of it. I've had too much experience of boards to think otherwise."

"You're right man. I'll let it ride until Friday. Then we put the managers in the picture. I don't understand why the chairman is playing hard to get. It's not like him."

Just before lunchtime a letter from his travel agency fetched up on his desk. Harry hastily opened it and read it. He sat back, glowing. At last. Their Californian holiday he and Doreen had dreamed of was about to become reality two weeks down the line. Just then his 'phone rang.

"I have something to show you," a plainly annoyed Victor Grey announced. "Can I come up to your office?"

"Of course."

Ten minutes later Victor strode in clutching an inter-office envelope.

"What's up Vic?"

"This!' he roared. "It's in this morning's *Financial Times*. I thought you'd want it before the managers' meeting this afternoon. It's bloody dynamite!"

It had to be serious if normally phlegmatic Victor was so enraged. Harry soon saw why and lost no time putting Bruno in the picture.

One by one the managers trooped into Bruno's conference room aware that something serious was on the go. Des was the last to arrive and closed the door at Bruno's request.

"I made copies of this newspaper report. It was printed in the *Financial Times* this morning," Bruno said. "It's not the best news. I have not heard anything from head office on the subject."

"Andrew Keinander wrote this!" a visibly upset Walter Clark uttered minutes later. "Whenever his name appears in print he's bad news."

"Chater's sold us?" Des fumed. "Bloody sold us? Just like that? And we knew nothing about it beforehand?"

"I'm only he general manager here…why would anyone want to keep us informed?"

A despondent Bruno was a rare sight. "I took it for granted that our chairman would have informed us about moves of that magnitude. It's only good manners."

"*Gawd...*" Cecil muttered. "This is terrible news. We must get an urgent brief out to our workforce."

"And tell them what?" Des scoffed. "Hey you lot! Learn to sing the Canadian anthem! What possible assurances could we give them without us looking like prize fools? They'll never trust us again."

"Not much," Bruno broke in. "Just tell them what we know and that when more details are available we'll pass them on."

"I was hoping that when I came here Bruno I'd left this kind of double-dealing behind me. Again, I got it wrong. My faith in mining companies is now non-existent," Walter blurted out. "The sods! Shiny-arsed seat pirates are at it again!"

"Lovely...just as I was about to go on holiday," Harry moaned. "I suppose I have to cancel it."

"It might be wise Harry," Bruno said. "Sorry man. It's a bad blow for us all."

"I want to go on record," Des said coldly. "I think our non-esteemed chairman is a first-class cowpat!"

"He had me fooled," Bruno admitted. "I was in seventh heaven when he gave me this job. Now this! I just don't understand the man."

"Hear, hear," Cecil said sarcastically. "With only two weeks to Christmas...what jolly tidings we bring upon those who work here! I hope they don't overspend, because sure as eggs a lot of us are going to lose our jobs. Canadian cutthroats will come in here slashing. That's their style."

"It mightn't turn out that way," Harry said. "*Astarte Enterprises* is a rejuvenated finance house. I don't think we should over-react until we know the full picture."

"You seem well informed," Des butted in. "How come you know so much about this...this, *Astarte*?"

"An old colleague of mine works for it," Harry said, hoping Des would not pursue the subject.

"Oh yes, what does he do?"

"He's its financial controller. As announcements have been made I think I'll 'phone him. I'd like to know who is on its board. It might give us a hint of what's in store for us."

"You know what I find strange about all this?" a restrained Walter cut in. "Why does some other company buy us without knowing what they're buying? I mean no one I know of came here to size us up. Would you buy a car sight unseen? Or a house? No. It doesn't make sense to me."

"We can sit here and bitch all day," Cecil interrupted. "It doesn't matter what message we give out but *when* is important. A change of such scale results in good people having another think about staying on at the mine. They could argue its owners think so little of them that they were not counseled. I say we owe it to our employees to try and keep spirits up. That's why we're managers isn't it? Let's not give them ammunition so that they think we're in on the scheming."

Bruno nodded. "Cecil will you prepare that brief please and get it out before the end of the day shift?"

"I'll get on it."

"I need to put Gerard Dresser in the picture. If he doesn't know already," Bruno continued, "and prepare for the local press. They'll be wanting comment too."

"So," Des commented to a downcast Cecil on his way out, "those developments will certainly go down in the anals of South African mining history. Canadians taking over? How convenient—we sort this place out and they romp in and lord it over us. Where's the justice in that?"

"'*Justice?*' Des. Ask that slimy Hilton Walsh."

Predictably South African financial journals featured *The Thuringia's* sale in their pages. Harry accepted that the articles were written by headline seekers—except for one of their number. Damian Gattic of *The Weekend Herald* who made sense.

> *A Canadian finance house buys the Chater Metals uranium mine in South Africa—why? We await developments with interest.*

Truculent as always, Victor Grey nodded sagely when Harry confirmed to his superintendents that as yet no one from the London office had contacted Bruno to put him in the picture.

"I might have known," Vic said.

"What do you mean Vic?"

"I'd lay odds that when the chairman's daughter beat a path out here it wasn't for the reasons that we understood at the time."

"Ann Foster? You yourself know what she's about. She didn't find anything to carp about. Leastways not anything that I know of. Remember, we do keep a close eye on her."

"Don't you find that strange? Forgive me but I've had years at it so I can afford to be cynical. The only one who could have come here with that agenda was Ann Foster. Look at the facts. She had a detailed tour of the mine with Des Irwin panting in her wake. He even took her out to dinner. She had a good look at the figures let me tell you. Burt will confirm that."

"True," an alarmed Burt Burnett said while lighting a cigarette. "She knows her way round an income statement and a balance sheet. I wouldn't mind employing her myself."

231

"I chatted to the mayor about her," Vic went on. "She asked him no questions about her precious environmental issues but also did a lot of fact finding about the mine. This whole scene smells like a burning whore house."

Ann Foster. The thought had not entered Harry's mindset. "It sounds credible Vic when you put it like that. No one knows for sure what's going on. The chairman has to say something to us eventually."

After his department heads had left Harry rang Des Irwin.

"He's down in the open pit Mr McCrae," his secretary said. "Can I take a message?"

"Please. Ask him to ring me, or better still, to come and see me. If he prefers I'll drive down to his office to talk to him."

"Ann!" Des exploded. "Never! Not from what I saw and heard!"

"It didn't come from me Des. When you think about it, it's possible she was scouting the scene. Anyhow you spent the most time with her so you're in a better position to judge things." Harry noticed doubt flicker across Des's face.

"When she left here she did say something about wanting to come back at sometime in the future," Des muttered. "I'm beginning to wonder what she meant. I'd better see Bruno about this seeing that you've put doubts in my mind."

"Things change fast at your precious mine," Marlene goaded her workaholic husband during dinner. "Fancy that! When you least expect it, guess what? A takeover! Canadians taking over! Do you think they'll put in an ice hockey rink?"

"Very funny Marlene. Turning the knife already are you? Ta very much."

"Just making a point Cecil. Your sodding mine is living up to expectations. It became an obsession with you. Do you think your new masters will care what you achieved here? I lost out on time spent with you Cecil. Years of it. I became a mine widow. Why do you think Pam took off? Where did it get you if I might ask? You're about to get kicked out."

He stared at her disconsolately and put down his utensils. "You have a point much as I hate to admit it. I indulged myself and took you for granted. I overdid it. I apologize. All I can say is that it will never happen again."

She softened. "What are you going to do?"

"What any sensible person would do. My oath, from now on, I'm out the door at four-thirty and straight home. No more bringing stuff home. No more weekends shooting out to the mine. An odd game of mid-week golf won't go amiss either. Won't that be a luxury? I'll wait it out and see what happens. Perhaps I'll get a big pay-off? Who knows? It's out of my hands."

"At last!" she smiled. "At last you saw the light Cecil. Enjoy yourself for a change."

"I will Marlene, make no mistake. I'm ready for that holiday once we know what the hell is going on. Harry had to cancel his and he badly needs a break the poor man."

"That's a pity. Doreen must be disappointed."

"Among others. Who would believe that after what we did for Walsh that he'd turn around and kick us in the privates?"

"I would Cecil. You show me a mining company run by angels and I'll show you the Queen Mary sailing through the desert."

Cecil guffawed. "My oath," he gasped, "I've never seen this side of you before! I'm impressed!"

"Divisional managers are meeting at the club for the whole day on Thursday. Superintendents are required to join them on Friday morning first thing," Joey Schneider informed the managers' secretaries. "No excuses Mr Gerber says."

"What's it about?" she was asked. "You can tell me."

"The chairman will be arriving here next Monday. I expect it's to agree tactics in good time."

"How nice of Hilton Walsh," a sardonic Burt Burnett commented to Victor Grey, "to drop in and deign to talk to us at last. At our expense no doubt."

"Yes, but a bit late what? Stuff him!" Vic spat back.

"What do you think our managers are up to? Harry was mad as a snake but he's cooled down. Cecil's all smiles. The buggars are even playing golf after work now! You want to see Walter Clark swing a club? What a hoot!"

"How would you know?"

"I'm playing as well," Burt laughed. "Very nice too! Everyone's stampeding out the gate at four-thirty. And why not? It's about time that we looked after number one."

"They're up to something all right," Vic mused. "Harry's not one to be caught on the hop. He's been spending lots of time with Bruno. I get the impression some sort of war council is on the go. We'll get a good idea on Friday about what our managers think won't we?"

"Wasting precious Saturday recreation time on that goof-head from London" had spoilt Don's entire weekend. Rising at five-thirty, preparing the Piper and then flying to Kimberley to collect his unwelcome passengers soured him no end. Larry Foyer felt no different and suggested to Don that they fly back through bumpy air pockets to "to make them honk their guts up!" Worse was that later in the day that they had to fly their passengers back to Kimberley to board their connection to Cape Town.

Surly managers and their superintendents lined the entrance for a last minute smoke and chat while watching Don South deliver Hilton Walsh and his two sidekicks to the club, the only venue with a room big enough to seat up to fifty people.

"I did specify that we wanted only managers present," a plainly dismayed Hilton hissed at Bruno. "You got it wrong."

Bruno had no intention of allowing his chairman the safe ground. "I don't think so chairman. Our superintendents are the backbone of this mine. We are all interested in what you have to say."

Bruno's response was so strident that Hilton Walsh blinked in surprise and timidly followed Bruno to the conference room.

Once visitors had helped themselves to the top table and had played at drinking coffee, Hilton stood up. "Are we all present?"

"Yes," Bruno brusquely answered and nodded to Des Irwin to shut the doors.

"Good morning everybody," Hilton said. "Thank you for attending."

A few mutters passed for a communal reply and baleful faces fixed Hilton in their sights.

"There have been one or two corporate rearrangements recently that affect group mines," Hilton opened with. "This is why we are here to explain matters to you. Our shareholders received offers for all Chater Group's uranium mines. This suited the directors' future strategy. As mature managers our board felt that you would understand about the takeover of this mine. We could hardly have publicised the offer process because that will have jeopardized the sale of all the mining properties concerned."

"May I ask how?" Bruno responded, purposely omitting "Chairman" from his address.

"The risk of adverse publicity. Such aspects badly affect share price. Shareholders on both sides have to be happy for a deal to go through. Publicity is only in order after the event don't you see?" It came out so glibly Hilton cursed himself at the sight of rows of dismayed and disbelieving faces staring back at him.

"And labor unrest?"

"Yes. That too is a risk," Hilton Walsh ploughed on, his sensors on alert. No person before him exhibited servility, a state of mind that he had banked on to accept his "kiss-off" arrangements with minimum fuss.

"May I ask a question?" Cecil said and stood up. "Why did you want to sell all the uranium mines. Do you know something that we do not? Is the market for U3o8 collapsing for example? There's a lot of anti-nuclear publicity on the go after all." He found it hard not to add, *"Ask your daughter."*

"A substantial capital gain gave us cash infusion for deployment elsewhere so that we can improve on our return on capital invested. The Chater Group is diversifying to prepare for the next century."

Des stared back disbelievingly, muttering, *"Gobbledegook."*

"What a load of bollocks!" Cecil murmured. "Board room brain-deads blowing smoke."

Hilton took a haughty look at his audience and rocked back on his heels, satisfied that he'd got his message across. "I want to introduce Mr William Odger your new president as from March next year and Mr Dawson Davis, *Astarte Enterprises* chief financial officer both based in Montreal."

Odger's amply protruding stomach exhibited stark evidence of a practised restaurant trawler at company expense, as did bleary pale blue eyes befitting a man in his somnolent seventies. Dawson Davis had taken over the financial role from Harry's friend who apparently been dismissed with two weeks notice with no reason given. A bespectacled Davis's crew-cut hairstyle appeared odd for a man in mid forties anointed by a permanent triumphal sneer that accentuated his cadaver-like visage.

"What about the managing director of *Astarte Enterprises*? Aren't we going to meet her? Officially that is? *Miss Ann Foster?* Your daughter."

Bruno's question ensured that Hilton Walsh's mouth froze agape until he spluttered, "Well, you know, these things...what I mean is...perhaps we should..."

"Sorry," Bruno interceded, "we did not quite catch what you said?

We wondered whether there was a conflict of interest involved here."

"It is only a temporary measure," Hilton replied making an effort to assert himself. *You lost the high ground* an inner voice pounded. *How much do they know?*

"Oh that!" Odger drawled, "nothing to worry about let me say."

"Ditto," an alarmed Dawson Davis uttered while furiously scribbling notes to avoid catching anyone's eye.

"You must realize that in any transaction of this size new owners reserve the right to put in their own people. For those employees affected on site there will be severance packages."

The atmosphere descended into one of raw malice. Rows of disgusted faces stared back at him.

"What did you have in mind," Cecil enquired. "What kind of severance packages?"

That no one was bothering to address him as "Chairman" clearly annoyed Hilton Walsh.

"We'll attend to that later shall we?" he replied disdainfully.

"No. None of us think that's acceptable. All this secrecy. We believe we deserved better treatment from you. We prefer to have the details now." Cecil had made sure that his tone was not going to sound conciliatory no matter who Hilton Walsh though he was.

"Hey," Odger shouted, "let's not get hysterical buddy. We will *allow* them to receive accumulated leave pay and take their pensions out as cash. You know, employee contributions—after tax that is. And a week's pay for every year of service. Not bad huh!"

Bruno stood up. "We are not interested. Goodbye."

"But, I already explained..."an aghast Hilton stammered.

"We resign," Bruno coldly announced. "With immediate effect."

Bruno headed for the exit followed by his men.

"You can't do that!' Hilton Walsh shouted. "You can't just walk out! We need that production! Come back here! How dare you, you, you, you friggin' *scum!*"

Des was the last to leave. His tape recorder was switched on and he waved it at Walsh.

"Thank you for that thought," he smiled. "So that's what you think of us. *Chairman*."

"We've got them by the balls," an exhilarated Bruno burst out while gleefully rubbing his hands together. "And do you know what? I love it! Chairman or no chairman, Walsh is knee-deep in manure!"

Everyone assembled in the club bar and watched an irate Hilton Walsh and cohorts troop past towards the car park.

"Don will be pleased," a risible Cecil said. "He'll be back in for his game of golf this afternoon."

"We did our homework," Bruno said. "Thanks guys for your coaching. I never thought I could ever face down someone like Walsh."

"They thought they had us cold Bruno," Harry laughed. "Well done. I was proud of you standing up to that trio! The rotters got a huge fright."

Managers and superintendents broke a golden rule, *no liquor during working hours.*

"I'm paying for this lot," a sheepish Des said. "'That bitch fooled me. How did you find out about her Harry?"

"Vic Grey put me on to it. There's nothing that gets past that man. My contact in Canada telexed me with interesting stuff. I suppose that when you lose your job you'll want to warn an old friend about to be kicked out too. Walsh is buying this mine for himself. Then guess what? He's brokering it through his tame finance house, *Astarte*, in Canada to sell on at a premium price as and when it suits him. Guess who keeps the profit? Tax-free profit at that. He stuck his daughter in as MD at *Astarte* to oversee his interests. All that nonsense we heard about the two of them at each other's throats? Utter nonsense. The Press will kill for that information. Those three goons know that we're better informed than they ever dreamed of.

They know we can do them one hell of a lot of damage. In fact we just did. Isn't that one for the books now!"

"Yes, but we must use it to our advantage first," Bruno chirped. "Thanks to you Harry we own our own houses so we can sit tight while they sort out their damage control."

"I agree with you. Let Walsh sweat. He has to come back to us pretty smartly and then we can give him both barrels."

"I must say," Walter opined and signaled for another drink, "I'm impressed! I could have done with having you blokes around in my last job. I'd love to have given my directors corporate trots on a massive scale. What a pleasure to be attacking an ivory tower for a change. Are you going to tell the newspapers what's happening Bruno?"

"No not yet. That's what we all agreed if you recall. We will if and when we have to."

"Hopefully," Cecil cut in, "that old fella Odger has stroked out by now. As for *ditto four-eyes*, he'll be swallowing valiums by the dozen. They took us all for a bunch of desert dolts. What a pity Don can't eject them from the Piper at ten thousand feet."

"'*Friggin' scum*,' Walsh called us Bruno. That's what he thinks of us. Make him crawl. As for that Ann Foster, she really took me in."

"I believe you Des," Cecil smirked. "They're both good at that. Come on everyone. Lunch at my place. Our ladies are expecting us."

Amazed onlookers' jaws dropped at the sight of the entire mine brass driving through town to Cecil's house. *On a weekday? Friday?* Thankfully the weather had held tight allowing Marlene, together with other managers' wives, to prepare and lay out trestle tables and chairs in her garden.

"Man, just watching everyone enjoying themselves you'd think that we'd struck gold," Bruno laughed, "not just bladdy fired ourselves. If we don't see this thing through we're well and truly shafted in the mining business."

"You did see it through Bruno," Doreen told him. "You men stood up against a big mining house. I'd wish that I'd been there to see it. I bet it's the first time Hilton Walsh lost his way."

"He looked like he'd been electrocuted," Walter said. "That must have been a first for old steel-eater Hilton, being on the receiving end of his own medicine for a change."

"You have a way with words Walt," Harry laughed. "Yes, we were expendable when old Hilton decided as much. It's happened to me more times than I care to remember. *Sort it out, get it going* and *hey presto*, the 'boys' from head office take over at twice what you were paid. Typical. One thing for sure mining is not a sincere business to be in."

"No man, not this time Harry," Bruno said. "The old guy will have backed out. Walsh must be looking pretty stupid. He knows that he needs us more than ever."

"When do you think *phase two* starts Bruno?" Cecil enquired.

"What's phase two?" a quizzical Judy asked. "Wally? Explain!"

"Ah Judy my love, phase two is our masterstroke. If you like us now my love, after *phase two* you ladies will be kissing our feet. I promise you that!"

"Other way round buster!" Marlene chirped. "Chauvinist!"

"I'm lost," Judy confessed. "You're all speaking in codes."

"You didn't answer my question Bruno," Cecil said.

"It will go like we planned. Walsh has to 'phone me. I hope he's got sedatives with him. I took a few before the meeting. Man were my knees knocking!"

"We still don't budge an inch?"

"Definitely not," Harry replied. "Walsh either accepts our terms or we say bye-bye. He knows he can't let that happen."

"Walsh got it wrong," Bruno guffawed. "Tough on him hey!"

"Gerber? What the hell are you playing at?" an irate Hilton Walsh shouted.

Bruno heard jet noises and departure announcements in the background—*Cape Town Airport*. Ten minutes past five in the afternoon. The BA jumbo to London was only due to depart at nine. Walsh was giving himself bargaining time.

Don had reported back to Bruno on the furious row in the Piper. "The old guy screwed *goof-head* that's for sure. They were both screaming their nuts off."

Bruno put the 'phone down. "He's mad as a snake," he informed Marie"

"I bet he is! The old coot!"

The 'phone rang again.

"Don't put it down!" Hilton shouted

"What are you playing at Gerber?"

"Playing at what?" Bruno responded, making a superhuman attempt to hide concern in his voice. "What do you mean?"

"I'll have you in court, you, you…*bastard*."

Bruno put the 'phone down.

"Now he's really mad! Man, but these Aussies like to swear."

"I do to! Tell him to get lost!"

Minutes later the 'phone chirped again.

"Let it ring Mariette," Bruno said. "He can sweat for a while."

An hour later Bruno answered the 'phone.

"Gerber! What are you doing? Are you mad? I'll…"

Bruno put the 'phone down. "He's still screaming Mariette. The ex-big boss has no manners. Can I get you a drink?"

"Yes. Make it a big gin and tonic. Bruno, this is bad. I don't know what this *'phase two'* business of yours is all about, but you can never work for that man again. One of you will have to go after all this warfare."

"You're right my sweet. It's not going to be me or anyone else from this mine. We have him cornered."

"Will it get into the newspapers?"

"It might. If it does he's the big loser. Chater will get a panning. He knows that we control him. Not the other way round."

Bruno answered the 'phone.

"All right Gerber," a suffused Hilton Walsh panted, "enough of your games. What do you want?"

"*Mr* Gerber if you please. I take it that we remain part of the Chater Metals Group *Mr* Walsh?"

"You just bloody saw to that didn't you?"

"Just as well for your sake. We were aware of your real intentions."

Ten seconds of silence reigned before Hilton answered. "You're bluffing," he hissed. "What real intentions?"

"Try us, and find out. We all look forward to it."

"I repeat. What are you after?" The irate Australian magnate insisted. "What's your bloody game?"

Bruno inhaled deeply and crossed his fingers. "For starters, we want your resignation from the board."

"Did I hear right? What! I can't just resign, just like that!" the stricken man cried. "The City..., the banks will...no I won't do it."

Bruno put the 'phone down.

"He is still fighting is he?" Mariette enquired. "He must be thick."

"Now we wait," Bruno grinned. "He has to be a worried man. I'll get my papers ready. The next time he rings I will answer. Then he will hear what we want—in detail."

Eight thirty. The 'phone rang again.

"Have it your way. I'll go if you promise to keep away from the press," Hilton Walsh muttered when Bruno picked up. "Is that it?"

"No. Our managers and superintendents will not resume work unless we agree a ten-year management contract to run this mine. With guarantees for obvious reasons."

Even Mariette heard the thunderous gasp. "You can't be serious!"

"We are. We will work to the ten-year plan that we have already submitted to London office. Pension monies including company contributions are to be transferred to a fund of our choice and leave pay accumulation paid out in full. Tax-free. Another condition will insist on is no interference from London headquarters. That's the deal."

"And cruises on the Queen Mary while we're about it, and tickets to the boat race? What about the ballet too? You're off your conk mate. I can't sell that to my board. They'll toss it out."

"That's our final word. We will wait until Monday next at two o'clock in the afternoon for a written confirmation of our conditions signed by your board. You have the majority shareholding so there will be no excuses. I fly to London with Mr Lonsdale tomorrow. We will personally call at your office on Monday to collect it."

"How dare you order me about like a friggin' office boy! I'm your bloody chairman and don't you friggin' forget it! Your proposal is ludicrous I keep telling you. It can't happen!"

"We don't agree," Bruno said flatly. "Not when you tell your board *why* it isn't."

"No. My answer is friggin' *no*!"

"I repeat. We will call at your office on Monday. By then we will have nothing to lose. We will have plenty of time to visit the newspapers editors and television stations."

Commissionaires ushered Bruno and Cecil to the chairman's office.

Only his secretary was present. "The chairman said to give you this Mr Gerber," she grimly informed the duo. "He's gone home sick."

"Thank you Ma'am," Bruno responded smiled and shook her hand. "May I open it here if you don't mind?"

"Oh please, go ahead," she said, happy that at last someone within the corporate maelstrom that she worked in had paid her some old-world courtesy. "Meanwhile I'll get you both some tea," she said and made for the door. "And biscuits."

"It's a signed board meeting minute of a management contract offer," Bruno breathed when scanning the document and passed it to Cecil. "It covers everything that we asked for. He's directed us to lawyers waiting to notarize matters."

Cecil heaved a sigh of relief. "It's a bit of an anti-climax isn't it Bruno? I was enjoying the adrenalin rush. I looked forward to a shouting match where we at least could have punched Hilton's lights out. So no more are we *friggin' scum*? You mean he's backed off totally? Did he resign from the board?"

"He says so. It has to be in the press before long."

"Make sure we cover that Bruno, when we see the lawyers. I don't think Walsh will just creep into the woodwork to lie low. He's not that much of a loser. He will want to peg us out to dry that's for sure."

29

"Do you think Bruno and Cecil will pull it off?" Des mused. "If they do, they're going to rattle the mining world, turning the tables like that on old Walsh."

She'd made him a simple meal of scrambled eggs on toast late that evening and both of them sat in the kitchen smoking their Paul Revere's and enjoying their coffee.

"I do," Marlene replied. "Walsh was greedy. He got so big for his boots that he thought no one could or would have the nerve to challenge him. In his place I'd be going through some introspection. I'll bet he won't like the conclusions he arrives at. Cecil said that he'd 'phone me tomorrow to tell me what the score is."

"It's grim outside Marlene," Des said and peered outside at the dense fog settled on the town. "I'll have one last cup of coffee before I push off. I'm driving out to the mine. My chaps are blasting out a new bit of ground in the pit at midnight. I want to be there to see it."

"I thought you chaps had stopped work?"

'No. That was pure bluff. Imagine what people in town said when they saw us all trooping here on a Friday? Our section heads carried the day running things for three days after Walsh's departure. It

245

genuinely looked as if we senior guys had walked out. What do you call it in Bridge?"

"A finesse," she smiled and kissed him. "It's been fun Des. New ball game now so we have to break off."

"I know Marlene. I know. I'd better be on my way."

He gulped down the rest of his coffee and walked out and disappeared into the mist.

Rixon and Mason soon saw to notarizing the contract of acceptance and by early Tuesday evening had placed the complete document in Bruno's hands.

"Mr Anthony Scobar requested the pleasure of your company gentlemen, for dinner at the RAC Club tonight," their lawyer advised. "At nine if that suits you."

"Scobar?" Cecil probed. "Why would he do that? We can't be top of the pops in his eyes."

"He's the one who fast-tracked your document through all its board signatories. We know that he is a very powerful man in The City."

"We accept," Bruno replied. "We have no quarrel with him, whatever he thinks of us."

"Good. I'll inform him. Pleasure doing business with you gentlemen," Eric Rixon QC beamed.

"Hold on sir. We must settle your bill."

"No need Mr Gerber. No need. Mr Scobar took care of it."

Their host had left word with the frock-coated doorman who welcomed them and ushered them to the bar where Anthony Scobar was nursing a glass of red wine and scanning a racing journal.

"I'm glad you could join me," he smiled and beckoned his steward.

Cecil took in Scobar's body language. Perfectly poised. Immaculate appearance. In command. The man behaved as if he owned the place and judging from instant fawning attention he received, he would have been forgiven for thinking as much. Cecil had not taken to Anthony Scobar when meeting him at the mine. Condescension and veneer had oozed from the man...*yet another one who thinks he walks on water.*

Cecil opened dialogue on a neutral note. Pretending to be awestruck by the opulence surrounding him he declared as much. "Compared to this our little old desert club back home is a hovel."

"We do tend to take the facilities for granted right enough," Scobar replied. He was clearly happy that his visitors were impressed by his choice of venue. It made matters much easier for his game plan if visitors went away happy that they had been entertained by Chater's top brass *after* Hilton Walsh had got his unexpected comeuppance. "State matters are discussed here before they get to the Commons and the Lords. Wars formulated...it reeks of history. It's not as impersonal as an hotel. And much cheaper. The food's superb too!"

To Cecil, Scobar came across as a Walsh clone. He spoke like Walsh and was as direct as Walsh. His mannerisms too shouted *trained by Walsh*. If ever he ever ran a case study for aspirant young managers in the future he had masses of material as to how not to behave at corporate levels. Bruno by comparison, had stated that he endorsed Scobar's incisive approach.

Cecil waited for Bruno to take the initiative once they'd sat down and made menu choices. Bruno seemed intent on digesting his surroundings and sat mute, miles away in thought.

"Very nice Mr Scobar," Cecil reflected. "We were wondering what to do on our last night here. Might I ask you, to what do we owe this most welcome pleasure?" I *might as well join them* Cecil thought. *Fawn a little and break the ice.*

Scobar took his time answering, unblinkingly surveying his guests. "Surprised as I am about our recent turn of events I have to say that I owe Hilton Walsh a great deal despite the situation we find ourselves in. And the situation he is in."

"I'm sure he got his money's worth," a wary Bruno cut in, now suddenly in on the talk.

"I hope so. He was a great leader in my opinion."

"'*Was*'?" Cecil arched an eyebrow.

"Yes. He had The City at his beck and call and then he shot himself in the foot. The money boys never forget something like that."

"So, you know why he's really going?" Bruno probed.

"I do of course. It seems you weren't caught lagging in this entire opera. If it leaks out to The City, Chater will go belly-up. No financial institution would touch it. Hilton's official resignation as chairman and board member will be in the press tomorrow. If it becomes known that he unloaded his shares in one fell swoop it's a terrible signal to investors."

Bruno looked up, surprised. Scobar had gumption after all.

"What is it that you want from us?"

"Nothing. Walsh messed up, but he is a big loss to the company. That man's brain is so active he's a walking money-spinner. He will surface elsewhere in his own good time, catch the bourses by storm again and make another billion dollars."

"I'm sure he will," Cecil agreed. "Not that I'll lose any sleep over him. His name is non-existent where we come from."

"I believe you. You may or may not know," Scobar continued, "that the fact your mine exists is primarily due to Hilton Walsh. He's the one who rooted out questionable dealings among the previous board and recommended a second go for your mine. He may have queered himself since, but the fact is that you're here, with a management contract, because originally Hilton Walsh took a big chance keeping your mine open."

"With respect, we know that," Cecil said. "David Bradshaw and his team turned it round as a result. Is there a point you're about to make Mr Scobar?" He was glad that he saw surprise registered on Scobar's features at so direct a question.

"All I ask of you gentlemen, that for the good of Chater Metals PLC and your mine, we let matters rest. You have your own arrangement to set up. Our directors have to regroup to reappraise matters. Our board has to re-enervate an unsettled worldwide workforce and retain goodwill in The City. It therefore behoves us all not to create bad publicity."

"Now that we have our contract we did not intend taking matters further. By the way, who's standing in for Walsh until the next annual general meeting?"

Anthony Scobar raised his wine glass. "Would you believe Mr Gerber?" he chuckled. "Me."

Household staff at Hilton's Hampshire Victorian country home was aquiver. In the past Hilton dropped in by helicopter unannounced for a few days at a time and then disappeared back to London. When learning that he intended permanent residence, nervousness set in. All this on top of Ann Foster who had also waltzed in on the scene—master and daughter living in comprised a daunting duo to wait on.

Hilton kept to his study refusing all telephone calls. All that pressmen got was photographing trade traffic to and fro the main gates, but they persisted, swarming daily outside the entrance to

Glebe Manse vainly hoping for a shot of the big business guru who had gone to ground.

He was his own fierce critic. *I should have seen it coming he cursed. No wonder Scobar put up a solid show when I wanted to drop the mines. He was after my Chater chairmanship. 'Piece of cake. Leave it to me Hilton—you want quick cash to buy that newspaper group. I'll organize an outside loan into Astarte Enterprises. Astarte pays Chater out and you repay Astarte when you sell our South African U3o8 mine. Why not put Ann in as MD at Astarte? Her support signals to buyers and investors that environmental matters are kosher—big bonus that Hilton! After all, chairmen are supposed to think ahead are they not?'*

"The slimy devil!" Hilton shouted. "The low-down, low-life germ! He lined me up like a duck in a shooting gallery. The conniving bastard!"

"My, my. Such language daddy! Who's a bastard?" Ann enquired when she knocked and entered to see him. "Your favorite word these days it seems."

"Scobar! That devious rat! He set me up good and proper!"

"Daddy dear," Ann chided her father, "you are mixing your metaphors again. He learned from the master didn't he? Well, well, he outflanked you. That takes some doing. Good old *Brylcreemed* Ant must be preening himself."

"I'll nail him," Hilton glowered. "I'll nail him so hard he'll think crucifixion is a pleasure outing. And those desert dingoes in South Africa! Can you imagine? Dictating to me! Hilton Walsh! Someone must have put them up to it. Scobar...the bastard—it could only have been him...what a friggin' mess!"

She sat down in front of him and coolly lit a cigarette. "You are an old fusspot," she sighed. "So someone turned the tables on you. So what? You've been doing that to others all your life. Isn't it time to regroup? I'm sure your fertile brain will turn to other avenues of making money."

"Yeah, but I wasn't a crook! I was smart. Who would point fingers at me for that?"

"Oh come on daddy, admit it. You overdid it. This 'No crook' fable of yours is hogwash and you know it. You're a ruthless businessman. To survive in this cutthroat world you have to be a crook or as close to it as making no difference."

"God almighty Ann! What a cynic you are. Saying that about your own father!"

She puffed out a trail of blue smoke and lounged back in her chair. "I'm a chip off the old block daddy dearest. You keep reminding me of our mutual genes. Have you ever wondered why you have no friends? Entertainment here is only by command performance. Not that I'm doing too well myself. Who can you talk to? No one. You terrify people. Is it worth it? Why not take off somewhere and enjoy yourself? Become a *nobody* I say. A nobody with money. Keep out of the news. You'll soon learn to enjoy it. That's what I call *living*."

Her words hit him hard. In her mind she'd already consigned him to "nobody" status.

"A '*nobody*'? Listen to yourself Ann. Me a '*nobody*'? You of all people saying that to me? Oh yes, a lot of people would like me out the circuit, especially that pompous bunch in The City. Chinless bloody wonders all. Slinking away with my tail between my legs? Never! Not in a thousand years—never!"

Prior to boarding the Jumbo for the long flight home Bruno and Cecil bought a stack of British newspapers.

Barely five minutes after take-off the two men exchanged knowing glances.

"Hilton says he pulled out because the other party pulled out. What a joke!" Cecil heaved. "That man lies through his teeth."

"Look at this headline," Bruno smiled, and held up the headline he was reading.

Walsh? Welch? What's The Difference?

"Man, this guy is on a hiding to nothing," Bruno sneered. "Serve him bladdy right!"

"He's hurting. We'll have to watch our backs."

"I don't envy Scobar," Bruno confessed. "Chater Metals has got the spotlight on it."

"Walsh is one mean cookie," Cecil said. "He trained Scobar. I don't feel sorry for people like them."

"What do you think Hilton will do?"

The two men sat back while the captain made his announcements. Being aboard a South African Airways jumbo jet was home territory, inviting them to drop their guard.

With a glass of port in hand Cecil was totally relaxed. "What would I do if I was in the ex-esteemed Hilton's shoes?" he mused. "Mere mention of a certain uranium mine would infuriate me; it would be a permanent reminder of an outfit that brought me down. I'd pray for another fire there so I could say *'Couldn't have chosen a better mine!'* But that's not going to happen, not with the kind of safety precautions we've installed. What else would my evil mind turn to? I'd bank on something unexpected Bruno, like buying Chater Metals out in total? The big picture."

"Never!" Bruno scoffed. "That takes really big money man. He'd never have enough."

"What then?" Cecil continued. "I'd have a go in via the political route using my connections. You know, sanctions and all that goes with it. Red tape...bad publicity. More disasters. That would frighten shareholders and get so much rolling adverse press, Chater Metals directors will sprint for cover."

"Why?"

"Sales would plummet for one thing—then bang goes our ten year plan. That's how he could screw us."

"You forget," Bruno grinned, "if the press find out what really went on at *Astarte,* he's history. No man, he's the big *fool.* Hilton's blown it. We did our homework on him."

"That's what's probably what's driving him mad," Cecil said. "The fact that we have an inside track on him."

"And Scobar? His general factotum taking over the boss's job? How very convenient for *Ant?*"

"Yes, very convenient for good old Anthony as it turned out," Cecil chuckled. "He gloated when telling us that he'd taken over Walsh's mantle. Men like Scobar don't take prisoners."

Bruno sighed heavily, lay back and closed his eyes. "What a bladdy business!" he yawned. "I hope dinner is served chop chop. I'm going to sleep it off after a few glasses of good brandy."

Bruno woke early. Refreshed smiling cabin staff had begun to serve wake-up glasses of orange juice. Bleary-eyed, he watched the welcome African eastern sky gradually light up, racing through its rainbow of colors to reveal grey, but welcome, South Atlantic Ocean beneath the aircraft.

Arrival formalities in Cape Town were quickly dispensed with. Harry had instructed Don South to pick up the two men to fly them back to site.

"This ten-year plan becomes our master," Bruno informed his team three hours later. "Our new CEO and chairman is a finance guy. Scobar's bright but he's ruthless. If we don't deliver he'll go ape."

"So Hilton Walsh is really out the window?" a seemingly delighted Des piped in. "I'm not surprised."

"He is," Cecil answered. "He's totally out of Chater Metals. The new guy made sure of that."

"The good news," Bruno brightened, "is that if we beat plan

annually any savings we make are ours. But Chater Metals continues to handle final product sales."

"What about our pensions and leave pay?"

"Chater Metals will pay us out Harry. That lump sum must be finalized by you."

"So Bruno," Walter Clark smiled, "we're in total control? Other than sales, no more London whiz kids with egg stains on their ties slithering around here?"

"True. We're on our own."

Rather than get stuck behind or between mine busses Harry allowed them half an hour start before drove home. Combined with forty minutes morning driving time, he put it all to use mulling about mine matters. Occasionally Bruno or a manager asked him for a lift home, an opportunity to use each other as sounding boards seeing that their time on site was usually spoken for.

Bruno's news, a new chapter in the mine's life, was sufficient incentive to have 'phoned ahead to tell Doreen not to make dinner.

"Put on your glad rags Doreen. We'll go out tonight," Harry promised her. "To *The Pelican*."

He'd invited Bruno and Mariette but untypically Bruno demurred. "Too much paper work," he replied. "I put three baskets of stuff in my car boot."

Doreen needed no second bidding. No person in their right mind slopped it at the formal hostelry. Flaxen-haired German owners who sported starched collars and immaculately charcoal colored suits saw to that. For Harry, donning jacket, collar and tie constituted torture but, "What the hell," he muttered, "We survived! That's worth celebrating."

"Hello you two!" a joyful Cecil greeted them when they entered the dining room. "Join us please!"

"Great minds think alike," Marlene laughed. "Are we all basking in the good news?"

Cecil was already well past his first glass of late harvest wine. Unbidden, the wine steward sidled over with a second bottle and opened it in before a nodding Cecil.

"Try this nectar from the gods Doreen. You'll love it."

Harry read the label. *French*...ten times the cost of its best South African counterpart.

An obsequious maitr took the quartet's orders after being put through the mill by Cecil who had insisted on hearing about the "Chef's specials".

"*Mein Herr*, tell me this '*sweetmeat*' starter?" Cecil enquired and winked at Harry.

"Herr Lonsdale," the earnest young man explained while clutching the menu to his chest, "it is from the lamb. We fry it and then we..."

"Yes but what is it?" Cecil butted in. "What part of the animal does it come from?"

The embarrassed maitre leaned down and whispered into Cecil's ear.

Cecil grinned broadly. "Listen everyone Anyone for fried sheep's bollocks? Yum Yum."

Harry laughed so hard that Doreen elbowed him in his ribs. "Behave yourself!" she hissed. "You too Cecil!"

"All male species," a haughty Marlene drawled, "have a boobs and bum obsession, but now the vogue is sheeps' balls. What next?"

Both men were so creased with laughter that their ladies did a premature Ladies' Room retreat.

"It worked out well for us all didn't it?" Marlene said later as she toyed with her food. For her, eating was a chore. She'd long since disciplined herself to consuming as little as possible. "Health fanatic" her friends had labeled her, not that she minded. She felt good and she knew that she looked like a million dollars.

Doreen detected different beats. Cecil was over-animated and Harry…introspective. Marlene? She was her usual effervescent, superbly groomed self. "So it seems Marlene."

"I'm hoping Cecil will think about taking us on a nice long holiday. My skinflint must have run out of excuses by now not to think about it."

"No fear," Cecil joked in mid gulp. "That costs serious money."

"But you're all rolling in it Cecil. Go on Harry, support me! Get your miser friend to pull out his wallet so we can see the moths fly out."

"She's right Cecil," Harry said and nudged his friend who pretended to be in a state of mock horror. "She's the brains in your family. Did you forget that?"

"Getting money out of old Cecil?' Cecil smirked. "You can't get money out of a Lonsdale! Better men have tried. I finally yield to she who must be obeyed. Yes. Time for a trip. Where shall we go? To sample the heady delights of Kimberley? Looking down the big hole what?"

"Oh you!" Marlene laughed and dug her husband in the ribs. "Spain it is and you know it buster!"

Pelican Hotel staff eschewed hurried service and each plate of food bore chef's final inspection prior to being served. Working through three courses took three hours, during which time the foursome found plenty to talk about.

By the time herb tea for Marlene had arrived and coffee for everyone else, Cecil was beating Doreen's ears with snippets of his eventful trip to London with Bruno.

Marlene patted Harry's hand. "Why so quiet old friend?" she whispered.

"Oh, no reason Marlene. So much has happened so fast, I'm still catching my breath. I must say that I feel more settled now that we know we won't be kicked out. Cecil and Bruno brought home the bacon."

"That's life Harry. Twists and turns when we least expect it. What a bore it would be if we always knew what was in store for us."

"You're right. I admire the way you sail through it Marlene. Cecil is a lucky man to have you by his side."

"He has his moments too," she said. "As we've all just seen. When he's in the mood, Cecil's great company. I couldn't stand being married to someone with no SOH."

"'SOH'?"

"You know…Sense of humor."

"He missed his vocation. He has a gift for spontaneous humor. I read somewhere that behind a comic face is a character of tragedy. If that's true Cecil must have paid in spades."

"You don't know do you?" Marlene whispered. "Cecil was abandoned at birth. He was brought up in foster homes all over England. So you're right. He defines tragedy." She sat back and swept over him with her huge brown eyes. "Are you still looking for that special something Harry? I remember what you told me on the beach. You seemed so distracted then. What would make you happy?"

He thought long and hard before answering. "Long term. Marlene, I really don't know. Doesn't that sound silly? I'm supposed to be a professional, able to plan my life with certainty and I can't. Our ancestors did us no favors by coming out here looking to make a new life for themselves. They kidded each other that they were giving their children better opportunities. What a laugh that is as it turns out."

"Future's dim is it?"

"Africa's sell-by date in Western terms has arrived, to answer your question. Long term, I suppose that I'm waiting for something to happen to our disadvantage but I don't know quite when and what it is."

"And short term?"

"That can only concern our mine and our lives here in *Thuringia Bay*. We're celebrating good news right now but I keep thinking about Hilton Walsh. None of us read him correctly when we met him. What else and who else are we misreading I ask myself?"

"Well," she sniffed and brushed her knee against his, "who cares? I don't! Live for the day! Come on, we should all take a walk down at the mole—mist and moon allowing."

"Agreed. I enjoyed our evening. Don't ever change Marlene," Harry smiled. "You're an original."

"What's happening?" Harry asked Bruno at their morning meeting. "Since we got our management contract we're spending big money that's got blow-all to do with production."

"What big money man?" a highly irritated Bruno replied. "What are you saying?"

"Here's a list Bruno. In the six months since we went it alone we sent eight people to overseas conferences. Cost? One hundred and thirty thousand rands. We have to ask what does that do for production? Every man and his dog on site is ordering fancy office equipment. Secretaries are competing to see who gets the nicest office and can you believe it, ordering flowers for their desks! Some superintendents bought paintings for their offices and reclaimed via expense accounts. This is the clincher Bruno," a suffused Harry barked, "an order placed by a mine official for a television and a hi-fi system for his office! And a pair of hand-made heavy duty boots! I stopped it and chewed Des's ears off. Expense claims have gone over the top. We're making restaurant owners in town millionaires. We've spent over a million rands on fripperies. It's a bad trend. Frank would have gone bananas if he saw this happening!"

"Yes," Bruno said when reading the list, "but I'm not Frank. I don't interfere with how managers run their divisions. If they come in under plan I don't get involved. On that subject I'm want a new auditorium built so that we can show visitors a film about our mine. I'm looking for half a million to build it."

"You can't be serious," a shocked Harry replied. "That's a complete waste of money! We'll become a laughing stock. Bruno, we're miners, not MGM Film Company! We have to stem this outflow. One can leave it too late and then what? Who bales us out? Also, is it fair on those areas of the mine that take their operating plans seriously?"

"Hey man! Since when are you bladdy General Manager?" Bruno snapped. His hostile expression shouted rejection of what Harry had to say. "I'll make the decisions here!"

"Bruno. Listen to yourself," Harry replied and shook his head. "What's happening to us? We can't talk any more. The managers behave like hallucinated robots when meeting with you. Everyone's jockeying for position and polishing their marble trying to impress you. What's happened to brainstorming and exchanging ideas without fear or favor?"

"Oh, I see," Bruno snarled, "you think I'm mucking it up."

"Bruno, it's my job to make sure that we don't have financial exposure. I have to tell you about alarming trends."

"*Ugh* man, you're just bladdy jealous!"

Harry sat aghast. *What's happened to him?* "Bruno, we're all marching backwards afraid someone is going to get kudos at the expense of another. I hate to say it but you brought a defensive management style to this mine, the very thing David fought hard to reject and remove. The system appears to be, 'Cover your arse with Bruno'."

"Yes yes. So that's what you think. Anything else?"

Harry stood up to take his leave but turned to face Bruno. "I don't like what's going on and I want you to know it. I came here in a climate of transparency and I'm not going to change now. Not for you or anyone who ignores what's bad for this mine. You've put yourself before the mine. If that continues employee morale is going to sink to new depths. It's not right."

Pushed to an emotional precipice by Harry's unexpected verbal broadside, a white-faced Bruno stuttered, "Such speeches. Clap clap. You know you're talking mutiny man. I could fire y'you. I could fire you f'for what you just said. Who the hell do you th'think you are p'preaching to me?"

"If that's what you want Bruno, then do it." *So it's come to this Harry thought. I'm not backing off.* "Fire me. Be honest with yourself. Do it. Put it in writing and say why you are getting rid of me. What's more is that I'll go. I'll be happy to tell everyone why I left. My conscience is clear. I won't have to hold my nose because of the stink around here. I don't think you can say the same in a month of Sundays."

"Just 'b'bladdy get out of my office," a clearly unstable Bruno shouted. "Get lost!"

"Gladly," Harry replied. *"Mr Gerber."*

The following day Bruno chaired the monthly capital expenditure meeting. Harry's men had prepared schedules that had been circulated to the managers two days previously. Taking account of commitments all replacement and additional projects were badly overspent. When Bruno openly instructed Walter Clark to hide two million rands worth of unnecessary capital expenditure that he, Bruno had incurred, in metallurgical operating costs, Harry objected strenuously.

"Not only is it unethical, it's illegal," Harry fumed. "Our auditors will go mad. That's the sort of behavior that earns us qualified accounts and court appearances."

Bruno stared at him and wagged his forefinger. "Man, it's about time you bean counters were bladdy brought down to size. Just do what I tell you. I'm sick of number crunchers throwing their weight about here."

"No," a defiant Harry replied. "It's not on. For your information I don't take to being bullied. I intend to inform the auditors of my concerns."

An infuriated Bruno grabbed his schedules and threw them into the air.

"Man, these figures are just bladdy rubbish. I'll do my own in future," he shouted and stormed out of the room. "You can go to hell."

When Bruno began to wear pin-stripe suits to work and chose to host lunches in his new boardroom with willing supplicants, including fawning luminaries from *Thuringia Bay* who were ecstatic at being wooed, Harry was at his wits end trying to understand his boss's errant behavior. A complete personality change had taken place before his eyes. Harry wondered whether Bruno had a doppelganger hidden away for unleashing on certain occasions. Certainly the version that constituted his boss bore no resemblance to the jovial individual he'd met when first arriving at the mine. Cecil too felt the chill, particularly when it dawned on him that he and Marlene had been dropped from the Gerbers' social list. At a stage when he and Harry were the only two out of six managers partaking in what used to be the normal managers' lunch, they decided to drop it.

Bruno trod his increasingly capricious path and began to absent himself from the formerly mandatory Friday manager's round-up meeting. On that day he preferred lunching in *Thuringia Bay*, handy when arranging fishing trips with townies leeching on to him and saw no reason to return to his office. Paperwork shot up exponentially because of Bruno's insistence for written reports from his managers in place of verbal versions.

Harry's forecasted financial projections were ignored by Bruno who commented that that his production managers would "come right" in good time. As funds sank to perilously low levels Harry tried to see Bruno but was rudely rebuffed, a scene enacted in front of

Joey Schneider whose expression told Harry that she too was not having an easy time of it.

To evade fingers pointing back at him, Harry zealously shepherded the promised pension and leave pay payments from Anthony Scobar into an account with a South African bank, payments from it to be managed by Cecil. As far as he was concerned, Harry's own divisional disciplines had not relaxed but it was plain that his employees did not take kindly to excesses and lax behavior they saw propagated elsewhere on site and not a few of them were mocking Bruno.

With only two months to go Harry reminded Bruno of their contractual liabilities via an internal memorandum; six million rands overspent with no likelihood of eliminating it before the end of the financial year.

For his trouble Harry earned a severe written reprimand. Then Professor Koenig's letter arrived.

Dear Mister McCrae,

I received no responses from Mr Gerber to my letters. You are my last resort. I have expressed disappointment that during my last visit I saw for myself that against advice, your mine is high-grading. This is unprofessional and in the absence of a reply do hereby formally withdraw from supplying services to your mine. I have posted this as registered to be certain that it did arrive safely. Kindly inform Mr Gerber and Gerard Dresser,

Yours sincerely,
Prof. E. Koenig

Harry talked it over with Doreen when he got home. "Let's face it, Bruno's changed. It's like a different person has taken his over his body and his name. He's not the same easy-going fellow I used to fish with and trek out into the Kalahari with. He was a friend and now I can't discuss anything with him. I have to write memoranda to him. Can you believe it? His office is twenty meters from mine and I have to *write* to him! Financially, the mine is on a spending spree it can't afford but he won't listen to me. He thinks he's bigger than the mine. The money's a huge problem and we're into overdraft. I'm getting signal after signal that he doesn't value my advice. Obviously he wants to see the back of me."

"That's bad," Doreen said. "You don't have any choice do you? Being a part of breaking all the rules is professional suicide."

"I was afraid you'd say that," her glum husband responded. "I did not ever count on running away Doreen, I mean moving again and all the upheaval that goes with it. I can't stand the thought of it."

"Hold on a second! Who said anything about moving? This past five years has flown by and I've enjoyed it. I *really* do like it here. *Thuringia Bay* has everything that I want. We live by the sea. We're not short of money. Our girls' education is provided for. What more could we ask for? It's about time you let up and enjoyed yourself Harry. My goodness you have certainly earned it."

Her reaction took him by surprise. "Are you sure Doreen? I assumed that you'd have preferred to go back to Jo'burg."

"Of course I'm sure. Why should we leave? Everyone who matters knows that you did a good job here. You have principles and people respect you. Don't let Bruno manipulate you. I've heard the stories too. Bruno is off his head to say the least. He's living in a parallel universe and doesn't know it. I think that he's shrink material. We'll stay right here enjoying our lovely home and I'm sure we won't be the only ones to do so. To be honest, I'm happy that you won't be flogging yourself so hard in future. You're almost back to your old self. Don't let odd-ball Bruno take you down. He's damn well not worth it."

"I have to see him. It's important," Harry informed Joey Schneider next morning.

She saw that he was agitated. "Hold on Mr McCrae. I'll pop my head in and tell him."

"'No!" he heard Bruno shout. "Tell that man to send me a memo if he's so desperate."

"Thanks Joey,' Harry said. "I heard what he said. Just give him this letter please. It's my resignation. To take effect three months from today's date."

"Oh no!" the dismayed woman gasped and stared at the envelope. "Oh no Mr McCrae! This is bad news. I'm very sorry to hear it."

Bruno's reply, a written memorandum, took barely ten minutes to land on Harry's desk. "…*and leave site at once…*"

Over five years service had come to an ignominious close. Harry summoned his department superintendents to explain his position. Next to be advised were the company's auditors who readily agreed to provide him with a written acknowledgement of good order. By the time he drove out the mine gates an hour later ten security men stood smartly to attention to salute him.

"This is history is repeating itself," the senior audit partner lamented to him the following day. He had come to Harry's house to get the full story from Harry's lips. "You made life a lot easier for us after you arrived here Mr McCrae. It will all surely go to pot again and then I'll have to fly in extra people; it's fast heading back to the days of qualified accounts. That's not healthy. I'm very sorry to see you go. By the way, what are you going to do with your house?"

Two nights after Harry's sudden severance, a despondent Cecil and Marlene called on the McCraes'.

"I don't know what's come over Bruno," Cecil sighed. "Since we got the management contract, he's become a law unto himself. He behaves as if he owns the place."

Harry poured them all a glass of wine. "It's not a French one Cecil but it's good. Bruno? What can I say? I'm convinced that I'll never be able read people well. Bruno's just another corporate victim who lost his way."

"If it's any consolation," Cecil said while holding up his glass, "I jacked it in too. I can't understand the need for all this bravado, formality and outright pigheadedness. Being told to make an appointment to see him was the last straw for me. Who does he think he is?"

"Resigned! You too?" a shocked Harry retorted. "When?"

"This afternoon. He wouldn't see me so I left my letter with Joey. He 'phoned me and told me to get off the mine site immediately. You must have known it was inevitable Harry. Bruno's been pushing Des and talking me down. I saw less of him that you did Harry. He couldn't wait to get me into the history pages as well."

"I don't know why they avoid us," Doreen commented. "Mariette ignored me in town this morning."

"You men," Marlene said, "can be so stupid. It's all about power. Bruno's puffed out his chest because he thinks he alone got the better of Hilton Walsh. He didn't. You two did that. In his mind, if you snap at Bruno you're expendable. He'll pile in his mates to replace you. It's all so predictable, surely you must see through him by now? Mariette is just following her husband's lead, so don't come down too hard on her. She snubbed me too when I complimented her on her expanding wardrobe. I have to laugh about it."

A telephone rang and Doreen went to answer it. Minutes later she returned, grim-faced. "That was Vic Grey. He says to tell you Harry that he's written to Bruno. He's resigned. He was told to remove from site."

"Oh no!" Harry exclaimed. "He shouldn't have done that."

"That's not all. Don South and Larry Foyere did likewise. Burt Burnett called it quits and your other department heads are meeting right now at the club. They'll be off too. Now that's what I call a first-class uprising."

"In that case," Cecil groaned, "my guys will also take the hint. I don't see the mine surviving this time round. It's well and truly stitched up."

Inevitably it got into the newspapers.

"Senior Men Desert Desert Jonah Mine" one headline quipped. "Management Contract At The Thuringia Backfires" another headlined.

"We're making money for local newspapers," Cecil grimaced when the two men met for morning coffee in town. "Out of our misfortune they make money. How about that? Gross isn't it?"

"As Marlene says Cecil, 'Who cares?' I like living in *Thuringia Bay*. Perhaps I have a disingenuous streak in me too, standing on the sidelines watching Bruno and his custrels running amok."

"'*Custrels*?' I never head that word before Harry. Speak English please."

"*Attendants to a knight*, alias the lord of the manor, Gerber! If Bruno doesn't meet production targets Scobar will eat him alive."

"I'm not sure Bruno understands that too well," Cecil frowned. "If he looks for more loans to subsidize operations he can't use mine assets as collateral because they're vested in Chater Metals. In other words Chater Metals calls the tune."

"Yes but you do realize that there is another source he can get his hands on? Fifty million rands of it."

Cecil blanched hoping that the answer he was about to get differed to that he expected. "Not..."

"Yes. Those pension and leave pay accruals. A cash mountain.

And he knows it. We're lucky to have got our got our personal cash out when we did."

"He wouldn't!"

"He's probably managed to swipe it by now," Harry foamed. "He wouldn't have given a flying fig about what the auditors will say. He has access as a signatory."

"Do you think he'd be that stupid? That's tantamount to stealing. Surely not?"

"He's off his rocker," Harry sighed. "Bruno's former version curled up its toes ages ago. To think we used to drink Jagermeisters together on the beach. Where's that man gone? Answer me that?"

The morning coffee circle was surprised by another recruit to its ranks when Des Irwin arrived on the scene.

"I can't stand it any longer. Bruno's insisting that we mine out the high grade eye of the ore body. I made an appointment to see him and he ducked it. Twice. Wally's going with the flow. He tells me, 'You send it, I'll treat it!' Eventually I just left my written resignation on Joey Schneider's desk."

"We were laying bets when you would see the light," Burt Burnett commented. "The coffee's good here!"

"Bad luck Des," a sympathetic Cecil said. "By the way, is Joey on leave?"

"No. Bruno told her to get lost. It had to do about not reminding him about an appointment. She just upped and left town. The grapevine says that as of yesterday morning she's in Cape Town briefing her lawyers."

"Crikey! She worshipped that man at one time," Don South commented. "It must have been bad for her to have pulled up her tent pegs."

"You bet," Des said. "If you even look at Bruno in the eye these days he goes ape. I've had enough. I wrote to Gerard Dresser and told him why I resigned. I don't want Bruno blaming me later for desecrating the pit. It's his doing. If it gets into the mining gossip columns, the stink will kill the mine."

"Any response from Dresser yet?" a suspicious Cecil asked. *Des? Resigned? Bruno's blue-eyed boy?* "Things must have really worsened on site seeing that every man and his dog who knew what they were doing have pushed off."

"'I don't expect to hear from Dresser. He'll only deal with Bruno. I hear Bruno jumped about smartly lining up one of his old chummies from the gold mines to replace me. Good luck to whoever it is, because if he does what Bruno wants, bang goes his credibility as a mining engineer. What with seven of his relatives on site, Bruno has got quite a family following dogging his footsteps."

"How's Wally doing?" Harry enquired of Des. "We don't see much of him and Judy these days."

"He hates it but the poor guy's broke. He has to stick it out until he finds another job."

Don South shook his head. "Bruno's definitely lost his marbles I tell you. He's driving guests around the desert in his new Range Rover bought at company expense. The club's preparing hampers fit for a king. Roger Lacy is highly embarrassed about it but he just does as he's told otherwise Mariette goes for his jugular. Everyone is talking. Champagne and crystal glasses on the beach...chartering 'planes at the drop of a hat! I shudder to think what it's all costing. One operator is shooting off his mouth to me about 'Avian harvest time!'"

"Last days of the Reich?" a subdued Vic Grey commented. "To think that once I fired a man for pinching a tin of coffee."

"Ah yes Vic,"' Cecil joked, "but you had grounds for dismissal."

Harry couldn't help laughing. "Anyone listening to this conversation would think we don't have a care in the world. I have a pretty good idea where that extra cash is coming from," Harry said and stole a glance at Cecil.

"We don't have long to wait," Cecil retorted. "It has to implode sometime. Then we'll see how *Sir Bruno* fares. Hey Don, give your wallet some air! Order another round, oh tight one!"

Another death at *The Thuringia* resulting from a locomotive collision and a series of serious accidents ensured that Gerard Dresser spent a lot more time at the mine site. Before, from his office in Kimberley, he'd planned once a month routine visits seeing that mine officials were well on top of safety issues. A five star safety rated mine had sunk to inordinately shallow depths and he was not at a loss to put his finger on the cause. Bruno was the common denominator and it was amply obvious from the stream of derogatory comments on site about *Sir Bruno's* behavior that few employees had respect for him. A motivator? Not in a million years.

Bruno assured the hapless mines inspector that "All would come right"…"…just a bad run hey…don't worry man…" but his excuses hardly recompensed stricken families who had to cope with the disasters.

The Saturday morning coffee club in town had grown to three tables of ex-employees swapping mine horror stories.

"Our insurers pulled the plug," Burt Burnett tossed in as an aside. "Premiums doubled. That's expensive. The auditors put in one of their top men to do your job Harry. He doesn't know his rear end from his elbow. Idiot material he is, but boy is that going to cost big!"

"A wagonload of yellowcake disappeared between the mine station and the town's shunting yards. The police are running around like Keystone Cops looking for it. Some wag mentioned that it will probably fetch up in the Middle East so the police have gone bananas."

"That's damn serious Vic," a worried Harry said. "If the press get hold of that snippet there'll be hell to pay."

"Oh, don't worry they already have. I told them," Vic exulted. "Let *Sir Bruno* take some heat. Not that I think he's overly concerned. It will probably be in all the Sunday 'papers."

"My contact at the travel agents mentioned that Bruno's off to London tomorrow night," Don South said. "Mariette's going with him. They're both traveling first class too if you please. That's twenty-five thousand grand down the drain. They're booked in at a five star hotel penthouse overlooking Regent's Park. Very nice for some don't you agree?"

"Not on holiday surely," Cecil said.

"It's supposed to be on business."

"Listen to us prattling on," Harry cut in. "Like fishwives gossiping. Come on you guys. David Bradshaw always left business out his private life. It was a damn fine example to us all."

"You're right Harry," Des yawned. "I'm overdoing the *Gyppo PT*. I think I'll have a go at fishing. My problem is that I might run into Sir Bruno on the beach. He thinks he owns that too."

"What a good idea,' Cecil said. "Let's talk golf. Don! Your twelve handicap old man? You're a *ringer*; put in some proper scorecards won't you?"

"Look who's talking," Don guffawed. "Arithmetic's not your strong point is it Cecil? You play like a champ out the rough. Your caddie has the longest toes in the business. I think Vic here needs to keep an eye on you."

Hilton Walsh was well pleased with his "Ops' Room" at *Glebe Manse*. Latest communication equipment provided instant access to global events facilitating his newspaper takeovers with consummate timing. By working through an offshore company he shrouded purchaser details avoiding financial premiums that would have been levied had his name been mentioned.

He replaced editors with businessmen versed in printing gossip alongside profuse infusions of titillating pictures for mass illiterates to slaver over. So what if most of it was manufactured? They could always hide behind the age-old defence of "...*not obliged to reveal our sources...*" Yes, an odd defamation suit happened along but was easily paid for from exponential circulation increases. Additionally, massaging notoriety appetites of politicians hungry for publicity had opened myriads of political doors on five continents for him.

"This attempt at a silver monopoly," Hilton absently commented to Ann, "is headed for disaster. Whoever's behind it wants to control world price; the US government won't have it. Whoever's behind it didn't do the homework."

She'd wondered what had kept him up past midnight these past two weeks. He'd been monitoring his screens. "Silver? Are you poking your nose in there too father? My God, you're a devil for punishment."

"A watching brief only. Relax my little daughter. I wouldn't do that because I'd have you shouting at me at AGM's. Sometimes I think my editors need a good kick up their jacks. They should be putting up headlines that ask questions, enraging people and informing others. Remember that we mine information now. That's what makes big money."

"If you say so. You enrage people all the time don't you? You enjoy putting people down. Your forte. Like a Roman emperor itching to point his thumb down before lions are let loose on hapless victims."

"The things you say about me...my own daughter..." he mocked. "What's important is that I can open any door I want anywhere I want to whenever I want to."

"That's because you inspire *fear* daddy dear. But don't let me stop you. You're the expert. The world needs people like you. Some jerk back at that uranium mine of yours in South Africa told me that once. He told me that the world '*needs people like me*'. Not bad coming from a khaki clad troglodyte in love with pulling rock out the ground."

"At that damn South African uranium mine? You must be talking about that fellow Des Irwin. He knew his stuff. I don't forget names, especially of that lot of pirates. Chater's got a failing mine on its hands," he gloated. "For that, I'm pleased! My 'papers are going to lay it open like a slit eel."

"Why be so spiteful?" she frowned. "Why hurt a lot of innocent people. Where would they find jobs?"

Image, overt success and money represented her father's credo. People were just a means to an end and if it wasn't for the fact that she was his daughter, she felt he'd have got shot of her at birth. The fact that her mother had died in the process seemed to have been held against her.

"That's their lookout, not mine. Anything that nails Scobar is manna from heaven for me. I'm watching him. Sooner or later he'll wrong-foot himself and I'll be waiting for him. I live for it. Then it will be my turn to roast him good and proper."

"I believe you. No church will ever have you father. I enjoyed my visit to South Africa," she uttered dreamily recalling her magical days with Des. "I want to go back there for a holiday sometime. The Cape is a marvelous place to visit in summer."

"You're a big girl," he sniffed. "Go whenever you want. Haven't you got work to do? Go out eat and eat a few chairmen."

Buying a British Financial Times was a big cost so Harry treated himself to the Friday edition that arrived four days later in his post box. Reading the journal was first on his agenda when pitching up for his morning coffee session.

He had more than a casual interest in "Situations Vacant" and absorbing the small print of company announcements and financial results.

"I don't believe it!" he burst out after opening his latest edition and scanning the "Movements" column.

"What's wrong?"' Cecil enquired. "Bad news is it?"

Harry sat back and had a good think before answering. "Do you remember me mentioning my contact at *Astarte Enterprises*?"

"I do. Why? Don't tell me that *Sir* Bruno did him in as well?"

"The last time Chris Stevens telexed me he implied that he was about to get the axe."

"I remember that. What of it?"

Harry pointed to a column in his FT. "This says he's Chater's Metals new financial director in London. He took over from Scobar! I don't believe it!"

Cecil could not understand why Harry was so perturbed. "Bully for him. He got a good job. What's wrong with a chance to crack the whip?"

"Don't you see?" Harry cried. "On the one hand he works for *Astarte* and informs us that Chater Metals is quietly selling its uranium mines to it, the intention being for Walsh to sell them on later and make a big killing for himself. Then it all collapses and Chris gets an executive job with Chater Metals? *The enemy*?"

Cecil sat back and whistled derisorily. "Wow! Some friend! A turncoat!"

"Is it possible that Chris Stevens was put up to it by Scobar? Feeding us all that guff to wrong-foot us?"

"Set and match to Scobar," Cecil said. "He pulled our strings. We cry foul, Walsh gets into a corner pushed there by Scobar. Out goes Walsh and Scobar gets the chairman's job. Lovely. Lovely. Then your mate succeeds Scobar. Very nice too. Who said there was no honor among thieves?"

Harry ordered another round of coffee. "Am I wrong Cecil? Did we jump to conclusions about Hilton Walsh?"

"Maybe. I'm not beyond thinking Walsh could have played Scobar in turn. Deviousness to these blokes is second nature. London breeds people like that. That's why it's the world's most successful financial centre. You have to be a combination of rogue and blue blood to stay the course. I mean look how the big banks rip investors off by using offshore subsidiaries. Old Hilton was given the push so taking on that old boys club is asking for trouble."

"But," a dismayed Harry murmured, "if he didn't and the reverse happened, Scobar ousting him, Walsh won't be his big fan that's for sure. That's not a scenario that I would want to be part of."

"Too true. Slugs the lot of them aren't they? Let them get on with it I say. It's beyond my febrile brain to comprehend such low backstabbing norms."

"What a business! So that's how The City works? Backstabbing rules the roost! I wish I knew what the hell is going on."

"Forget it Harry," Cecil sighed. "Leave the devils to their own mischief. It's outside our league. We should content ourselves knowing that we did a fine job rescuing the mine. If that's how they operate in London they're welcome to it. We were unsuspecting soldiers in a game we didn't remotely understand."

"Perhaps we still are and don't know it," Harry said through pursed lips. "Anything's possible these days."

33

"Yes! I've got it!" Hilton shouted and excitedly turned to look for Ann.

She wasn't there. He'd forgotten that she was out demonstrating somewhere. She'd left the house two days previously to rally her troops. He'd lost count of the number of annual general meetings she had appeared at. He'd hoped that "doing her thing" would have palled by now.

Ridding herself of her hanger-on husband after only six months of marriage, Hilton took for granted. The poor man's undeveloped brain had turned out to be a grain of sand compared to her iceberg-sized mental abilities. Surely, Hilton told himself, that his daughter was aware of how desperately he wanted her in his enterprises, near him, preparing to take over when he finally decided to opt out. Her's was the anodyne influence he needed to back him up. Otherwise what was it all for? Ann, Ann…he yearned. The TV companies, his included, he assumed knew where she was so he reached for his remote control.

Meeting on a Sunday morning at his Mayfair residence? They appeared none too pleased but he knew that without Chater Metals PLC's coat tails to cling to they were financially marooned aside from their reputations hurtling down the pan.

"Let's get down to it. Hilton Walsh taught us the importance of global outlook. No one expected him to disappear when he did. What thoughts might I ask myself does he harbor about us and this company?"

"I wouldn't say he considers us the best of friends," Edward Fuller answered. "If I were him I'd celebrate for a week, were this entire board to disappear in circumstances most foul."

Edward had two years to go on Chater's board before coming up for re-nomination. Then, aged seventy, he had every intention of standing down to hightail it to his Northumberland cottage nestling beside its own trout stream. He had not acquired Scobar's canny knack of sliding into top-dog positions at every turn. Besides, every corporate animal accepted that non-executive directors were facing increasing legislative and press scrutiny and to worsen matters, Scobar was making his board members dance on eggshells. Edward wanted none of that. No, no…his time was looming up fast. Even if he got his marching orders right now, he felt emboldened to speak his mind.

"My sentiments exactly," Scobar smiled but his steely gaze broadcasted censure of his board members. "We all know that Hilton is a quintessential planner. He's busy gentlemen, very busy indeed, in the process of creating a cash mountain. He's raising capital globally but outside of The City. He's into communications and judging from the results, it seems we're back to days of back-street gossip, innuendo and half-truths in the media. He's changing the face of newspapers with one objective—to print his own money; he's taking over TV companies and reformatting them. He's in a prime position to manage public opinion without them even realizing it, so making more cash while he's about it. He's getting money men behind him. He's getting investors lined up to hand him their cash. Mind you, when his minions don't perform, he eradicates them and they come running to me to spill the beans. Hilton Walsh is on a mission gentlemen and I have not the slightest doubt that we figure highly in it. Where and what may this mission be?"

"Who would disagree with you Chairman?' Edward Fuller retorted. "You know him better than anyone else. Why don't we save ourselves the trouble and shop him? He was going to sell Chater's uranium mines twice over and keep the profits wasn't he?"

"Who knows? It certainly appeared so. The problem is that if that snippet got out gentlemen, we would all be under suspicion, labeled as pariahs in The City. What would our dear old shareholders say? We don't want that did we? It would be the end of Chater Metals if our financial brethren gave us a cold shoulder."

"You must have an indication of what he's gearing up for us."

"Seeing that you mention it, I suppose I do," Scobar purred. "I suppose I do at that. I'm asking you gentlemen what do you think he has in store for us? When we establish that, it will be our turn to plan, will it not?"

Scobar hadn't been marking time since seeing the back of Hilton Walsh. His contacts had kept him informed about Walsh's physical movements but before spewing out his thoughts he wanted his board members to take the lead. Old Edward Fuller seemed strident enough but he could see that the other duffers were there under sufferance waiting to sign the register before running away waving their attendance cheques. He wanted to frighten them off one by one then install his hand-picked nominees. Putting his greybeards under the spotlight to trawl their brains for innovative comment was futile; Scobar understood as much but he wanted his somnolent squad to squirm with embarrassment and stress themselves at being so pointedly labeled as near brain-dead as possible, until sheer strain forced them to do the honorable thing and stand down.

Five minutes elapsed while members present stared absently into the air or pretended to scribble notes. One member Scober noticed was bordering on falling asleep.

"Come now gentlemen," Scobar taunted. "Speak. Anything? Anything at all?"

It seemed the right place to do it. A misty grey Atlantic rolled in and his innards were warmed by a few Jagermeisters. His bag of fish was testimony to his angling rewards for the day. Land Rovers parked up as windbreaks where tall tales about 'the one that got away' were in full swing under a tarpaulin. Des Irwin dropped his bombshell.

"I always wanted to do my PhD," he announced while gutting a steenbras he'd just taken off the hook. "I'll remember these days in *Thuringia Bay* all my life."

"That sound ominous. Are you leaving us?" Harry enquired. He'd just poured himself a mug of coffee and fortified it with a shot of whisky before lolling back in his canvas deck chair.

"I decided that since I had some money behind me now would be a good time to do it. I've got the experience. And I've got plenty of original material to explore. I should get on with it while I have the motivation."

"Where do you intend doing it?"

"In London. At the Royal School of Mines. Two years it will take me. The good thing about it is that Prof Koenig will be my leader and tutor."

"Good on you Des!" Harry smiled. "Congratulations! What then *Doctor* Des? After you finish?"

"I have plenty of time to think about that. I'll be thirty-seven when

I get my cap. Living here on the coast has spoilt me. I can't imagine working on a mine in the jungle in Papua or Brazil. Chile? Too rarified for me not to mention its politics. Canada doesn't grab me and neither does America. Australia....that's a maybe. Who knows, perhaps the prof might have a spot for me in Oxford? I like the idea of a civilized base and sloping off to the wilds for short periods at a time. Frank did very well with the prof until he set up on his own. That might be an option too. I know plenty of mines that would fall over themselves to install mine planning like we did here."

"A lot can happen in two years right enough," Harry mused and cradled his mug to warm his hands. "Reading for a PhD? Good! That's a constructive move. You'll do well *Doctor*. Not a few people say that you're a good mining engineer. I'm sure you'll get what you want."

"That's nice of you Harry. Thanks a bunch. What's your plan?"

"I'm staring at forty-eight next birthday. I can hang up my spurs but I'd prefer to work for a bit longer. In the right environment of course without any crazies on the scene. I suppose the truthful answer to your question is that I'm unsure. There are few as nice places to live in while I make up my mind. I have to factor in Doreen's needs as well. She loves living in *Thuringia Bay*."

"'*Nice places*'?" Des murmured. "You're right there. No complaints from me."

"When do you plan on going Des?"

"Next week. I'm not selling my house. This location is a jewel. Wild horses wouldn't make me sell it. My agent found me a good tenant. An auditor in fact. I won't have any rent problems then will I?"

"We'll keep an eye on it for you," Harry said, "just in case you do."

An evil grin, spread across Des's face. "I had something made for Bruno. It's a sort of parting present from me, for him to remember me by. I'll send it in to his office the day before I go."

"He should be giving you a parting present," Burt commented, "after all you did for him."

"What till you see it," Des grinned. "You might change your opinion Burt. I'll fetch it from my Landie."

Minutes later he was back and unfurled a white T-shirt. On its front and back, was emblazoned, *"The Only thing I Miss Is...My Mind."*

The roar of laughter emanating from the Bon Marchë Café must have been heard for miles down the beach.

Doreen wasn't surprised when Harry told her the news about Des. Her rapier-like response surprised him. "If he ever comes back to live here,' she said, "he'll need to be married. This is a small town and Des was its number one Lothario. Women lapped him up. A lot of husbands didn't. Sooner or later he was headed into very messy divorce proceedings."

"I don't want to know Doreen," Harry said, "whose beds he was in. I've long since discovered that unless you see it for yourself, don't believe it. Anyway at least Des fancies women," Harry twitted his wife. "When I read newspapers these days they're full of at rear end spoiler antics."

"What on earth are you talking about?"

"Never mind. Hey, it's my turn to make dinner. I invited Des to join us. He'll be here about seven. Cecil and Marlene are coming too. How about some nice *galjoen* on the coals, *Sir Bruno* style? Fancy that Doreen do you, and a bottle of Constantia red to wash it down?"

"Oh good! Constantia's fine," she sniffed. "I'll settle for a simple steak. I'm a little off stuffed *galjoen* at the moment Harry, seeing whose favorite meal it is."

Cecil enjoyed his meal preceded by the noisy, affable build-up when the men stood around the fire and chatted. It couldn't have been a nicer evening suffused by western skies redolent with dying red and orange colored sunrays. It gave the ladies an opportunity too to catch up on each other's activities.

"That was great," a contented Cecil resonated when pushing his plate away. After three helpings he didn't dare to ask for more, risking Marlene's reproving gaze and inevitable verbal barb about his fast-expanding waistline.

"You're losing it on top," she was fond of telling him, "and putting on your middle".

"I'm pleased to hear that, Marl. Don said I'm losing it in the middle and putting it on up top!"

They sat on the veranda quizzing Des about his intended new lifestyle. "By the time you come back here old son, the only lateral thinking we'll be doing is while we're lying down and sun tanning on the beach," Harry murmured. "We're sorry to see you go."

Cecil had wanted to say, *Are you nuts? Going to an English winter?* but desisted from mouthing his mordant words.

"We'll miss you Des. Do write and tell us all about it won't you?"

"It's the least I can do Marlene. I'll miss you guys too. But I can't live on hold indefinitely. I have to have something to aim for."

"I think your timing's good Des," Harry said. "My last FT had a piece in it about the mine. It's news again for all the wrong reasons. Whoever wrote it is well informed. 'An exercise in futility' the guy who wrote the piece labels it."

"That probably why Bruno took off all of a sudden," Cecil said. "He's got to be in Scobar's bad books. He's due back next week; something will leak out then for sure."

"If he does go down the tubes what then?" Des enquired. "Does the mine close down?"

"That's the strange part…"

"I thought we weren't supposed to talk business,"' Doreen said. "Coffee everyone? Come on Harry, what about liqueurs? Stop talking shop."

Harry rose, gave his wife a sheepish smile and disappeared to fetch his drinks trolley. No person knew the state of the mine's finances better than him. He had to assume Bruno had played himself out the door after six months of runaway company expenditure. It was no secret that production was way behind plan and that immense stock control difficulties were cause for concern. Devious as Scobar had appeared, he had not been thought stupid. Surely the man had to rein Bruno in? A mixture of trepidation and plain inquisitiveness coursed through Harry. If anyone has asked him what exactly it was that he was waiting for he couldn't have answered — that was the strange part.

Des was happy with his accommodation arrangements. The distance between his comfortable bed-sitter in Russell Square and the Royal School of Mines boiled down to an easy bus-ride. Driving a car and garaging it was out of the question because parking was an eternal bugbear and besides, he enjoyed the sights and the people thronging the pavements. He'd learned to appreciate colors again and revel among facilities that had not altered in centuries. This was his heritage and he was in prime position to enjoy it.

Years had flown by since Des had visited Oxford's grey environment as a gangly barely solvent student chasing a redheaded girl he'd met at a London dancehall. He had to smile when thinking about her now — she was in Commons, a researcher for an opposition shadow minister. A mother of three children.

Late August had brought a window of welcome hot weather, an opportunity to dress lightly and take a train to Oxford. He thanked his Maker that half of England's population had decamped for Europe taking for granted that they were vacating rainy, cold weather in exchange for two weeks of sun overdose. On a Saturday morning the station platform seemed only to have attracted elderly American tourists absently gazing at arrival and departure boards.

From his window seat, despite grey skies, he sated on the green of England anew. What few doubts that had lingered within him were dispelled. He was *home*. He was of an age to enjoy it, more so because he had no money problems.

"I must say you look very well young man," the Prof beamed after welcoming him. "More assured. Your last job was good for you."

"It was Prof. I owe David Bradshaw and Frank Fielding a lot. My friends there were very special too. They gave me a break. And you Prof. You taught me much. Thank you for taking on my PhD mentoring."'

Professor Koenig's consultancy occupied an entire four-storey building on the ancient city's outskirts. Des had pictured a successful practice though nothing remotely on so large a scale. This was a multi-million pound business employing, he estimated, over two hundred full-time professionals. Fee income to pay for that salary bill had to be monumental.

"You might not be complimentary as you develop your researches young man."

"Why is that Prof?"

"You must understand that you and I launch a new relationship. As mentor I oversee your academic growth for the next two years. My role is to ensure originality of your premises and to vouch their added value to our mining profession. I shall guide you so that you do not tread up dead-ends. If deserved, you will receive the sharp edge of my tongue. Do not be offended. We share a joint objective to achieve excellence. Your success reflects on this consultancy. It will not be an easy two years for you. Do you accept that?"

"I expect no less Professor Koenig. My sole objective is to get that PhD behind me. There are no higher priorities. I shall do whatever it takes."

The Prof nodded. "Good. We understand each other. Excepting for periods when I shall be overseas, I have programmed every Saturday morning from eight until lunchtime for us to review matters. You must get into the habit of defending your thesis as you progress it. Do you accept that?"

"I do."

"Today will be an exception. You will join me for lunch. I usually stop at a *trattoria* a short walk from here, on the Isis. We will sit outside away from noise so that we can have a good talk. I want to know what went wrong with my prize pupil…your mine. If ever I saw a great institution in its death throes it is that mine. So pointless…"

"I think we all do," Des smiled wryly. "It became a hot potato through no fault of its own."

It was "business as usual" for Bruno. He was particularly pleased that Anthony Scobar had glossed over his eighteen million rand overspend and granted his mine an interest-free loan.

"When you get your feet well and truly under your desk my dear fellow, things will improve for you. Just try and make up your production shortfall as swiftly as you can."

Lunch at the RAC again as Scobar's guest had also taken him by surprise, most enjoyable it was too, hobnobbing with City luminaries like they were old pals.

"Mariette!" Bruno laughed when bounding back into their hotel room, "Mariette, this is the place to live! Not hiding away in the desert any more. Anthony Scobar says that I'll go far! Isn't that something to crow about!"

His welcome words were music to her ears. She had expected Bruno to have received congratulations for doing so well, but moving to London had not occurred to her. She stood speechless. Joining and mixing with the big boys at last? No more *piss willy* gold and uranium mines in deadbeat surroundings entered their final equation; thoughts of taking in boutiques on the King's Road and in Carnaby Street, resonated so strongly she became breathless. London's sophistication had attracted yet another moth to its light. *Wait till the girls back home get a load of my wardrobe. Wait till I see the looks on their faces when I invite them to tea in London!*

"You mean, to actually live here Bruno! In London! You're pulling my leg! No man—I don't believe you!" she cooed.

"I'm serious! He says my experience is needed at head office. Who would have thought that a barefoot little Eastern Cape boy would make good here? With all the new mines opening up around the world he says he needs more experienced people in London who appreciate the problems in the field. Great isn't it? We'll be finished with living in the sticks."

"I'm proud of you Bruno," Mariette trilled. "I can't wait to tell everyone back home about it."

"Hold on. No. Not just yet my sweet. I must give this Scobar chap time to find me a slot. Nothing definite is agreed yet. When I know for sure, then yes, tell whoever you want to."

"Oh! I'm so excited Bruno!"

"When we do come and live here," Bruno said, "there will be one big problem."

Her face drained. "On no Bruno! What's that?"

"When the Springbok rugby team comes to England who do I shout for?"

34

"I invited a guest who you know to join us for lunch," Professor Koenig announced as they wound up their Saturday session. "You did well today young man. Keep it up."

Des had been diplomatically "guided" on a number of issues and was about to return to London with a lot more work to do than he'd counted on.

"That's nice Prof," he replied absently. "Who is it?"

"It's a surprise. I trust a pleasant one for you. I booked a table just to be sure that we would get into the restaurant."

Des was preoccupied. The Prof had pointed out several glaring errors in his statistical significance testing hypotheses. It meant that he needed more sustained concentration on what he was doing and to never to accept facts as read. *It's not going to happen again* he promised himself. The point at which open pit mining became uneconomic to be succeeded by deep-level shaft mining was new territory to explore and define. His mathematics had been found sorely lacking and his level of metallurgical knowledge required substantial reinforcement.

Drizzle had forced them to eat indoors where close-set tables ruled out any prospect of any serious conversation. Des saw the Prof's face light up and followed him to their table.

"Hello Professor. Hello Des. What a lovely surprise." Ann Foster's white teeth glowed in the gloomy surroundings.

"It must be a ghost! **Ann!** What are you doing here?" Des bellowed. He wasn't sure whether to hug her or castigate her. "You look well."

"Always the charmer," she chuckled. "Professor Koenig invited me. We met yesterday and he mentioned that you'd be here today. So I stayed on to see you. Pleased to see me?"

"That depends," Des smiled wryly.

"Well now young people," the courtly professor broke in, "I will take bar orders and leave you to chat. Getting past that mob," he nodded at the six-deep throng around the bar, "will take me a while."

Ann asked for a gin and tonic and Des plumped for a pint of lager. They watched their host slide into the bar crowd.

"The prof told me what you were doing. That's good. Being tutored by him will open important doors for you. I was surprised to hear that you'd left the mine. You were so much a part of it. You hardly talked about anything else."

Des looked at her disbelievingly. If she was fishing, she certainly came across as an innocent. "Left the mine? As it turned out I had no choice in the matter. But that's water under the bridge Ann. Tell me what have you been up to since we last met?"

"Quite a lot. My father's had a few problems as you probably know. But he's not one to lie down and give up. He's canny when it comes to spotting winners. As for me, yes I still bad-mouth the characters that pay slave wages, abuse employees and receive huge packages for their incompetence. In my book, such corporate rapists should go to jail."

"Interesting. I've read the odd article about you in my mining journal. As I told you before," he grinned, "you're good at getting under people's skins. Where are you based?"

"I'm dry," she gasped and turned to look for the professor. "I hope the prof won't take long. 'Based'? I'm living with my father. It's a lot less strain for me. I'm writing for a few magazines and newspapers and appear on odd television debates. Believe it or not, I pay my own way. I spend a good deal of time with donors. They need reassurance that our protests don't damage their pitch. For them, it's all tax-deductible of course."

Their drinks arrived none too soon.

"I hope you don't mind. I ordered food for us," the said. "Otherwise we will be here all day waiting to be served."

By unspoken consent conversation veered toward safe topics. An hour later, shepherds' pie had been gratefully consumed and coffee served. Professor Koenig had a function to prepare for and bade the couple goodbye.

"I'll give you a lift back to London," Ann offered Des. "It's no bother for me."

"Thanks," he said and stood up. "We need to chat about a few things."

"I don't understand it. I really don't," a glum Cecil commented to Harry just before they teed off. Obtaining a regular tee-off time had taken some effort on Harry's part seeing that the town's doctors, dentists and lawyers were thronging the course on Wednesday afternoons.

"Are you trying to put me off?" Harry complained as he bent to insert his tee and take a few practise swings. "What do you mean? Foul tactics? We're only playing for a ball!"

"I'll shut up. Go on…hit the ball. I'll wait till we're on the fairway before I tell you what I heard."

"Okay!" a satisfied Harry said when watching his second shot land on the green. "What is it that you don't you understand Cecil?"

"Mariette was hardly back in town on Monday and put it about that Bruno's been offered a big job with Chater Metals in London. That's news!"

"Very funny," Harry laughed. "Ha ha. And your punch-line is?"

"I'm serious Harry. What do you make of it?"

Harry turned to stroll towards the green. "Utter nonsense. The mine got a qualified audit report because of Bruno. Production is shot to ribbons, it ran out of cash and Bruno's been kicked upstairs? No way. Someone must have got the wrong end of the stick."

"So! Like old times Ann."

This time she'd recommended their rendezvous spot—a quaint hostelry nestling in the New Forest well off tourist trails. Professor Koenig was setting him a furious pace and time was his enemy. Ann wasn't taking "No" for an answer from Des.

"Bring your stuff with you and work away at the inn. I've got plenty to read. Come on…a change of setting will do you good."

Work? While she was with him? *Who am I kidding*? Des thought. They had no sooner shut the door and rushed into each other's arms. Lunch was forgotten and by early evening they lay exhausted beside each other.

"The prof's going to be mad with me," Des sighed contentedly.

She nestled up into the crook of his arm and raised her head to stare at him. "I bet you say that to all the girls."

"Be serious!"

"Honest?"

"Yes."

"That's good. I'm starved!" she sparred and disentangled herself. "Let's stoke up. We have a whole night ahead of us to make up for lost time. I'm not going to let you get away so easily this time lover boy!"

"I bet you say that to all the boys," Des grinned and got up. "I can't wait."

"The last time your father visited our mine Ann he had some pretty harsh words for us. You do know about it that don't you?"

Two days of exploring each other during their every waking moment had drained them. They sat in the downstairs pub, nestled in a dimly lit corner, nursing their drinks.

"I do. He hasn't said so in as many words but I know that he regrets it. From what I gleaned you chaps caught him by surprise."

"I was livid with you. It all went crook after your visit to the mine."

"You think I had something to do with it?"

"Did you? You must have expected that question. It's important to me."

"No Des, I was not spying for my father if that's what you're implying. I don't think mining activity wherever it may be is worth the price our planet and its peoples pay. Mining companies have been raping the earth, wasting natural assets and moving on to new areas of plunder when they've taken what they want; all orchestrated by commodity mandarins sitting in plush offices in London or New York. My father knows how I feel. I won't change my view, even for him. I do love him though and admire him. He's a fantastic man."

"'Fantastic'?"

"I think so. He understands the fabric of life. He wasn't satisfied with just a handkerchief—he went out and grabbed the whole damn blanket! He understands emotions and reacts accordingly."

"I don't know what you're getting at," a plainly mystified Des said.

"I'll give you an example. Once at a formal dinner at Glebe Manse he spotted one of his guests' wives slipping a bone china saucer into her handbag. Next day he sent her the complete set of crockery and attached a note that said, 'I thought you might appreciate the rest of it'. Imagine her shock! Her husband must have blown his top too when he got to the bottom of it."

"Wow! That seems a bit harsh."

"Maybe. Guess what? Her husband never shaped after that event. He's drying out in a country retreat somewhere. I suppose what I'm saying is that if you get on the wrong side of my father, well, be warned. He's a man who takes kindly to people who tell it like it is. The slightest evidence of trickery or underhand tactics, it's the best way to make a serious enemy for life."

"Oh really? He's no angel on that score. He did very well as far as making enemies is concerned."

She drew her knees up beneath her chin. "I expected you to say so Des. What I think he's battling with now is that he finds it hard to admit that he made a mistake concerning the uranium sell-off. He must be mulling over how to get over that hurdle with some degree of dignity. Despite his failings, I still think that he's great."

"We thought so too until he tried to dump us, and you were part of the plot with *Astarte*," Des replied making no effort to soften his words." I won't tell you what we called him."

"I can imagine. It's one of the few mistakes he's made. Another was him involving me with *Astarte*. I knew nothing about that and put a flea in his ear. He's convinced that his successor set him up in a cleverly orchestrated campaign without realizing what Scobar was really after. My father's chairmanship. It typifies the kind of behavior I just mentioned. Scobar's made a big mistake, take it from me. Thinking about it, perhaps father did get a message."

"What message?"

"He's divested himself of all his mining interests."

"It's difficult to accept right enough. Hilton out of mining? It's like Pele swapping over to netball. What's he doing now?"

"You know what Des? I prefer not to get too involved with his businesses. I know that he wants me to, and I suppose I'll have to give in at some time in the future. When he does say something about 'business' I listen with half an ear. I do know he operates through offshore companies and he spends a lot of time with investors in

Germany. A few weeks ago he was having a good look at the silver business. That cartel that tried to get off the ground? He said it would fail and it did. He's planning strategies for twenty years ahead. He has to be a few steps ahead of the game. That's what he wants me to inherit."

Des mulled over what she'd told him. He wasn't keen to take it as gospel but there was one spark of curiosity he had to explore. "He's definitely out of the uranium business?"

"To the best of my knowledge. He keeps reminding me that the only mining he's interested in is 'Mining the mind'."

"Profound stuff," Des murmured. "In a way I'm sorry that we're not under his wing any longer. I could have learned a lot from him. When Frank Fielding was general manager he had the measure of your father. He said old Hilton had no sentiments. Everything he did was for the benefit of his shareholders. To be like that? You have to make a lot of enemies in the process. But we don't forget…he tried to dump us. I could never trust him again."

"He's human," Ann replied sharply. "Perhaps others say the same about us because at the end of the day we're all looking after ourselves aren't we? If the chips are down Des, you save your own soul. I'll bet that if you think for a moment at some time you had friends who eventually dropped you after they got what they wanted from you? They stole your ideas, sometimes even your job, gossiped about you and you took them as friends?"

"Now that you mention it…"

"'*Trust* Des'? In a pig's eye! You have to take what you want and do what you want. People are just a means to an end. If you ever get an opportunity to work for him, or someone like him, grab it. Learn. Learn all about control. Learn how to manipulate. That's survival…otherwise just become part of the landscape. People will look at you, use you and move on. The trick is to get others to remember you for the right reasons. Did you bring a spark into their lives? Or did you just make small talk. Wake up Des! Boundaries have changed and that includes behavioral patterns. *'Trust'* in today's world? You really are behind the times aren't you?"

Des looked at her wide-eyed. She'd refined humanity into a new, crueler context, one so insincere and devoid of his norms that his brain locked, unable to cope.

"Congratulations," he eventually said and kissed her hand. "What a masterpiece of cynical reality. When you take over your old man's estate, there'll be no surprises for you. I'd work for you, strange as that may seem. Do you know why Ann?"

"I don't. Tell me why Doctor Des."

"I don't think you have ever said that to anyone before. That was brutal honesty. I'm truly honored. I know where I stand with you."

Anthony Scobar's third floor office enjoyed a good view across Onslow Gardens. "Damn!" he frowned, "only tenants who live on the square are supposed to have keys to the gardens! Look at it…it's a dashed camp site these days!"

Professor Koenig leaned across and had a cursory glance. "It does appear somewhat over-run."

"I've been thinking about what you said Professor Koenig," Scobar probed. "This Cartel? Hilton Walsh probing silver market machinations? The price plummeted since the Bunker brothers tried to muscle in and set the pace. Walsh is not a man to waste his time running up and down blind alleys."

"I agree with you. I cannot gainsay him. He moves in circles that most of us don't even know exist. I observe that he avoids London's financial district. I confess that I'm not an entrepreneur Mr Scobar. Hilton Walsh is. One thought that repeats in my head is why a top mining professional has no interests in mining any longer? He has expertise, money, resources and contacts, but no mining interests? This interests me."

"Me too Professor. Time will tell will it not? Now tell me—about that emerald field in Brazil you've been assessing. Do you have any news for me? I need to know whether that outcrop is fractured in any way before I make representations to finance a pilot plant and make noises to the Brazilian government."

The professor smiled and opened his satchel to withdraw a sealed white canvas folder. "In there," he said, "you will find all the information you require. It is a pleasing picture. You will have access to gemstones of princely quality and size to satisfy discerning markets for years."

"Good. Good," Scobar beamed. "In that case professor I look forward to receiving your bill for your services. Thank you very much indeed."

Professor Koenig shook his client's hand and let himself out.

Scobar wasted no time opening the report and reading its conclusions. *Wonderful. Just the sinecure that Edward Fuller is looking for in his old age. And me. Forty percent for him and sixty for me. Must think of a name—piece of cake. Register a company in Luxembourg and Bob's your uncle,* he gloated while picturing his new forty meter racing yacht that he was about to lift his telephone to order.

His board members knew better than to duck attendance at a hastily called meeting by their chairman. Two days notice was hardly enough time for them to rearrange their appointment schedules.

"What's on the agenda?" Edward Fuller asked his wife who also doubled as his personal assistant.

"He wants to talk energy and suggests that you all come prepared."

"I'll head for the London flat now," Fuller exclaimed. "Then I won't be in your way."

Heaven she thought, ecstatic that her old *Mr Methane Gas* with the sour breath was not going to be underfoot expecting to be waited on night and day.

"If you say so dear," she replied, already planning her shopping trip for that afternoon. Then dinner with her sister Flora—just the two of them out on the town in Basingstoke.

"Our last attempt to strategize gentlemen was not successful. You promised to submit ideas to me in writing. After three months I am none the wiser. No input from any of you."

"Do you have something on the table chairman?" a fawning Chris Stevens enquired in what sounded like too practised a tone.

"I do Mr Stevens. Kindly minute this meeting will you? It's about power generation. Mark you, cheap coal is not going to last forever," Anthony Scobar pontificated. "If it did, the environmentalists will have our guts for garters. The civilized world will need more and more clean power and that will only be supplied by nuclear sources."

"What about wind-driven energy Mr chairman?" Edward Fuller piped up. "And tidal energy?"

"Bah! A drop in the ocean! World consumerism needs more than wind, gas, bio-what's-it, hydro, coal, tidal energy and crude oil together could ever produce."

"What point are you making chairman?" Chris Stevens asked.

"I'll get straight to it. Far from being the millstone that Hilton Walsh had ordained, uranium offers an opportunity to increase our profits. How? We make a quick kill buying up all available uranium oxide spot market stocks, that's how. Then we dole it out in a rising price market. As energy demand increases, more uranium is needed for reactors. If we control supply, we decide price. Gentlemen," Scobar preened, "that is what I call real power!"

"In other words, a cartel?" Fuller exclaimed.

"I'll thank you not use that word," Scobar replied. "It's frowned upon in certain countries. Let us rather think of it as commodity speculation. No different to how the gemstone business is run."

"I'll do some quick sensitivity analyses," Stevens volunteered and pulled out his calculator from his satchel. "Let me see…if we clear out existing spot stocks, hmmm, and sell at normal sales prices we could make, ah, yes…three hundred and forty million dollars over and above plan; not a bad windfall."

"No utility supplier could risk closing down," Scobar continued. "They must have assured stocks of nuclear fuel. The cost of closing down a reactor and reopening it is calamitous, aside from damage done to its power users. Closing reactors willy-nilly would bring down governments. There's also the question to consider of where to store spent nuclear fuel."

"Will we have enough cash to buy the stuff in the first place?" Fuller queried. "We're talking big money here."

Chris Stevens did some quick sums. "It will be tight until we sell the stuff, but I should be able to broker a bridging loan to cover stock purchase and holding costs."

"I like it," Scobar said, his strident tone implying that everyone present had to agree with him. "It's simple and easy to carry out. We have to be careful. Buying quietly without disclosing our identity."

"Where will we stockpile the stuff?" Edward Fuller enquired. "It's not exactly easy to hide."

"My dear fellow," Scobar replied, "we'll arrange with suppliers to use their facilities and consign it from there via a middle man, so confusing the yellowcake trail even more."

Scobar waited for voices of approval. "Hands up those of you who agree with me?"

35

Bruno needed no prompting to get himself on to the first 'plane to London that he could manage.

"Bring your wife with you,"' Anthony Scobar had bidden him. "It should be a big day for her too."

"He's going to tell me about my new job. I just know it!" Bruno bubbled. "I can't wait. Imagine my sweet! Me working in head office as a consultant!"

Boutiques shimmered in Mariette's mind. Five star hotel on the park...sizing up houses to buy...holidays on the continent...her Audi convertible and Gucci scarf streaming in the wind...

"It's like a dream Bruno! That man knows talent when he sees it. Gosh man, but you have done well."

Both of them dined well and slept well during the flight. Flying first class meant that Bruno would arrive at Heathrow rested and raring to go.

"It happened!" Don South breathlessly informed his three colleagues while they waited to tee off.

"What happened?" Vic Grey said. "You had your handicap cut? About time too. No don't tell me—you paid for a round of drinks! That's it isn't it? Wow, it's going to snow!"

"Always the wit aren't you? For your information *Sir Bruno* dashed off to London. The talk is that he's landed a top job with Chater Metals."

"In that case good luck to him," Harry said. "I don't understand it but good luck to him."

"The next job that I get," Cecil said, "I'm going to set out from day one to make such a mess, I'll probably be elected chairman within a month and be paid off with millions. That's the way it's done these days."

"Forget him," shouted Walter Clark, whose conscience had finally driven him to resignation. "I don't give a toss what he's up to. Let's play golf! Get your money ready."

Bruno felt self conscious within the Chater Metals head office. It's Marbled precincts generated exquisitely attired persons and the hush in its corridors induced automatic deference to his hallowed surroundings.

Man he told himself, *I'm going to be a big noise here too. Just like these people sliding around the place. That crowd back home will never believe it.*

"Thank you for coming so promptly Mr Gerber," Anthony Scobar oozed when Bruno was shown into his office. "I have some news for you."

"Thank you sir," Bruno meekly replied noticing the immaculate charcoal striped suit Scobar was wearing. He felt like a country clod in his creased off the peg nylon special.

"I want to offer you a consultant position within our London office. I need input from someone fresh from the field. What do you say?"

Bruno's head was in a whirl. *It's happened!* "Thank you very much sir. It is an enormous opportunity for me. I will do my best."

"I'm sure that you will. I have arranged an offer of employment for you to sign. We need it to acquire a work permit for you. We will settle your remuneration details later. Be assured that your remuneration will be appropriate for a man of your obvious talents."

"Thank you sir," a servile Bruno replied, accepted Scobar's pen and signed the document.

"Good man," said. "Good man. I suggest that you return to your hotel. I shall be in touch with you tomorrow."

"Man, sir, I mean Mr Scobar, thank you, well..." Bruno stammered.

"Until tomorrow then," Scobar curtly cut in and swiftly ushered Bruno to the door.

The miserable amount of sterling currency that Bruno got in exchange for his South African rands did not put him off spending a few bob on himself. Mariette had never given a thought about warming up her plastic, so now it was his turn to spend. Off to Saville Row and Jermyn Street it was for him. He'd show Scobar a thing or two about dress sense. By tea time he was six thousand pounds lighter in wallet.

"I have to look the part," he later informed his surprised wife when entering their suite carrying his parcels. "These people are all so bladdy smart."

Lashing out thirty pounds for a haircut made his Adam's apple bounce like a golf ball, but his ballooning self-esteem knew no bounds, particularly after treating himself to a manicure costing twenty pounds.

Dinner in the revolving restaurant atop their hotel turned out to be a magical experience; the décor took his breath away and profusion of cutlery and crystal glasses made him falter. Three hundred pounds that gastronomic diversion cost, without tips, and he signed the bill with a flourish. He was uncertain about reclaiming his outlay on expenses but Mariette soon abated his worries when she promised to later show him her new French black, ultra-thin negligee. He recognised a Tory minister holding court in a corner while two young women hung on to his every word. A three-piece band struck up dulcet tones but the couple felt too intimidated to get up and dance.

They did splash out on a bottle of 1929 Tattinger champagne in their suite before retiring, wishing the time away until Bruno received further news from Scobar.

Bruno was first to wake. Nine o'clock. It was bright for October though brisk, with a light Autumnal wind blowing. Thank heaven he'd treated himself to a heavy cashmere overcoat boasting the famous extra "Prince Charles side pocket". It was a "Glad-to-be-alive day" one that he was sure would prove to be the prime milestone in his life.

He pulled on his robe and padded through to the sitting room to retrieve the newspaper under his door. It was there as ordered, as was a white envelope addressed to him. Tremulously he opened it.

Dear Mr Gerber it read under a Chater Metals PLC letterhead.

The terms of your management agreement with Chater Metals PLC are clear. All original parties to the agreement, namely the managers of Chater Mines SA Limited at the time of its signing, have exited Chater Mines SA Limited uranium mine in South Africa.

The terms of your intended employment with Chater Metals PLC signify one month's notice by either party. I exercise this right. You are hereby informed that my company has no wish to continue your services. Enclosed is a cheque comprising one month's salary less tax for your services.

This is based on ruling consultant remuneration rates in this country. The management agreement is therefore null and void and administration of this latter property reverts to Chater Metals PLC. Steps will be taken immediately to assume control of the Chater mine in South Africa. No compensation is therefore payable to any party.

Be advised that with immediate effect your services will not be retained at the mine in any guise whatsoever. You are instructed not to re-enter mine premises or conduct any proceedings in its name forthwith. Under the circumstances, no application will be made to secure a United Kingdom work permit for you,

> *Yours faithfully*
> *Anthony J. Scobar*
> *Chairman of the Board*

Mariette heard a strangled sound and dropped her cosmetic routine. She found Bruno sitting in an armchair. Sobbing.

"Oh, shit hey…look at this! Look what they did to me Mariette Oh no! Why? What have I done?"

"Very well," a smirking Scobar informed Chris Stevens, "we did him in this morning. That country cretin clodhopper will probably be banging on our doors within the hour. Make sure that our security people see him off."

"He certainly brought new dimension to the word 'stupid' didn't he?" Stevens opined. "Paying him off was a damn sight cheaper than paying out according to that management contract."

"I drafted it," Scobar laughed. "Dressed up in legalese. Gerber was so easy to manipulate, I almost feel sorry for him. A stand-up fall guy to be sure. If he decides to play us in court we'll crush him. His loss, our gain. He got lucky with Hilton Walsh. Not with me. Just looking at the figures, that mine is a disgrace. I have to get someone in there fast who knows what he's doing."

"Anyone in mind?"

"I'm working on it. In the meantime would you put that Mines Inspector in the picture? Gerard Dresser is his name. I asked for a caretaker management crew to fly out there from our Australian operation to put a hand on the rudder out there. Tell Dresser that they're on their way."

Ann knocked on his study door and entered. "Chef says you're not eating your food dear father. Are you sick?"

Ann Foster seldom ate with her father. She disliked the idea of being pinned down to routine and she knew full well how Mrs Robbins in the kitchen fulminated if she prepared food that no one ate. Ann normally snacked out something for herself from the refrigerator but Hilton had insisted on his three-course repast every night. Oddly enough, he dressed formally for the occasion too, a lone figure sitting at the end of a long thirty-six-seat table listening to Pavarotti warbling in the background while sipping the best red wine the Hunter Valley had to offer. To forsake his baronial regimen meant that something was drastically amiss.

"How solicitous of you Annie," he smiled despite his creased and unshaven appearance. "Quite the contrary. I'm bursting with energy. These kept me going," he said and held up a *Mars Bar*.

"Why did you duck your dinner then," she enquired and shook her finger at him. "Naughty man. Three nights running you did that."

"Annie, listen to me, I'll tell you when I'm finished what I started. Right now I have to monitor those commodity tapes coming in. When I see what I want, I have to move fast."

"Okay daddy. Just as long as you know what you're doing because I haven't the faintest idea what you're up to."

"Keep it that way my little Sheila. It won't be long, I hope, before, even you will be patting my back."

"This I must see," she mocked and left him to his devices. "Don't overdo it."

A day later, his patience paid off. "Yes Yes My turn now mate," he mumbled as he dialled his Luxembourg bank manager.

"Hess ," an imperious Herr Jurgen Hess replied within seconds.

"Jurgen?" Hilton pictured his banker standing stiffly to attention beside his desk.

"Ah Herr Walsh, how may I be of service to you?"

"Thanks. This is what I want you to do…"

Bruno slunk back into *Thuringia Bay*.

Mariette had refused to accompany her distraught husband, choosing to lodge with her parents in Krugersdorp one of the country's less salubrious residential localities, over a thousand miles away in Transvaal territory where no one knew her.

Worse for Bruno was being blandly informed by the mine telephone operator that his instructions by "the new bosses" were to not to accept any calls from him.

Besides their almost Herculean size and strange accents, the four

Australian newcomers to the mine stood out for their brutal honesty.

"Gerber was a prick," the clone in Bruno's chair was told by Ray King the team leader. "He's out. You! F*** off! We have to undo all your f*****g' damage! What did he do here? Stuff the place full with extended hillbilly family? Getting this mess right will be about as possible as stuffing a pound of melted butter up a wildcat's arse with a red hot hairpin "

As always, Don South was first to hear about new developments at the mine and unloaded his dramatic news within the hour at the Bon March cafe.

Cecil was thunderstruck and searched Don's face trying to decide whether it was a feeble attempt at misplaced raillery.

"Australians you say?" an amazed Harry spluttered. "Over here? When did that happen?"

"It's all over town by now!" Don gushed. "They waltzed in yesterday and Gerard Dresser was with them. They're grabbing the whole thing by the knackers. Sir Bruno's sulking at home 'phoning furniture movers. He's not heading to some top job in London according to Gerard Dresser. God knows where he's heading but it's certainly nowhere near London."

"Where's he going then?" a still suspicious Cecil asked Don.

"Can you believe it? He's heading for Krugersdorp! Ask Dresser he'll tell you. That's where Mariette is."

"Are the Aussies taking over? Is that the plan? Just like that?"

"Seems so," Don laughed, "by ten this morning they've told what pass for managers and half the superintendents to take a holiday with sex as of right now. We might see a few of them troop in here. *Geez* this place gets busy when people are fired doesn't it?"

"About time too," Vic Grey commented with the broadest smile anyone had seen on him in months. "Serve 'em 'effing right!"

"I think," Harry said as he finished his coffee, "there's only one thing for us to do."

"Yes maestro?" Cecil replied. "Aside from screaming 'Fantastic!' what?"

"Eighteen holes. Then a few drinks at the club. If someone can tell the Aussies, I want to buy them all the beer they can drink."

"*Barbie* at my place tonight. Aussies included," Cecil added. "Marlene will be over the moon when she hears about this. I have to make sure we get some sweetmeats. Aussies love sheep by all accounts!"

"Leave it to me," Don volunteered. "I'll be at the golf course in half an hour. Don't tee off without me!"

"This is amazing," Chris Stevens informed his boss. "Spot market uranium oxide supplies have gone up despite us buying its entire offering last month. All of a sudden there's another three thousand tons on the market. At twenty-five dollars a pound."

"Where from?" Anthony Scobar enquired.

"The broker says Australia. No problem stockpiling it is there?"

"Buy it," Scobar ordered. "We'll flog it soon enough at a profit don't you worry."

When Hilton received the news he was waiting for he called all his editors.

"Put out special editions…the Berlin Wall is coming down within days. Just dress it up and make it look good. No catch—I got the word. Just do it! Move!"

Anthony Scobar felt he'd had a heart attack when he heard it on the ten am TV news.

"What's our U3o8 stockpile standing at?" he shouted when a sweating Stevens entered his office.

"Twenty-two thousand tons. Coming up to six hundred million dollars worth."

"Bloody hell! Sell it! Sell it fast. With that Berlin Wall coming down the Soviets are going to disarm. The market's going to be flooded with redundant nuclear material!"

Stevens swiftly retreated to his office and 'phoned the commodity brokers.

"Are you kidding?" they all uniformly answered. "You couldn't give the stuff away if you tried."

In a sweat he dashed out to consult Chater's bankers.

"We have long since discounted your paper Mr Stevens to another client. I am informed that repayment is required as per agreement. Your next repayment is due in ten days time."

"Extend us another loan," Stevens pleaded. "Go up a percentage point. Chater's banked with you for years."

"I am sorry sir. We are not in a position to oblige you. Is there anything else that I can do for you?"

Hilton joyfully reverted to eating his dinners again. There was a glow about him that household staff had not witnessed for years.

Ann noticed his sudden bout of bonhomie and joined him

"You look like a nice Sheila tonight," he said as he got up to pull out a chair for her. "Going out on the town are you?"

"No father. I'm glad to see that you are up and about. Mrs Robbins is like a dog with two tails. She's pulled out all the plugs for you in her kitchen."

"She is good isn't she? No one makes a steak and kidney pie as good as hers."

Ann agreed with him after she sampled hers.

Unbidden he got up and opened a bottle of Chardonnay and poured her a glass.

"Thank you. Okay daddy, tell me what you've been up to. It must have worked out well because I like the new Hilton," she smiled conspiratorially. "stay that way old man. It's nice to see you laughing for a change."

"Is that so young miss?" His face was alive again. His eyes were at their sparkling best and his demeanor animated. He was back to his old self and he knew it. "How much time have you got?"

"As much as you need. Go on. Impress me."

It was his first visit to *Glebe Manse*. Des reveled in the sheer space of the house and its tasteful contents. A cold November evening meant that five fires in various hearths were blazing. Ann had arranged for drinks in the library before settling down to Mrs Robbin's carefully prepared dinner.

"Where's your old man?"

"Where he hasn't been for ages," she bantered, "in The City repaying old scores and rapping a few naughty gents over the knuckles. Then he's staying at his club tonight to wine and dine an old pal of his from your part of the world."

"Oh! Who might that be?"

"He didn't say. Daddy plays his cards very close to his chest. He'll tell me in good time."

"I'd like to believe you," Des replied.

"Talking about staying overnight dear boy, Mrs Robbins prepared a guest suite for you. Sorry about that. No naughty naughty. I'm still her baby you know."

"That's perfectly plain. Can I at least flirt with you?"

"Daddy's very pleased with himself I have to say. It's the first time I remember him ever being a father in the real sense of the word."

"What happened? I'm dying to know."

When she finished telling him he flopped back on the couch and whistled softly.

"Factoring Chater's uranium oxide clients' books? The wily old devil…that gave him a good idea what the price range was! No wonder he knew when to buy up stocks on the spot market…and then sell. He was manipulating Chater Metals…what flipping idiots. He bankrupted it and hung it out to dry. Your old man must have enjoyed his feeding frenzy."

"He always said one had to work hard at making contacts. Imagine getting the nod before the Wall fell? That's what I call *connections*."

"Sure enough, he was in the know days ahead of the mass media," Des said, still shaking his head in amazement. "He strategized everything to perfection."

"I can't get over it," Ann said. "Making the prof drop a few words about cartels in Scobar's office. The idiot took the bait. He assumed father was brushing up on a silver deal so as not to make the same mistake cornering the U3o8 market. Scobar technically bankrupted Chater Metals."

"So Hilton climbed in and got the majority clout back. Imagine that? Scobar was buying bogus spot stock from Hilton without knowing it!"

"That's my old man all over," Ann said proudly. "He's back at Chater in the chair and Scobar and his pals ran for cover. They have a few other problems too, like bribes to Brazilian officials and spending Chater money on an emerald prospect that he and that old fool Edward Fuller opened between them. My old man can prove it and told both those jokers never to so much appear on any board ever again otherwise his own newspapers would spill the sordid details about them chapter and verse. I'm sure Scotland Yard would get in on the act too if they knew what those two crooks were up to."

"That's what comes from screwing Hilton," Des opined. "He must be crowing."

"He is and he isn't," Ann said and sipped from her glass. "What are you doing this week-end?"

"Why do you ask Ann? You know darn well that every Saturday morning that I have to meet with prof. In two days time. If I can manage what he 'advises' within the next three months, I can spend six months in the field afterwards and then write it all up. Crudely put, I'll be working my backside off. Haven't you noticed how thin I am? And it's not only food I'm missing if you get my drift."

"Yes yes. Poor you. You're breaking my heart. But you won't be seeing Professor Koenig this Saturday Des. He's coming with me. And my father."

"Okay. I give up. Fill me in on the mystery. I'll never be able to out-think you three. What's going down?"

"He's chartered a business jet to flying non-stop to *Thuringia Bay*. Do you want to come with us?"

Des's eyed lit up and he punched the air in delight. "Do I ever! Professor Koenig can't object! For how long?"

"That depends. Come on poor boy, let Mrs Robbins feed you up. She can't wait to impress you, so be nice to her and pop your head into the kitchen to tell her not only that is she a lovely woman, but a fantastic cook as well. After all you've had plenty of practise getting your way with women."

"Ah, but she's not the only fantastic woman in the vicinity," Des chortled as he got up. "Lead on Miss McDuff!"

Any aircraft landing at mine's dormant airport was a huge event. Don South had volunteered his services to the Australian team to check over the airstrip and talk the newly resumed chairman's aircraft down. The strip was just big enough to take a twelve-seater Mystere jet for which he'd had to arrange return aviation fuel.

First on the agenda for Hilton was that wanted to address the entire mine personnel.

"What's he up to this time?" Cecil asked Harry as they compared invitations to be at the mine site when Hilton and his party arrived. Walter did not appear all that sure either what their visitors were up to. Vic Grey and Burt Burnett too were asking questions of each other. Uniformly, all men were of a mind that whatever news awaited them it was going to be to their liking.

"Nothing Hilton Walsh says or does will surprise me," a wary Vic announced.

"I have a good feeling about it all," Marlene had told her husband. "Don't ask me why, I just do."

Don couldn't believe his eyes when Des stepped off the aircraft last. "Des!" he shouted excitedly. "Hi!"

The two men shook hands and Don got in a quick, "What's going on?"

Des wiped sweat from his face. "I'd forgotten how hot it is here. Don, don't worry, Hilton's on a mission. Just tell the coffee club members that they're in the pound seats."

Don's smile was sunlight itself as he rushed to his car leaving it to Ray King to drive Hilton and his two guests to site.

By the time they reached the assembly area beside the open pit all the busses had parked nearby and curious employees were milling around trying to find out what was going on.

Hilton stepped up onto a dais and took the microphone.

"Good morning everyone. I'm Hilton Walsh. I was your chairman for a while and now I am happy to say that I am back at Chater Metals and will be your chairman again. Presently I am acting in the job, until the next annual general meeting when confirmation will be automatic. For obvious reasons…"

Some employees let out a nervous laugh.

Hilton looked down and drew a deep breath before facing the sea of faces giving at him. "When one has to say sorry it is best to do it in front of all the people involved. Just over a year ago, I confess that I made a bad mistake. I did what I thought best at the time for the

Chater Metals group by trying to sell some mines. Unexpected repercussions arose when I discovered that I had received questionable advice prior to the sales. Only then did I discover how many people I had let down and resigned my chairmanship for fear of worsening matters."

"This is sounding better and better," a wary Cecil murmured to Harry. "What now from the sweet talking Aussie?"

"I can tell you now without fear of contradiction that all the men concerned who deliberately misled me have been suitably dealt with," Hilton continued.

"It pained me to receive reports of how good solid people here were mistreated after my departure, individuals who must have assumed that I had done the dirty on them. I am sorry for the misunderstanding and the damage done to this mine. I have come here to make amends."

A spellbound audience began to drop their sour expressions. A few employees slow clapped.

Hilton held his hand up. "Call me what you will. I probably deserve it. I want nothing more than to see this mine back on a sound footing. My conscience will allow nothing less."

Applause interrupted, this time accompanied by a few happy souls giving each other thumb's up signals.

"'*Amends*' I said. Don King followed orders. He and his men were not part of the original plot. Three out of the four of the interim team will be heading back to Australia, reluctantly I might tell you, because they know what a great mine this will become again."

"Oh, here it comes," Cecil muttered to Harry. "Who's he bringing in now?"

"Mr Frank Fielding. Remember him?" Hilton smiled.

"Yes!" a thousand excited employees shouted. "We do!"

"He's back. On the first of next month. As your Managing Director, based here in *Thuringia Bay*. He will also be responsible for all Chater Metals mining activities in Africa."

Rapturous employees shouted, screamed, ululated and danced. "Frankie...Frankie's back..."

"I'll be buggared!" a delighted Walter laughed. "That's a great move!"

"I haven't asked them yet—I want your rebuild managers back where they belong. What do you say?"

"Yes!" the crowd thundered. "We want them!"

"I also want them to recall whomever they want from their old teams whose service will be treated as unbroken. Cecil Lonsdale, please join me."

Cecil all but sprinted to the dais and on the way had his back heartily slapped by well-wishers.

"Harry McCrae—we need him to keep those books straight."

Harry found it hard to stem his tears while picking his way through the throng. His faith in human nature was restored.

"Des Irwin...Oh he's right here!" Hilton laughed and in turn had his audience giggling. "I want to keep his seat warm, as general manager, until he finishes his studies in England. Mr Fielding has offered to run both portfolios in the interim period."

Again loud cheers went up.

"Walter Clark has to rejoin us. No one else knows how to run that process control computer of his!"

Cheering Metallurgy staff escorted their former boss to the dais.

"Now we come to the Engineering Manager's position."

Silence. Everyone knew that was the job associated with the late *Sir Bruno*.

"Blimey!" Cecil whispered to Harry. "If he's bringing Bruno back he's mad. I'll be off for sure."

"Mr King expressed interest in the job. He likes it here. He likes you. Could you work with him?"'

"Yes!"

"You remember Professor Koenig?"

"Yes!"

"He's our consultant. Our referee. We need him. He's back for as long as this ore body is mined responsibly."

The visiting professor received sustained applause from an upstanding audience.

"Before I boarded the 'plane, I had no idea about what I am about to tell you now. It is that you will be getting a further very willing member of the community. My daughter Ann and Des Irwin want to be married while they are here in *Thuringia Bay*. I can't stay for the ceremony. I'm sure you will wish them both well."

"Amazing!" Harry blurted and turned to shake Des's hand. "You sly fox! Congratulations! Geez...the chairman's daughter no less...what do we have to call you? Not another *Sir*?"

Hilton had a hard time settling his audience down. "Nothing will please me more than to see you in your rightful jobs. No decisions, I promise you, will be made about this mine's ownership in future without extensive counseling with and involvement by its employees."

Hilton stepped down into the crowd and found himself hoisted onto the shoulders of two very tough looking miners who jubilantly ran with him to his car.

"S'trewth!" Hilton laughed when he got off, "I thought I was going to be chucked into the pit!"

"I'm sure they thought about it," Ann told him. "These are the people that you called *friggin' scum*. Remember?"

"I do. You know how deeply I regret that."

"Well Des, Doreen will be happy that you're getting married," Harry informed his friend. "A lot of other ladies in town will be too," he winked. "and their husbands."

"Harry, Cecil, come here," Des invited his colleagues and put his arms across their shoulders. "Walter! You too. I want Ann to take a photo of us."

The quartet looked quizzically at the camera.

"I wonder if Sir Bruno ever wore that shirt on that you gave him Des?" Cecil cackled.

Hilton broke up the reverie. "Why don't you chaps and your wives join me for dinner tonight? In Cape Town at the mount Nelson. We'll use my jet. Let's call it a sort of overdue reunion and to celebrate Des and Ann's good news."

Don South submitted the flight plan by telephone to Kimberley airport. "Yes, Mr H. Walsh, Mr and Mrs H. McCrae, Mr and Mrs W. Clark, Mr and Mrs C. Lonsdale, Mr D. Irwin and Miss A. Foster. With two pilots that makes eleven all told. Okay?"

From the driver's seat of the fire tender Don watched the sleek beauty rise steeply. He never tired of the sight and sound of a 'plane in the air, particularly the elegant Mystere, a famed French aircraft of excellence for which, one waited five years to come off the assembly line.

Then there was silence. And a flash. Then a rumbling boom.

"No!" he screamed "No!", as he smashed the gear stick into "Drive" and raced out across the tarmac.

Three months later a disconsolate Don South and Frank Fielding stood outside the court building in Kimberley. "Open verdict" the chairman of the commission of enquiry had ruled. Eleven people killed.

"I don't believe it. Experienced pilots don't make those kinds of errors."

"What can I say? Don," Frank replied. "We can't blame anyone. 'Open verdict' the judge said. That's the ruling. We have to live with it."

Back in *Thuringia Bay* Victor Grey heard the news. It suited him that most individuals took for granted that terrorists were responsible for such outrages. It suited his masters too. Not that Vic knew who they were—or where they were based. As long as substantial sums were deposited in his Swiss account he was happy.

He had never openly voiced his thoughts that the only reason for him lingering in Africa was to make money. After tampering with the jet's fuel pumps he decided that it was time for him to slide out and take up a quiet existence well away from the seething continent heading for oblivion.

His masters had spoken. This time *The Thuringia* had to go belly-up for good. Not even Frank Fielding's genius stood a ghost of a chance of resurrecting it.

Printed in the United Kingdom
by Lightning Source UK Ltd.
108502UKS00001B/322